Samuel H. Brooks

Rudimentary Treatise on the Erection of Dwelling-Houses

illustrated by a perspective view, plans, elevations, and sections of a pair of

semi-detached villas with the specification, quantities, and estimates and every

requisite detail, in sequence

Samuel H. Brooks

Rudimentary Treatise on the Erection of Dwelling-Houses
illustrated by a perspective view, plans, elevations, and sections of a pair of semi-detached villas with the specification, quantities, and estimates and every requisite detail, in sequence

ISBN/EAN: 9783337393052

Printed in Europe, USA, Canada, Australia, Japan

Cover: Foto ©Andreas Hilbeck / pixelio.de

More available books at **www.hansebooks.com**

RUDIMENTARY TREATISE ON THE

ERECTION OF
DWELLING-HOUSES

ILLUSTRATED BY

A PERSPECTIVE VIEW, PLANS, ELEVATIONS, AND SECTIONS
OF A PAIR OF SEMI-DETACHED VILLAS

WITH

The Specification, Quantities, and Estimates

AND EVERY REQUISITE DETAIL, IN SEQUENCE, FOR THEIR
CONSTRUCTION AND FINISHING

By S. H. BROOKS, ARCHITECT

NEW EDITION, WITH ADDITIONS

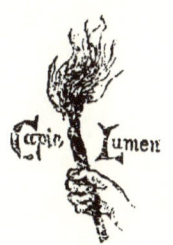

LONDON
LOCKWOOD & CO., 7, STATIONERS' HALL COURT
LUDGATE HILL
1874

PREFACE.

In our professional practice we have frequently been applied to for a treatise on Building, to which the young student in Architecture, as well as in Building, might refer and see, in an erection of simplicity or splendour, the necessity of studying all the details essential for such erection. In the office of the Architect, it frequently occurs that Buildings, from the variableness of practice, are only taken in detached parts as the work proceeds; and in the workshop of the Builder (*where they have drawings and specifications to work from*), the workman, or pupil, is seldom allowed to see them, but takes his instructions from the foreman for the portion of work to be executed; consequently he has little opportunity of acquiring the combined information requisite for the artisan in the building department to possess.

Under such considerations the present work was projected by Mr. Weale, the publisher of the rudimentary works on the Arts and Sciences.

We have, in this sketch of a pair of dwellings, endeavoured to show and describe the manner in which a building, from the commencement of it to its com-

pletion, should be dissected and studied in its various
mechanical departments, and how they work and combine with each other.

We first submit a set of probationary drawings, all
drawn to the same scale, and then show the requisite
details, as they would generally occur, for the completion of the carcass, and, lastly, the finishings. We
have also divided the specification, quantities, and
estimates, into corresponding parts. It may not always
be desirable to make such a distinction, but this being
a rudimentary work, we have adopted this method in
order to make it as intelligible as possible to the student in the Building art. We have also given as
much attention to the drainage, supply of water,
ventilation, &c., as the importance of such an erection
demands.

It may be proper to observe, that we have not
strictly conformed to the Metropolitan Building Act,
but have endeavoured to show how to erect a substantial building with every attention to the prevention
of such casualties as buildings of this class are frequently liable to.

In submitting this as one of a series of designs with
their details, allow us to acknowledge the information
quoted from the rudimentary series of scientific works
before alluded to, as we have freely referred to any of
them that would assist us in conveying our views in
the theoretical and practical construction of buildings.
Perhaps no one is more liable to criticism than the
architect for domestic arrangements ; consequently

there are few who devote their time to it. An archi
tect justly observes: to produce a building fit for its
purposes, and substantially beautiful at the same time,
is a good step towards perfection. And probably the
allusion to street architecture might with benefit be
here quoted.

It is stated that, in alluding to the building at the
corner of Fleet Street and Chancery Lane:—"It is a
good step towards that perfection which the commercial
architecture of the metropolis may reach. Fleet Street
and the Strand, transformed into a succession of such
edifices, might become a worthy Corso for the trading
Rome, and make a grand connecting point between
the region of docks and warehouses at one end, and of
mansions and palaces at the other."

The building referred to is an example of a commercial edifice. It were better, indeed, that the elements
of mercantile life were exemplified in its habitations.
We have surely had enough of doubtful objects in
stucco, &c. : sober and straightforward, not uncomely,
are the operations of upright tradesmen ; so let their
offices, warehouses, and shops, be truthful, substantial,
cheerful, ornamental piles. Thought is not thrown
away when applied to the improvement of our streets
and mercantile edifices. A man will carry on his
affairs with a healthier and clearer mind, surrounded
by buildings of the class we are now writing about,
than in such dens of darkness as some of the buildings
in the neighbourhood of Chancery Lane.

There is such correspondence between outward forms

and shows, and inner feelings and emotions, in all truthful matters, that it is far from an affair of indifference in what manner of form we transact our commerce, with what impress of form we endow our churches, or in what fashion of apartments we meet our friends and children. Providence has arranged this world upon these considerations (*so to speak*), and surrounded parts of the earth with cheerfulness and healthful beauties.

We, who in our offices and ledgers have often little enough thought of Providence, shall we esteem it indifferent whether we follow *His* precepts here, where, perhaps, we need their healthful influence most ?

To architects, at least, this question is not unimportant, in an architectural point of view ; for it is in such we speak. As a sanitary question, these things are happily decided.

The importance of domestic architecture must be held in a very different estimation to what it has been, by any one who hopes to assist in the revival of all architecture, dead since the sixteenth century in our country.

We are a commercial people, and a common-sense trading race ; he who can find a brotherhood in architecture with the great republics of mediæval Italy, the commercial communities of Florence, Genoa, Sienna, will perceive nothing but a source for the highest gratulations. We shall have our San Michele, Sansovino, &c. We, too, may become, amid this Kaleidoscope Europe, a stand-point of light for the after-times to reckon from ; but, to achieve this we must recognise and know ourselves. We must develop and not conceal our nationality, in arts as in all things else. From the streets of our cities and manufacturing towns, our wealth and power proceed. Let these become the stepping-stones to our temples ; as they must do, if our temples and our worship are to be sincere. It is not by forgetting, but remembering, our commercial street-life that we shall become a people great in wisdom as in wealth.

And, indeed, why should words be multiplied about the matter ? It is from these things that we are growing a wise, and, so much as there is of it, a holy people. From counting-houses, offices, warehouses, and chambers, come the schemes for baths and wash-houses, and model dwellings, ragged schools, and reformatory asylums. There on one side the genius of the shop-keeping people make them; beyond them burns the glory of future England. What if, on the other side, those who have no work to do embroider mediæval patterns and multiply Gothic churches over the land? Let us be grateful that they do so much.

But meanwhile the architects have work to do ; the public demands its streets and warehouses. Let us bear in mind how great these things are in their destinations—not, truly, all cheating and adulteration —let us remember that we are erecting buildings to-day through which the future contemplate, and the dwellers therein are preparing the paths of truth by their duties and their charities.

Let us then look upon those buildings and streets in their proper light, and build as if building for honourable men : to give our minds tone, let us discipline them to see in this shop-keeping what promise of greatness it encloses ; and, recognising the nature of the times, perceive that it is in these very streets that the way is opened for us to commence our stone daguerreotype of the nineteenth century.

Architects are the limners for the future; to them is perhaps entrusted the verdict which remotest times will form. All else will go, as it has gone, of Art and man's production. But Architecture, that substitute for Nature, is nourished by time as the fossil history of mankind; and as the shells which the nautilus and ammonite of the primæval world have formed, become to us the sure records and interpreters of their far-departed times; so these shells under which animal life has dwelt, which religion has formed and inhabited, will become, may-be, to future races the only and fossil records whence the epoch of man shall be clearly read. For us, then, who have to mould these latest medals of creation, there is the responsibility that we rightly represent our race—our age; it is not surely all untruthful. We forge the long chain of antique history link by link—almost from architectural remains : from these we deduce a people and a history for our edification, instruction, and example. Regarded in this light, study will soon disclose to us what valuable and unique opportunity domestic architecture affords in our time. There are yet higher

views, under whose radiance the architect begins to
perceive the great influence and responsibility of his
work. But the consideration of what, and how great
effect upon the mind, external objects exert, may be
explained on another occasion.

After thus adverting to street and mercantile architecture, we would solicit some little attention to that
style suitable and applicable for domestic purposes or
dwellings, that may be proposed to be erected in the
suburbs or environs of such as Cities, Towns, or
Boroughs, before alluded to. For wherever our places
of business assume a different and more healthy character for their various purposes, and in their erection a more permanent and architectural feature, the
dwellings, cottages, villas, mansions, &c., of the surrounding country approximate, in a corresponding
extent, with such improvements, and, consequently,
the buildings for domestic purposes become equally
combined with other classes of architecture, a reflection
and monument of the people, and a key to the date
of their erection. It was by witnessing this laudable
improvement that is daily taking place in this City
and other parts of the country, and in acquiescence
with numerous applications for a series of designs
suitable for the domestic arrangement and social comfort of all grades of society, the present works were
projected. It is admitted that much ignorance exists
as to the necessary knowledge in the erection of an
edifice, however simple: and this is a powerful draw-
back to the execution of such undertakings. It is

also proverbial that false estimates, which are frequently tendered, dishearten many from the prosecu-
tion of their plans, in the well-founded suspicion that
the expenditure will exceed the means appropriated
for that purpose.

In the erection of an edifice, much depends on the
choice of materials, whether for fitness or durability;
and a correct guide in the selection of them, on the
most cheap and economical principles, cannot therefore but be regarded as a desideratum by every one
connected with or concerned in building, whether
for profit or private purposes. An elaborate and explanatory specification, with the quantities of the
various materials required in each department, their
prices, the amount of labour and price required for
working them, with accompanying design, so that any
one about to build may arrive at the total expense
before commencing; the most approved and efficient
methods of water supply, drainage, warming, ventilating, according with the magnitude of the design,
will form an important feature of *the work*. We have
commenced our *series* with a design for a pair of semi-
detached dwellings, the estimated expense of each of
which would be about £400, or £800 the pair; thereby
giving a selection for the retired tradesman, or the
gentleman of moderate wealth who may wish to build
over his own demesne, fully detailing the most approved and efficient methods of construction, as well as
finishings, as a guide to the various trades employed
in the building art.

Each design is exemplified with a perspective view of the building, accompanied with all requisite plans, elevations, sections, and details, drawn to a large scale; thereby making this volume a work of instruction to the student and builder, and one of reference to the professional practitioner in all his requirements.

THIS SECOND EDITION has been carefully revised, and the Appendix to the former impression, " On the best form of Protractors essential for laying down Angles," placed immediately after the chapter which treats of Drawing instruments for producing geometrical figures, which it was intended to supplement.

Together with Mr. C. BRUCE ALLEN's " Cottage Building," of which a new edition is just issued with an additional chapter on " The Erection of Suburban Cottages for Tradesmen and Persons of limited incomes," this volume will furnish to members of Building Societies and others every information as to the best means of erecting such a dwelling-house on their land as is best suited to their means.

OCTOBER, 1867.

CONTENTS.

ERECTION OF DWELLING-HOUSES.

CHAPTER I.

WHEN it is determined to erect an edifice of any description, the first and primary consideration should be the money intended to be expended ; the next, when possible, the choice of situation, not only as respects its efficient drainages, dryness, and general healthiness, but also as regards its relative position with other buildings, and, when a number are proposed to be erected on a new site, to their being so placed as not to interfere with or injure the effect of the surrounding scenery. Consequently, it is desirable, after a space of ground has been appropriated for building purposes, surveyed, levelled, plotted, &c., that a perspective bird's-eye view should accompany the plans, not so much that the design there exhibited should be carried into execution, but that they shall not interfere with the principal prospect, and as little as possible intercept the view or prospect of each other.*

The "lamentable way in which the beauty and loveliness of the finest landscape may be injured or destroyed by buildings and grounds is exemplified by the far-famed view from the top of Richmond Hill. What it

* Mr. C. B. Allen's " Cottage Building " vol. 42 of this series.

B

was when Thomson wrote it would perhaps be difficult
to say; but now—instead of the houses and villas, and
the gardens about them, harmonising with and forming
a part of the general view to be examined in detail—
after the eye is satiated with the whole, it is first struck
with the glaring newness (*for they all seem as if they
were painted and pointed regularly once every year*) of
first one and then another of these regularly built boxes
placed in the middle of a large square garden or lawn,
and surrounded by a high fence, and the country round
being thickly wooded close up to the wall, the formality
of the grounds is rendered truly distressing."

A landscape made up of a collection of square fields,
surrounded by regular hedge-rows, and dotted here and
there with cubical, newly-painted boxes and straight
roads, may satisfy, as it commonly does, the owners of
the several lots, but can never be otherwise than pain-
ful to the eye of an artist. But what is called landscape scenery in England is mostly of this description,
and appears to be admired on the ground of its cultiva-
tion and plenty, qualities perfectly distinct from it,
considered as a beautiful object.

If any general rule could be given for the laying out
of building grounds, it would be to avoid everything
considered essential—long rows of houses all of the
same height, semi-circular rows with a tall house in the
centre, &c. The unsightliness of the common plan will
be seen by contrasting the picturesque cities of York
or Lincoln with the formal and uninteresting appearance of Bath or Cheltenham, or they may be seen side
by side in the old town of Hastings and the modern
Eversfield, with the adjoining triumphal-arched town of
St. Leonards. From this cause, London, though the

largest, is probably the least picturesque city in Europe. Mr. Disraeli, in his "Tancred," has ably contrasted the old part of London with the new, and has pointed out the absence of all interest of character in the modern portions. Strange that he should have been able to see so clearly that which professors of the art have not only been blind to, but are continually helping to increase.

If the building is proposed to be placed by the side of a public road, it would be desirable to erect the principal front facing the south-east or south-west as nearly as possible. The principal front, therefore, can only in certain situations be parallel to the public road, but the preference should be given to the south-east. The complete drainage of a house is a point of the utmost importance, as upon it mainly depends the health and comfort of its inmates—and not only is it requisite that the drainage be perfect; but it must be as little liable as possible to get out of order, and when disturbed for the purpose of cleaning, should be capable of reinstatement with the materials at first used. The most essential points to be attended to in the drainage of buildings generally, where main sewers are formed, are the following:—Assuming in this plate that the main sewer is constructed in the front or principal road—and we desire to convey all our soil, waste water, &c., into it. On the block plan in Plate III., upon which are shown the grounds, buildings, &c., mark the most accessible places for fixing the tank, gulleys, traps, siphons, &c.; and then upon a skeleton block-plan and section, Plate II.; show the principal pipes for the conveyance of water to the tank, and the waste and soil drains, into the principal sewer, with the necessary falls, traps, and gulleys required.

Soilage-drains are sufficiently large for the passage of the soil and water when their diameter is 6 inches. They should have a fall of not less than 6 inches in every 100 feet, and more where possible. They should be made water-tight in order to prevent the liquid portions of the soilage from escaping and so leaving the solid matters in the drain. The waste water passed through should be amply sufficient to carry the soilage onward. To prevent the foul air generated in, or re-turning by the drains, the waste ways should be double-trapped by a bell-trap at the sink where the waste water enters, and by a well-trap short of the inlet to the drain.

All drains should be so constructed as to admit of being opened for the purpose of cleansing without breaking them, and of the displaced portion being after-wards replaced. A great defect in the common soilage drains, whether built in brick work or earthenware pipes, is, that they have to be broken up whenever they require cleansing; this might be obviated by using drains of the form represented on Plate XIII., Fig. 1.

The upper tile a, in the diagram, could at any time be lifted off, and the drain cleansed, without the neces-sity of breaking the drain, or of removing any por-tion of the earth, except that immediately covering it. Fig. 1.

A simple kind of trap, applicable to this form of drain (*its transverse section being the same*), and equally effective as regards its capability of being readily cleansed, is shown in Fig. 2.

A section and plan of a drain-trap, to be formed of iron or earthenware, is shown in the same plate, Fig. 3; the tile a should not be fixed down, but be left loose, so as to allow of its ready removal, and the cleansing of the trap. It would, perhaps, be as well to leave the whole of the trap loose, which would allow of its being lifted out, and any obstruction removed. This form of drain-trap is suitable for yards, areas, &c., and, slightly modified, for streets. Figs. 4 and 5.

The waste water from sinks does not seem to be sufficient to cleanse these drains thoroughly; but this may be effected, and at little expense, by simply shortening by one or two inches or more the waste-pipes of the cistern in each case. For as the water runs off by the waste-pipe, the cistern would continue to fill from the main faster than it runs off, till the rate of its coming in (which is *always regulated* by the ball-cock, and becomes gradually less as the ball rises) became exactly equal to the quantity running off; and this it would continue to do until stopped at the main, the quantity of water running off being regulated by the length of the waste-pipe.

By this plan every house-drain might be daily cleansed with water, and kept at a low temperature at a trifling expense, that is, at merely the cost of water from each cistern; *though small,* it would in each street amount to a considerable body; it would serve to cleanse the main sewers themselves without the necessity of any separate apparatus as proposed above. As before remarked, the air of a house can never be kept pure unless the bell and water traps act perfectly, which they seldom or never do as at present constructed; for the bells of the traps in common use for sinks and other places are usually left loose for the convenience of cleansing them, as various matters find their way into the trap, and the escape becomes choked; and unless the bell is immediately replaced after the foreign matter is removed, the trap becomes, of course, useless. To remedy this defect, the bell is sometimes soldered down, when the trap, after a time, becomes filled up, and the bell is forcibly moved and laid aside. A simple apparatus for cleansing the traps when the bells are soldered down has been contrived,* which would be perfectly effective if its careful preservation and use by servants and others could be relied on. But the bell-traps in common use may be much improved, and made to answer all the uses required of them; be always certain of action, and yet admit of occasional cleaning, by fixing the bell to the trap by a hinge, as shown at Plate XIII., Fig. 5, with a projecting piece of metal to prevent its being but partially raised; so that the bell, being held up while the trap is cleaned by the knob *b*, as indicated by the dotted lines, falls into its place by its own weight, and can consequently never fail. The use of the metal top *a* is to prevent the bell being thrown back and left so; it is on this plate shown in section, Fig. 5. The sink may be of wood, lined with lead, of stone, or slate; or, perhaps, better than those, of earthenware, which, among other advantages, would allow of the trap being made with it, and forming a part of itself, as shown in Fig. 6.

Supply of Water.

The arrangements for distributing a supply of water over the different parts of a building will depend very materially on the nature of the supply, whether constant or intermittent. The most common method of

---

* By Mr. Hosking.

supply is from water-works, by pipes which communi-
cate with private cisterns, into which the water is
turned at stated intervals.

A cistern in a dwelling-house is always more or less
an evil; it takes up a great deal of space, costs a great
deal of money in the first instance, and often causes
inconvenience from leakage, from the bursting of the
service pipes in frosty weather, and from the liability
of self-acting cocks to get out of order. The common
material for the cistern itself is wood lined with sheet
lead; but slate cisterns have been much used of late.
The service or feed-pipe for a cistern, in the case of an
intermittent supply, must be sufficiently large to allow
of its filling during the time the water is turned on
from the main. The flow of water into the cistern is
regulated by a ball-cock, so called from its being opened
and shut by a lever with a copper or zinc ball which
floats on the surface of the water. The surface pipes
to the different parts of the building are laid into the
bottom of the cistern, but should not come within an
inch of the actual bottom, in order that the sediment,
which is always deposited in a greater or less degree,
may not be disturbed : the mouth of each pipe should
be covered by a rose, to prevent any foreign substance
being washed into the pipes and choking the taps. To
afford a ready means of clearing out the cistern, a waste-
pipe is inserted quite at the bottom, sufficiently large
to draw off the whole contents in a short time when
required ; into this waste-pipe is fitted a standing waste
which reaches nearly to the top of the cistern and
carries off the waste water, when from any disarrange-
ment in the working of the ball-cock the water con-
tinues running after the cistern is full. To prevent

any leakage at the bottom of the standing waste, the latter terminates in a brass plug which is ground to fit a washer inserted at the top of the waste-pipe.

Where the supply of water is constant, instead of being intermittent, private cisterns may be altogether dispensed with; the main pipes not being required to discharge a large quantity of water in a short time, may be of smaller bore, and consequently cheaper, and a considerable length of pipe is saved, as the water can be laid on directly to the several taps, instead of having to be taken up to the cistern and then brought back again. The constant flow of water through the pipes also much diminishes the risk of their bursting in frosty weather from freezing of their contents, when there is not a regular supply of water from the mains of water works, if any, as it frequently occurs. In new localities, wells are sunk, and the water raised by means of pumps, and conveyed by pipes to its required destination; and as rain-water is considered the purest of all water, it may be considered desirable to construct a filtering tank for its reception; and where there is a want of wholesome water, a tank might be constructed large enough to receive the rain-water from the roofs of a number of houses. This would insure a constant supply of soft and pure water for all domestic purposes.

The same would apply where there is no complete system of sewerage; a large manure tank might be constructed.

It is calculated that the average quantity of water which falls on a square yard of surface in Britain, in a year, amounts to about 120 gallons, which, for a building containing 100 square yards of roof, gives 12,000 gallons, an ample quantity for all purposes. Rain-

water tanks are generally constructed in the following
manner :—The ground being excavated, the bottom is
laid with one or two courses of bricks, upon which two
or three courses of tiles are laid in cement, and the
sides and ends are formed with brickwork in cement,
and the whole is then rendered with cement about an
inch in thickness. The top is either domed or covered
with a flat stone. To filter water into a tank of this
kind a small well or cistern is constructed, the bottom
of which is perforated to admit the water upon which
the charcoal is laid, and then covered over with
another perforated plate, as shown and described on
Plate XIV. ; a pump is then applied to the smaller
cistern or filter for the supply. This, as will be
perceived on inspection, would admit of ready cleaning,
as the filter could at any time be lifted out. Plate XIV.,
Fig. 1, is a section of the rain-water tank ; H the
cistern ; A the stone cover to the same ; E E the portion for the filtered water ; F filtering medium ; c c the
perforated portion for allowing the water to force itself
through the filtering medium F ; J rod for lifting the
filters out of cistern when it requires cleaning ; c the
supply pipe ; D waste ditto. Fig. 2 is a plan of the
same tank ; A cistern ; B slate or earthenware filter.
A modification of this arrangement may be adopted
for smaller buildings, and a bucket may be applied for
dipping the water from the filter.

CHAPTER II.

BRICKLAYER.

Our drainage, water supply, &c., having been considered as far as relates to our design, perhaps the next
consideration would be for the erection of the carcass of
the building, and probably we cannot do better than
commence with the bricklayer.* The business of a
bricklayer consists in the execution of all kinds of work
in which brick is the principal material; and in London
it always includes tiling, and paving with bricks or
tiles. Where undressed stone is much used as a building
material, the bricklayer executes this kind of work
also; and in the country the business of the plasterer
is sometimes connected with the above-named branches.
And here, perhaps, we cannot do better than give the
list of tools required, and the classification of them.

The tools of the bricklayer are—the *trowel*, to take up
and spread the mortar, and to cut bricks to the requisite
size; the *brick-axe* for shaping them to the required
bevel; the *tin-saw* for making incisions in them to be
cut with the *axe;* and a *rubbing-stone* to rub the bricks
smooth after being roughly axed into shape. The
jointer and the *jointing-rule* are used for running the
centres of the mortar joints; the *raker* for raking out
the joints of old brickwork, previous to repointing; the
hammer for cutting chases and splays; the *banker*,
which is a piece of timber about six feet long, raised on
supports to a convenient height, to form a table on

* Consult Mr. E. Dobson's four volumes in this series. I. "Art of
Building," No. 22; II. "Bricks and Tiles," No. 23; III. "Masonry
and Stonecutting," No. 25; and IV. "Foundations," No. 44.

which to cut the bricks to any gauge for which moulds and bevels are required. The *crow-bar*, *pick-axe*, and *shovel* are used in digging out the foundation ; and the *rammer* in punning the ground round the footings, and in rendering the foundation firm where it is soft, by beating or ramming.

To set out the work and keep it true, the bricklayer uses the *square*, the *level*, and the *plumb-rule*. For circular work he uses *templets** and *battering-rules; lines* and *pins* are used to lay the courses by, and *measuring-rods* to take dimensions when brickwork has to be carried up in conjunction with stonework ; the height of each course must be marked on a *gauge-rod,* that the joints of each may coincide.

The bricklayer is supplied with bricks and mortar by a labourer, who carries them in a *hod ;* the labourer also makes the mortar, and builds and strikes the scaffolding. The bricklayer's scaffold is constructed with *standards, ledgers,* and *putlogs.* The standards are fir poles, from forty to fifty feet long, and six or seven inches in diameter at the butt ends, which are firmly bedded in the ground. When one pole is not sufficiently long, two are lashed together, top and butt, the lashings being tightened with wedges. The ledgers are horizontal poles, placed parallel to the walls and lashed to the standard for the support of the putlogs. The putlogs are cross pieces, usually made of birch, and about six feet long, one end resting in the wall, the other on a ledger. On the putlogs are placed the scaffold boards, which are stout boards hooped with iron at the ends, to prevent them from splitting.

* The templet should be carefully cut to the form of the work to be executed. For description of the tools used, see Weale's " Technical Dictionary," No. 36 of this series.

A bricklayer and his labourer will lay in a day about 1000 bricks, or about two cubic yards.

The tools required for tiling are the *lathing-hammer*, with two gauge marks on it, one at 7 and the other at 7¼ inches; the iron *lathing-staff*, to clinch the nails; the *trowel*, longer and narrower than that used for brick-work; the *bosse*, for holding mortar and tiles, with an iron hook to hang it to the tiles or to a ladder; and the *striker*, a piece of lath about 10 inches long, for clearing off the superfluous mortar at the foot of the tiles.

Brickwork is measured and valued * by the rod or by the cubic yard, the price including the erection and use of scaffolding, but not centering to arches, which is an extra charge. Bricknogging, pavings, and facings by the superficial yard. Digging and steining of wells and cesspools by the foot in depth according to size, the price increasing with the depth. Plain tiling and pantiling are valued per square of 100 feet superficial.

A journeyman bricklayer receives from 4*s*. to 5*s*. 6d. and a labourer from 2*s*. 6d. to 3*s*. 6d. per day.

The following memoranda may be useful :—

WEIGHTS OF DIFFERENT KINDS OF EARTH.

13 cubic feet of chalk	weigh	one ton.
17 ,,	clay	,,	. . . .	
18 ,,	night soil	,,	. . . .	one ton
21¾ ,,	gravel	,,	. . . .	each.
23½ ,,	sand	,,	. . . .	

Twenty-seven cubic feet, or 1 cubic yard, is called a single load, and 2 cubic yards a double load.

A measure of lime is 27 cubic feet, and contains 21 strike bushels.

A bricklayer's hod measures 1 ft. 4 in. × 9 × 9, and contains 20 bricks.

* See Mr. A. C. Beaton's "Measurements and Quantities," in this series.

A rod of brickwork measures 16½ ft. square, 1½ brick thick (*which is called the reduced or standard thickness*) or 272 ft. 3 in. superficial or 306 cubic feet, or 11⅓ cubic yards.

A rod of brickwork, laid four courses to a foot in height, requires 4,353 stock bricks.

Ditto 11½ inches to four courses, 4,533 stock bricks.

These calculations are made without allowing for waste, which is necessary, because the space occupied by flues, bond-timber, &c., and for which no deduction is made, more than compensates for any waste; and in building dwelling-houses, 4,540 stocks to a rod is sufficient.

If laid dry, 5,370 to the rod.

4,900 ditto in wells and circular cesspools.

A rod of brickwork, laid 4 courses to gauge 12 in., contains 235 cubic feet of bricks and 71 cubic feet of mortar, and weighs about 15 tons.

A rod of brickwork requires 1½ cubic yards of chalk lime, and 3 single loads of sand, or 1 cubic yard of stone lime, and 3½ loads of sand or 36 bushels of cement, and an equal quantity of sharp sand.

A cubic yard of mortar requires 9 bushels of lime and 1 load of sand.

Lime and sand, and likewise cement and sand, lose one-third of their bulk when made into mortar.

The proportion of mortar or cement, when made up, to the lime or cement and sand before made up, is as 2 to 3.

Lime or cement and sand to make mortar require as much water as is equal to one-third of their bulk.

A cubic yard of concrete requires 34 cubic feet of material; or if the gravel is to the lime as 6 to 1, a concrete will require 1·1 cubic yard of gravel and sand, and 3 bushels of lime.

Facing requires 7 bricks per foot superficial.

Gauged arches 10 ditto, ditto.

Bricknogging, per yard superficial, requires 30 bricks on edge, or 45 laid flat.

PAVING.

Stock bricks laid flat require 36 per yard superficial.

Paving ditto on edge	,, 52	,,
Paving ditto laid flat	,, 36	,,
Ditto on edge	,, 82	,,
Dutch clinkers	,, 140	,,
12-inch paving tiles	,, 9	,,
10-inch ditto	,, 13	,,

TILING.

Description.	Gauge in Inches.	No. required per Square.
With pantiles	12	150
Ditto	11	164
Ditto	10	180
Ditto	4	600
Ditto	$3\frac{1}{2}$	700
Ditto	3	800

N.B.—A square of pantiling requires one bundle of laths, and 125 sixpenny nails.

A TABLE

Of the Sizes and Weights of various Articles employed in Building.

Description.	Length.		Breadth.		Thickness.		Weight.	
	ft.	in.	ft.	in.	ft.	in.	lbs.	ozs.
Stock-bricks . . . . each	0	$8\frac{3}{4}$	0	$4\frac{1}{4}$	0	$2\frac{1}{2}$	5	0
Paving ditto . . . . ,,	0	9	0	$4\frac{1}{2}$	0	$1\frac{3}{4}$	4	0
Dutch clinkers . . . ,,	0	$6\frac{1}{4}$	0	3	0	$1\frac{1}{2}$	1	8
12-inch paving-tiles . ,,	0	$11\frac{3}{4}$	0	$11\frac{3}{4}$	0	$1\frac{1}{2}$	13	0
10-inch ditto . ,,	0	$9\frac{3}{4}$	0	$9\frac{3}{4}$	0	1	8	9
Plain tiles . . . . ,,	0	$10\frac{1}{4}$	0	$6\frac{1}{2}$	0	$0\frac{5}{8}$	2	5
Pantile laths, per 10-feet bundle	120	0	0	$1\frac{1}{4}$	0	1	4	6
Ditto, 12-feet ditto . . .	144	0	0	$1\frac{1}{2}$	0	1	5	0
N.B.—A bundle contains twelve laths.								
Plain tile laths, per bundle .	500	0	0	1	0	$0\frac{1}{4}$	3	0
Thirty bundles of laths make a load.								

To ascertain the quantity of brickwork* contained in a well, take the diameter, allowing the thickness on one side, three times of which, and one-seventh, will be the circumference. This should be multiplied by the depth, and the contents brought into brick and half work.

To find what quantity of water a well will hold, multiply half the circumference by half the diameter; this should be multiplied by the depth, and will give the number of cubic feet which will contain 6 gallons and 1 pint each.

Having explained the various tools and principal materials used in the trade of a bricklayer, we would impress upon the young artisan to give some attention to geometrical drawing, without which he will never be enabled to read or comprehend the design he may be entrusted with to execute. For, even in the simple turning of an arch over a centre already fixed for him, unless he knows that every brick should radiate to a centre and knows how to find that centre, he will never be certain of making sound work to his arch. We have endeavoured to show this in two diagrams shown on Plate XVI., Figs. 4 and 5. Let 1—2 be the opening or span of the segment of an arch; E F the rise; stretch a line, or apply a straight edge, from 2 to F, and mark the centre c; apply the square, and the point where it intersects the centre of the rise B F will be the centre for the arch; consequently, B will be the converging point for all the bricks on that arch. Fig. 5 merely exemplifies the same principle applied to the ellipse.

* Much time will be saved by using the *Slide-rule* in making these calculations. See "The Slide Rule, and its Use," by Mr. C. Hoare, in this series.

CHAPTER III.

CARPENTER.

THE business of the carpenter consists in framing timber together for the construction of *floors, partitions, roofs, &c.**

The carpenter's principal tools are the *axe*, the *saw*, and the *chisel*, to which may be added, the *chalk-line*, *plumb-rule*, *level*, and *square*. The work of the carpenter does not require the use of the *plane*, which is one of the chief tools of the joiner; and this forms the principal distinction between these two trades, the carpenter being engaged in the rough frame-work, and the joiner on the finishings and decorations of buildings.

Probably the first occupation a carpenter will have in a building is the preparation and laying of bond-timber, making and fixing of centres, &c. Bond-timber and wood-bricks were formerly used as the only means for providing against irregular settlement in the brick-work. There is, however, a great objection to the use of timber in the construction of a wall, as it shrinks away from the rest of the work, and often endangers its stability by rotting. Instead of bond-timbers, hoop-iron bond is now very generally used. This is formed of iron hooping tarred, to protect the iron from contact with the mortar, and laid in the thickness of the mortar joint. This forms a very permanent longitudinal tie, and has all the advantages, with none of the disadvantages, of the bond-timbers.

* "Carpentry and Joinery," founded on Robinson and Tredgold, No. 123; and "Roofs for Public and Private Buildings," No. 24 of this series.

Floors.

The assemblage of timbers forming any naked floor-ing may be either single or double. Single flooring is formed with joists reaching from wall to wall, where they rest on plates of timber, built into the brickwork, and called wall-plates. The floor-boards are nailed over the upper edges of the joists, whose lower edges receive the lathing and plastering of the ceilings. Double floors are constructed with stout binding joists, a few feet apart, reaching from wall to wall, and sup-porting ceiling joists, which carry the ceiling, and bridging joists, on which are nailed the floor-boards. In double framed flooring, the binders, instead of rest-ing on the walls, are supported on *girders.* Single flooring is in many respects inferior to double flooring, being liable to sag or deflect, so as to make the floors concave; and the situation of the joists occasions injury to the ceilings, and likewise shakes the walls. This may be prevented in single floors by herring-bone, trussing them, and introducing an iron rod from wall-plate to wall-plate, as shown and described on Plate XIX., Figs. 1, 2, 3, and 4. Fig. 5 shows the method of applying sound boarding puggings, &c., to prevent any sound passing between the upper and lower floors. In double floors, the stiffness of the binders and girders prevents both deflection and vibration, and the floors and ceilings hold their lines, that is, retain their in-tended form much better than in single flooring.

If it were not for the increased expense, it would be much better for all the joists of a single floor to be laid on a plate supported by projecting corbels, which prevents the wall being crippled in any way by the in-

sertion of the joists. The plates of basement floors
are best supported on small piers carried up from the
footings. This is an important point to be attended to,
as the introduction of timbers into a wall is nowhere
likely to be productive of such injurious effects as at
the foundations, where from damp and imperfect ventilation all woodwork is liable to speedy decay.

Partitions.

The partitions forming the interior divisions of a
building may be either solid walling of brick or stone,
or they may be constructed entirely of timber, or they
may be frames of timber, filled in with masonry or
brickwork. It would always be best for durability,
and security against fire, to make the partitions of
solid walling; but this is not always practicable;
and in the erection of houses they are generally made
of timber.

The principles to be kept in view, in the construction
of framed partitions, are very simple. Care must be
taken to avoid any cross strain, and they should not in
any way depend for support upon subordinate parts
of the construction, but should form a portion of the
main carcass of the building, and quite independent
of the floors, which should not support, but be supported by them.

When a partition extends through two or more
stories of a building, it should be as much as possible
a continuous piece of framing, with strong sills, at
proper heights, to support the floor-joists.

Where openings occur, as for folding-doors, or where
a partition rests on the ends of the sill only, it should

be strongly trussed, so that it is as incapable of settlement as the walls themselves.

From want of attention to these points, we frequently see in dwelling-houses floors which have sunk into curved lines, doors out of square, cracked ceilings and broken cornices, and gutters that only serve to conduct the roof-water to the interior of the building, to the injury of ceilings and walls, and the great discomfort of the inmates.

Roofing.

In roofs of the ordinary construction, the roof-covering is laid upon rafters, supported by horizontal purlins, which rest on upright trusses, or frames of timber, placed on the walls at regular distances from each other. Upon the framing of the trusses depends the stability of the roof; the arrangement of the rafters and purlins being subordinate matters of detail. The timbering of a roof may be compared to that of a double-framed floor; the trusses of the former corresponding to the girders of the latter, the purlins to the binders, and the rafters to the joists.

Timber roofs may be divided into two heads :—

First. Those which exert merely a vertical pressure on the walls on which they rest.

Secondly. Those in which advantage is taken of the strength of the walls to resist a side thrust, as in many of the gothic open-timbered roofs.

Trussed roofs exerting no side thrust on the walls consist essentially of a pair of principals, or principal rafters, and a horizontal tie-beam, and in large roofs these are connected and strengthened by king and queen posts and struts.

The collar beam roof is the most simple truss, in which the tie is above the bottom of the feet of the principal, which is often done in small roofs for the sake of obtaining height. In this roof the feet of both common and principal rest on a wall-plate, and the tie is called a collar. The purlins rest on the collar, and the common rafters butt against a ridge running along the top of the roof. This kind of truss is only suited for very small spans, as there is a cross strain on that part of the principal below the collar which is rendered harmless in a small space by the extra strength of the principal; but which, in a larger one, would be very likely to thrust out the walls.

In roofs of larger spans the tie-beams are placed below the feet of the principals, which are tenoned into and bolted or strapped to them. To keep the beam from sagging, or bending by its own weight, it is suspended from the head of the principal by a king-post of wood or iron. The lower part of the king-post affords abutments for struts, supporting the principals immediately under the purlins, so that no cross-strain is exerted on any of the timbers in the truss, but they all act in the direction of their length, the principals and struts being subjected to compression, and the king-posts and tie-beams to tension. The common rafters butt on a pole plate, the tie-beams resting either on a continuous wall-plate, or on short templates of wood or stone. Where the span is considerable, the tie-beam is supported at additional points by suspension pieces called queen posts, from the bottom of which spring additional struts; and by extending this principle *ad infinitum* we might construct a roof of any span, were it not that a practical limit is imposed by the nature of the materials.

Having in a cursory manner described the principles of framing, we will now endeavour to describe some of the principal joints made use of in framing. Timbers that have to be joined in the direction of their length, are what is termed scarfed together, that is, an oblique cut is made across the width of one piece at the end, proposed to be joined, and a corresponding one to the piece proposed to be added to it, with bird's-mouth bevels at each end and notches in the middle to admit of oak or iron wedges; these are then placed together and secured either by iron bolts or straps. The king-post is connected with the tie-beam by a tenon and mortice, and the post should be cut somewhat short, to give the power of screwing up the framing after the timber has become fully seasoned. The tie-beam may be suspended from the king-post either by a bolt or by a strap passed round the tie-beam, and secured by iron wedges or cotters passing through a hole in the king-post; this last is the more perfect, but at the same time the more expensive of the two methods.

The king-post is generally cut with joggles for the principal rafters and struts to abut against and frame into. The ends of the principal rafters and struts should be cut off as nearly square as possible, and tenoned into the joggles—otherwise when the timber shrinks, which it will more or less, the thrust is thrown upon the edge only, which splits or crushes under the pressure and causes settlement.

The wall-plates are halved and dove-tailed together, and the tie-beams cogged upon them, the purlins bridged upon the principal rafters, and the common rafters notched upon the purlins. And it should be observed, as a general rule, all timbers should be notched down to those on which they rest, so as to prevent their being moved either lengthways or sideways. Where an upright post has to be fixed between two horizontal sills, as in the case of the uprights of a common framed partition, it is simply tenoned into them, and the tenons secured with oak pins driven through the cheeks of the mortice.

The carpenter requires considerable bodily strength for the handling of the timbers on which he has to work; he should have a knowledge of mechanics, that he may understand the nature of the strains and thrusts to which his work is exposed, and the best method of preventing or resisting them; and he should have such a knowledge of working drawings as will enable him, from the sketches of the architect, to set out the lines for every description of work for centering, framing, &c., that may be entrusted to him for execution.

In measuring carpenter's work, the tenons are included in the length of the timber. This is not the case in joiner's, in which they are allowed for in the price. Carpenter's work is generally measured by the square of 100 feet, and the cubical contents of every square taken out; and nothing is to be deducted for chimneys, as the extra thickness of the trimmers will make up the deficiency, and in a quarter partition the braces and extra thickness of the door-posts will make up for the opening, but the head and sill must be taken separate; and if the joists or quarterings in roofs or partitions are 13 inches asunder, one-twentieth of the quantity found is to be taken off—but if placed within 11 inches, one-twentieth must be added. And in measuring the work for labour, only take the extreme verge, including the bearings, one way, and make no deductions for well-holes, chimney-breasts, doorways, &c. The timber to be collected the full length and size, and charged as " cube fir," without labour. The following tables should be constantly borne in mind by the young carpenter :—

Lineal or running measure contains 12 inches in 1 foot, 3 feet in 1 yard, 2 yards 1 fathom, and 1,760 yards or 5,280 feet in one mile.

Superficial measure contains 144 square inches in 1 foot, 9 feet in 1 yard, and 100 feet in 1 square of flooring, roofing, partitioning, &c. ; 272¼ feet in 1 rod or pole, and 160 poles in 4,840 yards, or 43,560 feet in 1 acre.

Cubic measure comprises the length, breadth, and thickness, and contains 1,728 inches in 1 cubic foot, 27 cubic feet in one cubic yard, 282 cubic inches in 1 gallon, and 6 gallons and 1 pint in each cubic foot.

To measure round timber, multiply the mean or quarter girt by itself, and that product by the length by cross multiplication, and the cubical quantity will be ascertained. For instance : suppose a piece of timber to girt 6 feet, one-quarter of this will be 1 foot 6 inches, which, multiplied by 1 foot 6 inches, will give 2 feet 3 inches superficial, which, multiplied by the length (say 20 feet), will give the contents—45 feet cube ; and in the same way for any other size.

A TABLE

Of quantities of Timber each making One Load.

50 cubic feet of square timber.	600 sq. feet of 1-inch planking.
40 ditto of round or rough.	30 12-feet 3-inch deals.
150 sq. feet of 4-inch planking.	26 14-feet ditto ditto.
170 sq. feet of 3½-inch ditto.	18 20-feet ditto ditto.
200 sq. feet of 3-inch ditto.	25 12-feet 3-inch plank.
240 sq. feet of 2½-inch ditto.	21 14-feet ditto ditto.
300 sq. feet of 2-inch ditto.	18 16-feet ditto ditto.
400 sq. feet of 1½-inch ditto.	15 20-feet ditto ditto.

The following quantities of Material will each, on an average, weigh One Ton :—

39 cubic feet of oak timber.	35 12-feet 2½-inch deals.
50 ditto of fir ,,	30 ditto 3-inch ditto.
60 ditto of elm ,,	46 12-feet 2½-inch batten
45 feet of ash ,,	38 ditto 3-inch ditto.
60 feet of beech ,,	

The number of Cubic Feet in every Square of Flooring, Roofing, or Quarter Partitions of the following different dimensions, the timbers whereof are one foot apart, which should not be more in either.

ROOFS AND QUARTER PARTITIONS.

inches.	cubic ft.	in.	inches.	cubic ft.	in.
2 by 2½	2	10½	3 by 4½	6	10
2 ,, 3	3	4	4 ,, 2½	5	8
3 ,, 2½	4	3½	4 ,, 4	8	4
3 ,, 3	5	0	4 ,, 4½	9	1
3 ,, 3½	5	7	4 ,, 5	9	9½
3 ,, 4	6	8			

NAKED FLOOR WITHOUT GIRDER.

inches.	cubic ft.	in.	inches.	cubic ft.	in.
5 by 2½	7	2¼	9 by 2½	12	11¼
5 ,, 3	8	4	9 ,, 3	15	0
6 ,, 2½	8	7½	10 ,, 2½	14	4½
6 ,, 3	10	0	10 ,, 3	16	3
7 ,, 2½	10	4½	11 ,, 2½	15	9½
7 ,, 3	11	8	11 ,, 3	18	4
8 ,, 2½	11	6	12 ,, 2½	17	3
8 ,, 3	13	4	12 ,, 3	20	0

The above tables of different scantlings will be found

very useful to those who are unacquainted with taking, squaring, and cubing dimensions; as also to such as have to make an estimate in a hurry, as they are the common dimensions of fir scantling for joists, rafters, and quarters for roofs and partitions, of second, third, and fourth-rate houses : but we would advise the young carpenter to take the dimensions of the timber required for any stated work, and square and cube them himself.*

CHAPTER IV.

MASON.

THE business of the mason consists in working the stones to be used in a building to their shape and setting them in their places. The works connected with the trade of the mason are those of the stone-cutter, who hews and cuts large stones roughly into shape preparatory to their being worked by the mason, and of the carver, who executes the ornamental portions of the stone-work of a building, as enriched cornices, capitals, &c. Where the value of stone is considerable it is sent from the quarry to the building in large blocks, and cut into slabs and scantlings of the required size with a stone-mason's saw, which differs from that used in any other trade in having no teeth. It is a long thin plate of steel, slightly jagged on the bottom edge, and fixed in a frame, and, being drawn backwards and forwards in a horizontal position, cuts the stone by its own weight. To facilitate the operation a heap of

* See "Quantities and Measurements," by Alfred Charles Beaton, and "The Slide Rule and its Uses," by Charles Hoare, both in this Series.

C

sharp sand is placed on an inclined plane over the stone, and water allowed to trickle through it so as to wash the sand into the saw cut. Of late years machinery worked by steam-power has been used for sawing marble into slabs as well as stone to a very great extent, and has almost entirely superseded manual labour in this part of the manufacturing of chimney-pieces.

Some freestones, as Bath stone, are so soft as to be easily cut with a toothed saw worked backwards and forwards by two persons. The harder kinds of stones, as granites and gritstones, are brought roughly into shape at the quarry, with an axe or *scappling* hammer, and are then said to be *scappled*.* The tools used by the mason for cutting stone consist of the *mallet* and chisels of various sizes. The mason's mallet differs from that used by any other artisan, being similar to a dome in *contour*, excepting a portion of the broadest part, which is rather cylindrical ; the handle is short, being only sufficiently long to enable it to be firmly grasped. In London the tools used to break the faces of the stone are the *point*, which is the smallest description of *chisel*, being never more than a quarter of an inch broad on the cutting edge ; *the inch tool;* the *boaster*, which is two inches wide, and the *broad tool*, of which the cutting edge is three and a-half inches wide. The tools used in working mouldings, and in carving, are of various sizes according to the nature of the work. Besides the above cutting tools, the mason uses the *banker* or bench, in which he places his stone for convenience of working, and straight-edges, squares,

* Reduced to a straight surface without being worked smooth. (See " Technical Dictionary.")

levels, and templets, for marking the shapes of the blocks, and for trying the surfaces as the work proceeds. Any angle greater or less than a right angle is called a bevel angle, and a bevel is formed by nailing two straight-edges together at the required angle; a bevel square is a *square* with a shifting back, which can be set to any required bevel. A templet is sometimes called a mould, which moulds are commonly made of sheet zinc carefully cut to the profile of the mouldings with shears and files. For setting his work in place the mason uses the trowel, lines, and pins, the square and level, and plumb, and battering rules for adjusting the faces of upright and battering walls.

The mason's scaffold is double, that is, formed with two rows of standards, so as to be totally independent of the walls for support, as putlog holes are inadmissible in masonry.

Of late years the construction of scaffolds with round poles lashed together with cords, has been superseded in large works by a system of scaffolding of square timbers connected together by bolts and dog-irons. The hoisting of the materials is performed from these scaffolds by means of a travelling crane, which consists of a double travelling carriage running on a tramway formed on straight sills laid on the top of two parallel rows of standards. The crab winch is placed on the upper carriage, and by means of the double motion of the two carriages can be brought with great ease and precision over any part of the work lying between the two rows of standards.

The facilities which are afforded by these scaffolds and travelling cranes for moving heavy weights over large areas have led to their extensive adoption, not only in the erection of buildings, but on landing wharfs, masons' and iron-founders' yards, and similar situations, where a great saving of time and labour is effected by their use. Scaffolding of square timbers appears to have been little used in England before 1837, when Messrs. Cubitt, of Gray's Inn Road, applied it to the erection of the entrance gateway of the Euston Station of the North-Western Railway. Since then it has been very generally used in large works, amongst which may be mentioned the Reform Club House, and the Nelson Column,—where it was carried up in perfect safety to the height of 180 feet; and it was used on a very large scale at the new Houses of Parliament.

The movable derrick crane is also much used in setting mason's work. It consists of a vertical post supported by two timber back-stays, and a long movable jib or derrick hinged against the post below the gearing. By means of a chain passing from a barrel over a pulley at the top of the post, the derrick can be hoisted to an almost vertical, or lowered to nearly a horizontal position, thus enabling it to command every part of the area of a circle of a radius nearly equal to the length of the derrick. This gives it a great advantage over the old gibbet-crane, which only commands a circle of a fixed radius, and the use of which entails great loss of time from its constantly requiring to be shifted as the work proceeds.

Derrick cranes appear to have been first introduced at Glasgow, in 1831, by Mr. York, since which time their original construction has been greatly improved upon, and they are now very extensively used.

In hoisting blocks of stone they are attached to the tackle by means of a simple contrivance called a *lewis*, which consists of the following arrangement:—A taper-

ing hole is cut in the upper surface of the stone to be
raised; the two side pieces of the lewis are inserted
and placed against the sides of the holes (which being
made in the form of a dovetail, and the aperture in the
stone made to correspond), a centre parallel piece is
then dropped in and secured in its place by a strong
pin passing through all three pieces, and the stone
may then be safely hoisted, as it is impossible for the
lewis to be drawn out of the hole. By means of a lewis,
slightly different in form from that just described,
stone can be lowered and set under water without difficulty, the lewis being disengaged by means of a line
attached to the parallel piece, the removal of which
allows the other to be drawn out of the mortice.

In stone-cutting the workman forms as many plane
faces as may be necessary for bringing the stone into
the required shape with the least waste of material and
labour, and on the plane surface, so formed, applies the
moulds to which the stone is to be worked.

To form a plane surface the mason first knocks off
the superfluous stone along one edge of the block until
it coincides with a straight-edge throughout its whole
length—this is called a *chisel draught*. Another chisel
draught is then made along one of the adjacent edges,
and the ends of the two are connected by another
draught. A fourth draught is then sunk across the
last, which gives another angle point in the same plane
with the other draughts, and the stone is then knocked
off between the outside draughts until a straight-edge
coincides with its surface in every part.

To form cylindrical or moulded surfaces, curved in
one direction only, the workman sinks two parallel
draughts at the opposite ends of the stone, to be worked
until they coincide with a mould cut to the required

shape, and afterwards works off the stone between these draughts by a straight-edge applied at right angles to them.

The formation of conical or spherical surfaces is much less simple, and requires a knowledge of the scientific operations of stone-cutting, a description of which would be unsuited to the elementary character of these pages. The reader who wishes to pursue the subject is therefore referred to the writer's volume (25) of this series on Masonry and Stone-cutting, where he will find the required information.

The finely grained stones are usually brought to a smooth surface, and rubbed with sand to produce a perfectly even surface.

In working soft stones the surface is brought to a smooth face with a drag, which is a plate of steel, indented on the edge like the teeth of a saw, to take off the marks of the tools employed in shaping it. The harder and more coarsely grained stones are generally tooled; that is, the marks of the chisel are left on their face. If the furrows left by the chisel are disposed in regular order, the work is said to be *fair-tooled;* but if otherwise, it may be *random-tooled,* or *chiselled,* or *boasted,* or *pointed.* If the stones project beyond the points, the work is said to be *rusticated* or reticulated.

Granite and gritstone are chiefly worked with the scappling hammer. In massive erections, where the stones are large, and effect is required, the fronts of the blocks are left quite rough, as they come out of the quarry, and the work is then said to be *quarry pitched.*

Many technical terms are used by quarry-men,* and

* See "Technical Dictionary of Terms used in Architecture, Building," &c.

others engaged in working stone; but they need not be inserted here, as they are mostly confined to particular localities, beyond which they are little known, or perhaps bear a different signification. When the mason requires to give the joints of his work greater security than is afforded by the weight of the stone and the adhesion of the mortar, he makes use of *joggles, dowels,* and *cramps.* Stones are said to be joggled when a projection is worked out on one stone to fit in a corre- sponding hole or groove in the other; but this occasions great labour and waste of stone. Dowels are chiefly made use of, which are hard pieces of stone cut to the required size, and let into corresponding mortices in the two stones to be joined together.

Dowels may be pins of wood, metal, or stone, used to secure the joints of stone-work in exposed situations, as copings, pinnacles, &c. The best material is copper; but the expense of this metal causes it to be seldom used. If iron be made use of it should be thoroughly tarred, to prevent oxidation, or it will sooner or later burst or split the work it is intended to protect. Dowels are often secured in their places with lead poured in from above, through a small channel cut in the side of the joint for that purpose; but a good workman will eschew lead, which too often finds its way into bad work, and will prefer trusting to very close and workmanlike joints, carefully fitted dowels, and fine mortar. Dowels should be made tapering at one end, which ensures a better fit, and renders the setting of the stone more easy for the workman.

Iron cramps are used as fastenings on the tops of copings, and in similar situations; but they are not to be recommended, as they are very unsightly, and if they once become exposed to the action of the atmosphere, are powerfully destructive agents. Cast iron is, however, less objectionable than wrought for this purpose.

In measuring mason's work, the cubic contents of the stone is taken as it comes to the *banker*, without deduction for subsequent waste. If the scantlings are large, an extra price is allowed for hoisting. The labour in working the stone is charged by the super-*ficial* foot, according to the kind of work, as plain work, sunk work, moulded work, &c. Pavings, landings, &c., and all stones less than three inches thick, are charged by the superficial foot. Copings, curbs, window-sills, &c., are charged per lineal foot. Cramps, dowels, mortice holes, &c., are always charged separately.

A journeyman mason will receive from 4s. to 5s. 6d. per day, and the labourer from 2s. 6d. to 3s. per day; but masons working piece-work, or at any work requiring particular skill, will often earn much more. The remuneration of a stone-carver is dependent on his talent, and the kind of work he is engaged upon.

The following table of the weights of the different kinds of stone will convey an idea of their relative hardness, and of the labour required to work them :—

TABLE

Of the Weights of different kinds of Stone.

13 cubic feet of marble	weigh one ton.		
13½ ,, of granite	,,	,,
14 ,, of Purbeck stone	,,	,,
14½ ,, of Yorkshire stone	,,	,,
16 ,, of Derbyshire grit	,,	,,
17 ,, of Portland stone	,,	,,
18 ,, of Bath stone	,,	,,
58 feet superficial of 3-inch York paving .	,,	,,
70 ,, of 2½-inch ,, . .	,,	,,

PLUMBER.

The work of the plumber chiefly consists in laying sheet lead on roofs, lining cisterns, laying on water to the different parts of a building, and fixing up pumps and water-closets. The plumber uses but few tools, and those are of a simple character, the greater number of them being similar to those used by other artificers, *hammers, mallets, planes, chisels, gouges, files,* &c. The principal tool peculiar to the trade of the plumber is the *bat,* which is made of beech. It is about eighteen inches long, and is used for dressing and flattening sheet lead. For soldering, the plumber also uses iron ladles of various sizes for melting solder, as well as lead, and *grozing-irons* for smoothing down the joints. The sheet-lead used by the plumber is either *cast* or *milled,* the former being generally cast by the plumber himself out of old lead taken in exchange, whilst the latter, which is cast lead flattened out between two rollers in a flatting mill, is purchased from the manufacturer. Sheet-lead is described, according to the weight per superficial foot, as 5 lb. lead, 6 lb. lead, &c.

Lead-pipes, if of large dimensions, are made of sheet-lead dressed round a wooden core and soldered up. Smaller pipes are cast in short lengths, of a thickness three or four times that of the intended pipe, and either drawn or rolled out to the proper thickness.

Soft-solder is used for uniting the joints of lead-work; it is made of equal parts of lead and tin, and is purchased of the manufacturer, by the plumber, at a price per lb., according to the state of the market.

Laying of Sheet-lead.

In order to secure lead-work from the injurious effect of contraction and expansion where exposed to the heat of the sun, the plumber is careful not to confine the metal by soldered joints, or otherwise. All sheet-lead should be laid with a slope sufficient to keep it dry; a fall of one inch in ten feet is sufficient for this purpose, if the boarding on which the lead is laid be perfectly even.

Flashings are pieces of lead turned down over the edges of other lead-work, which is turned up against a wall, and serve to keep the wet from finding its way between the wall and the lead. The most secure way of fixing them is to build them into the joints of the brickwork, but the common method is to insert them about an inch into the mortar joint, and to secure them with wall hooks and cement.

A very important part of the business of the plumber consists in fitting up cisterns, pumps, and water-closet apparatus, and in laying the different services and wastes connected with the same.

Plumber's work is paid for by the cwt.; milled-lead being rather more expensive than cast. Lead pipes are charged per foot lineal, according to size.

Pumps and water-closet apparatus are charged at so much each, according to description, as also basins, air-traps, washers and plugs, spindle valves, stop-cocks, ball-cocks, &c.

TABLE

Of the Weight of Lead Pipes per Yard.

Bore.	lbs.	ozs.	Bore.	lbs.	ozs.
½-inch	3	3	1¼-inch	11	0
¾-inch	5	7	1½-inch	14	0
1-inch	8	0	2-inch	21	0

The wages of a journeyman plumber are from 5*s.* to 6*s.* per day, and the plumber's labourer receives from 3*s.* to 3*s.* 6*d.* per day.

ZINC-WORKER.

The use of sheet-lead has been to a certain extent superseded by the use of sheet-zinc, which, from its cheapness and lightness, is very extensively used for almost all purposes to which sheet-lead is applied. It is, however, a very inferior material, and not to be depended on. The laying of it is generally executed by the plumber, but the working of zinc, and manufacturing of it into gutters, rain water-pipes, chimney-cowls, and other articles, is practised as a distinct business.

SMITH AND IRON-FOUNDER.

The smith furnishes the various articles of wrought iron work used in a building, as pileshoes, straps, screw-bolts, dog-irons, chimney-bars, gratings, wrought-iron railing, and iron balustrades for staircases. Wrought-iron was formerly much used for many purposes, for which cast-iron is almost exclusively employed; the improvements effected in casting during the present century having made a great alteration in this respect. The operations of the iron-founder have been much improved since the middle of the last century, when the smelting of iron was carried on with wood charcoal, and the ores used were chiefly from the secondary strata, although the clay iron-stones of the coal-measures were occasionally used. The weald of Kent and Sussex contained many iron-works during the seventeenth century. The one formerly situated at Lamberhurst, near Tunbridge Wells, Sussex, is noted as having furnished the cast-iron railing round St. Paul's Cathedral. The tilt hammers used in forging bar-iron were chiefly worked by water power. A large pool in Beeding Forest, near Horsham, Sussex, still retains the name of the Hammer Pond, and the former sites of many old forges in the Wealden district may still be traced by the heaps of cinders which yet remain here and there, and by the local name to which the works gave rise.

The introduction of smelting with pit-coal coke during the last century caused a complete revolution in the iron trade. The ores now chiefly used are the clay iron-stones of the coal measures, and the fuel pit-coal or coke.

Steam power is almost exclusively used for the production of the blast furnaces, and for working the forge hammers and rolling mills. For the production of wrought-iron in the ordinary manner, two distinct sets of processes are required: 1st, the extraction of the metal from the ore in the shape of cast-iron; 2nd, the conversion of cast-iron into malleable or bar-iron by remelting, puddling, and forging. The conversion of bar-iron into steel is effected by placing it in contact with powdered charcoal in a cementing furnace.

Cast-iron is produced by smelting the previously calcined ore in a blast furnace along with a certain quantity of limestone and coke; the former acts as a flux, while the combustion of the latter supplies the heat. The metal when fused sinks to the bottom, while the limestone and the impurities rise to the top, and are allowed to run off, forming slag or cinder. The melted metal is run off from the bottom of the furnace into moulds in the case of castings, and into furrows made in a level bed of sand, when the metal is required for conversion into malleable iron; the bars thus produced being called *pigs*.

In the year 1827 it was discovered that by the use of heated air for the blast a great saving of fuel could be effected as compared with the cold blast process. The hot blast is now very extensively used, and has the double advantage of requiring less fuel to bring down an equal quantity of metal, and of enabling the manufacturer to use raw pit-coal instead of coke; so that a saving is effected both in the quantity and cost of the fuel.

For a considerable time after its introduction it was held in great disrepute; which, however, may be chiefly attributed to the inferior quality of ores used, the power of the hot blast in reducing the most refractory offering a great temptation to obtain a much larger product from the furnaces than was compatible with the good quality of the metal.

The use of the hot blast by firms of acknowledged character has greatly tended to remove the prejudice against it, and in many iron-works of high character nothing but the hot blast with pit-coal is used in the smelting furnaces, the use of coke being confined to the subsequent processes.

It may be laid down as a principle, that in architectural structures, at least where a proper margin of safety has been provided in determining the scantlings of either cast or wrought-iron to resist known stresses in construction, that it is practically unimportant at present (1867) to the architect whether the metals he specifies or employs be hot blast or cold blast.

The temperature of the hot blast has been lately considerably intensified by the use of Siemens's regenerative furnace. The reader wishing further information respecting these furnaces will find a description of them in the articles *Heat* and *Iron* in "Tomlinson's Cyclopædia of Useful Arts." The results obtained are an increased temperature, a saving in the amount of fuel used per ton of iron obtained, and a better quality of iron.

Cast-iron is divided by the iron-founder into three qualities:—No. 1, or dark grey cast-iron, is coarse-grained, soft, and not very tenacious. When remelted, it passes into No. 2, or grey cast-iron. This is the best quality for castings requiring strength. When repeatedly remelted, it becomes excessively hard and brittle and passes into No. 3, or white cast-iron, which is only used for the commonest castings, as sash weights, cannon balls, and similar articles.

White cast-iron if produced direct from the ore is an indication of derangement in the working of the furnace, and is unfit for the ordinary purposes of the founder, except to mix with other qualities.

Girders and similar solid articles are cast in sand moulds enclosed in iron frames or boxes, each mould requiring upper and lower boxes. A mould is formed by pressing sand firmly round a wooden pattern, which is afterwards removed, and the melted metal poured into the spaces thus left through apertures made for that purpose.

The moulds for ornamental work and for hollow castings are of a more complicated construction, which will be better understood from actual inspection at a foundry than from any written description. Almost all irons are improved by admixture with others, and therefore where superior castings are required they should not be run direct from the smelting furnace, but the metal should be remelted in a cupola furnace, which gives the opportunity of suiting the quality of the iron to its intended use. Thus for delicate ornamental work a soft and very fluid iron will be required, whilst for girders and castings exposed to cross strain the metal will require to be harder and more tenacious. For bed-plates and castings which have merely to sustain a compressing force, the chief point to be attended to is the hardness of the metal.

Castings should be allowed to remain in sand until cool, as the quality of the metal is greatly injured by the rapid and irregular cooling which takes place from exposure to air if removed from the moulds in a red-hot state, which is sometimes done in small foundries to economise room.

Staffordshire, Shropshire, and Derbyshire afford the best iron for castings. The Scotch iron is much esteemed for hollow wares, and has a beautifully smooth surface, which may be noticed in the stoves and other articles cast by the Carron Company. The Welsh iron is principally used for conversion into bar-iron.

The conversion of forge pig into bar-iron is effected by a variety of processes, which have for their object the freeing of the metal from the carbon and other impurities combined with it, so as to produce as nearly as possible the pure metal.

Besides cast-iron columns, girders, and similar articles which are cast to order, the founder supplies a great variety of articles which are kept in store for immediate use, as cast-iron palings, balconies, rain water-pipes, and guttering, air-traps, coal-plates, stoves, stable-fittings, iron sashes, &c., &c.

Both wrought and cast-iron work are paid for by weight, except small articles kept in store for immediate use, which are valued per piece :—

One cubic foot of cast-iron	. . . .	weighs about 450 lbs.
Ditto ditto of wrought.	. . . . .	,, 475 ,,
Ditto ditto of closely-hammered	.	,, 485 ,,

The coppersmith provides sheet copper for covering roofs, copper-gutters, and rain water-pipes; washing and brewing coppers; copper cramps and dowels for stone-mason's work, and all other copper work in a building; but the cost of the material in which he works prevents its general use, and the washing-copper is frequently the only part of a building which requires the aid of this artificer. Sheet copper is paid for by the superficial foot, copper in dowels, bolts, &c., at per pound.

Warming apparatus, steam and gas-fittings, and similar kinds of work are put up by the mechanical engineer, who also manufactures a great variety of articles which are purchased in parts, and put together and fixed by the plumber, as pumps, taps, water-closet apparatus.

SLATER.

The business of the slater chiefly consists in covering the roofs of houses with slates; but it has of late years been very much extended by the general introduction of sawn slates as a material for shelves, cisterns, baths, chimney-pieces, and even for ornamental purposes.

We propose here to describe only those operations of the slater which have reference to the covering of roofs. Besides the tools which are in common use among other artificers, the slater uses one peculiar to his trade called the *zax*, which is a kind of hatchet with a sharp point at the back. It is used for trimming slates and making the holes by which they are nailed in their places.

Slates are laid either on boarding or on narrow battens from two to three inches wide, the latter being the more common method on account of its being less expensive than the other. The nails used should be either copper or zinc; iron nails, though sometimes used, being objectionable from their liability to rust. Every slate should be fastened with two nails, except in the most inferior work. The upper surface of a slate is called its *back*, the under surface the *bed*, the lower edge the *tail*, the upper edge the *head*, the part of each course of slate exposed to view is called the *margin* of the course, and the width of the margin is called the *gauge*.

The *bond* or *lap* is the distance which the lower edge of any course overlaps the slates of the second course below, measuring from the nail-hole.

In preparing slates for use, the sides and bottom-edges are trimmed, and the nail-holes punched as near the head as can be done without risk of breaking the slate, and at a uniform distance from the tail.

The lap having been decided on, the gauge will be equal to half the distance from the tail to the nail-hole, less the lap; thus a countess slate measuring nineteen inches from tail to nail, if laid with a three inch lap, would show a margin of eight inches. The battens are of course nailed on to the rafters at the gauge to which the slates will work. If the slates are of different lengths, they must be sorted into sizes and gauged accordingly, the smallest size being placed nearest the ridge. The lap should not be less than two inches, and need not exceed three inches.

It is essential to the soundness, as well as the appearance of slater's work, that the slates should all be of the same width, and the edges perfectly true. The Welsh slates are considered the best, and are of a light sky-blue colour; the Westmoreland slates are of a dull greenish hue.

Slater's work is measured by the square of 100 superficial feet, allowance being made for the trouble of cutting the slates at the hips, eaves, round chimneys, &c.

Slabs for cisterns, baths, shelves, and other sawn work, are charged per foot, superficial, according to the thickness of the slab, and the labour bestowed on the work. Rubbed edges, grooves, &c., are charged per lineal foot.

A journeyman slater receives about 5s. per day, and his labourer about 3s. per day.

TABLE

Of the Sizes of Roofing Slates.

Description.	Size.		Average Gauge in Inches.	No. of Squares 1200 will cover.	Weight per 1200 in Tons.	No. required to cover one Square.	No. of Nails required to one Square.
	Length.	Breadth.					
	ft. in.	ft. in.					
Doubles	1 1	0 6	5½	2	¾	480	480
Ladies	1 4	0 8	7	4½	1¼	280	280
Countesses	1 8	0 10	9	7	2	176	352
Duchesses	2 0	1 0	10½	10	3	127	254
Imperials	2 6	2 0					
Rags and Queens . .	3 0	2 0	A Ton will cover 2¼ to 2½ squares.				
Westmoreland of various sizes							

Inch slab per foot superficial weighs 14 lbs.

We have now endeavoured to explain the various trades employed, and the materials required for the carcass of a building, and will commence with the finishings.

Finishings.

The work of the plasterer consists in covering the brickwork and native timbers of walls, ceilings, and partitions with plaster, to prepare them for painting, papering, or distempering, and in forming cornices, and such decorative portions of the furnishings of buildings as may be required to be executed in plaster or cement.

The plasterer uses a variety of tools, of which the following are the principal ones :—

The *drag* is a three pronged rake, used to mix the hair with the mortar in preparing coarse stuff.

The *hawk* is a small square board for holding stuff on, with a short handle on the under side.

Trowels are of two kinds, the *laying and smoothing tool*, with which the first and the last are laid, and the *gauging trowel* used for gauging fine stuff for cornices, &c., &c. : these are made of various sizes, from three to seven inches long.

Of *floats*, which are used in floating ceilings and other work, there are three kinds, viz., the *Derby*, which is a rule of such a length as to require two men to use it ; the *hand-float*, which is used in furnishing stucco ; and the *quirk-float*, which is used in floating angles.

Moulds, for raising cornices, are made of sheet copper cut to the profile of the moulding, to be formed and fixed in a wooden frame.

Stopping and *picking out tools* are made of steel, seven or eight inches long, and of various sizes. They are used for modelling, and for finishing mitres, and returns to cornice.

Materials.

Coarse stuff, or lime and hair, as it is usually called, is similar to common mortar, with the addition of hair from the tanner's yard, which is thoroughly mixed with the mortar by means of the drag.

Fine stuff is made of pure lime, slaked with a small quantity of water; after which sufficient water is added to bring it to the consistence of cream. It is then allowed to settle, and the superfluous water being poured off, it is left in a bin or tub to remain in a semi-fluid state, until the evaporation of the water has brought it to a proper thickness for use. In using fine stuff for setting ceilings, a small portion of white hair is mixed with it.

Stucco is made with fine stuff and clean washed river sand. This is used for finishing work intended to be painted.

Gauged stuff is formed of fine stuff mixed with plaster of Paris, the proportion of plaster varying according to the rapidity with which the work is required to set.

Gauged stuff is used for running cornices and mouldings.

Enrichments, such as pateras, centre flowers for ceilings, &c., are first modelled in clay, and afterwards cast of plaster of Paris in wax or plaster moulds.

Papier maché ornaments also are much used, and have the advantage of being very light, and being easily and securely fixed with screws.

The variety of compositions and cements made use of by the plasterer is very great. *Roman cement, Portland cement,* and *lias cement,* are the principal ones used for coating buildings externally. Martin and Keene's cements are well adapted for all internal plastering where sharpness, hardness, and delicate finish are required.

Operations for Plastering.

When brickwork is plastered, the first coat is called *rendering.*

In plastering ceilings and partitions, the first operation is *lathing.* This is done with *single, one-and-a-half* or *double* laths, these names denoting their respective thicknesses. Laths are either of oak or fir; if of the former, wrought-iron nails are used, but cast-iron nails may be employed with the latter. The thickest laths are used for ceilings, as the strain on the laths is greater in a horizontal than in an upright position.

Pricking-up is the first coat of plastering of coarse stuff upon laths; when completed, it is well scratched over with the end of a lath, to form a key for the next coat.

Laid work consists of a simple coat of coarse stuff over a wall or ceiling.

Two-coat work is only roughed over with a broom, and afterwards set with fine stuff, or with gauged stuff in the better description of work.

The laying on of the second coat of plastering is called *floating,* from its being floated or brought to a plain surface with the float.

The operation of floating is performed by surrounding the surface to be floated with narrow strips of plastering called *screeds,* brought perfectly upright, or level, as the case may be, with the level or plumb rule; thus, in preparing for floating a ceiling, nails are driven in at the angles, and along the sides, about ten feet apart, and carefully adjusted to a horizontal plane, by means of the level. Other nails are then adjusted opposite to the first, at a distance of seven or eight inches from them. The space between each pair of nails is filled up with coarse stuff, and floated perfectly true with a floating rule; this operation forms a screed, perfectly level throughout. Other screeds, are then formed, to divide the work into bays about eight feet wide, which are successively filled up flush, and floated level with the screeds.

The screeds for floating walls are formed in exactly the same manner, except that they are adjusted with the plumb rule instead of the level. After the work has been brought to an even surface by the floating rule, it is gone over with the hand float and a little soft stuff, to make good any deficiencies that may appear. The operation of forming screeds and floating work, which is not either vertical or horizontal, as a plaster floor laid with a fall, is analogous to that of taking the face of a stone out of winding, with chisel, drafts, and straight edges in stone-cutting, the principle being in each case to find three points in the same plane, from which to extend operations over the whole surface.

Setting.

When the floating is about half dry, the setting or finishing coat of fine stuff is laid on with the smoothing trowel, which is alternately wetted with a brush, and worked over with the smoothing tools, until a fine surface is obtained.

Stucco is laid on with the largest trowel and worked over with the hand-float, the work being alternately sprinkled with water and floated until it becomes hard and compact, after which it is finished by rubbing it over with a dry stock brush. The water has the effect of hardening the face of the stucco, so that after repeated sprinklings and trowelling, it becomes very hard, and smooth as glass.

The above remarks may be briefly summed up as follows. The commonest kind of work consists of only one coat, and is called *rendering*, on brickwork, and *laying*, if on laths. If a second coat be added, it becomes two-coat work, or *render set*, or *lath lay* and *set*. When the work is floated it becomes three-coat work, and is *render, float*, and *set* for brickwork, and *lath, lay, float*, and *set* for ceilings and partitions; ceilings being set with fine stuff and a little white hair, and walls intended for paper with fine stuff and sand; stucco is used where the work is to be painted.

Rough stucco is a mode of finishing staircases, passages, &c., in imitation of stone. It is mixed with a large proportion of sand, and roughened by the hand-float, to give it the appearance of stone.

Rough-cast is a mode of finishing outside work, by dashing over the second coat of plastering, whilst quite wet, a layer of rough cast, composed of well-washed gravel mixed up with pure lime and water till the whole is in a semi-fluid state.

Pugging is lining the spaces between floor joists with coarse stuff, to prevent the passage of sound, or between two stones, and is done on laths or rough boarding.

In the midland districts of England reeds are much used instead of laths, not only for ceilings and parti-

tions, but for floors, which are formed with a thick
layer of coarse gauged stuff upon reeds.   Floors of
this kind are extensively used about Nottingham, and,
from the security against fire afforded by the absence
of wooden floors, Nottingham houses are proverbially
fire-proof.

Plasterer's work is measured by the superficial yard,
cornices by the superficial foot, enrichments to cornices
by the lineal foot, and centre flowers and other decorations at per piece.

Memoranda.

The wages of a journeyman plasterer are from 4s. 6d.
to 5s. 6d. per day; those engaged on modelling and
ornamental work will earn much more.   A labourer
receives from 2s. 6d. to 3s per day; and a plasterer's
boy about 1s.

Lathing.—One bundle of laths and 384 nails will
cover 5 yards superficial measure.

Rendering.—187½ yards require 1½ hundred of lime,
2 double loads of sand, and 5 bushels of hair.

Floating requires more labour, but only half as much
material as rendering.

Setting.—375 superficial yards require 1½ hundred of
lime and 5 bushels of hair.

Render Set.—100 yards superficial require 1½ cwt. of
lime, 1 double load of sand, and 4 bushels of hair, and
the work of plasterer, labourer, and boy, for 3 days
each.

Lath, Lay and Set.—130 yards superficial of lath, lay
and set require I load of laths, 10,000 nails, 2½ cwt. of
lime, 1½ double load of sand, and 7 bushels of hair.
Plasterer, labourer, and boy, 6 days each.

Twenty per cent. profit is allowed upon all materials.

JOINER.

The work of the joiner consists in framing and joining together the wooden finishings and decorations of buildings, both internal and external; such as floors, staircases, framed partitions, skirtings, solid door and window frames, hollow or cased window frames, sashes and shutters, doors, columns and entablatures, chimney-pieces, &c.

The *joiner's* work requires much greater accuracy and finish than that of the carpenter, and differs materially from it in being brought to a smooth surface with the plane wherever exposed to view, whilst with the carpenter's work the timber is left rough as it comes from the saw.

The *joiner* uses a great variety of tools: the principal cutting tools are saws, planes, and chisels.

Of saws there are a great variety, distinguished from each by their shape and by the size of their teeth. The *ripper* has 8 teeth in 3 inches; the *half ripper* 3 teeth to the inch; the *hand-saw*, 15 teeth in 4 inches; the *panel-saw*, 6 teeth to the inch. The *tenon-saw*, used for cutting tenons, has about 8 teeth to the inch, and is strengthened at the back by a thick piece of iron to keep the blade from buckling. The *sash-saw* is similar to the tenon-saw, but is backed with brass instead of iron, and has 13 teeth to the inch; the *dovetail-saw* is still smaller, and has 15 teeth to the inch. Besides the above named, other saws are used for particular purposes—as the *compass-saw* for cutting circular work, and the *keyhole-saw* for cutting small holes. The *carcase-saw* is a large kind of *dovetail-saw*, having about 11 teeth to an inch.

D

Planes are also of many kinds: those called *bench planes*—as the *jack-plane*, the *trying-plane*, the *long plane*, the *jointer*, and the *smoothing-plane*—are used for bringing the stuff to a plane surface. The jack-plane is about 18 inches long, and is used for the roughest work. The trying-plane is about 22 inches long, and used after the jack-plane for *trying-up*—that is, taking off shavings the whole length of the stuff. Whilst using the *jack-plane*, the workman stops at every arm's length. The *long-plane* is about 2 feet 3 inches long, and used when a piece of stuff is to be tried-up very straight. The *jointer* is about 2 feet 6 inches long, and is used for trying-up or *shooting* the *joints*, in the same way as the *trying-plane* is used for trying-up the face of the stuff. The *smoothing-plane* is small, being only about 7½ inches long, and is used on almost all occasions for cleaning or smoothing-off finished work. *Rebate-planes* are used for sinking rebates, and vary in their size and shape according to their respective uses. *Rebate-planes* differ from *bench-planes* in having no handle rising out of the stock, and in discharging their shavings at the side. Amongst the rebate-planes may be mentioned the *moving fillister* and the *sash fillister*, the uses of which will be better understood from inspection than description. *Moulding-planes* are used for *sticking mouldings*, as the operation of forming mouldings with the plane is called. When mouldings are worked with chisels instead of with planes, they are said to be worked by *hand*. Of the class of moulding-planes, although kept separate in the tool chest, are hollows and rounds, beads, &c., of various sizes.

There are other kinds of planes besides the above-named, as the *plough*, for sinking a groove to receive a projecting tongue ; the *bead*, for sticking beads ; the *snipe's-bill*, for forming and cleaning out quirks ; the *compass-plane* and the *forkstaff-plane*, for forming concave and convex cylindrical surfaces. The shape and use of these and many other tools used by the joiner will be better understood by inspection than description.

Chisels are also varied in their form and use : some are used merely with the pressure of the hand, as the *paring chisel;* others by the aid of a mallet, as the *socket chisel* (so named from the iron at the top forming a socket to receive an iron handle), for cutting away superfluous stuff; and the *mortice chisel,* for cutting mortices : the gouges are curved chisels.

The joiners use a great variety of boring tools, as the *brad-awl, gimlet,* and *stock and bit.* The last form but one tool, the *stock* being the *handle,* to the hollow of which may be fitted a variety of steel bits of different bores and shapes, for boring and widening out holes in wood and metal, as *countersinks, rimers,* and *taper shell-bits.*

The *screw-driver, pincers, hammer, mallet, hatchet,* and *adze* are too well known to require description.

The *gauge* is used for drawing lines on a piece of stuff parallel to its edges.

The *bench* is one of the most important of the joiner's implements. It is furnished with a vertical *sideboard,* perforated with diagonal ranges of holes, which receive the *bench-pin,* on which to rest the lower end of a piece of stuff to be planed, whilst the upper end is firmly clamped by the *bench-screw.*

The *mitre-box* is used for cutting a piece of stuff to a mitre, or an angle of forty-five degrees, with one of its sides.

The joiner uses for setting out and fixing his work the *straight edge*, the *square*, the *level* or square with a shifting blade, the *mitre square*, the *level*, and *plumb rule*.

In addition to the tools and implements above enumerated, the execution of particular kinds of work requires other articles, as *cylinders, templets, cramps,* &c., the description of which would unnecessarily extend the limits of our present object.

The principal operations of the joiner are sawing, planing, dovetailing, morticing, and scribing.

The manner of forming a dovetail is by inserting a wedge-shaped projecting piece, called the pin, into a corresponding hole made to receive it, which is called a *socket*.

Morticing is executed by forming a hole in a piece of timber to receive the end of another piece, called the *tenon*. The tenon is sometimes *pinned* in its place with oak pins driven through the checks of the mortice; but in forming doors, shutters, &c., the tenon is secured with tapering wedges driven into the mortice, which is cut slightly wider at the top than the bottom, the adhesion of the glue with which the tenon and wedges are first rubbed over making it impossible for the tenon afterwards to draw out of its place.

Joints in the length of the stuff may be either *square, rebated,* or *grooved and tongued,* which is executed by a groove made with a plough and iron on each edge of the two pieces of stuff, and then a slip of wood, which is called the *tongue,* being inserted before the joint is glued up.

Scribing is the drawing on a piece of stuff the exact profile of some irregular surface to which it is to be made to fit; this is done with a pair of compasses, one leg of which is made to traverse the irregular surface, the other to *describe* a line *parallel* thereto along the edge of the stuff to be cut.

In the execution of *circular work,* or as it is frequently termed *sweep work,* there are four different methods by which the stuff can be brought to the required curve:—

Firstly. It may be steamed and bent into shape.

Secondly. It may be glued up in thicknesses which must, when thoroughly dry, be planed true, and, if not to be painted, covered with a thin veneer, bent round it.

Thirdly. It may be formed in thin thicknesses bent round and glued up in a mould. This may be considered the most perfect of all the methods in use.

Lastly. It may be formed by sawing a number of notches on one side, by which means it becomes easily bent in that direction, but the curve produced by this means is very irregular, and it is an inferior mode of execution compared to the others.

When a number of boards are secured together by cross pieces or *ledges* nailed or screwed at the back, the work is said to be *ledged;* ledged work is for common purposes, as cellar-doors, outside shutters, &c.

Framed work consists of *styles* and *rails* morticed and tenoned together, and filled in with panels, the edges of which fit in grooves cut for the purpose in the *styles* and *rails.*

Work is said to be *clamped* when it is prevented from

warping or splitting by a rail at each end. If the ends of the rail are cut off it is said to be *mitre-clamped*.

There are several ways of laying floors practised by joiners. In laying what is called a *straight-joint floor*, from the joints between the boards running in an unbroken line from wall to wall, each board is laid down and nailed in succession, being first forced firmly against the one last laid with a flooring cramp.

Folding floors are laid by nailing down first every fifth board, rather closer together than the united widths of four boards, and forcing the intermediate ones into the space left for them by jumping on them. This method of laying floors is resorted to when the stuff is imperfectly seasoned and is expected to shrink, but it should never be executed in good work. The narrower the stuff with which a floor is laid the less will the joints open, on account of the shrinkage being distributed over a greater number of joints. The floor boards may be nailed at their edges, and grooved and tongued or dowelled, if a perfect floor is wanted. Dowelling is superior to grooving and tonguing, because the cutting away the stuff to receive the tongue greatly weakens the edges of the joint, which are apt to curl.

Glue is an article of great importance to the joiner, the strength of his work depending much upon its adhesive properties. The best glue is made from the skins of animals, that from the sinewy or horny parts being of inferior quality. The strength of the glue increases with the age of the animals from which the skins are taken.

Joiner's work is measured by the superficial foot, according to its description. Floors by the square of 100 feet superficial. Hand-rails, small mouldings, water-trunks, and similar articles, per lineal foot. Cantilevers, trusses, cut-brackets, scrolls to handrails, &c., are valued per piece.

The wages of a joiner are from 5s. to 6s. per day.

The following memoranda relative to joiner's work may be found useful :—

One Square of Flooring will take—

24	10-feet boards at	. .	5-inch gauge.	
20	„ „	at . .	6-inch ditto.	
17	„ „	at . .	7-inch ditto—10 in. wanted.	
15	., „	at . .	8-inch ditto.	
13	„ „	at . .	9-inch ditto—2 ft. 6 in. wanted.	
12	„ „	at . .	10-inch ditto.	
20	12-feet boards at	. .	5-inch gauge.	
14	„ „	at . .	6-inch ditto—4 ft. wanted.	
12	„ „	at . .	7-inch ditto—2 ft. wanted.	
12	„ „	at . .	8-inch ditto—4 ft. wanted.	
12	„ „	at . .	9-inch ditto—1 ft. wanted.	
10	„ „	at . .	10-inch ditto.	

N.B. One square of flooring will take 200 nails. To make them tough they should be heated in a fire-shovel or the like, with a bit of tallow or grease in them.

120 twelve-feet deals make one hundred; and the readiest way of calculating the price of a single one is to consider every pound per hundred as two-pence per deal: thus if deals are £40 per hundred, they are 40 times two-pence each, or 80 pence, which is 6s. 8d. for each deal; or if £36 10s. per hundred, they would be 36½ times two-pence each, double of which, for pence, would be 73, or 6s. 1d. each deal, and in the same way for any other given price.

120 12-feet 3-inch deals equal 5⅔ loads of timber.
400 superficial feet 1½-inch deals weigh 1 load.

Planks are 11 inches wide.			
Deals	„	9	„
Battens	„	7	„

A reduced deal is 1½ in. thick, 11 in. wide, and 12 feet long.

A square of flooring laid rough requires 12¼ floor-boards. Ditto, edges shot, 12½. Ditto wrought and laid folding, 13. Laid straight joint, 13½. Wrought and laid straight joint, and ploughed and tongued, 14. If laid with 12 feet battens, wrought and laid folding, 17, and with straight joint, 18.

Sawing.

The *sawer* is to the carpenter and joiner what the stone-cutter is to the mason.

The pit saw is a large two-handed saw fixed in a frame, and moved up and down in a vertical direction by two men called the top-man and the pit-man, the first of whom stands on the timber that is to be cut, the other at the bottom of the saw-pit. The timber is *lined out* with a chalk line on its upper surface, and the accuracy of the work depends mainly on the top-man keeping the saw to the line, whence the proverbial expression *top-sawyer*, meaning one who directs any undertaking.

In sawing deals and battens into thicknesses for the joiner's use, the parallelism of the cut is of the utmost importance, as the operation of *taking out of winding* a piece of uneven stuff causes a considerable waste of material, and much loss of time.

Circular-saws, moved by steam-power, are now much used in large establishments, timber-yards, &c., and effect a considerable saving of labour over the use of the pit-saw, where the timbers to be cut are not too heavy to be easily handled.

The saw is mounted in the middle of a stout bench

furnished with guides, by means of which the stuff to be cut is kept in the required direction, whilst it is pushed against the saw, which is the whole manual labour required in the operation.

IRONMONGERY

Is charged for, generally, with the work to which it is attached; the joiner being allowed 20 per cent. profit upon the prime cost.

The principal articles of ironmongery used in a building consist of *nails, screws, sash-pulleys, bolts, hinges, locks, latches,* and *sash* and *shutter-furniture,* besides a great variety of miscellaneous articles which we have not space to enumerate.

Of the different kinds of hinges may be mentioned *hook-and-eye hinges* for gates, coach-house doors, &c.; *butts* and *back-flaps* for doors and shutters; *cross garnets,* which are used for hanging ledged doors and other inferior work; H *and* H-*hinges,* whose names are derived from their shape; and *parliament hinges.*

Besides these are used *rising-butts* for hanging doors to rise over a carpet or other impediment, *projecting-butts,* used when some projection has to be cleared, and *spring-hinges* and swing centres for self-shutting doors.

The variety of locks now manufactured is almost infinite. We may mention the *stock-lock,* cased in wood for common work, and *rim-locks,* which have a metal case or rim, and are attached to one side of a door; they should not be used when a door has sufficient thickness to allow of a mortice-lock, as they often catch the dresses of persons passing through the doorway. *Mortice-locks*, as the name implies, are those which are morticed into the thickness of the door.

The handles and escutcheons are called the *furniture* of a lock, and are made of a great variety of materials, as brass, bronze, ebony, ivory, and glass, &c.

Of latches, there are the common *thumb-latch*, the *bow-latch*, with brass knobs, the brass *pulpit-latch*, and the *mortice-latch*.

There are also a great variety of other articles, both useful and ornamental, kept in stock and supplied by the furnishing ironmonger.

GLAZIER.

The business of the glazier consists in cutting glass, and fixing it into *lead-work*, *wood-work*, or wood sashes. The former is the oldest method of glazing, and is still used, not only for cottage windows and inferior work, but for church windows and glazing with stained glass, which.is cut into pieces of the required size, and set in a leaden framework; this kind of glazing is called *fretwork*. Glazing in sashes is of comparatively modern introduction. The sash bars are formed with a rebate on the outside for the reception of the glass, which is *cut into* the rebate, and firmly *beaded* and *back-puttied* to keep it in its place. Large squares are also *sprigged* or secured with small brads driven into the sash bars.

Glazing in lead-work is fixed in leaden rods called *cames*, prepared for the use of the glazier by being passed through a glazier's vice, in which they receive the grooves for the insertion of the glass. The sides or checks of the grooves are sufficiently soft to allow of their being turned down to admit the glass, and again raised up and firmly pressed against it after its insertion. For common lead-work, the bars are soldered together so as to form squares or diamonds. In fret-work, the bars, instead of being used straight, are bent round to the shapes of the different pieces of glass forming the device. Lead-work is strengthened by being attached to *saddle-bars* of iron, by leaden bars soldered to the lead-work and twisted round the iron.

Putty is made of pounded whiting beaten up with linseed oil into a tough tenacious cement.

The principal tool of the glazier is the *diamond*, which is used for cutting glass. This tool consists of an unpolished diamond fixed in lead, and fastened to a handle of hard wood.

The glazier uses a *hacking-knife* for cutting out old putty from broken squares, and the *stopping-knife* for laying and smoothing the putty when *stopping-in* glass into sashes. For setting glass into lead-work, the *setting-knife* is used.

Besides the above, the glazier requires a square and straight edge, and a pair of compasses, for dividing the tables of glass to the required sizes. Also, a hammer for springing large squares, and brushes for cleaning off the work.

The *glazier's vice* has already been mentioned. The *latter-kin* is a pointed piece of hard wood, with which grooves of the *cames* are cleared out and widened for receiving the glass.

Cleaning windows is an important branch of the glazier's business in most large towns; the glazier taking upon himself the cost of all glass broken in the operation. Glazier's work is valued by the superficial foot, the price increasing with the size of the square. Irregular panes are valued according to the extreme dimensions each way.

Crown glass is *blown* in circular *tables*, from 3 feet 6 inches to 5 feet diameter, and is sold in *crates*, the number of tables in a crate varying according to the quality of the glass.

> A crate contains 12 tables of best quality.
> Ditto   ditto   15 „   second ditto.
> Ditto   ditto   18 „   third ditto.

Plate glass is cast in large plates on horizontal tables, and afterwards polished.

The manufacture of sheet or spread glass, which was formerly considered a very inferior article, has of late years been much improved. Much is now sold, after being polished, under the name of patent plate.

PAINTER, PAPER-HANGER, AND DECORATOR.

The business of the house-painter consists in covering with a preparation of white lead and oil such portions of the joiner's, smith's, and plasterer's work as require to be protected from the action of the atmosphere. Decorative painting is a higher branch, requiring a knowledge of the harmony of colours, and more or less artistic skill, according to the nature of the work to be executed.

The introduction of fresco painting into this country, as a mode of internal decoration, has led to the employment of some of the first artists of the day in the embellishment of the mansions of the nobility, and the example thus set will no doubt be extensively followed.

The principal materials used by the painter are— *white lead,* which forms the basis of all the colours used in house-painting; *linseed oil* and *spirits of turpentine,* used for mixing and diluting the colours; and *dryers,* as *litharge, sugar of lead,* and white vitriol, which are mixed with the colours to facilitate their drying. *Putty,* made of whiting and linseed oil, is used for *stopping* or filling up nail holes and other vacuities, in order to bring the work to a smooth face.

The painter's tools are few and simple: they consist of the *grinding-stone* and *muller,* for grinding colours; *earthen pots,* to hold colours; *cans* for oil and turps; *pallet knife,* and brushes of various sizes and descriptions. In painting wood, the first operation consists in killing the *knots,* from which the turpentine would otherwise exude and spoil the work. To effect this, the knots are covered with fresh slaked lime, which dries up and burns out the turpentine; when this has been on twenty-four hours, it is scraped off, and the knots painted over with a mixture of red and white lead mixed with glue size. After this, they are gone over a second time with red and white lead mixed with linseed oil; when dry, they must be rubbed perfectly smooth with pumice stone, and the work is then ready to receive the priming coat.

This is composed of red and white lead, well diluted with linseed oil.

The nail holes and other imperfections are then stopped with putty, and the succeeding coats are then laid on, the work being rubbed down between each coat with pumice stone, to bring it to an even surface. The first after the priming is mixed with linseed oil and a little turpentine; the second coat with equal quantities of linseed oil and turpentine.

In laying on the second coat where the work is not

to be finished white, an approach must be made to the required colour. The third coat is usually the last, and is made with a base of white lead, mixed with the requisite colours, and diluted with one-third of linseed oil to two-thirds of turpentine.

Painting on stucco, and all other work in which the surface is required to be without gloss, has an additional coat mixed with turpentine only, which from its drying of one uniform *flat* tint is called a flatting coat. If the knots show through a second coat they must be carefully covered with silver leaf. Work finished as above described would be technically specified as knotted, primed, painted three oils, and flatted. Flatting is almost indispensable in all delicate interior work, but it is not suited to outside work, as it will not bear exposure to the weather. Painting on stucco is primed with boiled linseed oil, and should then receive at least three coats of white lead and oil, and be finished with a flat tint.

The great secret of success in painting stucco is, that the surface should be perfectly dry, and as this can hardly be the case in less than two years after the erection of a building, it will always be desirable to finish new work in distemper, which can be washed off whenever the walls are sufficiently dry to receive the permanent decorations.

Graining is the imitation of the grain of various kinds of wood, by means of *graining tools*, and, when well executed and properly varnished, has a handsome appearance, and lasts many years. The term graining is also applied to the imitation of marble.

Clear coling is a substitution of size for oil, in the preparation of the priming coat. It is much resorted to by painters on account of the ease with which a good face can be put on the work with fewer coats than when oil is used, but it will not stand damp, which causes it to scale off, and it should never be used except in painting old work, which is greasy or smoky, and cannot be made to look well by any other means.

Distempering is a kind of painting in which whiting is used as the basis of the colours, the liquid medium being size; it is much used for ceilings and walls, and will require two, and sometimes three coats, to give it a uniform appearance.

Painter's work is valued per superficial yard, according to the number of coats, and the description of work, as *common* colours, *fancy* colours, *party* colours, &c.

Where work is cut on both edges, it is taken by the lineal foot. In measuring railings, the two sides are measured as flat work. Sash panes are valued per piece, and sashes per dozen squares.

The manufacture of *scagliola*, or imitation marble, is a branch of the decorator's business which is carried to very great perfection. Scagliola is made of plaster of Paris and different earthy colours, which are mixed in a trough in a moist state, and blended together until the required effect is produced, when the composition is taken from the trough, laid on the plaster ground, and well worked together with a wooden beater and a small gauging trowel. When quite hard, it is smoothed, scraped, and polished, until it assumes the appearance of marble.

Scagliola is valued at per foot *superficial,* according to the description of marble imitated and the execution of the work.

Gilding is executed with leaf-gold, which is furnished by the gold-beater in books of twenty-five leaves, each leaf measuring 3½ by 3 inches.

The parts to be gilded are first prepared with a coat of gold-size, which is made of Oxford ochre and fat oil.

The operations of the paper-hanger are so simple as to require little description. There are as great a variety of patterns as there are of prices, and the expense of hanging them is generally regulated by the value of the paper, as the most expensive papers require more time and attention than the plainer sorts.

A piece of paper is twelve yards long, and is twenty inches wide when hung, and covers six feet superficial, hence the number of superficial feet that have to be covered divided by sixty, will give the number of pieces required for any description of work.

CHAPTER V.

ARCHITECTURAL DRAWING.*

HAVING thus far described most of the principal tools and materials used in the several trades engaged in the erection of dwelling-houses, it is necessary that the young artisan should now give attention to lineal drawing. We are now desirous of conveying our opinion (founded upon many years' experience, both theoretically and practically) of its utility and importance ; and in doing so, we may not probably assume too much, by stating that not any mechanic in the building department, or in fact in any other, can ever be efficient in his

* See Heather's "Descriptive Geometry," and his "Mathematical Instruments," both in this series.

business unless he comprehends the application of scales and the elementary principles of geometrical drawing.

Until late years there was not that attention paid to this art which its general application and usefulness demanded, it being considered more an acquisition for the mathematician, artist, or amateur, than the mechanician. But the progress that has been made within the last half century in every branch of mechanical art has rendered necessary a practical and theoretical knowledge of at least the rudiments of mechanical drawing; and the want has been met by the Schools of Art, which afford, at a comparatively low cost, instruction in this important auxiliary to the various arts of design and ornamentation.

That geometrical drawing to the young mechanic may at first be considered a dry and useless study is admitted, but he must recollect that no one ever rose to eminence in any of the arts or sciences without perseverance and intense application, and although the study here particularly alluded to may be considered dry and uninteresting at first, it will be rewarded by the pleasure and confidence it gives to its possessor hereafter.

It is a well-known fact that without a knowledge of scales and their application, and an elementary acquaintance with the principles of geometry, no one, however well-informed on other subjects, can convey the emanation of his mind for any practical mechanical purpose.* He certainly may be enabled in a cursory manner to sketch out his ideas, but they cannot with any certainty be carried into practical execution, unless they are geometrically delineated to a scale. Having

* See Warren's "General Problems of Shades and Shadows," one of the best books on the subject.

thus expressed our views upon the usefulness and application of drawing, we will now endeavour to explain
the paper in general use for drawing, and the particular
use of such scale and mathematical instruments as
are essential for him to possess.

A TABLE OF THE DIMENSIONS OF DRAWING-PAPER.*

		Inches.		Inches.
Demy		20	by	15½
Medium		22¾	„	17½
Royal		24	„	19¼
Super Royal		27¼	„	19¼
Imperial		30	„	22
Elephant		28	„	23
Columbier		35	„	23½
Atlas		34	„	26
Double Elephant		40	„	27
Antiquarian		53	„	31
Emperor		68	„	48

HINTS ON THE MANAGEMENT OF DRAWING PAPER.

The first thing to be done preparatory to the commencement of a drawing is the preparation of the paper,
that is, the stretching it evenly upon a drawing-board.
The edges of the paper should first be cut straight, and
as near as possible at right angles with each other.
Also the sheet should be so much larger than the intended drawing and its margin, as to admit of being
afterwards cut from the board, leaving the border by
which it is attached thereto, by glue or paste, as we
shall next explain. The paper must be thoroughly and
equally damped with a sponge and clean water on the
opposite side from that on which the drawing is to be
made. When the paper absorbs the water, which may
be seen by the wetted side becoming dried, as its surface
is viewed slant-ways against the light, it is to be laid

---

* It is assumed that the student is fully acquainted with the use of
the drawing-boards, T-squares, set squares, and parallel rulers.

on the drawing-board with the wetted side downwards, and placed so that the edges may be nearly parallel with those of the board, otherwise in using a T-square an inconvenience may be experienced. This done, lay a straight-edge on the paper with the margin parallel to and about half an inch from one of the edges of the paper. The straight-edge or ruler must now be held firm while the said projecting half-inch of paper is turned up against it; then a piece of glue, previously softened by a few seconds' exposure to the steam from a basin of hot water, must be passed once or twice along the turned up edge of the paper, after which, by sliding the ruler over the glued border, it will again be laid flat, and the ruler or straight-edge being pressed down upon it, that edge of the paper will adhere to the board. If sufficient glue has been applied the ruler may be removed directly, and the edge finally rubbed down by an ivory book-knife, or any clean polished substance at hand, which will then firmly cement the paper to the board. This done, another but adjoining edge of the paper must be acted upon in a like manner, and then the remaining edges in succession ; we say the adjoining edges, because we have occasionally observed that when the opposite and parallel edges have been laid first, without continuing the process progressively round the board, a greater degree of care is required to prevent undulations in the paper as it dries.

Sometimes strong paste is used instead of glue; but as this takes a longer time to set, it is usual to wet the paper also on the upper surface to within an inch of the paste mark, care being taken not to rule or injure the surface in the process; the wetting of the paper in either case is done for the purpose of expanding it, and

the edges being fixed to the board in its enlarged state
acts as stretcher upon the paper while it contracts in
drying, which it should be allowed to do gradually.
All creases or undulations by this means disappear from
the surface of the paper, and it is a smooth plane to
receive the drawing.

In mounting paper upon canvas, the latter should be
well stretched upon a smooth flat surface, being damped
for that purpose, and its edges glued down as was
recommended in stretching drawing paper; then with a
brush spread strong paste upon the canvas, beating it
in until the grain of the canvas be all filled up; for
this, when dry, will prevent the canvas from shrinking
when subsequently removed. Then, having cut the
edges of the paper straight, paste one side of every
sheet and lay them upon the canvas, sheet by sheet,
overlapping each other a small quantity. If the drawing
is strong it is best to let every sheet lie five or six
minutes after the paste is put on it, for as the paste
soaks in, the paper will stretch and may be better
spread smooth upon the canvas, whereas, if it be laid
on before the paste has moistened the paper, it will
stretch afterwards and raise blisters when laid upon the
canvas. The paper should not be cut off from its extended position till thoroughly dry, which should not be
hastened, but left in a dry room to do so gradually if
time permit, if not, it may be exposed to the rays of
the sun, unless·in the winter season, when the assistance
of a fire is necessary, provided it is not placed too near
a scorching heat. In joining two or more sheets of
paper together by overlapping, it is necessary, in order
to make a neat joint, to feather-edge each sheet, this is
done by carefully cutting with a knife half-way through

the paper near the edge and on the sides which are to overlap each other, then strip off a feather edge or slip from each, which, if done dexterously, will form a very neat and efficient joint when put together. The following method of mounting and varnishing drawings or prints may be considered useful. Stretch a piece of linen on a frame, to which give a coat of isinglass or common size, paste the back of the drawing or print, which leave to soak and then lay it on the linen. When dry give it at least four coats of well-made isinglass size, allowing it to dry between each coat. Take Canada balsam diluted with the best oil of turpentine, and with a clean brush give it a full flowing coat.

Pencils.

In selecting black pencils for use, it may be remarked, that they ought not to be very soft nor so hard that their traces cannot be easily erased by the India rubber. Great care should be taken in the pencilling, that an accurate outline be drawn, the pencil marks should be distinct, yet not heavy, and the use of the rubber should be avoided as much as possible, for its frequent application ruffles the surface of the paper and will destroy the good effect of shading or colouring, if any is afterwards to be applied.

DRAWING INSTRUMENTS.

The Compasses.

The compasses or dividers are instruments so well known, that it would be superfluous to enter into a lengthy description of them, or of the various uses to which they may be applied. The best are constructed with joints of two different metals, as steel and brass, whereby the wear is more equal, and the motion of the legs uniform and steady, and not subject to sudden jerks in opening or shutting; this motion will occasionally require some adjustment to render it uniformly smooth, and to move stiffer or easier at pleasure; but so that they may keep steadily any position that may be given to them, the adjustment is performed by the application of a turn-screw to this axis of the joint. In the common compasses a simple screw forms the axis upon which the legs move, and may be turned with a screw driver of the ordinary construction; but in the best made instruments a steel pin passes through the joints, having at one end a head of brass riveted fast upon it, and on the other end a similar plate is screwed, which is therefore a nut, on a diameter of which is drilled two small holes for the application of a lever of a particular description.

The points of a well-made instrument should be of steel, so tempered as neither to be easily bent or blunted; not too fine and tapering, and yet meeting closely when the compasses are shut. As some of the numerous uses to which this instrument may be applied, the following may be mentioned:—To take any extent or length between the points of the compasses, and to set it off or to apply it successively upon any line. To take any proposed line between the points, and by applying it to the proper scale, to find its length. To set off equal distances upon a given line, to describe circles, intersecting arcs, &c. To make an angle equal to any given angle; to lay off an angle of a given quantity upon an arc of circle from the line of cords, &c.; to construct any proposal in plotting, or drawing plans, &c., &c.

The Hair Compasses.

This instrument is represented in the adjoining engraving, and is constructed in the same manner as those above described. The only difference consists in a contrivance *b*, whereby the lower point, or half one shank, can be moved a very small quantity, either towards or from the other point, which is useful when a distance is required to be taken with the utmost possible exactness. This contrivance consists of a fine spring and screw, by which, when the compasses are opened nearly to the required extent by the help of the screw *b*, the points may be set to the greatest precision, which cannot be done so well by the motion of the joints *alone*.

Compasses with movable points.

In the smaller and more portable cases of drawing instruments, it is customary to insert a larger sized pair of compasses, of which the point of half of one of the legs is never movable, to admit of adapting singly a pen or pencil, or dotting points. The pen point is used for drawing circles or arcs with ink, and is constructed like the drawing-pen, which will be hereafter described; the pencil point is alike adapted to hold a piece of black lead pencil or crayon for describing circles or arcs that are not to be permanent, and the dotting point consists of two blades similar to those of the drawing pen, but rounded at the points, between which revolves a small wheel with numerous points round its circumference resembling the rowel of a spur. The space between the blades being supplied with Indian ink, and the wheels rolled upon paper, as the compasses describe a circle or arc, each point as the wheel revolves will pass through the ink and transfer it to the paper beneath, making equi-distant dots in the circle which the compasses describe.

The movable points have a joint in them just under that part which locks into the shank of the compasses, by which the part below the joint may be set perpendicular to the plane on which the lines are described when the compasses are open. An additional piece, called a lengthening bar, is frequently applied to these compasses, which by lengthening the movable leg

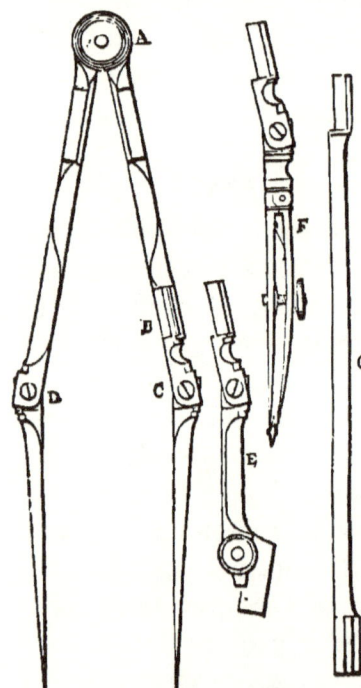

enables them to strike larger circles, or measure greater extents than they otherwise would perform. When this is applied, the movable part has a joint similar to those on the pen and pencil points, and for a similar purpose the annexed diagram represents this instrument and its appendages.

A the compasses with a movable point at B; c and D, the joints to set each point perpendicular to the paper; E the pencil point; F the pen point (this is represented with a dotting wheel, the pen point and the dotting point are similar in shape to each other);
G the lengthening bar.

Bow Compasses.

These are a small pair having a point either for ink or pencil. They are used to describe small arcs or circles, which they do more conveniently than large compasses, not only on account of the size, but also from the shape of their head, which rolls easily between the fingers and can be turned round as delicately as they require to be moved for drawing very minute circles.

The adjoining figures represent the pencil bow as suited for describing arcs of different radii. Fig. 1 is a construction adapted for describing arcs of a radius intermediate between those described by the above-named compasses, and those capable of being produced by the bows represented by Fig. 2.

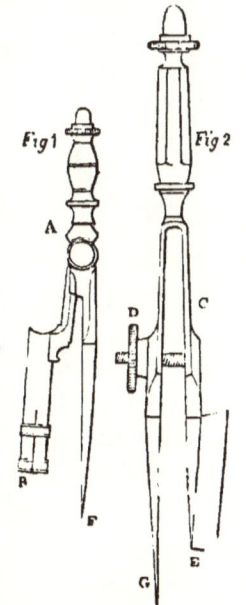

In Fig. 1 the pencil point B, and the centre point F, can be opened a considerable width by the joint A, whilst in the other construction, Fig. 2, the corresponding points E and G are limited in their opening, the two blades carrying the points, being formed out of one solid piece of steel, and tempered so as to form a spring at the upper part corresponding with the joint A in Fig. 1. The spring of the two blades is then kept in obedience by an adjusting screw D, by which the two points may be set to any required degree of minuteness, and very small circles may be described with a precision

E

that could not be expected or scarcely attempted by the construction of Fig. 1.

The pen bows are represented in the annexed engraving; their construction is similar to the pencil bows last described. In the pen point of

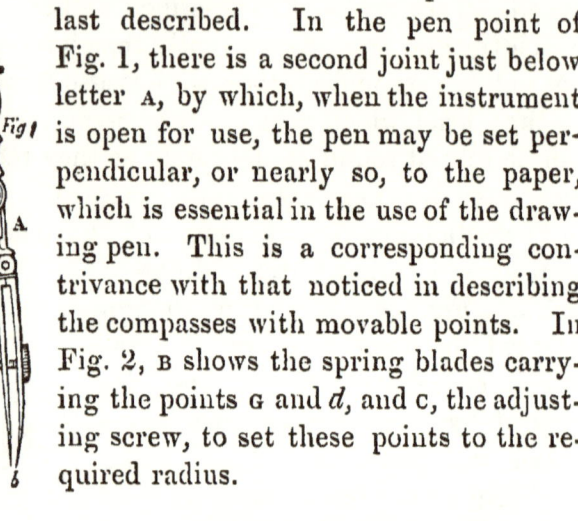

Fig. 1, there is a second joint just below letter A, by which, when the instrument is open for use, the pen may be set perpendicular, or nearly so, to the paper, which is essential in the use of the drawing pen. This is a corresponding contrivance with that noticed in describing the compasses with movable points. In Fig. 2, B shows the spring blades carrying the points G and d, and c, the adjusting screw, to set these points to the required radius.

Tubular Compasses.

The engraving on page 75 represents this instrument. It may be used as an ordinary pair of compasses, either with two fine points, a pen point, or a pencil point, and is capable of describing circles to any extent of radius from an eighth of an inch to fourteen inches and a-half, and with the advantage of reversing points which may be changed from pen to pencil, &c., without deranging the setting of the instrument when opened to any definite extent.

A and B are the two principal legs of the instrument, consisting of tubes movable about a very nicely constructed joint at c. Within these are two sliding tubes E and D, which draw out their whole length, and are accurately fitted to the principal tubes A and B, so that

they may be drawn out to their required extent with a smooth and steady motion, not subject to sudden stoppages, or to move with equally sudden jerks, a proof of bad workmanship, but uniformly, and not too easy.*
To assist in this, their inner extremities are made to act as springs within tubes, wherein they slide, thus increasing their friction.

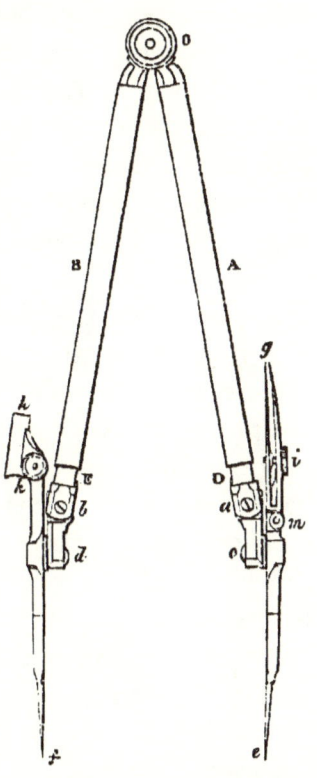

The outward extremity of each of the sliding tubes E and D terminates in a square headed joint, a and b; upon these move the pieces c and d, which carry the point limbs of the compasses. The joints a and b in this instrument correspond with the joints c and D of the compasses with movable points as before described, and are used for a similar purpose, namely, to set the point limbs perpendicular to the paper, and consequently parallel to each other, at whatever opening the legs of the compasses may be extended to.

In our engraving, the pivots of the two point limbs f, h and e, g to the two carrying pieces, which are jointed to the tubes at a and b, also give the means of inverting the position of the points; that is to say, the

* Messrs. Parkes and Son, of Birmingham, have introduced needle-points to their compasses, which greatly tend to facilitate accuracy in drawing.

limbs can be turned upon these pivots so as to make the points *e* and *g*, or *f* and *h* change places. By this simple and ingenious contrivance, the draftsman, after having used the two fine points *e* and *f*, for fixing with precision the opening of the compass to his required radius, may obtain a pencil point to describe a corresponding arc or circle, by simply turning the pencil limbs *h, f,* round on its pivot *d,* which will cause the point of a pencil or crayon placed in the tube *h,* to change places with the fine point *f* of the compasses, and as the pivot is (or ought to be) at right angles to a line connecting the points *f,* and of the pencil at *h,* the latter will exactly take the place of the former, at the same extent or opening, *e, f.* In like manner, by turning the pen limb *e, g,* round its pivot *c,* the pen point *g* may be made to occupy the position of the fine point *e,* or whatever the compasses may have been set to in the first instance. The milled-head screw, represented at *k,* is for the purpose of fixing a pencil firmly in its tube *h*; the screw *i* is for adjusting the blades of the pen-point *g,* between which the ink is inserted to any required degree of fineness, so as to produce a corresponding fine or coarse circular line. The joint *m,* by removing altogether the screw *i,* gives the means of opening the blades for the better cleansing them after use.

Portable or Turn-in Compasses.

This forms in itself a complete portable case of drawing instruments, consisting of a large pair of compasses with movable points, which are also so contrived that one forms in itself a small pencil bow and the other a pen bow; and when the whole instrument is put together and folded up (or the points turned in, from whence is derived the name of *turn-in compasses*) they occupy a space not more than three inches long, and may be carried in the pocket without being an incumbrance. The annexed engraving represents the instrument when all its parts are together. The principal

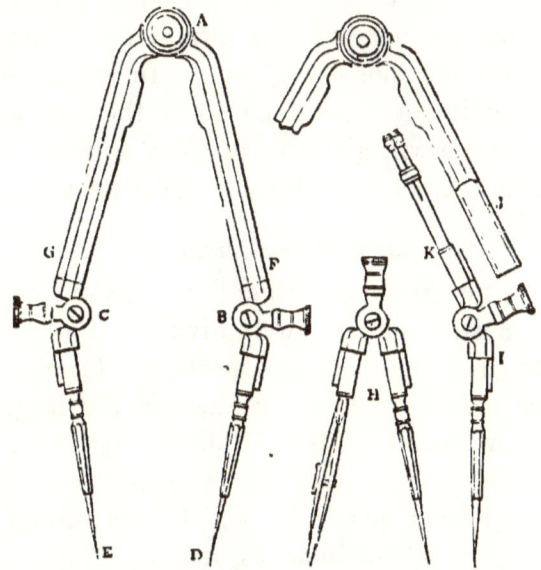

legs of the instrument are F and G, movable, as usual, by a joint at A. The lower joints, B and C, afford the means of setting the front limbs, D and E, perpendicular to the paper, as explained before when describing the last instrument. Each of the point limbs may be removed from the legs F and G, and by means of their joints B and C form perfect instruments—the one a pen bow, represented at H, and the other a pencil bow, shown at I K. The points of these lesser instruments are all adapted to slide into the principal legs, F and G, of the larger one, which are made hollow for their reception. A section of the limb F is shown at J, to convey to the reader a better idea of the arrangement.

It may easily be seen from the engraving, that by reversing either of the points in the principal instrument, the other point may be used as a centre. When not in use the instrument may be conveniently carried in a sheath or case provided for the purpose. There are also various forms and arrangements of the parts occasionally given to the instrument to suit the fancies of individuals; but the one we have described above will give the reader a correct notion of the general character of this class of instruments.

Large Screw Dividers.

We have now to describe another class of compasses, such as are used for accurately dividing lines, &c., into a definite number of equal parts, or for setting off equal distances. The first of these is the large screw divider represented in the adjoining figure: A is the centre, about which the legs A C and A B open or shut; B and C are joints by which the pointed limbs may be set perpendicular as usual. The extent or opening between the points is regulated by a screw passing through a socket, F, and terminated at the other extremity by a milled head, by which the screw is turned round. Between this milled head and the nearest pointed limb is fixed what is called a micrometer head, decimally divided round its outer or cylindrical edge. One turn of the screw carries the micrometer head completely round; therefore, when part of a turn only is given to the screw, the divisions on the head show what fraction of a turn has been given, and if it be known what number of turns or threads of the screw are equal to one inch, the points of these compasses may be thus set to any small definite measure of length with the utmost precision. The index or zero for reading the fraction of a turn of the screw is marked on the point limb below B : thus this instrument may be considered as a beam compass of small dimensions and minute accuracy.

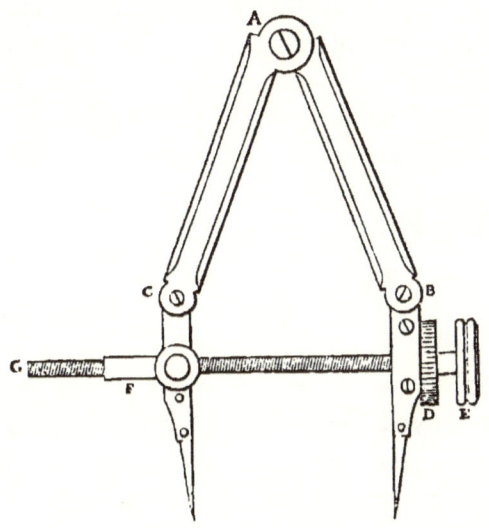

Spring Dividers.

This instrument, represented in the accompanying diagram, is particularly useful for repeating divisions of a small but equal extent—a practice that has the name of stepping, for which a small pair of hair compasses would also be found useful when the head is constructed as shown in the adjoining figure, or similar to that of the bow compass before described, and for reasons before stated. The upper part forming the handle is composed of brass or silver, whilst the lower part from A towards the points is made of one piece of steel of a spring temper, whereby the two points are always endeavouring to recede from each other, or open by their elasticity, which is counteracted by the adjusting screw B, by which it may be set to the required opening. This acts in the same manner as the micrometer screw, described as belonging to instruments before explained, but with this difference—that it has not the means of pointing out the measure of the material, or extent between the fine points of the compasses, which must therefore be taken from a suitable scale.

Wholes and Halves.

Having explained the general construction of the most approved instruments of the smaller kind for describing circles and dividing lines, we come now to allude to those employed in copying and reducing drawings. And first of the instrument represented in the annexed engraving, which is the simplest form of proportional compasses, and capable of reducing or enlarging in one proportion only—namely, one-half, from whence its name of wholes and halves is derived. The points A and E are one piece of metal : likewise the points B and D are at the extremities of another piece of metal, and straight lines connecting these points pass through the centre, c. The legs of the instrument are connected together by a joint of the usual form at c, placed one-third of the whole length from one extremity : consequently, whatever may be the extent of the opening of the points A and B, it will always be double the extent of the opening of the other two points, D and E. Therefore, if the whole

length of any line be taken between the opening of
the two former points, the interval between the two
latter points will be exactly one-half the length of
the same line; consequently, this instrument affords the readiest means of dividing a line into two equal parts, or *vice
versa.* Its usefulness in dividing lines
does not rest here; for, if the original
line has to be divided into any number
of parts—2, 4, 6, 8, &c., by constantly
taking the half of the half in the same
manner as taking the half of the original
line in the first instance, the requisite
number of subdivisions may be obtained.

Proportional Compasses.

This instrument is a very useful and
necessary appendage to a case of drawing
instruments, and although rather expensive
in its original cost, it very soon repays
its owner in saving both time and trouble. The proportional compasses consist of two equal and similarly
formed parts or limbs, A E and B D (see the accompanying engraving), which are represented as opening upon
a centre c, and forming a double pair of compasses or
points, A B, E D. When shut up, the two limbs appear
as one, and a small stud fixed on one fits into a notch
made in the other, and retains the instrument exactly
in its closed position, the two points also at each extremity then coincide and become as one point. When
thus closed the dove-tailed slits shown in the engraving
as made in each limb, being equal and similar, coincide
and appear as one slit, and in this position only can the

adjustment be made for any required proportion; that is to say, the instrument must always be closed in order to slide and fix the centre c in its proper place, and the opening of the small points E D at the other extremity.

The centre consists of a pivot or steel pin, which passes through the dove-tailed pieces of brass, nicely fitted to slide in the before-named slits, and also through a circular nut or collar on each face, which answers the double purpose of keeping the dove-tailed pieces of brass in their slits, and also firmly clamping them together by means of the milled head, c, when they are moved to the position where the centre is required; on the dove-tailed pieces a line is drawn for the zero to set the centre by, which in our engraving is represented as coinciding with the division on the limb marked 2, and nearly with the one marked 12. On the face of each limb there are two sets of division, one denominated lines, a second circles, a third planes, and the fourth solids. When the zero of the centre on the dove-tailed sliding-piece is set to the division marked 1, on the line of lines, then the proportion between any opening of the large points A B, will be two to one, or twice as great as the opening of the smaller points D E, and consequently any extent taken between the large points may be accurately divided into two parts by the smaller ones. Also when the zero is set to the division marked 3, on the same lines, the proportion of any opening will be three to one, or that of the smaller points will be one-third of the extent of the larger points, and the same of the remaining divisions on the line which extend to ten of the line marked " *circles*" on the opposite edge of the same face of the instrument; the divisions are numbered from 6 to 20, and the index of zero being set to any number, the points will open in proportion to the radius of a circle to the side of an inscribed polygon of that number of sides. Thus if it be set to the division marked 8, and the points A B are opened to the radius of any circle, the opening of the smaller points D E will divide the circumference into eight equal parts.

The other lines of divisions, namely, those marked "planes" and "solids," are on the other face of the instrument, these are in fact lines of square and cube roots. The line of "*planes*" or "*squares*" shows the proportion between the areas of similar plane figures. Thus, set the zero to the division marked 3, and measure the side of the square in the large points A B, the opening of the short ones, D E, will then be equal to the side of a square, which will be one-third the area of the other. The same of triangles, circles, or any other regular plane figure.

To find the square root of a given number, shut the compasses and set the zero to the number given upon the line of planes, open the instrument, and from any scale of equal parts take the number between the larger points A B, then apply the smaller points D E, to the same scale, and the distance between them will be equal to the square root of the distance between the points of the larger legs A B. The mean proportional between two given numbers is the square root of their product, and may be found by the proportional compasses ; thus, required the mean proportional between 2 and 4½. Open the compasses with the zero or index set against 9, the product of two given numbers, till the distance between the larger is equal to 9, taken from some scale of equal parts, then the distance between the smaller points will be equal to 3 of the same scale, and is the mean proportional between 2 and 4½, for as $2 : 3 :: 3 : 4\frac{1}{2}$.

The line of "solids" expresses the proportions between cubes or spheres. Thus, set the zero to the division marked 2 on the line of solids, then measure the diameter of any sphere, or the side of a cube which will have one half the solid content of the former. In like manner, by setting zero to the divisions marked 3, 4, &c., the interval between the larger and smaller points of the instrument will show respectively the diameters, &c., of spheres, of which one shall have three or four times the solid of the other.

Also the cube root of any number may be found by setting zero upon the given number upon the line of solids, &c., as described for obtaining square root by means of the line of planes; proportional compasses of the best construction are sometimes made with a clamp and tangent screw for setting the zero with the utmost precision; this, however, is seldom used, and the instrument we have described is the kind in general requisition.

Triangular Compasses.

The adjoining figure represents this instrument as it appears when closed up for packing in its case. That which appears in the engraving as one limb A, consists of a pair of compasses precisely of the ordinary construction; the single point limb B, has a compass joint at *a*, by which its points may be opened at right

angles to the plane of the pair of compasses A, when the
three points will form a triangle. The compass point at *a*
is firmly attached to the centre of the compasses A, which,
by means of a nut or screw *b*, may be turned round
without moving the limbs, of which it is the centre. The
double motion thus given to the point limb B (both right
angles to, and parallel to the plane of the compasses A), partake of the nature of an universal
joint, and enables the three points of the
instrument to be placed at the angular points
of any shaped triangle whatever, be it ever so
obtuse. Also, by the same means, the three
points may be brought into one straight line.
This instrument, it will be obvious from
the description, is chiefly useful in trans-
ferring points from one paper to another,
and is very serviceable in copying mechanical drawings. The two points of the compasses A being set upon such points of the
drawing as are already copied, the third
point, B, of the instrument may be moved
by its universal joint, *a b*, to rest upon any
other point, and then by similarly applying
the points of A to the corresponding points
on the copy, the new point of the original may be
correctly transferred to it by means of the limb of the
instrument B. Another form of tri-
angular compasses is represented in
the annexed engraving. *a, b, c* is a
solid tripod, having at the extremity
of each arm a limb, *c, d*, and *c*,
moving freely upon centres, by
which they may be placed in any position with respect

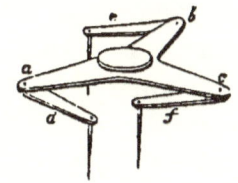

to the tripod and each other. These limbs carry points at right angles to the plane of the instrument, which may be brought to coincide with any three given points on the original drawing, and then transferred to the copy as above described.

Beam Compasses.

The accompanying diagram represents this instrument, which consists of a beam, A, A, of any length

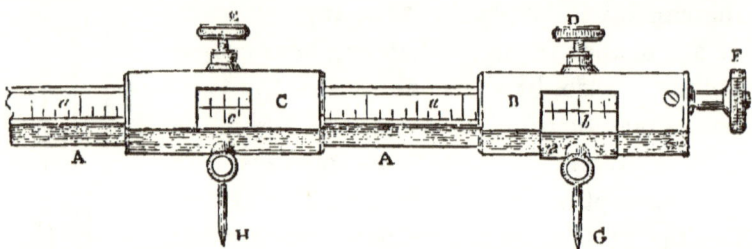

required, generally made of well-seasoned mahogany; upon its face is inlaid, throughout its whole length, a slip of holly or box-wood, a, a, upon which are engraved the divisions or scales, either feet and decimals, or inches and decimals, or whatever particular scale may be required : those made for use of the persons engaged on the ordnance survey of Ireland were divided to a scale of chains, 80 of which being equal to six inches, which therefore represented one mile, that being the scale to which the survey is being plotted. Two brass boxes, B and C, are adapted to the beam ; the latter may be moved by sliding to any part of its length, and fixed in position by tightening the clamp screw E. Connected with the brass boxes are the two points of the instrument, G and H, which may have any extent of opening by sliding the box C along the beam, and the other box B being firmly fixed at one extremity. The object to be attained in the use

of this instrument is the nice adjustment of the points
G and H to any distance apart; this is accomplished
by two verniers or reading plates, *b, c,* each fixed at
the side of an opening in the brass boxes to which they
are attached, and afford the means of minutely sub-
dividing the principal divisions, *a, a,* on the beam which
appear through those openings; D is a clamp screw for
a similar purpose as the screw E, namely, to fix the
box B, and prevent motion in the point it carries after
adjustment to the position; F is a slow-motion screw
by which the point G may be moved any very minute
quantity, for perfecting the setting of the instrument
after it has been otherwise set as nearly as possible by
the hand alone.

The method of setting the instrument for use may
be understood from the above description of its parts,
and also by the following explanation of the method of
examining and correcting the adjustment of the vernier
b, which, like all other mechanical adjustments, will
occasionally get deranged; this verification must be
done by means of a detached scale. Thus, suppose for
example that our beam-compass is divided into feet,
inches, and tenths, and subdivided by the vernier to
hundredths, &c. First set the zero division of the
vernier to the zero of the principal divisions on the
beam, by means of the slow-motion screw F. This
must be done very accurately. Then slide the box c
with its point G, till the zero on the vernier c exactly
coincides with any principal division on the beam, as
12 inches or 6 inches, &c., which must also be done
to a great nicety (in some superior kind of beam-
compasses the box c is also furnished with a tangent
or slow-motion screw, by which the setting of the
points or the divisions may be done with the utmost

precision in the same manner as the vernier *b*, by
means of the screw F), then apply the points to a
similar detached scale, and if the adjustment is perfect
the interval of the points G H will measure on it the
distance to which they were set on the beam. If they
do not by ever so small a quantity, it should be corrected by turning the screw F till the joints exactly
measure that quantity on the detached scale: then, by
loosening the little screws which confine the vernier *b*
in its place, the position of the vernier may be gradually
changed till its zero coincides with the zero on the beam,
and then, tightening the screws again, the adjustment
will be complete.

Knife, File, Key, and Screw-driver.

The annexed engraving represents a very useful appendage to a case of drawing instruments; its use will

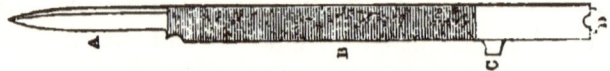

be too apparent to need much description. A is the
knife blade, B the file, C the screw-driver, and D the
key, which is adapted to fit the heads of the compasses
for tightening or loosening them as may be required.

Drawing Pens.

These are made as represented in the accompanying
engraving. The left-hand figure shows the form of
the best kind, the handle is of ivory, and the blades
have a joint whereby they may be opened for the purpose of more effectually cleaning them after use. The
right-hand figure, which is in two parts, shows an older
form of construction, the part A, to which is attached
a pricker or protracting pin, screws into the part

marked B, making the handle of sufficient length to
use conveniently as a drawing pen, thus combining two
instruments in one.

The milled head screw, which is represented as connecting the blades together,
is for the purpose of setting their points
at any opening to draw a line of an
assigned thickness. In using the pen,
it should be slightly inclined in the direction of the line to be drawn, taking
care, however, that the edges of both
the blades touch the paper. These observations are equally applicable to the
pen-point of the compasses before described, observing, as before stated, that
whenever a circle or an arc of more than
about an inch radius is to be described,
the point should be so bent that the
blades of the pen be nearly perpendicular to the paper, and both of them touched at the
same time.

The Road Pen.

This instrument consists of two pens, A and B, so
arranged with a spring which gives them a tendency
to separate from each other to the extent of about
half an inch, which tendency is counteracted by a
screw, c, whereby the pen-points may be set to any
required interval within the above limits. The screws
a and *b* are for the purpose of setting the points of the
blade to draw lines of any assigned degree of fineness, as
before explained for the ordinary drawing pen. The use
of this instrument is to draw two lines parallel and close
to each other at the same time, whereby perfect paral-

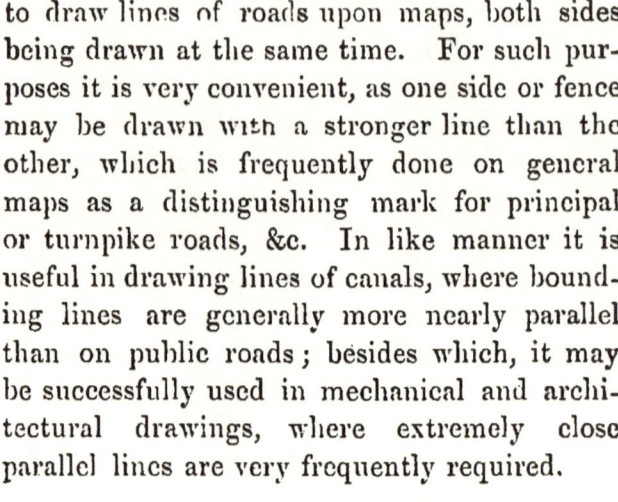

lclism may be secured. It is usually known by the name of the Road Pen, having been originally designed to draw lines of roads upon maps, both sides being drawn at the same time. For such purposes it is very convenient, as one side or fence may be drawn with a stronger line than the other, which is frequently done on general maps as a distinguishing mark for principal or turnpike roads, &c. In like manner it is useful in drawing lines of canals, where bounding lines are generally more nearly parallel than on public roads; besides which, it may be successfully used in mechanical and architectural drawings, where extremely close parallel lines are very frequently required.

The Dotting Point.

The great expense of time in dotting by hand such lines upon a drawing as may be essential to be shown and not drawn in full, may be obviated by the use of this instrument. It in all respects resembles a drawing-pen, except that the points are not so sharp, and the back blade, as seen in the engraving, is a pivot, on which may be placed a dotting-wheel, *a*, resembling the rowel of a spur; the screw, *b*, is for opening the blades to remove the wheel for cleaning after use, or replacing it with one of another character of dot. The cap, *c*, at the upper end of the instrument, is a box containing a variety of dotting wheels, each producing a different shaped dot. These are used as distinguishing marks for different classes of boundaries on maps; for instance, one kind of dot distinguishes *county* boundaries, another kind *parish* boundaries; a third kind distinguishes that which is both a county and a parish boundary. In using this instrument, the ink must be inserted between the blades of the dotting wheel, so that as the wheel revolves the points shall pass through the ink, each carrying with it a drop, and marking the paper as it passes. It is sometimes stated as an objection, that the wheel will often revolve many times before it begins to deposit its ink on the drawing, thereby leaving the first part of the line altogether blank, and in attempting to go over it again, the made dots are liable to get blotted; at all events, the line is likely to consist of dots of different sizes, which is at least unsightly. This evil may be mostly remedied by placing a piece of blank paper over the drawing at the very point the dotted line is commenced upon; then begin with drawing the wheel over the blank paper first, so that by the time it will have arrived at the proper point of commencement, the ink may be expected to flow over the points of the wheel, and make the dotted line perfect, as required.

The Pricking or Tracing Point.

This instrument consists of a pair of forceps, which firmly hold a needle point, or blunt point, *a*, by means of a sliding ring, *b*. Its use, which scarcely needs pointing out, is chiefly in copying drawings, the original being laid upon paper intended to receive the copy, and held down by weights or pins to prevent its shifting its position. The principal points are trans-

ferred to the copy by pricking through the origina.
with a very fine needle. This method of copying cannot be resorted to when the original is of considerable value. When such is the case, a common method of copying is by placing between
the drawing and the intended copy a sheet of
thin paper (such, for instance, as bank post paper),
one face of which has been sprinkled with black
lead and rubbed until it be uniformly covered,
and then as much wiped off as would come away
with gentle rubbing. This being placed with
the blackened part towards the intended copy,
a blunt point substituted for the needle point in
the instrument may be drawn with gentle pressure
over the lines of the original without damag-
ing it, and the blackened paper will leave corresponding lines on the fair sheet beneath ; by
reversing the needle in the instrument, leaving
the eye end instead of the point exposed, and
using it edgeways, it will be found a fine and smooth
tracer.

Drawing Pins.

These require but little explanation. They are used
to fix paper down upon a drawing or other board in any
required position, and in most cases answer better than

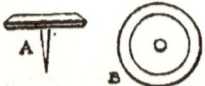

heavy weights, which are frequently
used for that purpose, as the board
may be shifted from place to place
without moving the paper. They consist of a brass
head with a steel point at right angles to its plane.
A represents it as seen edgeways, and B as seen from
above.

Having endeavoured to explain the construction of such instruments as are used for the purpose of drawing lines, whether straight or curved, and hence producing geometrical figures, we will now proceed to explain the best form of protractors which are essential for laying down angles.

Protractors.

The edge of the semicircular is divided into 180 degrees, and subdivided to half degrees, or 30 minutes, and numbered for the convenience of plotting. Round the edge is carried a vernier, which subdivides the principal divisions into single minutes. The vernier is attached to an arm, forming a radius to the semicircle, which is extended beyond the circumference, and has on the extended part a fiducial edge, on which the angular line is to be drawn.

The centre of the instrument, which is visible from above, by the centre upon which the vernier radius moves, is a ring placed concentric with the centre. To use this instrument, it is only necessary to set the vernier to the given angle, then place the protractors so that the fiducial edge may in every part exactly coincide with the line already given, and the centre with the given angular point. A line then being drawn along the fiducial edge will be the direction of the line forming the angle required ; and upon moving the protractor, such line may be produced and connected with the angular point. In adjusting the fiducial edge upon the given line, so that the centre may exactly coincide with the given angular point, there is a certain degree of practical difficulty (we are now alluding to whenever great accuracy is aimed at).

It is not, therefore, essential, in setting the instrument, to have any regard to the given angular point, but only to set the edge nicely upon the given line; then, with a needle point, make three punctures in the paper, one near the extreme point, a second at the circumference of the arc, and the third as nearly as possible at the centre. The protractor may then be removed; and if all has been accurately performed, these three points will be in one straight line, which may be transferred to pass through the given angular point by straight edge or ruler.

The Circular Protractor

Is a complete circle, connected in its centre by four radii. Like the instrument last described, the centre is left open, and surrounded by a concentric ring or collar, which carries two radial bars. To the extremity of one bar is a pinion, working in a toothed rack, quite round the outer circumference of the protractor. To the opposite extremity of the other bar is fixed a vernier, which subdivides the primary divisions on the protractor to single minutes, and, by estimation, to 30 seconds. This vernier, as may readily be understood, is carried round the protractor by turning the pinion. Upon each radial bar is placed a branch, carrying at their extremities a fine steel pricker, whose points are kept above the surface of the papers by springs placed under their supports, which give way when the branches are pressed downwards, and allow the points to make the necessary punctures in the paper. The branches are attached to the bars with a joint, which admits of being folded backwards over

the instrument when not in use, and for packing in
its case.

The centre of the instrument is represented by the
intersection of two lines, drawn at right angles to each
other on a piece of glass, which enables the person
using it to place it so that the centre, or intersection
of the cross lines, may coincide with any given point
on the plane. If the instrument is in correct order, a
line, connecting the fine pricking points with each
other, would pass through the centre of the instrument,
as denoted by the before-mentioned intersection of the
cross lines upon the glass, which, it may be observed,
are drawn so nearly level with the under surface of the
instrument as to do away with any serious amount of
parallax when setting the instrument over a point from
which any angular lines are intended to be drawn.

In using this instrument, the vernier should first be
set to —zero (or the division marked 360), on the divided
limb, and then placed on the paper, so that the two
fine steel points may be on the given line (from whence
other and angular lines are to be drawn), and the centre
of the instrument coincides with the given angular
point on such line. This done, press the protractor
gently down, which will fix it in position by means of
very fine points on the under sides. It is now ready
to lay off the given angle, or any number of angles
that may be required, which is done by turning the
pinion till the opposite *vernier* reaches the required
angle. Then press down the branches, which will
cause the points to make punctures in the paper on
the opposite sides of the circle; which being afterwards
connected, the line will pass through the given angular
point, if the instrument was first correctly set. In

this manner, at one setting of the instrument a great number of angles may be laid from the same point.

As described for the last instrument, it is not essential that the centre be over the given point when applied to the given line, provided the pricking points exactly fall upon the line; for an imaginary line, connecting the pricking points in this instrument, correspond with the line on the diameter of the protractor last described. Sometimes, instead of a rack and pinion motion, a third radial arm is attached to the centre at right angles to the other two, upon which is fixed a clamp and tangent screw, by which the vernier is not only fixed in position upon the circular limb of the instrument, but by the tangent, or slow motion screw, it may be set to the required angle with the greatest accuracy.

Plain, Circular, and Semicircular Protractors.

Other and very useful protractors are made, consisting of a circle or semicircle, without verniers, slow-motion screws, or any other appendages, having simply a fiducial circular edge, nicely divided to degrees and half-degrees, or more minute subdivisions, if the instrument is sufficiently large to admit of them. A very useful instrument of this kind has a diameter of six inches, and will be found sufficiently accurate for most ordinary purposes, and not above one-third of the cost of the above-named instrument, which, however, must be resorted to when the utmost attainable accuracy is required.

The Plain Scale.

This instrument is usually made of ivory, 6 inches long, and 1¾ inches broad; it has on it two diagonal scales, one half the size of the other, on the same plane or face of the instrument, which, for distinction-sake, we will call the upper side. These diagonal scales consist of eleven parallel lines, drawn equi-distant from each other, and divided by vertical lines into equal parts of an inch long, and numbered from right to left—1, 2, 3, &c. The top and bottom lines of the extreme half-inch space to the right is subdivided into ten equal parts by diagonal lines drawn from the tenth below to the ninth above, from the ninth below to the eighth above, from the eighth below to the seventh above, &c., till from the first below to the nothing above, so that by these means the half-inch space is subdivided into 100 equal parts. Thus, if each of the first divisions of the half-inch spaces be considered to represent unity, each of the first divisions will express $\frac{1}{10}$ of 1, and each of the subdivisions taken on the diagonal lines, counting from the top downwards, will express $\frac{1}{10}$ of the last subdivisions, $\frac{1}{100}$ of the half-inch spaces (or primary divisions). If each of the half-inch spaces (or primary divisions) be considered as representing 10, then each of the first subdivisions will express 1 (or unity), and each of the second $\frac{1}{10}$ of unity. Again, if each of the primary divisions (or half-inch spaces) be considered to represent 100, then each of the first subdivisions will express 10, and each of the second subdivisions 1, or unity, &c., &c.

The method of taking distances from the scale may be thus shown :—Suppose the distance to be 347 on the diagonal, lined, joined to the 4th subdivision on the top line, count 7 downwards, reckoning the distance of each parallel as 1; there set one point of the compasses, and extend the other till it falls on the intersection of the third primary division with the same parallel in which the other point of the compasses rests, and their opening will then express a line of 847, 34·7, or 3·47, according as we may have considered the primary divisions to represent 100, 10, or unity.

The smaller diagonal scale is formed by dividing the half-inch space into two, and the further or left-hand quarter of an inch space is then diagonally divided as above described.

On the same or upper face of the instrument, a protractor is formed round its edges, and after what has been stated upon that instrument, nothing more than the mention of it is requisite in this place. On the under surface of the instrument a variety of scales are engraved, among which are the following :—

Line of	Chords	marked	C or C H.
,,	Rhombs	,,	R H.
,,	Tangents	,,	T A.
,,	Sines	,,	S I.
,,	Secants	,,	S E C.
,,	Longitudes	,,	L O N.
,,	Latitudes	,,	L A.
,,	Inclination of Meridians	,,	I M.
,,	Hours	,,	H O.

Besides scales having the following number of equal divisions to the inch :—30, 35, 45, 50, and 60.

The line of chords serves either to set off an angle from a given point to any line, or to measure the quantity of any angle already laid down. The first is done by opening the compasses to the extent of 60 degrees upon the line of chords (which is always equal to the radius, the circle of projection), and setting one foot upon the angular point; with that extent describe an arc; then taking the angular quantity from the same chord line, set it off from the given line upon the arc described; a right line connecting the given point with that upon the arc will form the angle required. To measure an angle already laid down, describe as before an arc of 60 degrees; and then taking the extent with a pair of compasses between the lines which form the angle upon the said arc, the opening measured upon the same line of chords will denote the dimensions of the angle.

The line of rhombs serves to lay down or measure on a chart the angle of a ship's course in navigation.

The lines of tangents, sines, and secants, are used in the stereographical and orthographical projection of the sphere.

The line of longitudes, with the help of the line of chords, will show how many miles are contained in a degree of longitude at any latitude. Thus, with a pair of compasses take from the line of chords the number of degrees of the given latitude, and apply the opening of the compasses to the line of longitude, placing one point of the compasses on the last division, marked 60 on the longitudes, the other point will note upon the same line the number of miles in one degree of longitude at the given latitude. For example, if the given latitude be 60 degrees, take 60 from the line of chords, and applying one point of the compasses on the last division of the line of longitude (marked 60), the other point will fall upon the division marked 30 on the same line, showing that 30 miles is contained in one degree of longitude at the latitude of 60 degrees. The lines of latitude, inclination of meridian, and of hours, are

r 2

applicable to the practice of dialling, which does not fall within our present purpose.

Plotting Scales and Rules.

These need but few observations, as they are nothing more than scales of equal parts, the divisions being placed on a fiducial edge, by which any length may be pricked off on the paper without using the compasses, whose points, by frequent use, destroy the fineness of the graduation. Plotting scales are made of various dimensions, and of all varieties of graduation, to suit the purposes of the draftsman. Parallel rulers are also made of various constructions—some of them sliding, and others with rollers, each having its own advantages. The plain scale above described is frequently fitted with rollers, making it at the same time a convenient small parallel.

The Sector.

The sector derives its name from the fourth proposition of the sixth book of Euclid, where it is demonstrated that similar triangles have their like sides proportional.

This instrument consists of two rulers, movable round an axis or joint, from whence several scales are drawn on the faces of the rulers.

The two rulers are called legs, and represent the radii, and the middle of the joint expresses the centre of a circle.

The scales generally put upon sectors may be distinguished into single and double. The single scales are such as are commonly put on plain scales, and may be applied in the same manner. The double scales are those which proceed from the centre ; each scale is laid twice on the same face of the instrument, namely, one on each leg. From these scales, dimensions or distances are to be taken, when the legs of the instrument are in an angular position.

The Decimal Scale.

This scale lies on the edge of the instrument, and is of the same length as the sector when opened (one foot is the usual length for sectors placed in cases of instruments), and is divided into 10 equal parts or primary divisions, and each of these into 10 other equal parts, so that the whole (foot) is divided into 100 equal parts.

The Line of Artificial Numbers.

The line of numbers (marked N), or Gunter's Line, as it is commonly called, is a line of geometrical proportion divided into nine unequal parts, beginning at 1 towards the left hand, and numbered on with 2, 3, 4, 5, &c., to 10, about the middle of the line, where another radius begins, and the same divisions are repeated, numbered as before to 10, at the end of the line on the right hand. Each of these primes, or first grand divisions, are subdivided, according to the same ratio, into ten other parts, and each of these divisions (if the line be of sufficient length) should again be subdivided into ten lesser parts. But upon pocket sectors, which, when opened, are twelve inches in length, only the part from 1 in the middle to 2 towards the right hand is a second time divided, and that but into five parts instead of ten, every one of which must be accounted as two centesms in numbering ; therefore, upon the line the figures 1, 2, 3, &c., which denote the primes, may be taken arbitrarily, either as units, tens, hundreds, or thousands, or thousandth parts of an unit.

If 1, at the beginning of the line, be taken for unity, then 1 in the middle will be 10, and 10 at the end 100; but if the first 1 be accounted 10, then 1 in the middle will stand for 100, and 10 at the end for 1000. Again, if the first 1 be reckoned 100, then 1 in the middle will be 1000, and 10 at the end 10,000.

When, therefore, the first, or prime, represents 10 units, the figures 2, 3, 4, &c., to 1 in the middle, will stand for 20, 30, 40, &c.; and each tenth, or subdivision in the first radius of the line, will signify 1 unit; and each centesm in those tenths (if there be any) will be one-tenth part of an unit: 1 in the middle will be (as before observed) 100; and the figures 2, 3, 4, &c., following, 200, 300, 400, &c.; each tenth, or subdivision in the second radius, will denote 10 units; and each centesm 1 unit. Again, let the first 1 represent 100, then the 2, 3, 4, &c., following, 200, 300, 400, &c.; 1 in the middle 1000; and 10 at the end 10,000. According to this supposition, in the first, each tenth of a prime will be 10 units, and each centesm 1 unit; and in the second radius, each tenth of a prime 100, and each centesm 10.

In estimating decimal fractions upon the line, if 1 in the middle be accounted as unity, then will each prime in the first radius denote ·1, each tenth of a prime ·01, and each centesm ·001. If 10 at the end of the line to the right hand be accounted as unity, the whole first radius will represent 1, and 2, 3, 4, &c., in the second radius will represent 2, 3, 4, &c., every prime in the first radius, and every tenth of a prime in the second radius, wil' signify ·01, or one hundredth part of unity, or centesm; in the second, will denote ·001, or thousandth part of unity.

The numeration of the line thus explained, let it now be proposed to find the point thereon, answering to the number 436. For four hundred, take the first four primes next the left hand; for the second figure, 3, take three tenths of the grand division between 4 and 5; and for the six units, reckon six centesms, or six parts of the next tenth, so that the extent from 1 at the beginning of the line to that point, will express the number 436. The same point will likewise represent the numbers 43·6, 4·36, or 436; if the first be accordingly accounted 10, 1, or $\frac{1}{10}$ of unity.

To multiply upon the line, extend your compasses from 1 at the beginning, to the point representing the number of your multiplier. The same extent will reach from the number of your multiplicand to the product. Thus, if 125 were given to be multiplied by 42, extend the compasses from 1 to 42, and the same extent will reach from 125 to 5250.

To divide upon the line, extend your compasses backwards from the numbers of the division to unity. The same extent, laid the same way, will reach from the number of the dividend to the quotient. Thus, if 5250 were to be divided by 125, extend the compasses backwards from 125 to unity; the same extent will reach the same way, from 5250 to 42.

The Lines of Artificial Sines and Tangents.

The line of artificial sines (marked s) consists only of the logarithms of the natural sines, transferred from a table of logarithms to the scale. They are numbered from the left to the right, with the figures 1, 2, 3, &c., to 10, which stands about the middle of the line; and so forward with 20, 30, 40, &c., to 90, at the end on the right. In the first part of the line, the grand divisions each represent one degree; so that if each prime be subdivided into twelve parts (as they are commonly called upon sectors), each subdivision will represent five minutes. In the latter part of the line, the grand divisions, which are each ten degrees, being subdivided into ten parts, each of them will signify five minutes. In the latter part of the line the grand divisions, which are each ten degrees, being subdivided into ten parts, each of them will represent one degree; and according as they are again subdivided into four, three, or two parts, such second divisions contain fifteen, twenty, or thirty minutes each.

What has been stated of the line of sines is likewise to be understood of the line of artificial tangents, (marked T), whose divisions begin also at 1, and run on to 10 in the middle of the line, signifying degrees. In the second part it runs on with 20, 30, &c., to 45, which stands at the end of the line; then returns back again to 90, where it began.

The use of these lines is in working proportions, whether arithmetical or geometrical, as well as in trigonometrical solutions. Thus, in all proportions, three terms are given to find a fourth. Seek out, therefore, the first term, whether number, sine, or tangent, on its proper line; and in that point set one foot of the compasses, and extend the other to the second or third term, whichever of them is of the same name as the first; the same extent laid from the other term the same way will reach to the fourth term required.

Example.—As the sine of 52°. 30′ : 85 :: radius, or the sine of 90° to the fourth number required.

Set one foot of the compasses in the line of artificial sines on 52°. 30′, and extend the other foot to 90° on that line; the same extent will reach from 85 on the line of numbers to 107, the fourth term required.

The Double Scales.

These consist of the line of lines, or of equal parts marked L; the line of chords marked c; the line of sines marked s; the line of secants also marked s, but placed on the reverse side of the sector; the line of polygons marked Pol; a line of tangents to 45° marked T; and also a second line of tangents from 45° to 75°. Each of these scales begins at the centre of the instrument, and is terminated near the other extremity of each leg; viz. the lines at 10, the chords at 60, the sines at 90°, and the tangents at 45°; the remainder of the tangents, or those above 45°, are on other scales beginning at ¼ of the length of the former, counted from the centre, and marked with 45, and run to about 76 degrees.

The secants also begin at the same distance from the centre, where they are marked with 10, and are continued to as many degrees as the length of the sector will allow, which is about 75°.

The angles made by the double scales of lines of chords, of sines, and of tangents to 45 degrees, are always equal.

The angles made by the scales of upper tangents, and of secants, are also equal, and sometimes these angles are made equal to those made by the *other* double scales.

F 3

The scale of polygons is put near the inner edge of the legs; their beginning is not so far removed from the centre as the 60 on the chords is. The beginning of this scale is marked 4, and from thence is figured towards the centre of the instrument to 12.

From this disposition of the double scales, it is plain that those angles which are equal to each other when the legs of the sector are close, will continue equal to each other at every opening of the instrument.

Method of using the Double Lines on the Sector.

When a measure is taken on any of the sectoral lines beginning at the centre, it is called a lateral distance; but when a measure is taken from any point on one line, to its corresponding point on the line of the same denomination on the other leg, it is called a transverse distance.

The divisions of each sectoral line are contained within three parallel lines, the innermost being the line on which the points of the compasses are to be placed, because this is the only line of the three which goes to the centre, and is therefore the sectoral line.

Line of Lines.

Multiplication.—With the compasses, take from any convenient distance from the scale of equal parts the length of one of the factors, and open the sector until the transverse distance between 10 and 10 is equal to it; then the transverse distance of the other factor (*measured upon the same scale of equal parts*) will represent the product.

Example.—Multiply 4 by 5, expand the compasses from the centre of the sector to 4 on the primary divisions (*or take it from any other scale of equal parts*), and open the sector till this division becomes the transverse distance from 10 to 10 on the same divisions; then the transverse distance from 5 to 5, measured upon the same scale as the former, will equal 2 or 20, the answer.

Division.—Make the lateral distance of the dividend the transverse distance of the divisor; the transverse distance of 10 will be the quotient.

Example.—Divide 20 by 4. Make 20, taken from any convenient scale of equal parts, the transverse distance of 4, then the transverse of 10 (measured upon the same scale) will be 5, the answer.

It will readily be perceived for the multiplication or division of high numbers, aliquot parts of both factors must be taken, and the result multiplied by the same. The application of the sector to such common arithmetical operations is therefore very limited (and of doubtful utility).

Proportion.—Two lines being given to find a third proportional.

Example.—The given = 2 and 6, a third proportional required. Take between the compasses the lateral distance of the second term 6 (either from the line of lines on the sector, or any convenient scale), and open the sector until this distance becomes the transverse distance to the first term 2, then the transverse distance of the second term 6 measured upon the same scale as the former, will equal 18, the third proportional required.

If the legs of the sector will not open so far as to let the lateral distance of the second term fall between the divisions expressing the first term, then take $\frac{1}{2}$, $\frac{1}{3}$, $\frac{1}{4}$, or any aliquot part of the second term (such as will conveniently fall within the opening of the sector), and make such part the transverse distance of the first term; then, if the transverse distance of the second term be multiplied by the denominator of the part taken of the second term, the product will give the third proportional required.   Thus, in the above example, take $\frac{1}{3}$ of $6 = 2$, which make the transverse distance of 2 the first term; then the transverse distance of 6 the second term will be $= 6$, which multiplied by 3, will give 18, the answer.

Three lines being given to find a fourth proportional, open the sector until the lateral distance of the second term, or some aliquot part thereof, becomes the transverse section of the first term, or some aliquot part thereof becomes the transverse distance of the first term; then the transverse distance of the third term will be the fourth proportional required, or such a submultiple thereof as was taken of the second term.

Example.—To find a fourth proportional to the numbers 2, 6, and 10.

Take this lateral distance of the second term 6 from any convenient scale of equal parts, and open the sector until that quantity, or any aliquot part thereof, becomes the transverse distance of the first term 2, then the transverse distance of the third term 10, taken from the same scale of equal parts, will give 30, the fourth proportional required.

To diminish a Line in any Assigned Proportion.

Example.—Let it be required to diminish a line of 4 inches in the proportion of 8 to 7. Open the sector until the transverse distance of 8 is equal to a lateral distance of 7.

Mark the point where 4 inches will reach as a lateral distance taken from the centre, which will be in this case 6·86, and the transverse distance taken at the point will be 3 inches and a half, the proportion required, that is, 8 : 7 : : 4 : 3½.

We may remark, once for all, that in all problems with the sector, if any given line is too long for the legs of the instrument, take ½, ⅓, or ¼, &c., of it, and the result multiplied by 2, 3, or 4, will give the quantity required.

The use of the sector in reducing drawings may be thus shown :—Suppose a triangle was to be reduced to the proportion of 4 to 7.

Take the length of one side of the triangle in the compasses, and make it the transverse distance of 7 and 7 ; then take the transverse distance 4 and 4, which will be the length of the corresponding side of the reduced triangle. Next take the length of another side of the given triangles, and make the transverse distance of 7 and 7 as before. Then the transverse distance of 4 and 4 will be the length of the corresponding side of the reduced triangle ; one point of the compasses being placed at the proper extremity of the first reduced line, describe an arc with the length of the second line as *radius*. Lastly, the third side of the given triangle being made the transverse distance of 7 and 7, and that of 4 and 4 being taken, another arc intersecting the former one, described from the opposite end of the first reduced line, will give the point to be connected with each end of the first reduced line, and the triangle will be completed.

In the same manner, any right-lined figure, of how many sides soever, may be reduced in any given proportion or augmented by the same rule.

To divide a given line into any proposed number of equal parts :—

Make the length of the given line the transverse distance to the figures representing the number of parts required; then the transverse distance of 1 and 1 will divide the given line as required.

Example.—Suppose a line to be divided into 9 equal parts, take the length of the given line in the compasses, and open the sector until it becomes the transverse distance between 9 and 9; then the transverse of 1 and 1 will be ⅑th part of the given line, or such a sub-multiple of the ⅑th part as was taken of the given line. Or the ⅑th part will be the difference between the given line and the transverse distance 8 and 8.

The latter of these methods is to be preferred when the parts required fall near the centre of the instrument.

To make the line of lines represent any scale of equal parts for drawing, plans, elevations, &c. Thus, suppose a scale of one to five chains, or one inch to five feet were required. Take one inch in the compasses, and, by opening the sector, make it the transverse distances of 5 and 5, and then the transverse distance of any other corresponding points, as 6 and 6, 7½ and 7½ will be that number of chains, and links or feet, &c., to the scale required.

Line of Chords.

The double scales of chords upon the sectors are more generally useful than the single line of chords described on the plane scale : for, on the sector, the radius with which the arc is to be described may be of any length, between the transverse distance of 60 and of 60, when the legs are close, and that of the transverse of 60 and 60 when the legs are opened as far as the instrument will admit of. But with the chords on the plane scale, the arc described must be always of the same radius.

To protract or lay down a right-lined angle, which shall contain a given number of degrees, suppose 46°.

Case 1.—When the angles contain less than 60 degrees, make the transverse distance of 60 and 60 equal to the length of the radius of the circle, and with that opening describe an arc. Take the transverse distance of the given degrees 46, and lay this distance on the arc. From the centre of the arc draw two lines, each passing through one extremity of the distance laid on the arc, and these two lines will contain the angle required.

Case 2.—When the angle contains more than 60 degrees. Suppose, for example, we wish to form an angle containing 148 degrees. Describe an arc, and make the transverse distance of $\frac{1}{2}$ or $\frac{1}{3}$, &c., of the given number of degrees, and lay this distance on the arc twice or thrice. Draw two lines connecting them, and they will form the angle required.

When the required angle contains less than 5 degrees, suppose $3\frac{1}{2}$, it will be better to proceed thus with the given radius, and from the centre describe an arc, and from a given point lay off the chord of 60°, which suppose to give the point A; and also from the first point lay off in the same direction the chord of $56\frac{1}{2}$ degrees ($= 60°—3\frac{1}{2}°$), which would give the point B; then through these two points draw lines to the point A, and they will represent the angle of $3\frac{1}{2}$ degrees, as required. From what has been stated about the protracting of an angle to contain a given number of degrees, it will easily be seen how to find the degrees or measure of an angle already laid down.

Line of Polygons.

The line of polygons is chiefly useful for the ready division of the circumference of a circle into any number of equal parts from 4 to 12, that is, as a ready means to inscribe regular polygons of any given number of sides from 4 to 12, within a given circle. To which set off the radius of the given circle (which is always equal to the side of an inscribed hexagon), as the transverse distance of 6 and 6 upon the line of polygons. Then the transverse distance of 6 and 6 upon the line of polygons. Then the transverse distance of 4 and 4 will be the side of a square; the transverse distance between 5 and 5, the side of a pentagon; between 7 and 7, the side of a heptagon; between 8 and 8 the side of an octagon; between 9 and 9, the side of a nonagon, &c.; all of which is too plain to require an example.

If it be required to form a polygon upon a given right line, set off the extent of the given line as a transverse distance between the points upon the lines of polygons, answering to the number of sides of which the polygon is to consist, as for a pentagon between 5 and 5, or for an octagon between 8 and 8; then the transverse distance between 6 and 6 will be the radius of a circle whose circumference would be divided by the given line into the number of sides required.

The line of polygons may likewise be used in describing, upon a given line, an isosceles triangle, whose angles at the base are each double that at the vertex.

For, taking the given line between the compasses, open the sector, till the extent becomes the transverse distance of 10 and 10, then the transverse distance of 6 and 6 will be the length of each of the two equal sides of the isosceles triangle.

All such regular polygons, whose number of sides will exactly divide 360 (the number of degrees into which all *circles* are supposed to be divided) without a remainder, may likewise be set off upon the circumference of a circle by the line of chords. Thus, take the radius of the circle between the compasses, and open the sector till that extent is the transverse distance between 60 and 60 upon the line of chords; then having divided 360 by the required number of sides, the transverse distance between the numbers of the quotient will be the side of the polygon required. Thus for an octagon, take the distance between 45 and 45 : and for a polygon of 36 sides, take the distance between 10 and 10, &c.

Lines of Sines, Tangents, and Secants.

Given the radius of a circle (suppose to two inches); required the sine and tangent of 28°. 30' to the radius.

Open the sector so that the transverse distance of 90 and 90 on the sines, or of 45 and 45 on the tangents, may be equal to the given radius, viz. two inches; then will the transverse distance of 28°. 30', taken from the sines, be the length of that sine to the given radius; or if taken from the tangents, will be the length of that tangent to the given radius. But if the secant of 28°. 30' was required, make the given radius of two inches a transverse distance of 0 and 0, at the beginning of the line of secants, and then take the transverse distance of the degrees wanted, viz. 28°. 30'.

A tangent greater than 45 degrees (suppose 60) is found thus:—

Make the given radius, suppose two inches, a transverse distance to 45, and 45 at the beginning of the scale of upper tangents, and then the required degrees (60) may be taken from the scale.

Given the length of the sine, tangent, or secant of any degrees, to find the length of the radius to that sine, tangent, or secant.

Make the given length a transverse distance to its given degrees on its respective scale.   Then,

If a sine		the trans-		90 and 90 on the sines		will be
If a tangent under 45°	}	verse dis	{	45 and 45 on the tangents	}	the
If a tangent above 45°		tance of		45 and 45 on the upper tangents		radius
If a secant				0 and 0 on secants.		sought.

To find the length of a versed sine to a given number of degrees, and a given radius.

Make the transverse distance of 90 and 90 on the sine, equal to the given radius.

Take the transverse distance of the complement of the given number of degrees.

If the given number of degrees is less than 90, subtract the complement of the sine from the radius, the remainder will be the versed sine.

If the given number of degrees are more than 0, add the complement of the sine to the radius, and the sum will be the versed sine.

To open the legs of a sector, so that the corresponding double scale of lines, chords, sines, tangents, may make each a right angle.

On the line of lines, make the lateral distance 10, a

transverse distance between 8 on one leg, and 6 on the other leg.

On the line of sines, make the lateral distance 90, a transverse distance 45 to 45 ; or from 40 to 50 ; or from 30 to 60 ; or from the sine of any degrees to their complement.

On the line of tangents make the lateral distance of 45 a transverse distance between 30 and 30.

Having now endeavoured to describe the principal drawing instruments in general use, and the principal scales from which all others emanate, we propose at some future period to exemplify the simplicity of their application to all the trades engaged in the building art, accompanied by some useful diagrams and geometrical problems.

CHAPTER VI.

SPECIFICATIONS :—ARTIFICERS' WORK, AND QUANTITIES.

HAVING thus conveyed some preliminary notions as to the methods of designing architectural structures upon paper, and having also described the several materials and trades with their chief tools and methods of manipulation, which are employed in the construction of dwelling houses, we proceed to illustrate the design itself, which will be done most briefly by giving (with the necessary illustrations) an example in the following—

" SPECIFICATION of the different Artificers' Work required for the erection of two houses proposed to be erected on a plot of ground, situate

for

according with, and corresponding to the various drawings, comprising plans, elevations, sections, and details, made and combined with this specification for the purpose of such erection, and under the superintendence of   .

CARCASS OF BUILDING."

EXCAVATOR.

The ground is to be excavated to the whole of the extent of the principal building for the basement storey, and to the depth and dimensions shown, and described on the plans and section, Plates II. and III., which will average an area of about 50 feet by 50 feet, and 5 feet deep; and the trenches then to be dug out of sufficient breadth and depth for the construction of the foundations of the several walls, chimney breasts, piers for sleepers, &c. To excavate when and where directed, according to the dimensions, the earth required for the formation of the rain-water tank, being about 11 feet long, 8 feet deep, and 8 feet wide, as well as for all pipes, drains, traps, syphons, or cesspools, that are, or may be hereafter, described or necessary.

To fill in and well ram the earth or soil round all the foundations, piers, traps, gullies, syphons, &c., and to well puddle round and about the rain-water tank, sufficient to prevent the ingress or egress of water. To level all grounds and to cart away from time to time, as may be directed, all the superfluous earth or rubbish that accumulates round or in the buildings or grounds during their erection, and to leave them in a clean and perfect condition at the conclusion of the works.

BRICKLAYER.

Drains.

Provide and lay six-inch glazed earthenware socket-jointed pipes, for conveying soil and waste-water into principal drain or sewer, in the position and to the depth shown on the block-plan and section, Plate III., with a fall of not less than 6 inches to every 100 feet, and to fix and make perfect and secure, No. 8 15-inch earthenware gully-traps, and No. 4 syphons of the best and most approved description. To lay a 6-inch similar connecting pipe from principal and servants' water-closets, as well as 4-inch glazed pipes, from sink in back kitchens and front areas into the above-named or principal drain, with all necessary bends, traps, &c., to render the drainage perfect. Build in 9-inch sound stock brickwork, the rain-water tank, and complete the same in the manner shown and described, and to the dimensions exemplified on Plate XIV., viz. : The walls all round to be built in 9-inch brickwork in cement, and the bottom to be paved with two courses of bricks laid flat in the same material, upon which are to be two courses of tiles bedded in cement, and the whole to be rendered all round with compo $1\frac{1}{4}$ inch thick, and all the external portion to be well puddled. To lay and fix complete 4-inch glazed earthenware socket-pipes, from the zinc down-comers of roofs into the said tank, and a 6-inch waste ditto into the principal drain or soil pipe, with all necessary bends, neck, or traps, that may be requisite for the full completion of the conveyance of the water to and from the tank and the drainage.

Building.

The whole of the brickwork to be executed with sound hard-burnt stock bricks laid in well-made mortar, composed of Dorking lime (or any other that approximates to the same quality), mixed in the proportion of one measure of lime to three of clean sharp river or road sand, free from loam or earthy particles.

The whole of the external walls of the erection as high as the ground-floor line to be laid in old English bond and left rough for receiving Roman cement stucco, and from thence to the top of the building, to be carried up in Flemish bond and prepared and left for tuck pointing. No four courses in either bond to rise more than 12 inches in height, and all the several walls, chimney-breasts, piers, &c., with their various footings, to be built and finished in the manner and according to the dimensions shown and described upon the accompanying plates.

All openings below the ground-floor line to have rough skew-back arches turned over them, and all above, both to front and back elevation, to have 14-inch arches of the best picked malms rubbed and set in putty.

The foundations to be laid in three courses, and the piers for sleepers to be built 9 inches square, as shown and described on Plate XV. To provide and lay a course of slates between two beds of cement on all the walls at the level of the ground surface of the principal building to prevent the rising of the damp.

Each storey of the building to have two double tiers of hoop-iron bonds, of No. 12 gauge, properly tarred and bedded round and across all the walls of the building. To build up the bay-windows and porches to entrance-hall in cement, and according with the manner and dimensions shown and described on Plates XXII and XXIII.

No. 6 air bricks to be inserted between the floor joists of each storey in front, and the same number in the back elevations, for allowing ventilation to the floors.

To turn over all door and window openings 4½ discharging arches closely set, and to each fire-place a 4½ inch brick trimmer, and insert a wrought-iron chimney-bar 2 inches wide by ¾ of an inch thick, as shown on

Plate XVII., to all the chimney openings; the bars to have 4½ inch bearing, and to be turned up and down at the ends.

To carry up all the flues as shown on section, and in the direction thereon described, and to properly core and parget the same.

To thoroughly bed in mortar all the sleepers, wall-plates, wood bricks, bond-timber, lintels, and all others requiring to be set or bedded in mortar, and to fix in and point with lime and hair all the door and window frames.

A chasm in the brickwork of each house to be left where directed, from the ground to the principal water-closet, for soil and water-pipes.

Kitchen Offices.

The walls of these buildings to have two courses of footings, and carried up to their various heights one brick or 9 inches thick, and the flues to be taken as shown on the section, one tier of iron hoop bond, similar to that described for the principal building, to be inserted all round the party and external walls.

A 6-inch glaze earthenware soil pipe to be laid from servants' water-closet into principal or main drain, and a 4-inch ditto from sink in back-kitchen into waste-drain, properly trapped and in connection with waste or soil-pipe of the above-named closet.

To carry up 4½-inch division or protection walls between water-closet, coal-cellar, and back-kitchen. Also to 9-inch spandril brickwork, with necessary footings for the support of steps from ground-floor to garden.

CARPENTER.

All the timber used (*except for the sleepers*) to be the best Dantzic, Riga, or Memel fir. *The sleepers to be of well seasoned oak*, as free from knots, shakes, and sap as possible, and all the scantlings figured on the drawings or herein expressed to finish to their full dimensions. No ceiling joists, quarters, or rafters are to be more than 12 inches apart.

To provide and fix all wood bricks where and when required, as well as all necessary centres, screens, springing slips, and all other articles necessary for the due execution of the carpenter's work.

Basement Storey.

The sleepers to be of oak 5 × 3 inches, halved and spiked together, and bedded level and soundly on the brick piers, as shown and described on Plate XV.

The floor joists to be 4 × 2 inches, bridged and well nailed to sleepers.

Wood bricks to be inserted where requisite in jambs of doors, windows, &c., as well as round the walls for fixing the skirting and other joiner's work to.

Lintels to be inserted over all the door and window-openings, 3 inches thick, and the width of the jamb; and to have at least a 4-inch bearing on each jamb.

Ground Floor.

Wall-plates $4\frac{1}{2}$ × 3 inches to be inserted the whole length of front and back walls, to be halved and dovetailed at the angles of the two external flank walls, and return upon the same not less than 6 feet, to form a connecting bond with the front and back walls of the building. A wall-plate of the same scantling to be also

G

inserted upon the top of the wall dividing breakfast room from kitchens.

The floor-joists to be 9 × 2 inches, and to extend from front to back wall of building and over bay window, and to be bolted and spiked to the wall-plates. The joists to be herring-bone trussed, and to have on the floors of each house No. 3 1-inch wrought iron tension-rods inserted, as shown and described, with the trimmers on Plate XIX. It must be distinctly understood that before the herring-bone trussing and iron tension-rods are applied, the joists on each floor must be shored up in the centre to form a camber of at least 2½ inches, when, after the trussing is filled in, and the above-mentioned rods screwed up, the shoring may be taken away.

The wood trimmers before and on the sides of chimney-breasts to be framed and supported as shown and described on Plate XVI. It may, perhaps, be as well to state, that they are framed at one end into the front one, and rest upon a stone corbel inserted purposely for their support at the other; and after being properly applied to their places, are secured by an iron bar being well spiked to the end of each end trimmer.

The trimmers for well-hole of stairs to be of the same scantling, and supported from the flank walls in a similar manner.

Lintels, bond, wood bricks, and every other requisite to be inserted as before described for the basement floor.

First or Chamber Floor.

The wall-plates to be 4½ × 3 inches, and to extend the whole length of front and back walls of building, to be halved and dovetailed and well spiked at the angles, and to return upon the flank walls, not less than 6 feet, to form a connecting bond at the angles. The floor joists to be 9 × 2 inches, and to extend from front to back and over bay windows, and to be notched and spiked to wall-plates.

The joists to be herring-bone trussed, and wound up with wrought iron tension rods, as shown and described for the ground floor below.

Also, the trimmers to be framed, fixed, and supported in a similar manner; at the same time providing and fixing all necessary centres, bond, wood bricks, and every other requisite.

Attic.

The wall-plates of this floor to be of the same scantling, and to be fixed on the walls in a similar manner to that above described for the two floors below. The floor joists to be also 9 × 2 inches, and fixed, herringbone trussed with the iron rods applied in a like manner to those before described, as also the trimmers; with all the necessary auxiliaries alluded to for the before-named floors.

Quarter-partitions.

The partitions to be framed and fixed in the manner shown and described on the Plates XXIV. and XXV., and the floor joists notched and secured to the heads or sills thereof (*as the case may be*), which heads and sills are to rest on a stone corbel inserted in the party wall for that purpose, and connected together by iron straps, as shown and described at Fig. 2, Plate XXV. The scantlings to be of the following dimensions, viz.:—

heads and sills, 7 × 3 inches; side and door posts, 4 × 3½ inches; braces, 3½ × 3½ inches; filling in quarters, 3½ × 2 inches; with all necessary bolts, ties, straps, &c., fixed complete.

Cisterns.

A cistern to be framed and fixed in the roof over water-closet, and put together with white lead, as shown and described in Plate XXIV., Figs. 4 and 5, and to be of the following dimensions, viz. :—8 feet long, 6 feet wide, and 3 feet deep; the quarterings of the *heads, sills, sides,* and *bottom,* to be 3 × 3 inches, framed and put together in the usual manner, with 1½ by ¼ thick iron ties at all the angles, properly spiked thereto; the whole to be lined with 1½-inch ploughed and tongued yellow deal boarding.

A smaller cistern also to be prepared and fixed immediately under the one above described, but just above the water-closet, upon the quarter space of stairs between the ground and chamber floors, the size of which is to be 2 feet 6 inches long, 1 foot 6 inches wide, and 1 foot 6 inches deep—to be prepared from 1½-inch yellow deal, ploughed, tongued, dovetailed, and strapped in the usual manner

Roof to principal Building.

The roof to be framed and fixed with wall-plates, tie-beams, queen and king posts, principal rafters, half principal ditto, pole plates, purlins, common rafters, diagonal ties, slips, ridges, &c., as shown and described on Plates XX. and XXI., and with the accompanying explanation, viz. :—Two whole pair of principal rafters to be framed and fixed at the intersection of the hips,

and eight half principal rafters in the position shown
on plan of roof to be framed into them; the wall-plates
to be properly scarfed and wedged together with oak
or iron wedges, and to be halved, dove-tailed, and well
spiked at the angles, so as to form and be a continuous bond all round the external walls of the building; the tie-beam and angular ties to be properly
cogged down upon the wall-plate; the principal rafters
and half principal rafters to be framed with the necessary
draft, and in the usual manner, with all the requisite
iron bolts, clips, straps, wedges, &c., fixed thereon; the
pole plates to be scarfed and wedged together, and
tenoned and fixed at the angles, so that it may make
a continuous tie to the roof, in the same manner the
wall-plate does to the walls, and the purlins to be
scarfed where required, and fixed to hips in the usual
way—and to be bridged down upon principal rafters;
the hip rafter to be framed into the dragging tie, and the
common rafters to be notched on to purlins and pole
plate. The ridge board and hip rafters to rise full 2 inches
above the top or line of common rafters for dressing the
lead round. The scantlings of the timbers for this roof
are to be as follows :—

The plate for fixing brackets to	4½ by	3¼
Wall-plate	4½ „	4½
Cantilevers, to be halved and nailed to feet of		
common rafters	4 „	2
Tie beam	9 „	4
Principal rafters	7 „	4
Pole plate and purlins	7 „	4
Common rafters	4 „	2
Queen and king posts in clear of joggles	4 „	4
Braces or struts	4 „	3
Hips and ridges	12 „	2
Diagonal and dragging ties	4½ „	4¼

Battens for slates . . . . 2 by 0¾
Collar pieces . . . . 7 „ 3
To prepare and fix to collar pieces of roof ceiling ⎫ 4½ „ 2
    joists . . . . ⎭

And to fix, as shown in Plate XX., all canting fillets, facia, as
may be required, to their various sizes, &c.

Kitchen Offices.

To prepare and fix in jambs and other places required,
and, where directed, wood bricks for fixing and completing the joiner's work, and to prepare and bed
lintels over all door and window openings; the width
of the jambs 3½ inches thick, and to lay 4½ inches on
each jamb.

The servants' privy to have a wall-plate 4½ × 3 inches
inserted, and to have floor 4½ × 2 inches notched thereon,
and trimmed for pan of closet.

The roofs over these buildings to be plain lean-to
roofs, each declining from the party-wall, and to the
same inclination as that of the principal building, and
to comprise a *wall-plate, tie-beam, principal rafter,
forming common rafter as well,* a *purlin* supported by a
strut from the *tie-beam,* and a *pole plate;* the whole to
be battened for receiving slates, &c.

The scantlings for these offices are to be of the following dimensions, namely :—

Wall-plates, 4½ × 3 inches; tie-beams 8 × 4 inches;
pole plate, 4½ × 3 inches; principal rafter, 8 × 3 inches;
common rafters, 3½ × 2 inches; ridge-board, 6 × 1½
inches; and battens for slates, 2 × ¾ inches.

Two cisterns to be prepared and fixed in roofs over
the sinks for receiving the water from the service and
the rain-water tank; these cisterns are to be 4 feet
long, 3 feet wide, and 2 feet 6 inches deep, and framed

with skeleton angular framing; that is, to have a head and sill all round with quartering, at all the angles similar to that described for the cistern in principal roof, with one upright in the middle, and a corresponding piece across the bottom, the whole to be lined with 1½-inch yellow deal, ploughed, tongued, and put together with white lead. A partition in each cistern, prepared in the same manner, from 1-inch yellow deal, to be inserted and grooved into sides and bottom.

To provide and fix, when and where directed, all centres, bond, timber, wood bricks, springing pieces, &c., and set out all necessary work, and to do or cause to be done all and everything that is required of a carpenter in a building, providing all materials, the best of their respective qualities, and all requisite plant for the full completion of the work.

SMITH AND IRON-FOUNDER.

All the iron work, except that particularly described to be *cast*, to be of the best malleable metal, as free from blister or any other imperfections as possible. To prepare, deliver, and assist in fixing No. 16 wrought-iron chimney bars, of the dimensions of the opening shown on the various drawings, and of the form and manner described in the detailed Plates, each bar to be 2 inches wide, and ⅜th of an inch thick, to have a 4½ bearing on each joint, and to turn up and down 2½ inches at each end.

To prepare and deliver No. 8 iron straps, 2 feet 6 long, 2½ inches wide, and ¼-inch thick, punched with holes for the necessary spikes, &c., for tieing heads and sills of partitions together, and as shown on Plate XXIV., Fig. 2, prepare No. 6 iron clips for partition posts, 2 feet long, $3\frac{1}{2}$ clip, 2 inches wide, and $\frac{1}{4}$ inch thick.

To prepare, provide, and assist in fixing, No. 18 one-inch wrought iron tension rods, to extend from front to back walls of the building, three of which are to be fixed in each floor of each house of the building, with 2-inch head, one inch thick at one end, and taped up at the other end at least four inches, with a nut of the same size as the head, with a pair of washers to each rod, 6 inches by 3 and $\frac{1}{4}$ of an inch thick. See Plate XIX.

To prepare and deliver No. 12 iron clips for feet of principal rafter, as shown on Plate XXI., Fig. 1, 18 inches long, 4 inches clip, 2 inches wide, and $\frac{1}{4}$ inch thick, pierced for the necessary spikes, &c.; No. 4 clips for foot of queen posts, Figs. 3 and 4, 2 feet long, 4-inch clip, 2 inches wide, &c., $\frac{1}{4}$ inch thick, with mortice for wedges, $1\frac{1}{2}$ inches deep, and $\frac{3}{8}$ thick, and a pair of corresponding wedges to each clip.

No. 4 pairs of iron straps to fix on the heads of queen posts, *stretching piece* and head of principal rafter, made to the form shown on the same plate, 2 feet 6 inches long, 2 inches wide, $\frac{1}{4}$ inch thick, pierced for the requisite spike, &c.

No. 4 $\frac{3}{4}$-inch bolts for king posts, 2 feet long, taped down $3\frac{1}{4}$ inches, with 2 heads and washers, 4 inches by 3, and $\frac{1}{4}$ of an inch thick.

No. 8 clip similar to those described for the whole principal rafters, to be provided for the half principal rafter. No. 8 clips also to be provided for the heads of the same, 1 foot 6 inches long; clip 4 inches by 2 inches wide, and $\frac{1}{2}$ inch thick, with all necessary spikes, nails, wedges, &c., for making the work complete.

To provide and fix No. 8 angular irons to top and sill of cistern in roof, 1 foot 6 inches upon each return, 2 inches wide, and $\frac{1}{4}$ inch thick; and also No. 8 for the two smaller cisterns, 1 foot long, $1\frac{1}{2}$ inch wide, and $\frac{3}{16}$ inch thick.

STONEMASON.

To put to all the external doorways Yorkshire stone solid tooled steps, with mortice holes for receiving the ends of door-posts.

To provide and fix No. 8 properly dished and holed gully stones, 15 inches square and 3 inches thick, when and where directed; as also a 5-inch York landing, 10 feet long by 7 feet wide, or two stones to correspond to the same dimensions over the rain-water tank, with every preparation of receiving the slate filter, as shown on Plate XIV.

To prepare and bed No. 20 Yorkshire stones, 1 foot 3 inches square, and 1 foot 4 inches deep, for receiving trimmers to floors and heads and sills of partitions, tooled as shown on Plate XXIV.

To prepare and fix 100 feet run of York throated coping, 12 × 3, to area of front and back elevations, and to kitchen offices; also, 36 feet run of rough York, 1 foot 4 inches by 4 inches thick, to form core for the cornices of entrance porches and bay windows.

To prepare, provide, and fix tooled, rubbed, and throated window sills, 8 inches wide and $4\frac{1}{2}$ inches thick, properly dished, to all openings of windows in front and back elevations and kitchen offices, according to the dimensions shown on the various drawings.

To prepare and fix to the porches of entrance doors a 6-inch tooled and rubbed landing, with steps leading thereto, 12 inches by 6 inches, bedded to brick spandrils, as shown on Plate XXIII. Also, to fix a tooled landing 7 inches thick to the back or garden entrance, and the steps from thence to the garden, which are to be 2½-inch tooled treads and risers securely bedded on brick spandrils carried up for that purpose.

To provide and fix in back kitchen a stone sink, to size shown on plan and 6 inches deep, with a hole cut and dished to receive bell trap and waste water pipe.

To cut on the stonework all necessary holes, mortices, rebates, grooves, as required, and all other work pertaining to the trade of a mason.

PLUMBER.

All the slips and ridges of principal roof to be covered with 6 lb. milled lead, and to be laid down over the slate at least 6 inches on each side with the usual lap, and secured in the most approved manner. The dormer lights to attics to be also covered with 6 lb. lead, and the vertical sides of each with 5 lb. lead. All the flashings for this roof, as well as that over kitchen office, to be of 5 lb. lead, and to dress over the slates and up the side at least 6 inches, and where requisite to be let into the brickwork at least 1 inch, with all necessary solder, holdfast screws, nails, &c., with every other requisite for making the internal roofs impervious to wet, from rain, snow, or other causes.

SLATER.

The roof over principal building to be covered with duchess slating, with at least 3 inches lap, and the usual gauge of about 10½ inches securely fixed to the battens, with 2 copper nails to each slate; and to cover the kitchen office with lady slates, with the usual lap and gauge fixed to the battens, with 2 zinc nails to each slate, with all the necessary dressings to hips, valleys, and eaves, &c., and both roofs to be securely pointed with lime and hair.

To provide, prepare, and fix No. 12 3-inch slate cantilevers, to the size and form shown in the drawing of details for roof.

To provide and fix in the rain-water tank a $\frac{3}{4}$-inch slate filter, according with and to the dimensions described on the plan and section Plate XIV., with all necessary lifts, perforated plates, taps, &c., and apparatus complete.

ZINC WORKER.

To prepare and fix all round principal building a gutter of the best Belgian zinc of 15-inch gauge, to the form and dimensions shown and explained on Plate XXI., with all proper falls to the various dimensions, and so manufactured in external appearance as to be level with the soffit of the projecting cave of the building, as shown on the before-named plate.

To put up and securely fix No. 6 downcomers of 4-inch calibre in the position marked on plan of roof.

To provide and fix the said in the position marked on the plan of roof, and each to have a suitable cistern head, with all necessary shoes, laps, joints, holdfasts, and every requisite to connect them with the earthenware pipes laid for conveying the water into the rain-water tank.

The gutters and downcomers from the roof over kitchen offices of 3-inch calibre, with corresponding cistern-head.

Also to provide and fix a 2-inch downcomer, with every requisite bend from the flats of the bay windows and entrance porches to the drain in front area.

FINISHINGS.

JOINER'S WORK.

Attic Floor.

The dormer light in each room to be fitted up with two-inch beaded, and rebated frames, and 1½-inch chamfered sashes, suspended on pivots in the centre, with all requisite cords, pullies, fastenings, &c., for the opening and closing of the same, in an impervious and efficient manner.

Floor.

The floor to be 1¼-inch white deal, and laid folding; skirting ground 2 inches wide by ¾ thick, chamfered to receive plaster, and as shown on Plate XXVI., Fig. 2, to be fixed all round the rooms, and a similar description of ground to door and window joints, which are to be covered with a 1¼-inch moulding, to form an architrave and break the joints of plaster, and grounds, and to the ground round rooms, is to be fixed a 6-inch square skirting-board. The jambs of doors to have a ¾-inch beaded lining, and to have a slip braded on to form the rebate for doors, which are to be 1¼ inch; two panel square, hung with suitable butt hinges and fastenings.

Chamber Floor.

The floor to be 1¼-inch yellow deal, with a straight joint, and splayed heading, joints, with mitred borders to hearths, a ground 2 inches wide by 1 inch thick, chamfered, to be fixed all round the rooms for receiving the plaster and fixing the skirting to, and also one $3\frac{1}{2}$ wide of the same thickness round all door and window openings. The housemaid's small closet on this floor to be formed with a $1\frac{1}{2}$-inch square panelled partition, and the door to correspond with the other described for this floor.

The sashes and frames for the principal rooms on this floor, to be of the venetian character, with the centre sashes of each window, double hung, and side sashes fixed. The frame to be deal cased, with oak sunk sills, brass cased pullies, with $1\frac{1}{2}$-inch ovolo sashes hung with cast-metal weights, patent cord, &c., and the sashes and frames for dressing-room and stairs to be of a similar description and double hung. The finishing to all these windows to be as shown and described on Plate XXVI.

The jamb lining for doors to be $1\frac{1}{4}$ inch thick, beaded and single rebated, and to have $1\frac{1}{4}$-inch four-panel-square doors, properly hung with $2\frac{1}{2}$ butt hinges.

The skirting to be moulded 9 inches wide, and fixed in the manner shown at Fig. 2, Plate XXVI.

Ground or Principal Floor.

The floor to be $1\frac{1}{4}$-inch yellow deal, straight jointed, splayed heading, joints edge-nailed, and mitre borders to hearths.

Grounds.

Skirting grounds $2\frac{1}{2}$ inches wide, by 1 inch thick, to be fixed all round the floors for receiving the plaster, and fixing the skirting to the upper edge, to be ploughed,

and all angles to be dovetailed together, as well as the
ends secured in a similar manner to the vertical grounds
of doors and windows—(see grounds to venetian window)
Plate XXVI.

Entrance Hall.

The door frames to be 4 inches by $3\frac{1}{2}$ inches, rebated
and beaded, with double rebated transom head, and to
be tenoned into stone step.

The doors to be $2\frac{1}{2}$ inch, two panel bolection moulded
on both sides, $\frac{7}{8}$th panels, and to be hung with 3 pair
of $2\frac{1}{2}$ butt hinges.

The fan-light to be a 2-inch lamb's tongue moulded
light and fixed above door, with grounds, linings, and
architraves, corresponding with those shown and described for the floor on Plates XXVI. and XXVII.
To put up, with all the corresponding fittings, a pair of
2-inch sash doors, with a suitable light above, to divide
the entrance hall from passage and stairs.

Also to provide and fix a 2-inch sash door and partition to form the lobby under water-closet, and
divide the stairs from the garden or back entrance to
this floor, with all suitable finishings, and according to
the one above described for dividing the hall from the
stairs.   The door frame from lobby to garden to be
prepared for fan and side lights (*as shown on elevation
of back front*), the external posts and head to be $3\frac{1}{2}$
inches by 3 inches, and the two vertical posts, as well
as transom head, to be $3\frac{1}{2}$ inches by $2\frac{1}{2}$ inches, to be
beaded, rebated, and tenoned into step, in a similar
manner to that described for the front entrance door,
and to have a 2-inch sash-door fan and side-lights, with
$1\frac{1}{4}$-inch framed boxing shutters as high as the transom

head, the grounds, linings, and other finishings, to be similar to those shown on Plate XXVI, and described for the venetian window in the back parlour.

Bay-windows, Front Parlours.

These windows to be fitted up and finished in the manner shown and described on Plate XXVII., with deal cased frames, oak sunk sills, and the centre position to have brass cased pullies, patent cords, and cast metal weights, and prepared to receive the sashes, which are to be 2-inch lamb-tongue moulding, the middle sashes double hung, and those of the sides fixed. The other portions are to be prepared and fixed in the manner shown on the before-mamed Plate XXVII., for receiving metal, revolving shutters, and finished with the grounds, linings, soffit, skirting, architraves, as there shown and described.

Back Parlour.

The venetian window in this room to be fitted up in the manner shown and described in Plate XXVI., Fig. 4; the middle sashes to be double hung, and the side lights fixed. To have $1\frac{1}{4}$-inch moulded shutters hung with brass, cased pullies, patent cord, and cast metal weights; and to have $1\frac{1}{4}$-inch framed and moulded back. The grounds, linings, architrave, &c., in a corresponding manner to those described and shown for the front parlour or dining room.

Doors.

To prepare and fix $1\frac{1}{4}$-inch double rebated and beaded jamb-lining to the grounds for the folding-doors between the two parlours. The doors to be $1\frac{1}{2}$-inch double moulded, two panels in each door, and the grounds, architraves, &c., to be of the same description, and to correspond with those before described. The jamb-linings for the other doors to be of the same de scription as before stated, and to have 1¼-inch 4-panel doors moulded on both sides, with corresponding grounds and architraves.

Skirting.

All the skirting for this floor to be board wide and 1 inch thick, and to be surmounted with a 1½-inch rebated moulding.

Basement.

Breakfast Room.—The floor to be 1¼-inch yellow deal, straight joints and splayed headings, and mitred borders to hearth. The bay window to have sashes and frames similar to those described for dining-room above, and to have sliding shutters similar to those shown and explained for the back parlour windows, with door skirting, lining, and all others of a corresponding character.

Kitchen.

The floor to be 1¼-inch deal, folded and mitred border to hearth.

Sash Frames.

The sash frames to be of a similar description to those already described for the upper floor, and to have 1½-inch ovolo sashes, and 1¼-inch square framed sliding or hung shutters with 1-inch grounds and 1½ moulding to break the joint and form architrave, as those described for the attic storey.

Cellar Door

Under principal entrance and back entrance doors to have frame $3\frac{1}{2}$ by 3 inches, beaded and single rebated and tenoned into stone steps or sills, and to have a $1\frac{1}{2}$-inch 4-panel bead and butt door. The back entrance door frame to be of similar scantling, but framed with a transom head for a 1 fan light, and the door to this frame to be a $1\frac{1}{2}$-inch sash door with a lifting shutter; and all other doors on this floor to be $1\frac{1}{4}$-inch 4-panel square doors, with lining and finishing as above stated for the attics.

Stairs.

The stairs from basement to ground floor to have $1\frac{1}{4}$-wrought yellow deal strings, with $1\frac{1}{4}$-inch treads and 1-inch risers blocked and bracketed, and securely housed into the strings in the usual manner.

The partitions forming the spandril framing, as well as those forming pantries and store closets, to be $1\frac{1}{4}$-inch square panel, and to have a 6-inch $\frac{3}{4}$ skirting board, to correspond with others that are to run round the passage.

Stairs from ground floor to chamber storey to be geometrical, with one circular string and quarter circular on landing, as shown on Plan, and to have $1\frac{1}{4}$-inch yellow deal treads, risers, carriage and string boards, with all requisite carriage furrings to soffit, &c. The treads to have round and hollow nosings. The risers to mitre into the external string, which is to be dovetailed to receive the balusters and the return nosing; the other end of both treads and risers to be housed and securely wedged into the external string; a full scroll curtail step, with veneered riser and circular part to frame into external string, to be firmly fixed at the starting of the flight, and the succeeding step to be gradually carved until they join the straight flyers. (See Ground Plan, Plate V.) The whole flight to have $\frac{3}{4} \times \frac{5}{8}$ inch-square balusters dove-tailed into the end of tread and string, and covered with the mitred nosing. One ornamental iron baluster, taped, and to have nuts and screws complete, to be securely fixed in centre of scroll of curtail step, and No. 3 plain iron balusters, corresponding with those of deal before described, to be fixed where requisite on the flight. The whole to be surmounted with a $2\frac{1}{2}$-inch moulded Spanish mahogany hand-rail, sunk to receive the balusters and properly wreathed to well, and to have a corresponding mitred cap over curtail step. The same description of skirting as described for rooms of ground floor to be fixed all round hall and passage, and the same mouldings to continue up inside string of stairs : finding and applying all necessary joints, screws, and every other requisite to make the work complete.

Water Closet.

On quarter space.—The partition dividing stairs from water-closet to be a 2-inch framed and moulded sash partition with sash doors to correspond, prepared for receiving ground or stained glass, with the moulded skirting of stairs continued round on the stair side and the whole to finish in accordance with the stairs.

Inside.—The window-frame and sash to correspond with the one described for the chamber storey. To fit up the seat and riser with $1\frac{1}{4}$-inch Honduras mahogany, the riser to be properly dished out to the form of pan, and to have a beaded box for handle. This seat to be covered with a framed and beaded skeleton for the flap to hang to, which is to be 1¼-inch selected mahogany, hung with brass butts, and both frame and flap to have a projected moulded nosing; ½-inch beaded skirting 6 inches deep to be fixed round back and sides, as also on ground in front of riser. The whole to be fitted up with all necessary scantling, bearers, &c., for the support of pan and apparatus, as well as the efficient support of the seat and riser, in the most approved manner.

Also to fit up with 1-inch Honduras mahogany an angular wash-board and closet, the closet underneath with a 1-inch square panel-door, hung to a beaded and suitable skeleton frame, with all suitable appendages for receiving basins and depositing towels, &c., and also to fix over chasm of soil, waste, and supply-pipe, a 1-inch mahogany-framed skeleton-ground, rebated and beaded for a corresponding board, to be slightly screwed to the same for allowing easy access to the before-named pipe, a small moulding, to be fixed over ground, and plaster to break the joint; and to fix on all other articles that may be required for the full completion of the closet.

Kitchen Offices.

All the external door-frames to be 3½ × 3 in. yellow deal, beaded and rebated, and tenoned into stone sills or steps. Those to servants' water-closets, and to the lobby between kitchen and back-kitchen to be framed with transom heads, and to have 1¼ lights fixed therein. The whole of the external doors to be 1½-inch bead and butt, 4-panel doors framed flush on one side, and square panel on the other. All internal doors to be fitted up in the same manner as those described for the attic. The doors for coal-shoots to have a small 2½-inch × 2-inch frame rebated and beaded and 1-inch ledged doors.

The sash-frames and sashes for kitchens to be of a similar description to those described for chamber-floors; and each window to have a pair of 1¼-bead, bead and flush-panel shutters hung to the frame on the outside.

The small window to pantries, marked D D on the basement plan, to have 2½ × 2-inch beaded and rebated frames, and a 1½-inch sack hung upon centres for ventilation. The servants' water-closets, marked A on the same plan, are to have floor-joints 5 × 2 inches, and laid with 1¼ yellow deal. The seat and risers to be also of 1¼-inch deal, properly fixed and blocked to pan, and dished out in a corresponding manner; and a beaded box prepared for the pull; a movable ¾ beaded casing to be placed over pipes, with every article to make the work complete.

PLASTERER.

Attic.

Lath, plaster, and set the ceilings and partitions, and also render, and set the walls of the same.

Chamber Floor.

To lath, plaster, float, and set the ceilings and partitions, and render, float, and set the walls; run a plain moulded cornice round the porch room of this floor of 6 inches girth, and one round back room of 5 inches girth.

Ground Floor.

Entrance and passage—lath, plaster, float, and set the ceilings; the partitions to be lathed, floated, and set in stucco; and render, float, and set the walls in stucco; and finish the whole for painting; and a plain moulded cornice of 5 inches girth to be run all round so far as the break of stair will admit.

The front and back parlours to have their ceilings and partitions lathed, plastered, floated, and set, and to have a 10-inch plain moulded cornice run round both rooms.

Basement Floor.

The ceilings of this floor to be lathed, plastered, floated, and set; and the walls rendered, floated, and set; the front room, or breakfast parlour, to have a plain moulded cornice of 5 inches girth run all round.

Stairs.

The stairs from basement to ground floor and all other contiguous conveniences, not before alluded to, to be finished as the rooms of the attic floor: the next flight from ground floors to chamber floors, with the lobby and water-closet included: to finish in the manner described for the entrance halls, that is to say, the soffit of the stairs and ceilings to be lathed, plastered, and set, and partitions to be lathed, plastered, floated, and set with stucco; and all the walls rendered, floated, and set in stucco, and finished for painting. The stairs from chamber floors to attic to be finished in a corresponding manner to that already described for the chamber floor. All the ceiling and soffits to be twice lime-whitened.

Kitchen Offices.

To lath, plaster, and set all the ceilings, and to render and set the walls.

The ceiling and walls of these buildings to be twice lime-whitened.

Outside Work.

The tops of chimneys to be stuccoed in cement all round, with fillet moulding and blocking, as shown on front elevation, Plate IX.

The soffit of the eaves of principal building to have a sinking between each bracket to form a panel, as shown on section, Fig. 1, Plate XXI., and to be lathed, plastered, and set; the portion round flank and back to be finished plain. The string-course and frieze to be finished in stucco, with Atkinson's cement, and in the manner shown and described on the same Plate.

The entrance porches and bay-windows to be finished in stucco as shown and described on Plates XXII. and XXIII., with cornice, piers, pilasters, spandrils, &c., all complete. The whole of principal front from basement to ground-floor line to be stuccoed with cement, and have returned reveals, sides of steps to entrance hall, and party wall of area with sunk joints, as shown on Plate XXII.

MASON.

Attics.

To put to each fire-place in attic a hearth and back hearth of 3 inches Yorkshire stone, and to each opening jambs and head 5 inches wide and 1 inch thick, with a shelf of the same dimensions, properly cramped and fixed together.

Chamber Floor.

To provide and fix on this floor No. 4 marble chimney piece, with back hearths, slabs, and shelves complete, to the value of 40s. each.

Ground Floor.

Provide and fix on this floor No. 4 marble chimney pieces, with back hearth slabs, and mantel complete, to the value of £3 each.

Basement Storey.

To provide and fix in the breakfast-room No. 1 marble chimney piece, with back hearth, slab, and mantel complete, to the value of £2 10s.

Kitchens.

To fix complete, rubbed York chimneys, with mantels and hearths complete, to the value of £2 each, and to the back kitchen chimney pieces of the same description of stone to the value of 30s. each.

To pave the lobby leading from kitchen to back kitchen, and the whole of the kitchen offices, as well as the front and back areas, with 2½ tooled York paving.

FURNISHING IRONMONGER.

Attic Floor.

To provide and deliver for dormer lights on this floor No. 8 ¾-inch pivots, with side-plates, patent cord and pulleys for opening and closing the lights, as also No. 4 barrel 4-in. bolts, and requisite staples for fastening the same, with all necessary screws, nails, &c. Also to deliver No. 4 6-inch iron-rim locks, with box staples, keys, and brass furniture, with all necessary screws and nails complete for the doors to these rooms.

Chamber Floor.

To provide and deliver all the brass cased pulleys, patent cord, cast metals, weights, &c., shown on the drawings, and described in the joiner's work for this floor, as well as 2-inch spring fastenings to each sash.

To provide No. 16 pair of butt-hinges, with all necessary screws, &c., as well as No. 4 6-inch morticed locks, with brass furniture complete, for the principal doors ; No. 2 4-inch brass spring and bolt latches for dressing rooms, and No. 2 4-inch iron closet locks, with all requisite striking plates and furniture complete.

Water-Closet.

To provide the brass cased pulleys, cords, weights, fastenings, &c., for this window, as before described, as well as one pair of 2½ butt-hinges for door, and a 4½ brass spring and bolt latch with furniture complete for door.

Ground Floor.

To provide the brass cased pulleys, patent cord, weights, fastenings, &c., as before described for the sashes, as also a set of a similar description for shutters of back-parlour, and to provide and fix to the bay-window of this floor the metal revolving shutter shown on Plate XXVII., with all requisite machinery for their efficient action, as well as the necessary furnishing.

To provide for entrance doors to hall No. 4 pair of

4-inch butt-hinges, with all necessary screws, &c., and a best 10-inch draw-back mounted lock, with staple and all necessary furniture complete; as also a 12-inch door-chain, with brass knobs and asp complete, and two 10-inch barrel bolts, with staples and plates complete for top and bottom of door. The back entrance doors to have hinges, locks, bolts, and chain of a similar description; the shutters to have 18-inch bow-latch shutter-bars complete, with every necessary, &c., and to provide for doors dividing lobby from stairs, a 3-inch brass spring bolt latch.

To provide for shutters in back parlour No. 4 1-inch brass flush rings, with No. 2 brass clips for fastenings. To provide for doors not before alluded to on this floor No. 8 pair of 3-inch butt-hinges, with all necessary screws, &c., and for folding doors No. 4 12-inch brass flush-bolts, with all necessaries, &c., as also to provide No. 6 inch mortice locks, with brass striking plates and furniture complete.

Breakfast Room.

To provide for the sashes brass cased pulleys, patent cords, and fastenings, as described above for back-parlour; but the shutter will require three pair of brass cased pulleys with weights, fastenings, and cords, complete; the door of this room to be provided with a 6-inch mortice lock, and brass furniture complete.

To provide for kitchen window and shutters the same number of brass cased pulleys, cords, and fastenings, as before described for the back-parlour.

To provide for the six back-entrance doors 9-inch iron spring-stock locks with staples complete, No. 6 10-inch door chains, and No. 12 10-inch barrel-bolts and staples all complete, as also No. 6 6-inch iron rim stock locks with box staples complete for the other doors, and to provide No. 24 pair of 3-inch butt-hinges, as well as No. 8 pair of $2\frac{1}{2}$ ditto, with all necessary auxiliaries, &c.

To provide one ornamental cast-iron baluster, $1\frac{1}{4}$ diameter, 3 feet 6 inches long, tapped at one end, with nut and plates complete for curtail step, and three other, $\frac{3}{4}$ by $\frac{5}{8}$, two feet 5 inches long.

It is to be distinctly understood that the furnishing ironmonger is to deliver all articles here expressed, and all others that may be requisite for the due execution of the work into the possession of the joiner, who will apply and fix the same in their relative positions, providing and delivering, as may be required, glue, brads, nails, screws, and materials generally supplied by the ironmonger.

BELL-HANGER.

To provide and hang bells with all proper springs, cranks, wires, &c., of the size required, and in the position when and where may be hereafter directed, to the value of £10.

PLUMBER.

To line the cisterns in roof of principal building, as well as the four smaller ones described for supply of water-closet and kitchen offices, with six pounds milled lead, in the most efficient and workman-like manner, and to lay on from principal main to the large cistern in each house a $1\frac{1}{4}$-lead main supply-pipe, with a 6-inch ball-cock properly applied at the cistern end, with a standing waste of the same calibre to be taken down and connected with principal drains. The house-service, to be 1-inch calibre, to be taken into small cisterns over water-closets, and from thence into cistern in roof of kitchen offices; each of the small cisterns to be furnished with a suitable ball-cock, standing waste and service with rose-tops, and every other requisite article. The water-closets to be fitted up with Beetson's patent valve closets, with Warner's registered valves and patent regulators fitted up complete, and to have a 5-inch soil-pipe connected and continued perfectly sound into principal drain; and to complete the closet apparatus with all necessary bends, valves, traps, &c., to render them efficient and complete in all their actions, the service pipes to be brought from the small cistern above, as well as two ¾-inch service-pipes to supply the water to the washing-basins in corner; to provide and fix No. 2 10-inch wash-basins, and fix to the ¾ pipes suitable cocks, and to the basins a stop valve, with chain and waste pipe complete into principal drain.

To provide and fix to each house one of Warner's vibrating lift and force pumps, with all necessary pipe, bosses, and fastenings for supplying the filtered rain water into the cisterns situate in roof over kitchen offices, &c., and bring from the said cisterns two 1-inch service pipes to sinks in washhouse, with all proper taps, &c., as well as the waste pipes from cisterns, and all other articles that are requisite to make the supply of water complete; to provide and fit up in servants' privies two single-valve pan water-closets, with flushing apparatus, and pipes of 1-inch calibre for water brought from cisterns in roofs, with necessary bends, traps, joints, &c., for carrying soil into principal drain.

The plumber to furnish and provide the water-closets as described, with all necessary traps, syphons, bends, pipes, lead, solder, joints, taps, cocks, bosses, roses, and every other article that is necessary for the full completion of his work.

GLAZIER.

To glaze the windows in attics with good seconds Newcastle glass, properly beded and back puttied, and the window in chamber-floor and water-closet with good crown glass, which is to be well beded, braded, and back puttied.

Ground Floor.

All the sashes on this floor to be glazed with 20-ounce crown glass.

Basement Floor.

The bay-window in breakfast-room to be glazed with 20-ounce glass, and all the other windows to be with the best Newcastle seconds glass.

PAINTER.

To knot, prime, and paint in three oils all the outside wood and iron work, and to flat any of the inside work when and where directed, and to finish the other in any colour that may be hereafter decided on.

PAPER-HANGER.

To prepare and hang (*except the hall passage, staircase, water-closet, and landing, which are to be painted*) the whole of the chamber floor with paper hereafter to be chosen, to the amount of 1*s*. 6*d*. a piece, and the front and back parlour on the ground floor, and the breakfast room on the basement floor, with paper to the amount of 2s. 6d. per piece, hanging and bordering included.

General Conditions.

It is to be distinctly understood that the party or parties contracting for the erection of the buildings herewith described, are to provide and deliver on the premises, all the materials, the best of their respective qualities, also to provide and furnish all necessary plant, scaffolding, labour, and all other articles that are requisite for the full completion and finishing of the work, according with the accompanying drawings and this specification; and if anything should be shown in the drawings and not herein specified, or anything herein specified that is not shown on the drawings, the same to be executed as if fully shown and explained in both; and if any alteration from the drawings or this specification should take place during the progress of the work, such alteration not to make the contract or estimate null and void, but the expense of such deviation to be added to, or deducted from (*as the case may be*), such estimate.

It is requested that the amount for each particular trade, with a tariff of prices upon which such estimate is founded, shall accompany each tender.

Specifications are generally and should be always accompanied by a schedule or statement in an orderly and classified form, of the quantities of every material that will be required in the structure specified in the judgment of the architect. This is called the bill of quantities, of which the following is an example, as applying to the foregoing specification.

A bill of quantities is for the guidance both of the architect and of the artificer, as respects the estimates ; but errors or omissions in it are never to exonerate the artificer from the completion of his contract.

BILL OF QUANTITIES.

Quantities of the various Materials, and the Excavation necessary, for the erection of two Houses proposed to be built on a plot of ground situate

according to the various drawings (numbered from 1 to 17 inclusive) and specifications made for that purpose.

PRINCIPAL BUILDING—CARCASS.

EXCAVATOR.

Cube yards.		at		
		£	s.	d.
573	To be excavated and carted away . . . . Levelling, filling-in, pugging, ramming, and carting away earth, rubbish, &c. . .			

BRICKLAYER.

Rods.	Super.	Run.		at		
				£	s.	d.
		200	Of 6-inch glazed socket pipes, with requisite bends . .			
		200	Of 4-inch ditto . . .			
			No. 8 15-inch gully traps .			
			No. 4 6-inch syphons .			
28		..	Of reduced or standard brick-work			
	64	..	Of rubbed malm arches .			

CARPENTER.

Cube feet.	Super.	Run.		at		
				£	s.	d.
25	..	..	Of English oak, for sleepers .			
925	..	..	18½ loads of Riga timber, framed in floors, partitions, roof, cisterns, &c., according to drawings and specification*			

* It perhaps is necessary to observe that this calculation embraces the *net* quantity of timber required for the erection of the carcass of the buildings, exclusive of any other article.

SMITH AND IRONFOUNDER.

Weight.		at		
		£	s.	d.
1140	Hoop-iron bond			
160	Chimney bars			
110	Clips and straps for partitions . . .			
1080	For tension rods, &c.			
187	For clips and straps to roof			
26	For bolts, &c.			
56	Ties to cistern, &c.			
2759 lbs. = 24 cwt. 71 lbs.				
	Exclusive of all spikes, holdfasts, nails, screws, and every other article requisite for the sound fixing of the above-named works, which are to be calculated in the estimate.			

PLUMBER.

lbs. weight.		at		
		£	s.	d.
900	Of 6-lb. lead, for flashings, &c. . . .			
1728	Ditto, to dormer lights			
1320	5-lb. ditto, to sides of ditto . . .			
1050	6-lb. flashings to lights and chimney, &c. . .			
145	Ditto to cisterns			
5143 lbs. = 45 cwt. 3 lbs. weight of milled lead, exclusive of any other article.				

MASON.

Cube.	Super.	Run.		at		
				£	s.	d.
50	..	..	Of tooled steps for doors .			
			No. 8 15-inch gulley-stones properly dished, and five holes in each . . .			
	70	..	Of 5-inch York landing for rain-water tank . . .			
100	..	..	Of tooled York, for trimmers, of floors, and heads and sills of partitions, &c. . .			
		50	Of 12-inch × 3-inch throated coping, for area walls, &c. .			
		36	Of stone core for cornice, 1 ft. 4 in. wide, 4 in. thick .			
		60	Of dished and throated window-sills			
	30	..	Of 6-inch rubbed York landing, for entrance porches . .			
50	..	..	No. 20 tooled and rubbed York steps, for entrance doors .			
	36	..	Of 7-inch tooled landing . .			
		75	Of 2¼-inch tooled treads, 13 in. wide, and			
		71	Ditto, for riser, 7 in. wide, for steps from back entrance of ground-floor to garden . .			

SLATER.

Square.		at		
		£	s.	d.
24¼	Of Duchess slating, with all cuttings and pointings complete			
	No. 12 slate cantilevers or brackets, for principal elevation—(See details of roof, Plate XXI.)	.		
	No. 1 sawn slate filter, as shown and described on Plate XIV., with all necessary bolts, nuts, screws, rods, perforated plates, &c., complete			

ZINC WORKER.

Super.	Run.		£	at s.	d.
	168	Of 6-inch gutter, worked and fixed as shown on details of roof, Plate XXI. No. 6 octagon heads, with shoes, &c., complete			
	210	Of 4-inch piping, for down-comers, fixed complete			
	80	Of 3-inch ditto, for ditto of entrance-porches and bay windows . . .			

Quantities of the various Materials requisite for finish-ing and completing the Carcasses of two Houses, before calculated for.

JOINER'S WORK.

Feet Super.	Feet Run.	No.	FLOORS.	£	at s.	d.
1304	..	..	Or 13 square 4 feet of 1¼-inch white floor-boards, laid folding in attic and part of basement stories .			
3120	..	..	Or 31 square 20 feet yellow deal floor-boards, laid with a straight joint and splayed headings, for chamber, ground-floor, and part of basement stories . .			
			GROUNDS.			
	120	..	Of ¾-inch grounds 2-inch wide, faced and chamfered, for attic			
	250	..	Of 1-inch ditto, for chamber floor			
106	..	..	Of 1-inch splayed framed ground, 3½-inch wide, for chamber floors . . .			

JOINERS' WORK *continued.*

Feet Super.	Feet Run.	No.		at £	s.	d.
	330	..	Of 1-inch × 2¼-inch ploughed skirting grounds, for ground floor			
164	..	..	Of 1-inch ploughed and framed, and 5 inches wide, for door and windows (See Plate XXVI.)			
			SASHES AND FRAMES.			
54	..	..	Of chamfered and rebated lights, with frames and finishings made complete according to the specification			
			VENETIAN WINDOWS—CHAMBER FLOOR.			
120	..	..	To front and back windows, with frames 1½-inch, oval sashes, lining, and all finishing complete, as shown on the drawings and described in the specification . .			
120	..	..	Ditto for back-parlour and kitchen windows, with sashes, frames, suspended shutters, and all finishings complete			
52	..	..	Of small frames, sashes, and finishings complete, for small windows, &c. . . .			
			BAY WINDOWS.			
390	..	..	Of frames, sashes, lining, soffit, and all other finishings complete, except the metal shutters . . .			
390	..	..	With suspended shutters and finishings complete, for breakfast-room (see, for the finishings of these windows, Plates XXVI. and XXVII., and specification) . .			

JOINERS' WORK *continued.*

Feet Super.	Feet Run.	No.		£	at s.	d.
			JAMB-LININGS.			
60	..	..	Of 1-inch beaded linings, with stops braided on, for attic and part of basement storey			
256	..	..	Of 1-inch beaded and single rebated ditto ditto . . .			
106	..	..	Of 1¼-inch beaded and double rebated ditto ditto . .			
			DOOR-FRAMES, DOORS, AND FINISHINGS.			
75	..	..	Of 1¼-inch two-panel square doors, for attics and part of basement			
280	..	..	Of ditto four-panel square doors, for ground-floor and part of basement . .			
188	..	..	Of 1¼-inch four-panel, moulded on both sides, for ground-floor and breakfast room .			
95	..	..	For entrance-hall door-frames, transom-head, fan-light, doors, and finishings, all complete (see specification)			
126	..	..	For back or garden entrance, door-frame, sash-door, side-lights, fan-lights, boxing shutters, and all other finishings complete . . .			
40	..	..	Of door-frame, with 1½-inch four-bead and butt complete, for cellar			
40	..	..	Frame, with transom-head light and 1½-inch sash door, lifting shutters, and all other finishings complete .			
			FRAMED PARTITIONS, WITH DOORS COMPLETE.			
729	..	..	Of 1¼-inch square panel, including 6 two-panel 1¼-inch doors complete, for store-closet and pantries . .			
140	..	..	Ditto, sash-partition and doors,			

JOINER'S WORK *continued.*

Feet Super.	Feet Run.	No.		£	at s.	d.
			to divide stairs from lobby of garden entrance . .			
130	..	..	Of 1¼-inch sash partition, to divide stairs from water-closet			
			SKIRTINGS.			
160	..	..	Of ¾-inch skirting, six inches wide, for attic and part of basement floors . . .			
220	..	..	Of 1-inch ditto moulded, for chamber floors . . .			
270	..	..	Of 1-inch rebated ditto, for ground-floor and breakfast-room			
			MOULDINGS.			
	210	..	Of 1½-inch, to form architrave over grounds, and pilaster attic story			
	380	..	Of 2-inch, for chamber-floor .			
	280	..	Of 3¼-inch for ground-floor and breakfast-room . .			
	120	..	Of 1½-inch for basement . .			
			WATER-CLOSET.			
112	..	..	Of mahogany seat and riser, dished to basin and handles			
32	..	..	Ditto mahogany-framed top, with moulded nosing, lining complete, and finished with skirting all round . . .			
25	..	..	Of mahogany wash-stand, with closet and shelves, &c., underneath . . .			
7	..	..	Of mahogany doors to ditto .			
	3	..	Feet run of ½-inch skirting, six inches wide . . .			
8	..	..	Of rebated and beaded mahogany box, to cover service and supply-pipes . .			
			(See specification for these privies.)			

JOINER'S WORK *continued.*

Feet Super.	Feet Run.	No.		at £	s.	d.
			STAIRS FROM KITCHEN TO GROUND-FLOOR.			
80	..	..	Of 1¼-inch treads, properly blocked			
			Of 1-inch risers . . .			
40	..	..	Of 1½-inch string boards with bracket housings and carriage complete			
to 40	..	..				
			GEOMETRICAL CIRCULAR WELL-STAIRS, FROM GROUND TO CHAMBER-FLOOR.			
936	..	..	Of 1¼-inch yellow deal treads, risers, strings, and carriage ; the risers mitred into external string, and treads moulded and mitred to return nosings, and the whole completed as shown on and described in specification			
		1	Blocked and veneered curtail step, with return to join external string . . .			
	32	..	Of 2½-inch sunk mahogany moulded hand-rail, wreathed to circular well, as well as to curtail step, and to be mitred into a hand-work mahogany cap, with all balusters complete to chamber landing, comprising the fixing of one ornamental baluster to curtail, and three plain ones on the flight .			
			STAIRS FROM CHAMBER-FLOOR TO ATTIC-FLOOR.			
136	..	..	Of treads, risers, strings, and carriage complete . .			
			(See plan and specification.)			

PLASTERERS WORK.

Yards.	Superficial Feet.	Run.		£	at s.	d.
1018	..	..	Of lath, plaster, float and set to ceilings and partitions .			
484	..	..	Of render, float and set on walls			
		240	Of cornice, 10-inch girth . .			
		188	Of ditto, 6-inch ditto .			
		236	Of ditto, 5-inch ditto .			
			STAIRS.			
65	..	..	Of lath, plaster, and stucco, to hall, passage, and stairs .			
70	..	..	Of render, set and float in stucco, on walls, &c. . .			
598	..	..	Of lime whitening . .			
			OUTSIDE WORK, **IN ATKINSON CEMENT.**			
		50	Of cornice, 5-inch girth, &c. . .			
		50	Of ditto, 3-inch fillet, for chimney-top . .			
	200	..	Of string-course, frieze, avolo moulding, and sunk soffit, under eaves of front elevation			
		10	Of sunk dentules, to front elevation . . .			
	320	..	Of plain lathed and trowelled soffit, under eaves of sides and back elevation . . .			
			PORCHES.			
4	..	..	Of lath and float, to ceilings			
	46	..	Of cornice, on brickwork .			
	42	..	To caps and bases of pilasters			
	12	..	To bases of ditto . . .			
20	..	..	Of render, float, and jointed to spandrils of steps .			
9	..	..	Ditto, chamfered and worked to steps (see Plate XXIII.) .			
			BAY WINDOWS.			
3	..	..	With sunk joints to jambs .			
60	..	..	Plain work to top . . .			
		50	..	Of cornice		
34	..	..	To front, rendered, floated and sunk-jointed . .			
47	..	..	Ditto, to area walls .			
		44	Of 6-inch string-course . .			

MASON.

Feet Super.	No.		at £	s.	d.
10	..	Of 1-inch rubbed York stone, for chimney-pieces in attic . . .			
	4	Chimney-pieces for chamber-floors . .			
	4	Ditto ditto for ground-floors .			
	2	Ditto ditto for basement-floors . .			
397	..	Of 2½ tooled York, for paving to areas and cellars, including steps . .			

FURNISHING IRONMONGER.

No.		at £	s.	d.

ATTIC-FLOOR.
8   ¾-inch pivots, with patent cords, complete . .
8   pair of brass-cased pulleys . . . . .
24   yards of patent sash-cord . . . . .
16   metal sash-weights . . . . . .
8   2-inch spring sash-fastenings . . . .
16   pair of 2½ butt hinges . . . . .
2   4-inch leaf spring latches . . . . .
2   4-inch iron closet locks . . . .
4   6-inch mortice locks, with furniture, complete .

WATER-CLOSET.
4   pair of 2½ butts . . . .
2   4½-inch brass spring latches, complete . .

GROUND-FLOOR.
12   brass-cased pulleys . . . . . .
30   yards patent cord . . . . . .
12   metal weights . . . . . .
4   2-inch brass fastenings . . . . .
revolving shutters, with all requisite finishing, to be estimated at so much each.

ENTRANCE-HALL AND BACK ENTRANCE.
8   pair of 4-inch butt hinges . . . . .
4   best 10-inch draw-back mounted spring locks .
4   12-inch door-chains, brass-mounted, with asp, and all complete . . . . . .
4   10-inch barrel bolts . . . . . .
4   18-inch bow-latch shutter bolts . . . .
4   3-inch brass spring-locks . . . .

FURNISHING IRONMONGER *continued.*

No.	SHUTTERS IN PARLOUR.	£	at s.	d.
4	1-inch brass flush-rings			
4	brass clips for fastenings, with requisite pins . .			
8	pair of 3-inch butt hinges			
4	3-inch flush bolts			
6	6-inch mortice locks, with furniture, complete .			
	BASEMENT-STORY.			
10	pair of brass-cased pulleys			
30	yards patent cord			
20	metal weights			
2	6-inch mortice locks			
6	9-inch iron-rim locks, with furniture, complete .			
12	10-inch barrel bolts, complete . . .			
6	6-inch iron-rim locks, ditto			
24	pair of 3-inch butt hinges			
8	pair of 2½-inch ditto			
1	ornamental cast baluster			
3	plain ditto ditto, 2 ft. 6 in. high, $\frac{3}{4}$ in. $\times$ $\frac{3}{8}$ in.			

BELL-HANGER. *(See specification.)*

PLUMBER.

Feet Run.		£	at s.	d.
300	Of 1½-inch service-pipe to principal cistern, with fittings-up, complete			
140	Ditto of waste into water-closet . . .			
100	Ditto to water-closet cistern and kitchen . .			
	To fit up, complete, two of Warner's patent water-closets (see specification), and two single-valve closets, for secondary closets, in yard			
50	Of 1-inch service-pipe to the same . . .			

GLAZIER.

Feet Super.		at		
		£	s.	d.
233	Of Newcastle seconds glass, bedded and well back puttied			
861	Of 20-ounce glass, the greater portion to be bradded, as well as back puttied (see specification)			

PAINTER.

Yards.	No.		at		
			£	s.	d.
	4	Frames and sashes to attic . . .			
	8	Venetian frames and sashes . . .			
	11	Ditto, usual size			
346	4	Times in oil			
		OUTSIDE WORK.			
37	..	To eaves, &c.			
40	..	To doors, iron-work, &c. . . .			
	4	Frames and sashes to attic . . .			
	8	Venetian frames and sashes . . .			
	11	Ditto, usual size			
		All properly prepared and finished according to specification.			

PAPER-HANGER.

Yards.	Pieces.		at		
			£	s.	d.
	30	For chamber-floor . . .			
	27	For ground-floor . . .			
	14	For basement			

These quantities only apply to the principal buildings *(the kitchen offices not being included),* and which may be executed for about 400*l.* each, or 800*l.* the pair.

DESCRIPTION OF PLATES.

THE END.

VIRTUE AND CO., PRINTERS, CITY ROAD, LONDON.

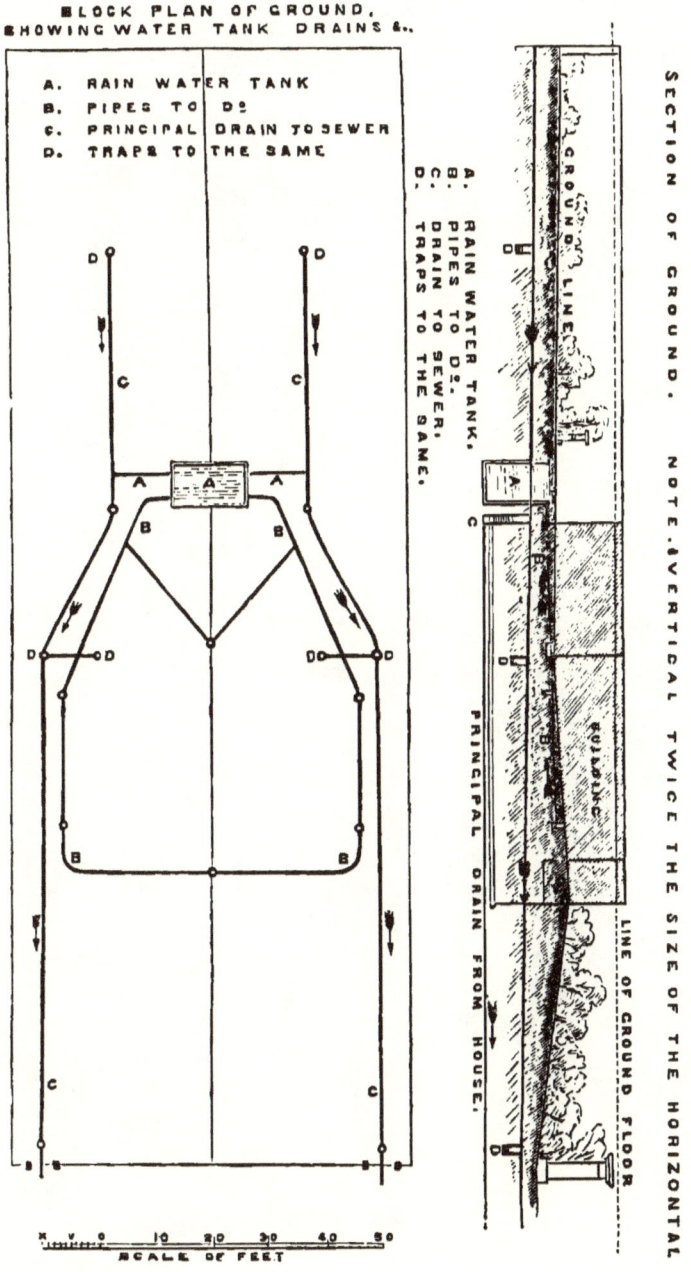

PLATE II.

BLOCK PLAN OF GROUND,
SHOWING WATER TANK DRAINS &.

A.   RAIN WATER TANK
B.   PIPES TO D°
C.   PRINCIPAL DRAIN TO SEWER
D.   TRAPS TO THE SAME

A.   RAIN WATER TANK.
B.   PIPES TO D°.
C.   DRAIN TO SEWER.
D.   TRAPS TO THE SAME.

SCALE OF FEET
0   10   20   30   40   50

SECTION OF GROUND.   NOTE. ¿VERTICAL TWICE THE SIZE OF THE HORIZONTAL

GROUND LINE.

PRINCIPAL DRAIN FROM HOUSE.

BUILDING

LINE OF GROUND FLOOR

PLATE III.

BLOCK PLAN. SHOWING BUILDINGS.&c.

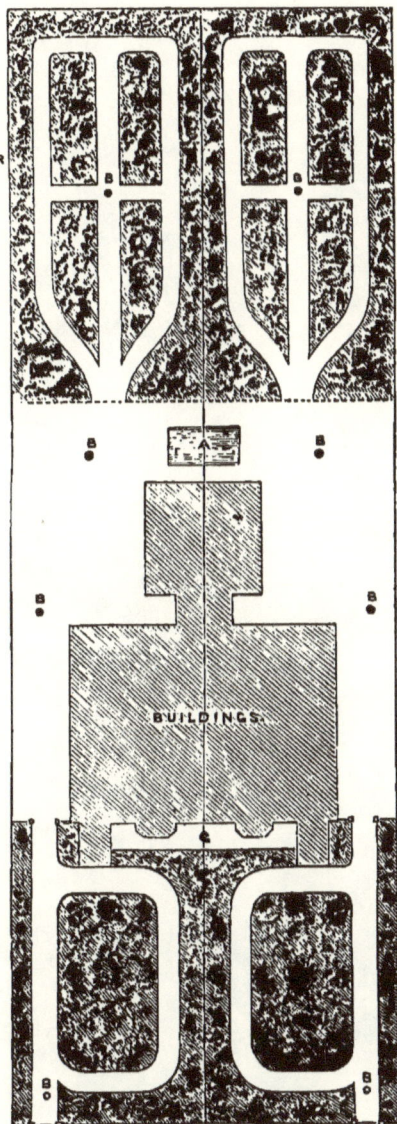

A. RAIN WATER
TANK.

B.B. TRAPS.
C. AREA.

BUILDINGS.

SCALE OF FEET

PLATE IV.

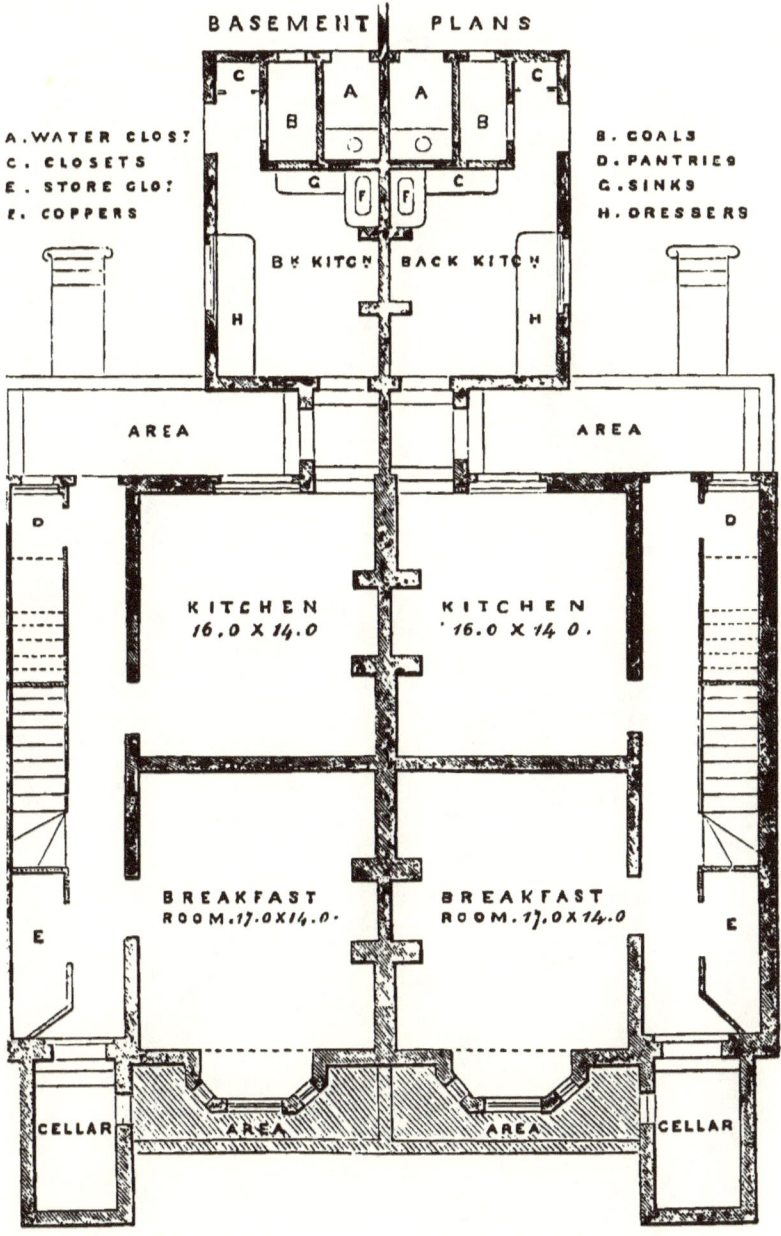

BASEMENT PLANS

A. WATER CLOS?
C. CLOSETS
E. STORE CLO?
F. COPPERS

B. COALS
D. PANTRIES
G. SINKS
H. DRESSERS

C
A
A
C
B
B
C
F
F
C
BK KITC? BACK KITCH

H
H

AREA

AREA

D
D

KITCHEN
16.0 × 14.0

KITCHEN
16.0 × 14.0

BREAKFAST
ROOM. 17.0 × 14.0

BREAKFAST
ROOM. 17.0 × 14.0

E
E

CELLAR

AREA

AREA

CELLAR

GROUND FLOOR PLANS

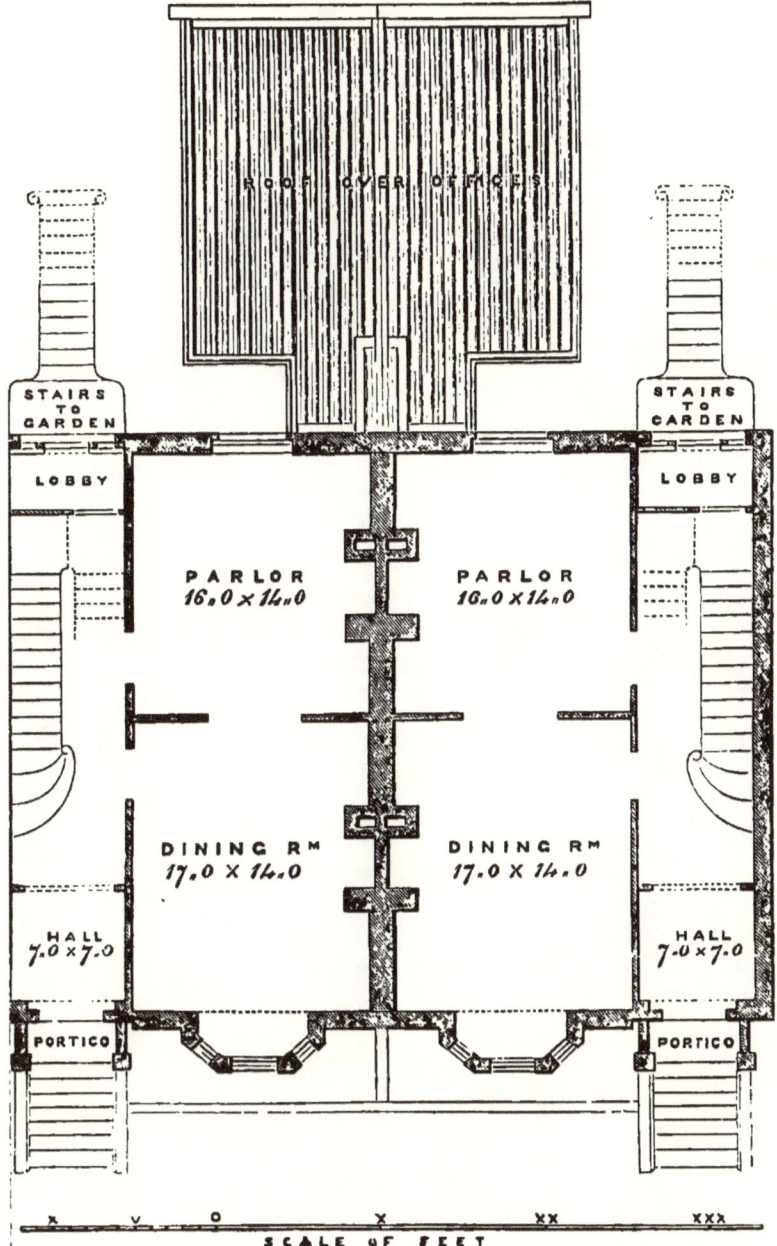

ROOF OVER OFFICES

STAIRS TO GARDEN

LOBBY

PARLOR
16.0 X 14.0

PARLOR
16.0 X 14.0

DINING R^M
17.0 X 14.0

DINING R^M
17.0 X 14.0

HALL
7.0 X 7.0

PORTICO

STAIRS TO GARDEN

LOBBY

HALL
7.0 X 7.0

PORTICO

X V O   X   XX   XXX

SCALE OF FEET

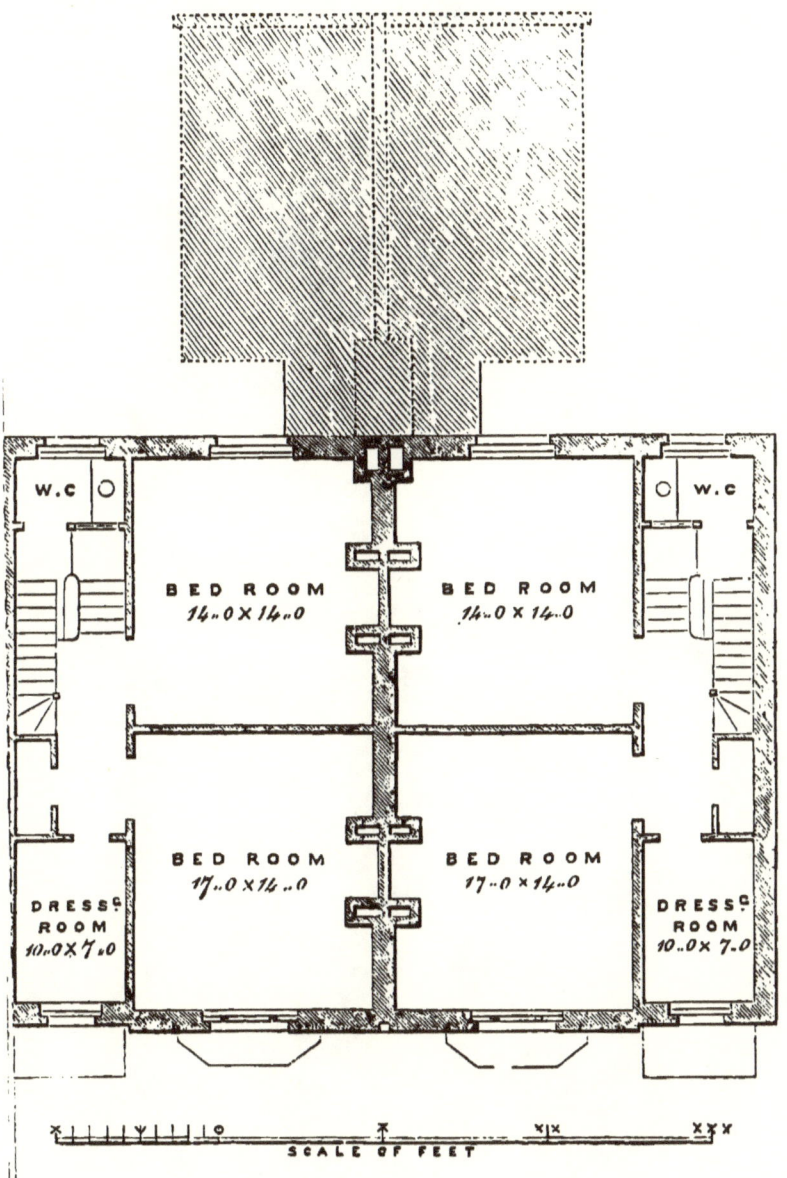

W.C

BED ROOM
14..0 × 14..0

BED ROOM
14..0 × 14..0

W.C

BED ROOM
17..0 × 14..0

BED ROOM
17..0 × 14..0

DRESS.
ROOM
10..0 × 7..0

DRESS.
ROOM
10..0 × 7..0

SCALE OF FEET

PLAN of ATTICS.

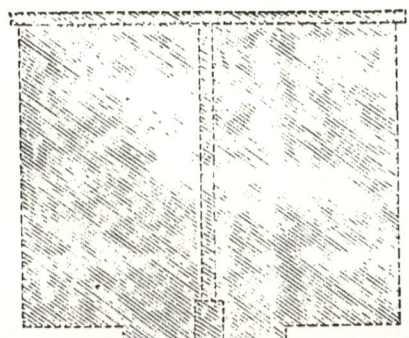

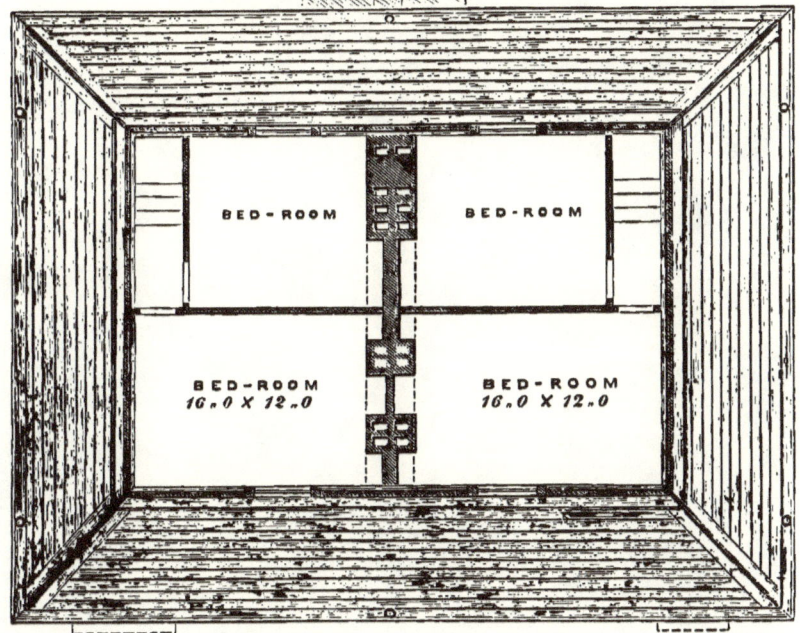

BED-ROOM

BED-ROOM

BED-ROOM
16,0 X 12,0

BED-ROOM
16,0 X 12,0

SCALE OF FEET.

PLAN OF ROOFS.

A. DOWNCOMERS
FROM GUTTER

NOTE. THE ARROWS
INDICATE THE
WATER-CURRENT

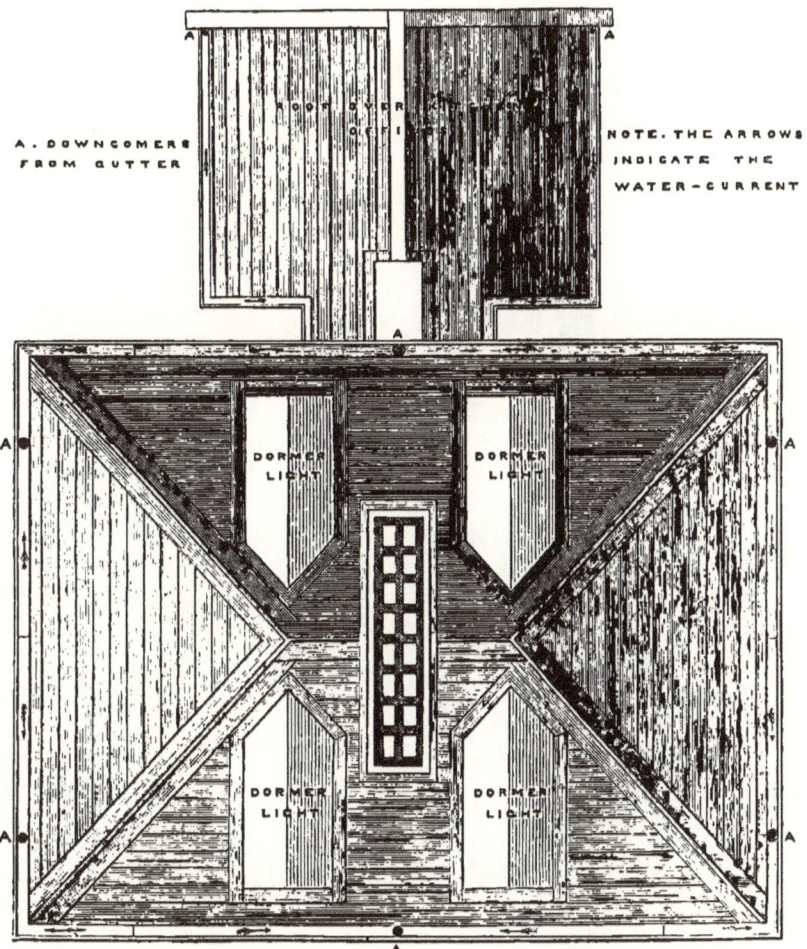

PLATE IX.

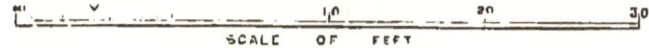

SCALE OF FEET

PLATE X.

BACK ELEVATION.

A.A. COAL SHOOTS

SCALE OF FEET.

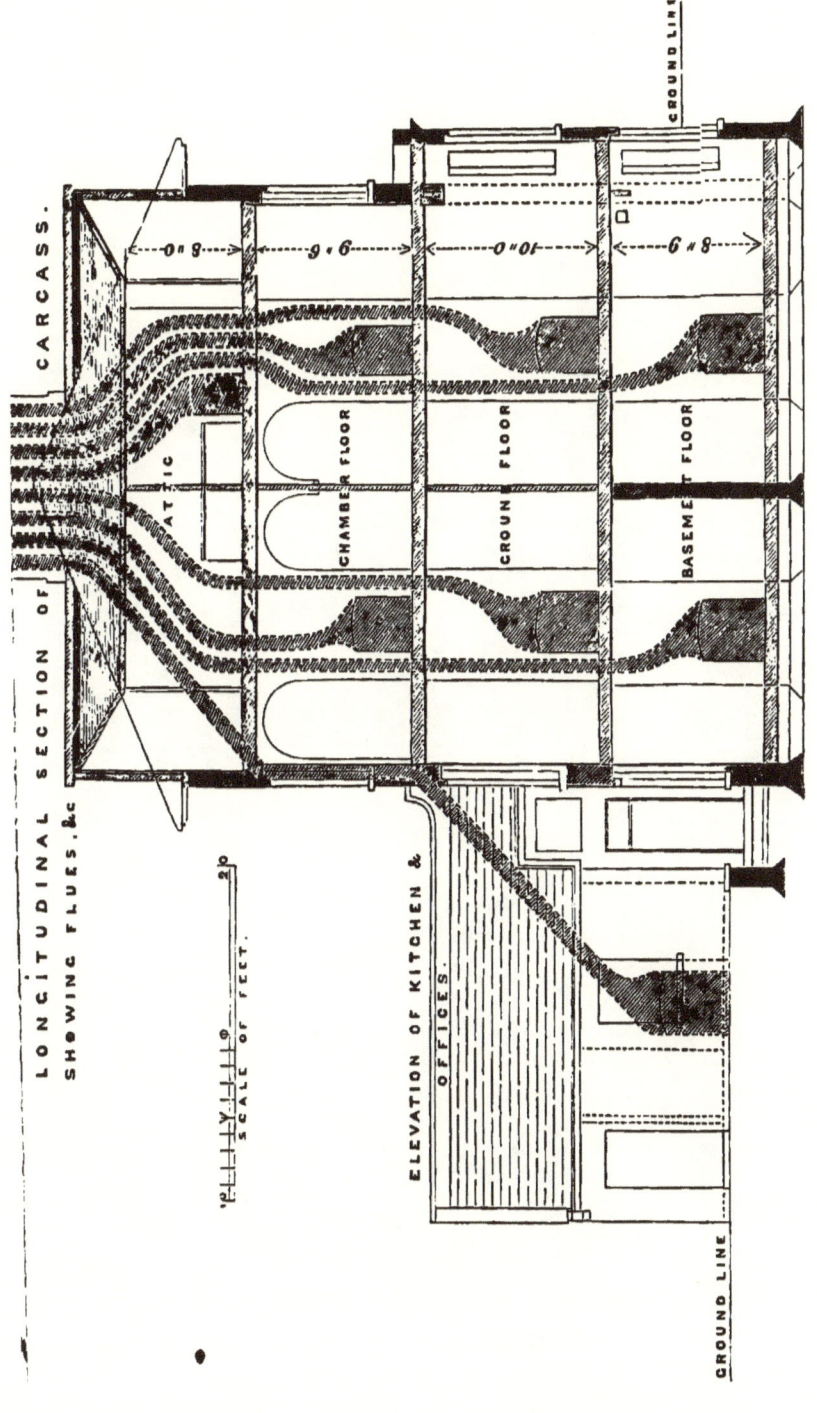

LONGITUDINAL SECTION OF CARCASS.
SHEWING FLUES, &c.

SCALE OF FEET.

ELEVATION OF KITCHEN & OFFICES.

GROUND LINE

ATTIC

CHAMBER FLOOR

GROUND FLOOR

BASEMENT FLOOR

8 · 0

9 · 6

10 · 0

8 · 6

GROUND LINE

Plate XII.

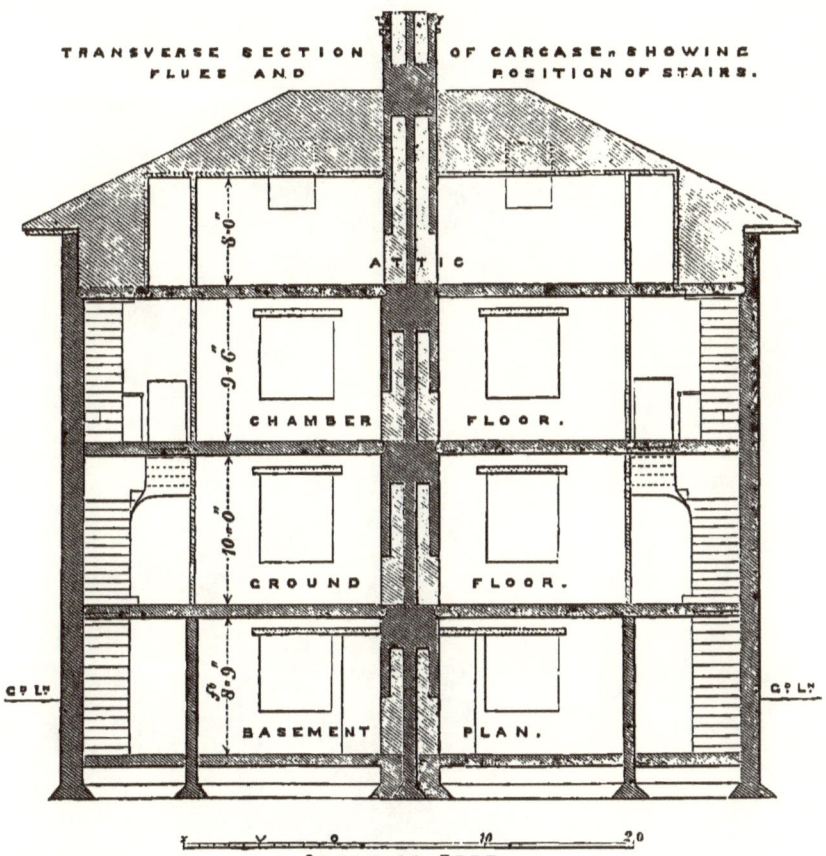

TRANSVERSE SECTION OF CARCASE, SHOWING
FLUES AND POSITION OF STAIRS.

ATTIC

CHAMBER FLOOR.

GROUND FLOOR.

BASEMENT PLAN.

SCALE OF FEET.

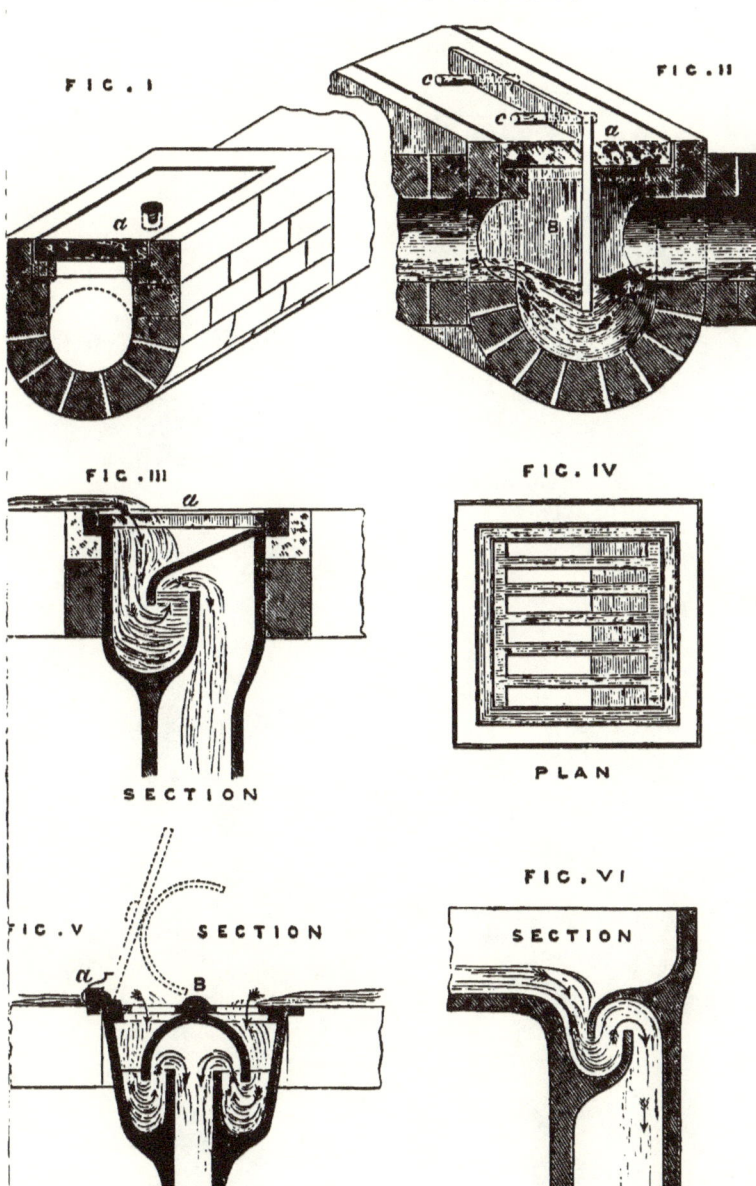

PLATE XIII.

TRAPS FOR DRAINS.

FIG. I   FIG. II

FIG. III

SECTION

FIG. IV

PLAN

FIG. V   SECTION

FIG. VI

SECTION

PLATE XIV.

FIG. I. SECTION OF RAIN WATER TANK

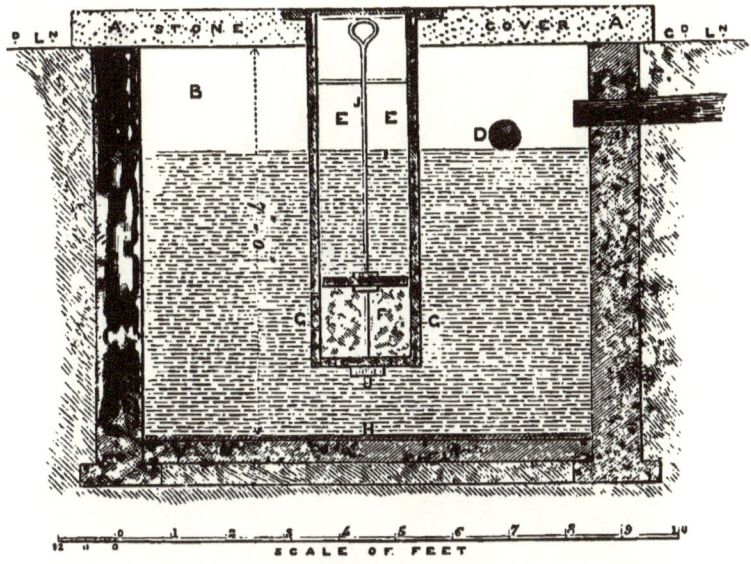

SCALE OF FEET

FIG. II. PLAN OF CISTERN

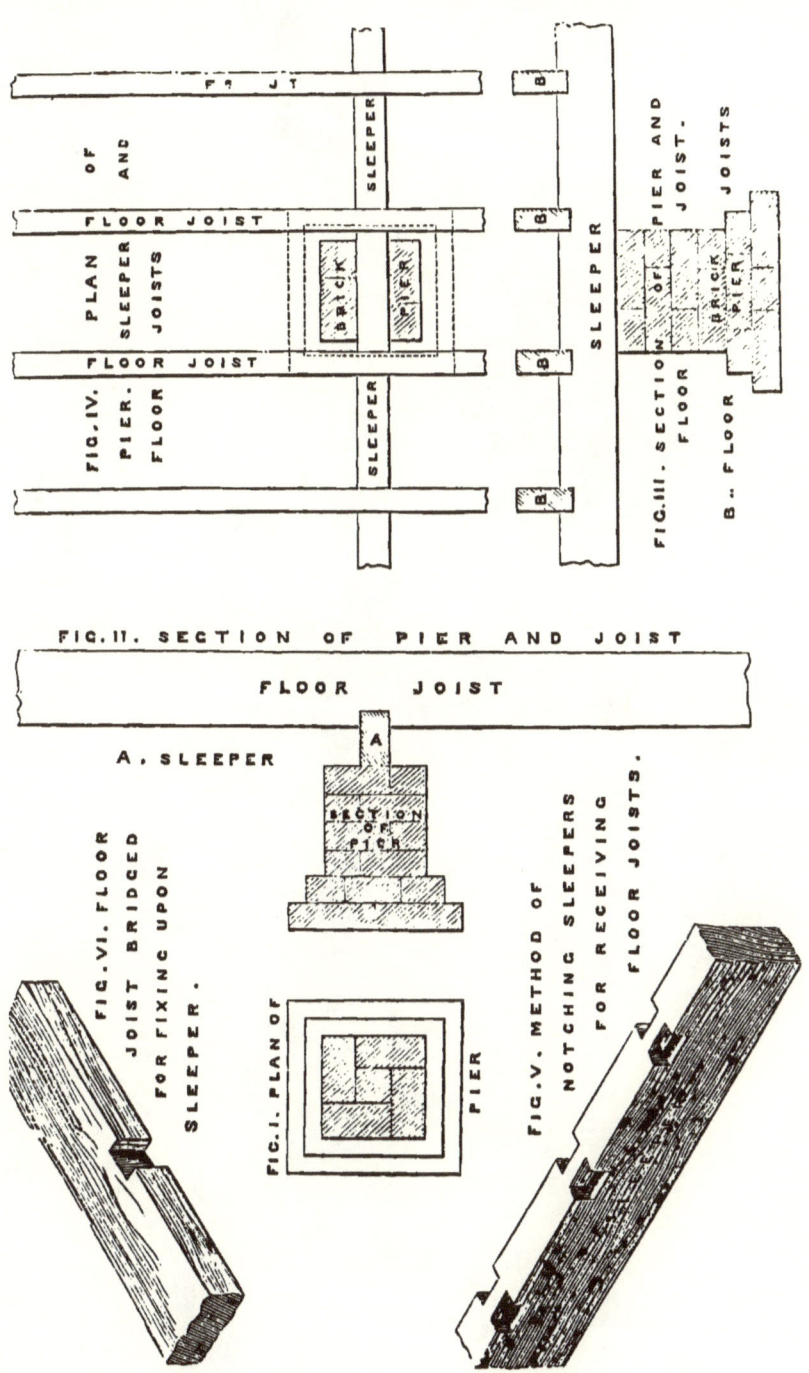

FIG.IV. PIER. PLAN OF SLEEPER AND FLOOR JOISTS

FL JT

SLEEPER

FLOOR JOIST

BRICK PIER

FLOOR JOIST

SLEEPER

B

SLEEPER

B

B

B

FIG.III. SECTION OF PIER AND JOIST.

BRICK PIER

B .. FLOOR JOISTS

FIG.II. SECTION OF PIER AND JOIST

FLOOR JOIST

A. SLEEPER

A

SECTION OF PIER

FIG.VI. FLOOR JOIST BRIDGED FOR FIXING UPON SLEEPER.

FIG.I. PLAN OF PIER

FIG.V. METHOD OF NOTCHING SLEEPERS FOR RECEIVING FLOOR JOISTS.

PLATE XVI.

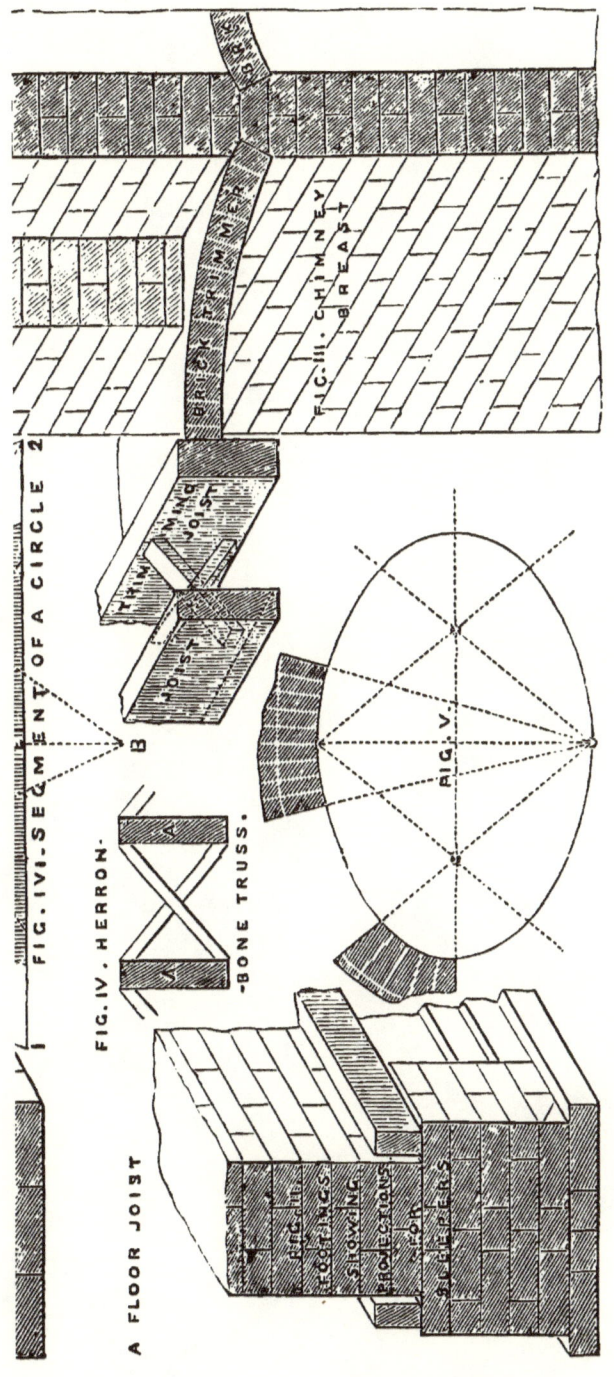

A FLOOR JOIST

FIG. IV. HERRON-BONE TRUSS.

FIG. IVI. SEGMENT OF A CIRCLE 2

B

A

FIG. III. CHIMNEY BREAST

BRICK TRIMMER

TRIMMING JOIST

JOIST

FIG. V.

FIG. II. SHOWING PROJECTIONS OF FLOOR JOISTS ON BUILDERS

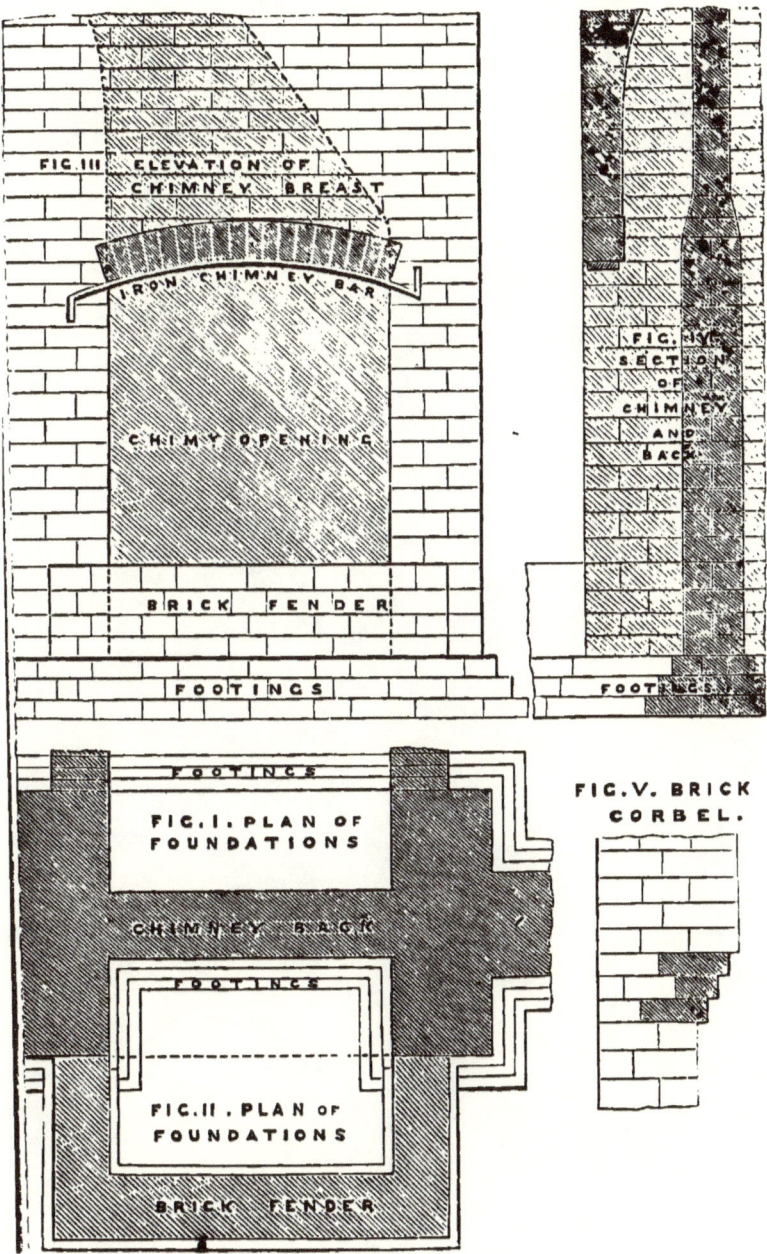

PLATE XVII.

DETAILS OF BRICKWORK FOR CHIMNIES

FIG.III ELEVATION OF CHIMNEY BREAST

IRON CHIMNEY BAR

CHIMY OPENING

BRICK FENDER

FOOTINGS

FIG. IV. SECTION OF CHIMNEY AND BACK.

FOOTINGS

FOOTINGS

FIG.I. PLAN OF FOUNDATIONS

CHIMNEY BACK

FOOTINGS

FIG.II. PLAN OF FOUNDATIONS

BRICK FENDER

FIG.V. BRICK CORBEL.

Plate XVIII.

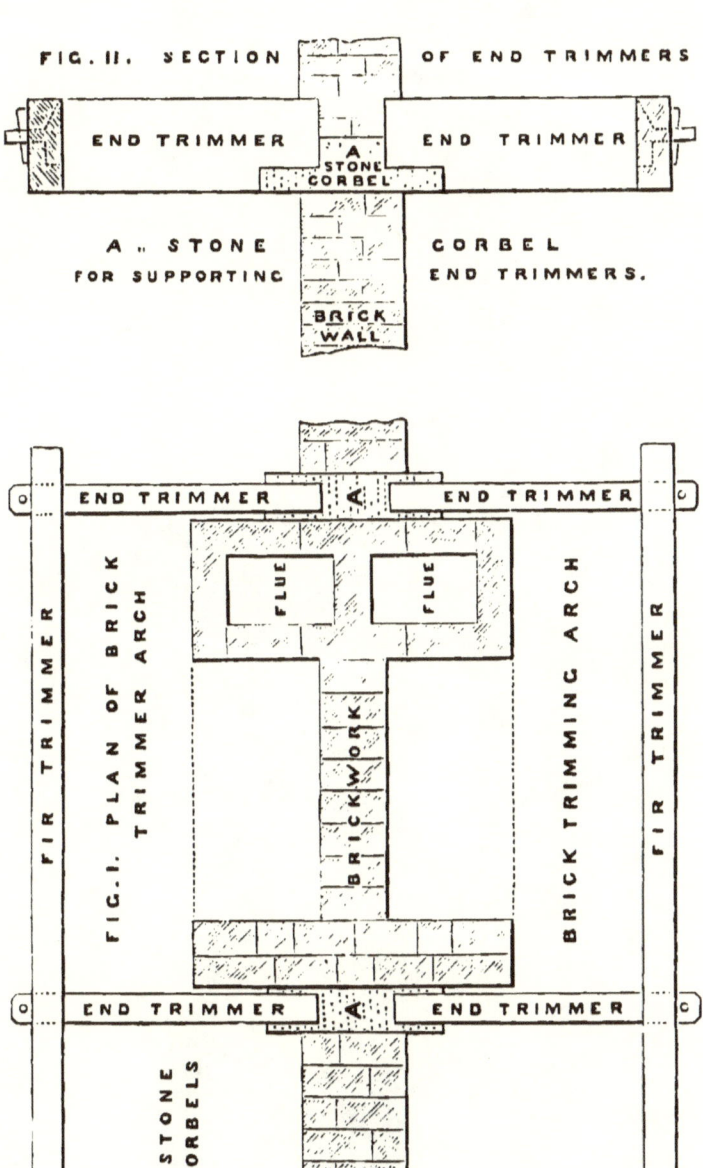

FIG. II. SECTION OF END TRIMMERS

END TRIMMER   A STONE CORBEL   END TRIMMER

A " STONE CORBEL
FOR SUPPORTING END TRIMMERS.

BRICK WALL

END TRIMMER   A   END TRIMMER

FLUE   FLUE

FIR TRIMMER

FIG. I. PLAN OF BRICK TRIMMER ARCH

BRICKWORK

BRICK TRIMMING ARCH

FIR TRIMMER

END TRIMMER   A   END TRIMMER

A.A. STONE CORBELS

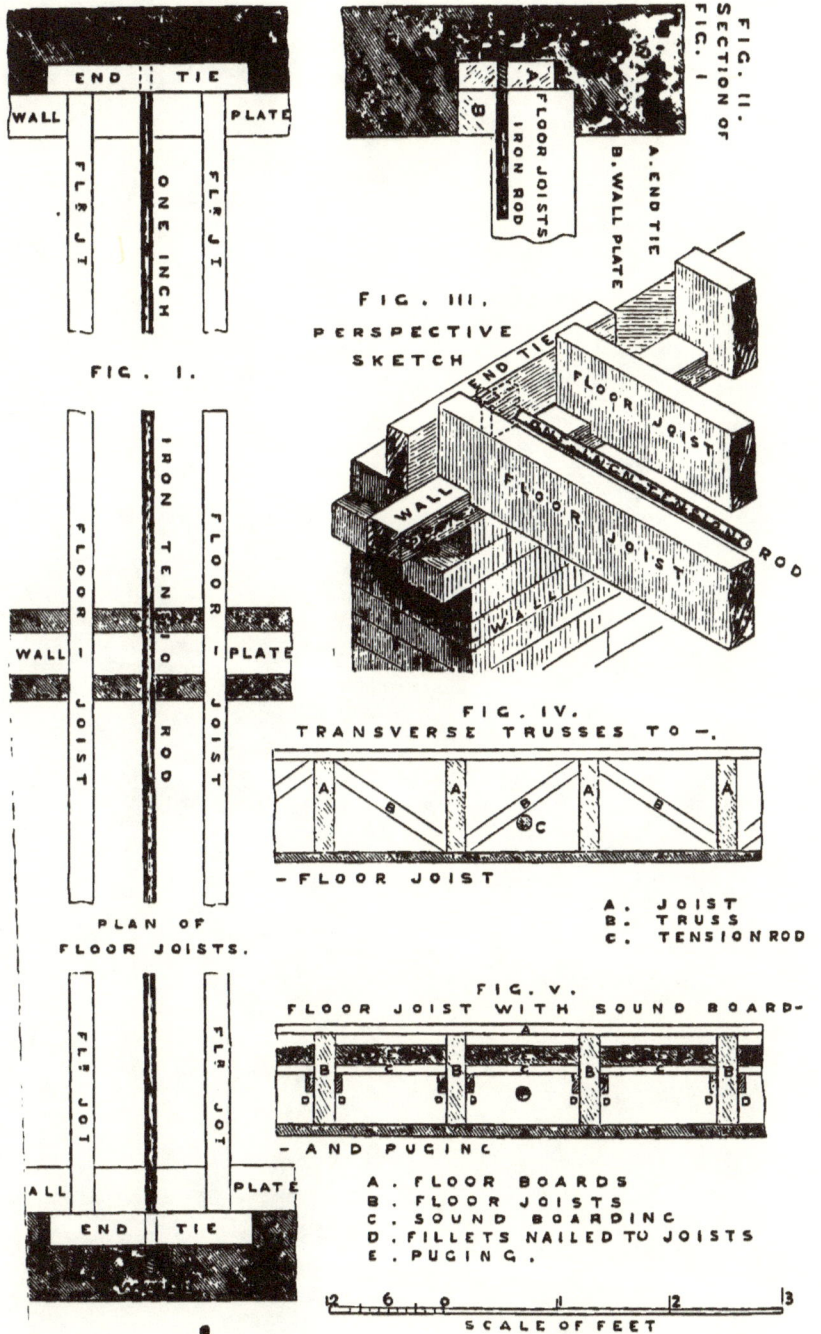

PLATE XIX.

FIG. II.
SECTION OF
FIG. I

A. END TIE
B. WALL PLATE

FLOOR JOISTS
IRON ROD

FIG. III.
PERSPECTIVE
SKETCH

END TIE

FLOOR JOIST

WALL

FLOOR JOIST

WALL

FLOOR JOIST

ROD

END ‖ TIE

WALL   PLATE

FLR JT   FLR JT

ONE INCH

FIG. I.

IRON TEN ·· O ROD

FLOOR JOIST   FLOOR JOIST

WALL   PLATE

FLOOR JOIST   FLOOR JOIST

IRON TEN ·· O ROD

PLAN OF
FLOOR JOISTS.

FLR JOT   FLR JOT

ALL   PLATE

END   TIE

FIG. IV.
TRANSVERSE TRUSSES TO —

A   B   B   A

C

— FLOOR JOIST

A. JOIST
B. TRUSS
C. TENSION ROD

FIG. V.
FLOOR JOIST WITH SOUND BOARD-

A

B   C   B   C   B   C   B

D   D   D   D   D   D   D   D

— AND PUGING

A. FLOOR BOARDS
B. FLOOR JOISTS
C. SOUND BOARDING
D. FILLETS NAILED TO JOISTS
E. PUGING.

12   6   0   I   2   3

SCALE OF FEET

PLATE XX.

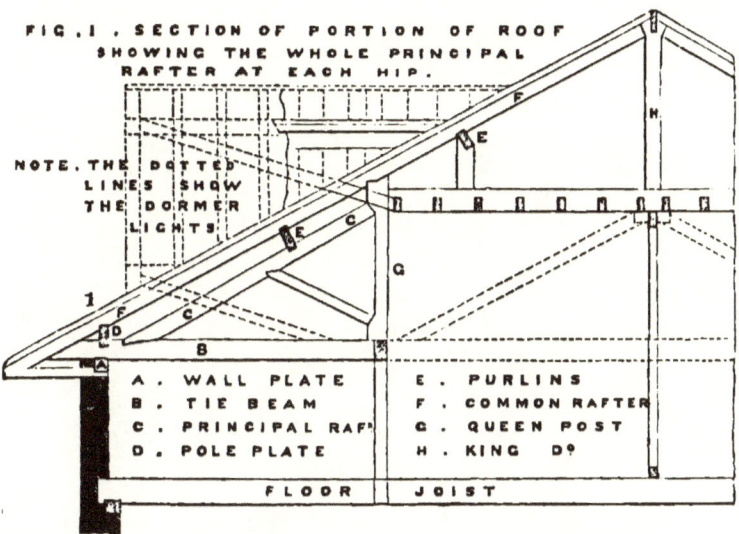

FIG. I. SECTION OF PORTION OF ROOF SHOWING THE WHOLE PRINCIPAL RAFTER AT EACH HIP.

NOTE. THE DOTTED LINES SHOW THE DORMER LIGHTS

A . WALL PLATE   E . PURLINS
B . TIE BEAM   F . COMMON RAFTER
C . PRINCIPAL RAF?   G . QUEEN POST
D . POLE PLATE   H . KING D?

FLOOR   JOIST

FIG. II. PLAN OF PORTION OF ROOF.

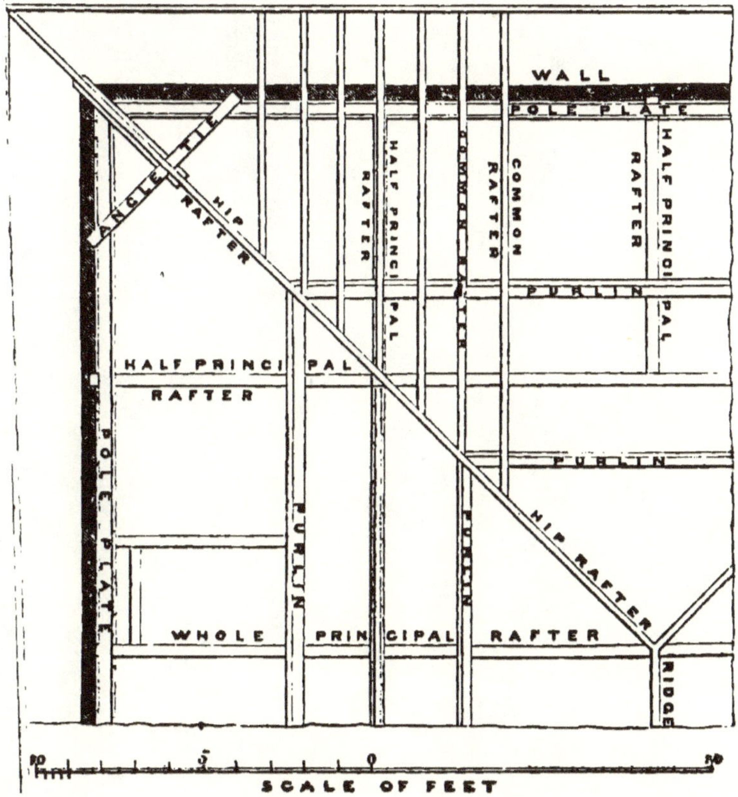

WALL
POLE PLATE
HALF PRINCIPAL RAFTER
HALF PRINCIPAL RAFTER
COMMON RAFTER
COMMON RAFTER
PURLIN
ANGLE TIE
HIP RAFTER
HALF PRINCIPAL RAFTER
POLE PLATE
PURLIN
PURLIN
PURLIN
HIP RAFTER
WHOLE PRINCIPAL RAFTER
RIDGE

SCALE OF FEET

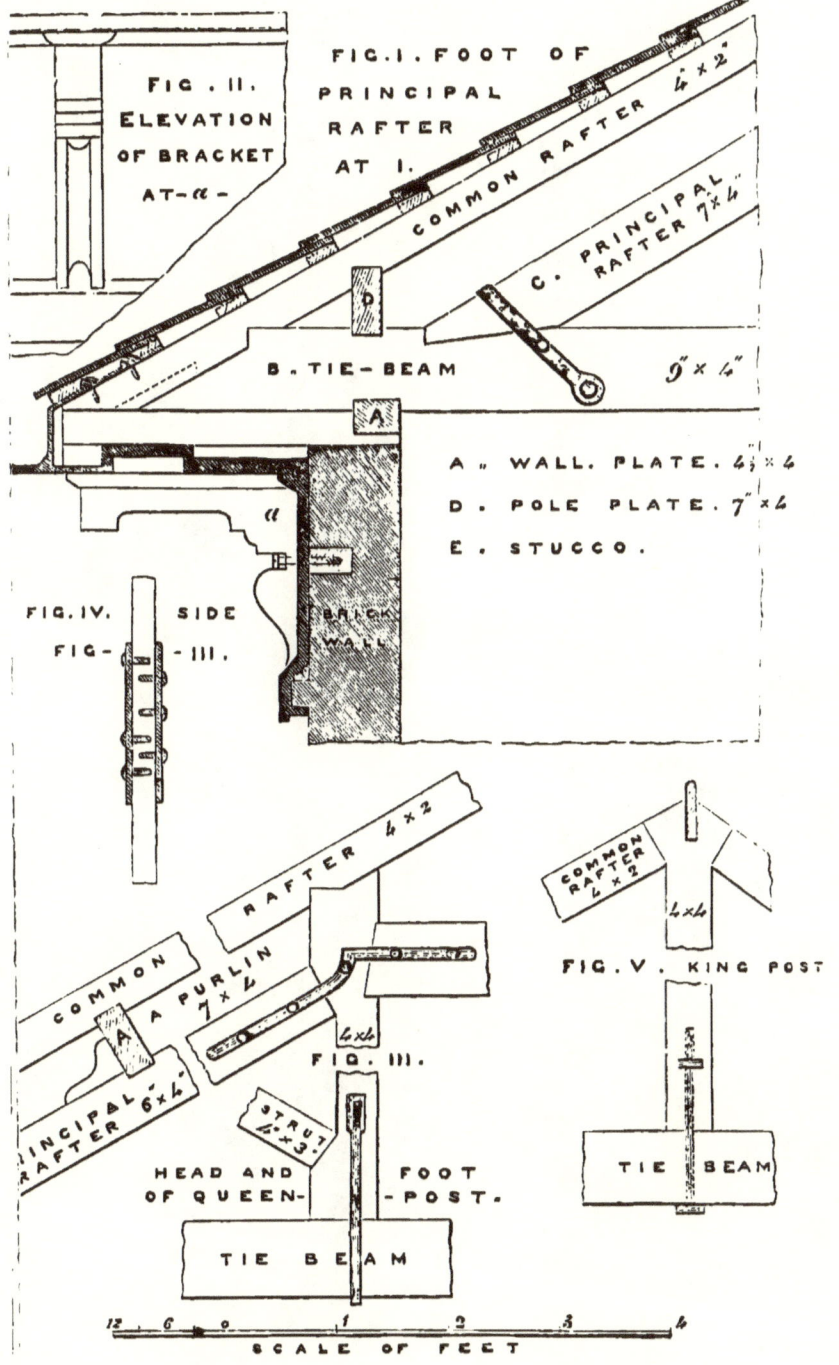

FIG. II.
ELEVATION
OF BRACKET
AT—α—

FIG. I. FOOT OF
PRINCIPAL
RAFTER
AT I.

COMMON RAFTER 4"×2"

C. PRINCIPAL RAFTER 7"×4"

B. TIE-BEAM

9"×4"

A " WALL. PLATE. 4½×4
D. POLE PLATE. 7"×4
E. STUCCO.

α

BRICK WALL

FIG. IV. SIDE
FIG—III.

RAFTER 4×2

COMMON

A PURLIN
7×4

PRINCIPAL RAFTER 6"×4"

4×4

FIG. III.

COMMON RAFTER 4×2

4×4

FIG. V. KING POST

TIE BEAM

STRUT 4×3

HEAD AND
OF QUEEN-

FOOT
-POST.

TIE BEAM

TIE BEAM

12 6 0 1 2 3 4
SCALE OF FEET

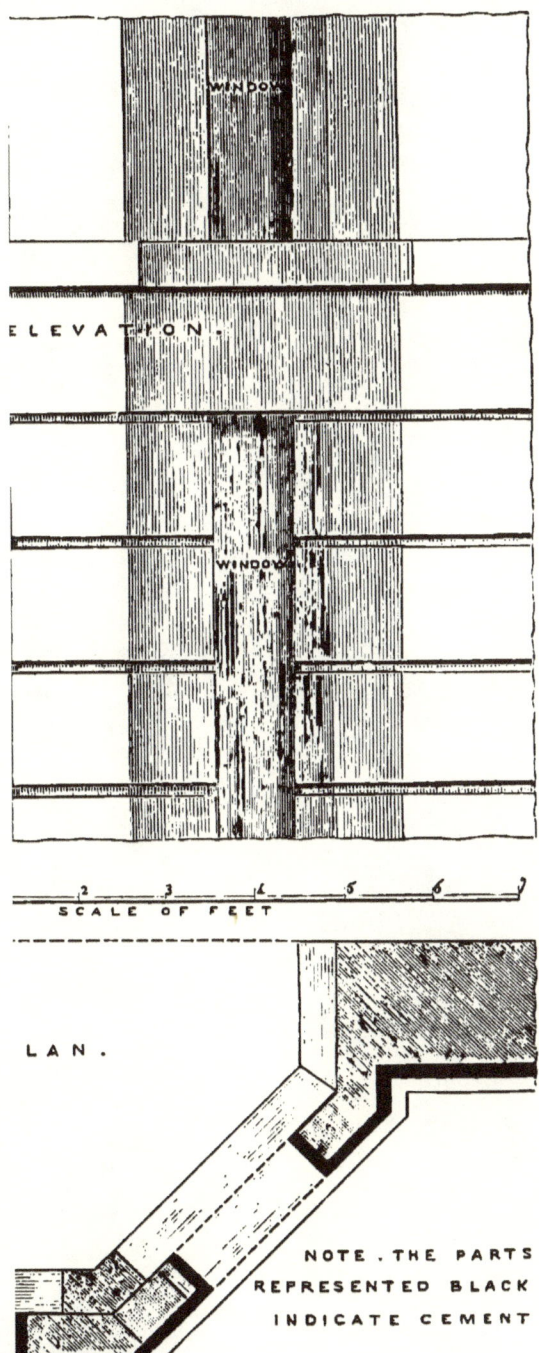

ELEVATION.

WINDOW

WINDOW

SCALE OF FEET

2   3   4   5   6   7

PLAN.

NOTE. THE PARTS
REPRESENTED BLACK
INDICATE CEMENT

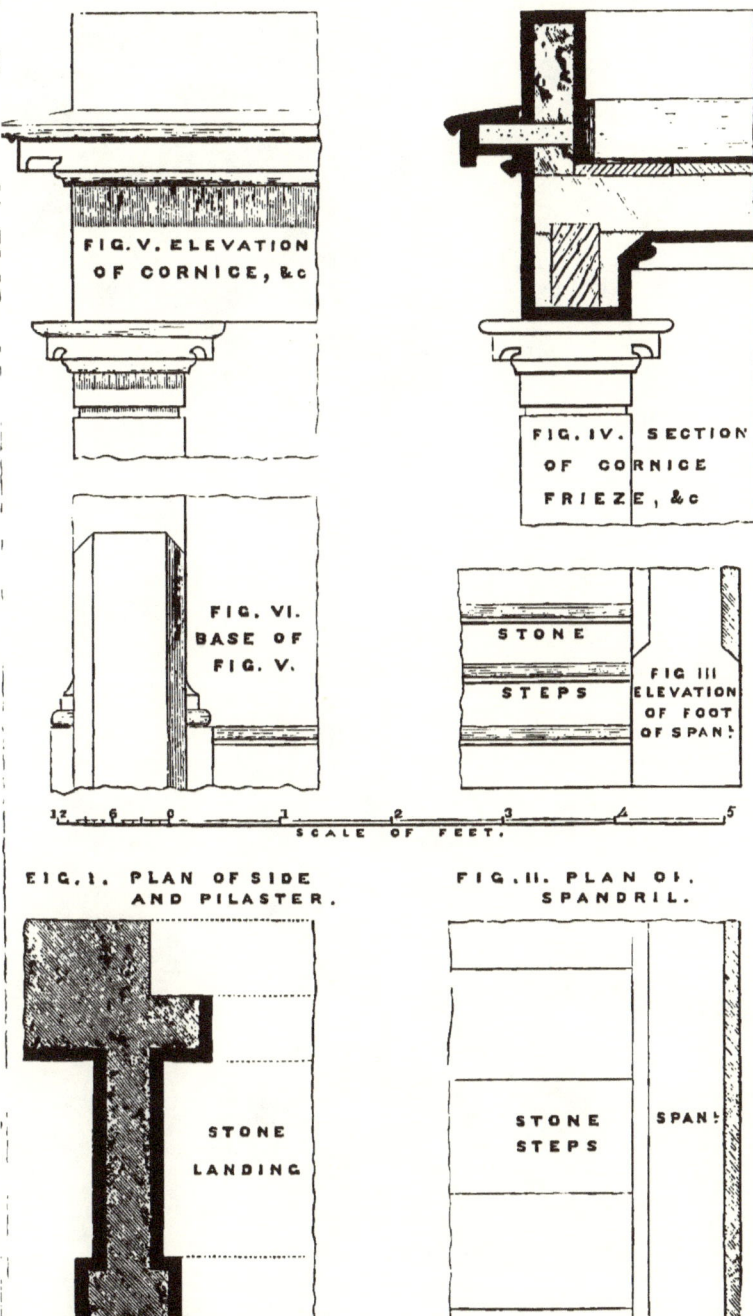

DETAILS OF ENTRANCE PORCH.

FIG. V. ELEVATION OF CORNICE, &c

FIG. IV. SECTION OF CORNICE FRIEZE, &c

FIG. VI. BASE OF FIG. V.

STONE STEPS

FIG III ELEVATION OF FOOT OF SPAN⁵

SCALE OF FEET.

FIG. I. PLAN OF SIDE AND PILASTER.

STONE LANDING

FIG. II. PLAN OF SPANDRIL.

STONE STEPS

SPAN⁵

PLATE XXIV.

TRANSVERSE SECTION SHOWING
PARTITIONS FROM A. TO B. ON PLAN.

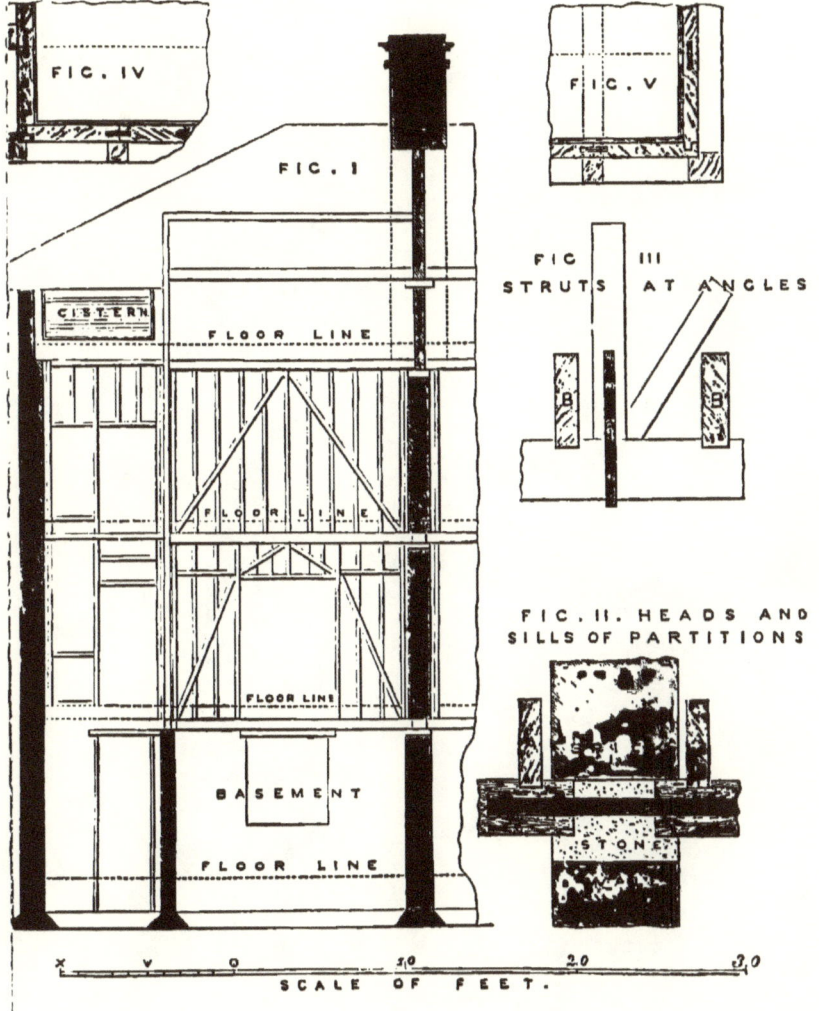

FIG. IV

FIG. V

FIG. I

CISTERN

FLOOR LINE

FIG III
STRUTS AT ANGLES

B   B

FLOOR LINE

FIG. II. HEADS AND
SILLS OF PARTITIONS

FLOOR LINE

STONE

BASEMENT

FLOOR LINE

X   Y   O   10   20   30

SCALE OF FEET.

PLATE XXV.

SECTION SHOWING PARTITIONS
FROM C. TO D. ON PLANS.

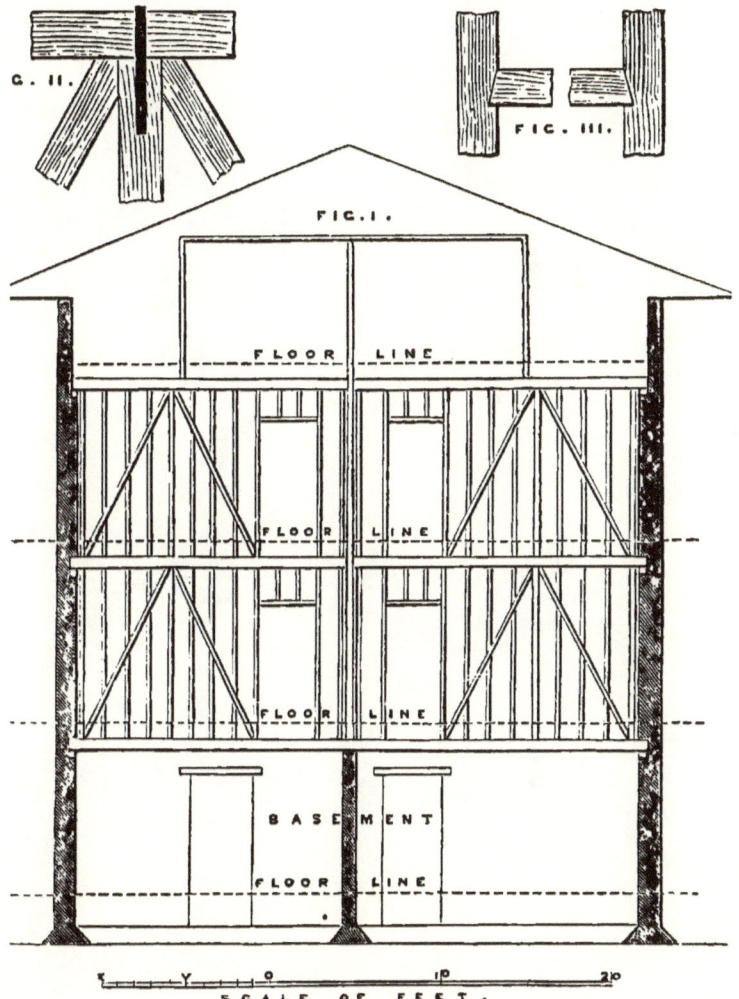

G. II.

FIG. III.

FIG. I.

FLOOR LINE

FLOOR LINE

FLOOR LINE

BASEMENT

FLOOR LINE

SCALE OF FEET.

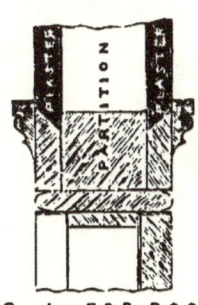

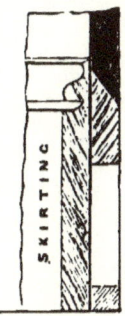

DETAILS FOR FINISHINGS CHAMBER AND ATTIC FLOOR.

PLASTER
PARTITION
PLASTER

FIG. I. FOR DOORS, WINDOWS ATTIC.

SKIRTING

FIG. II. SKIRTING CHAMBER FLOOR

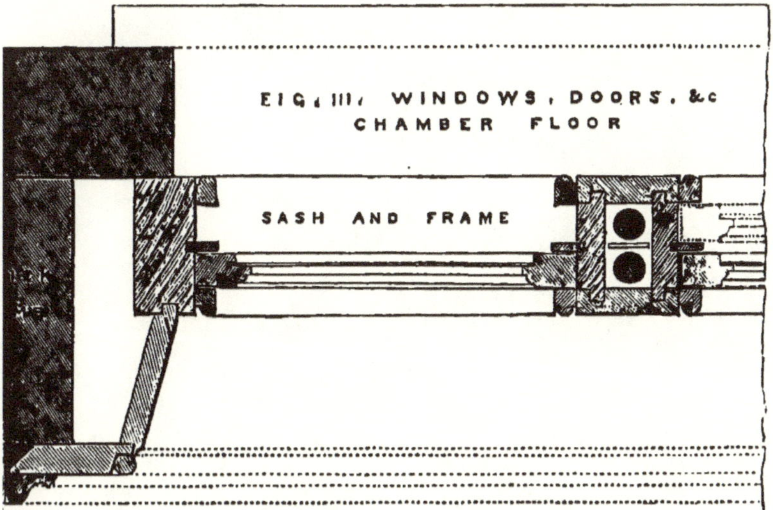

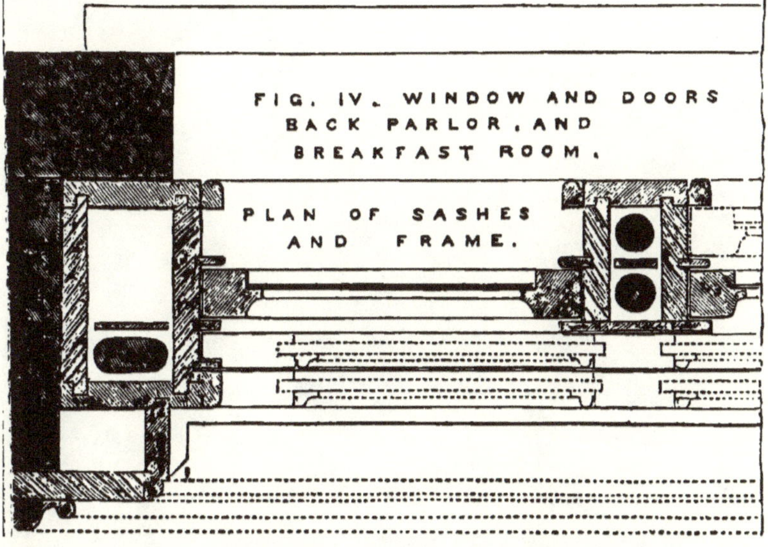

SASH AND FRAME

FIG. III. WINDOWS, DOORS, &c CHAMBER FLOOR

PLAN OF SASHES AND FRAME.

FIG. IV. WINDOW AND DOORS BACK PARLOR, AND BREAKFAST ROOM.

PLATE XXVII.

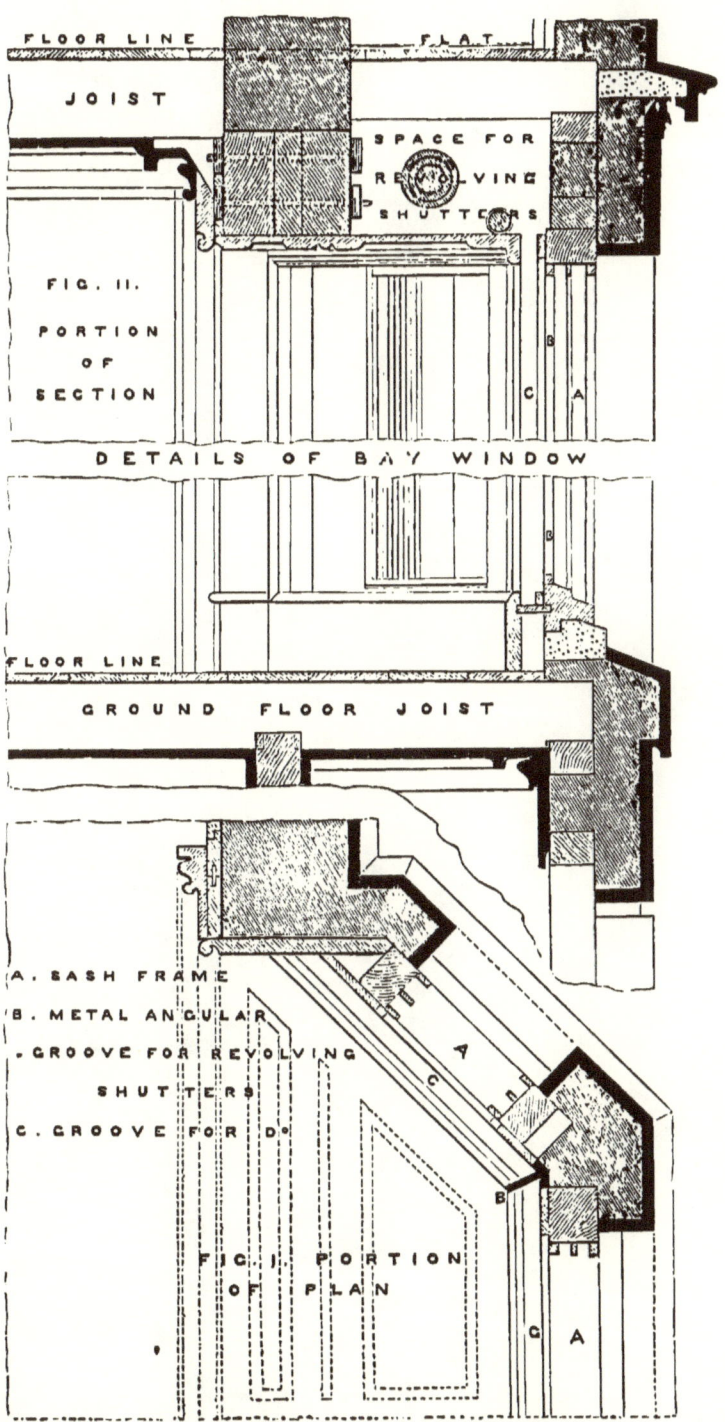

FLOOR LINE   FLAT

JOIST

SPACE FOR
REVOLVING
SHUTTERS

FIG. II.

PORTION

OF

SECTION

B

C   A

DETAILS OF BAY WINDOW

B

FLOOR LINE

GROUND FLOOR JOIST

A. SASH FRAME

B. METAL ANGULAR

. GROOVE FOR REVOLVING
    SHUTTERS

C. GROOVE FOR D°

A

C

B

FIG. I. PORTION
OF PLAN

G   A

A NEW LIST

OF

WEALE'S
RUDIMENTARY SCIENTIFIC, EDUCATIONAL,
AND CLASSICAL SERIES.

These popular and cheap Series of Books, now comprising nearly Three Hundred distinct works in almost every department of Science, Art, and Education, are recommended to the notice of Engineers, Architects, Builders, Artisans, and Students generally, as well as to those interested in Workmen's Libraries, Free Libraries Literary and Scientific Institutions, Colleges, Schools, Science Classes, &c., &c.

N.B.—In ordering from this List it is recommended, as a means of facilitating business and obviating error, to quote the numbers affixed to the volumes, as well as the titles and prices.

*** The books are bound in limp cloth, unless otherwise stated.

RUDIMENTARY SCIENTIFIC SERIES.

ARCHITECTURE, BUILDING, ETC.

No.

16. *ARCHITECTURE—ORDERS*—The Orders and their Æsthetic Principles. By W. H. LEEDS. Illustrated. 1s. 6d.

17. *ARCHITECTURE—STYLES*—The History and Description of the Styles of Architecture of Various Countries, from the Earliest to the Present Period. By T. TALBOT BURY, F.R.I.B.A., &c. Illustrated. 2s.
*** ORDERS AND STYLES OF ARCHITECTURE, *in One Vol.*, 3s. 6d.

18. *ARCHITECTURE—DESIGN*—The Principles of Design in Architecture, as deducible from Nature and exemplified in the Works of the Greek and Gothic Architects. By E. L. GARBETT, Architect. Illustrated. 2s.
*** *The three preceding Works, in One handsome Vol., half bound, entitled* "MODERN ARCHITECTURE," *Price* 6s.

22. *THE ART OF BUILDING*, Rudiments of. General Principles of Construction, Materials used in Building, Strength and Use of Materials, Working Drawings, Specifications, and Estimates. By EDWARD DOBSON, M.R.I.B.A., &c. Illustrated. 1s. 6d.

23. *BRICKS AND TILES*, Rudimentary Treatise on the Manufacture of; containing an Outline of the Principles of Brickmaking. By EDW. DOBSON, M.R.I.B.A. With Additions by C. TOMLINSON, F.R.S. Illustrated. 3s.

25. *MASONRY AND STONECUTTING*, Rudimentary Treatise on; in which the Principles of Masonic Projection and their application to the Construction of Curved Wing-Walls, Domes, Oblique Bridges, and Roman and Gothic Vaulting, are concisely explained. By EDWARD DOBSON, M.R.I.B.A., &c. Illustrated with Plates and Diagrams. 2s. 6d.

44. *FOUNDATIONS AND CONCRETE WORKS*, a Rudimentary Treatise on; containing a Synopsis of the principal cases of Foundation Works, with the usual Modes of Treatment, and Practical Remarks on Footings, Planking, Sand, Concrete, Béton, Pile-driving, Caissons, and Cofferdams. By E. DOBSON, M.R.I.B.A., &c. Third Edition, revised by GEORGE DODD, C.E. Illustrated. 1s. 6d.

LOCKWOOD AND CO., 7, STATIONERS' HALL COURT, E.C.

Architecture, Building, etc., *continued.*

42. *COTTAGE BUILDING.* By C. BRUCE ALLEN, Architect. Eleventh Edition, revised and enlarged. Numerous Illustrations. 1s. 6d.

45. *LIMES, CEMENTS, MORTARS, CONCRETES, MASTICS,* PLASTERING, &c., Rudimentary Treatise on. By G. R. BURNELL, C.E. Ninth Edition, with Appendices. 1s. 6d.

57. *WARMING AND VENTILATION,* a Rudimentary Treatise on; being a concise Exposition of the General Principles of the Art of Warming and Ventilating Domestic and Public Buildings, Mines, Lighthouses, Ships, &c. By CHARLES TOMLINSON, F.R.S., &c. Illustrated. 3s.

83**. *CONSTRUCTION OF DOOR LOCKS.* Compiled from the Papers of A. C. HOBBS, Esq., of New York, and Edited by CHARLES TOMLINSON, F.R.S. To which is added, a Description of Fenby's Patent Locks, and a Note upon IRON SAFES by ROBERT MALLET, M.I.C.E. Illus. 2s. 6d.

111. *ARCHES, PIERS, BUTTRESSES, &c.:* Experimental Essays on the Principles of Construction in; made with a view to their being useful to the Practical Builder. By WILLIAM BLAND. Illustrated. 1s. 6d.

116. *THE ACOUSTICS OF PUBLIC BUILDINGS;* or, The Principles of the Science of Sound applied to the purposes of the Architect and Builder. By T. ROGER SMITH, M.R.I.B.A., Architect. Illustrated. 1s. 6d.

124. *CONSTRUCTION OF ROOFS,* Treatise on the, as regards Carpentry and Joinery. Deduced from the Works of ROBISON, PRICE, and TREDGOLD. Illustrated. 1s. 6d.

127. *ARCHITECTURAL MODELLING IN PAPER,* the Art of. By T. A. RICHARDSON, Architect. With Illustrations, designed by the Author, and engraved by O. JEWITT. 1s. 6d.

128. *VITRUVIUS — THE ARCHITECTURE OF MARCUS VITRUVIUS POLLO.* In Ten Books. Translated from the Latin by JOSEPH GWILT, F.S.A., F.R.A.S. With 23 Plates. 5s.

130. *GRECIAN ARCHITECTURE,* An Inquiry into the Principles of Beauty in; with an Historical View of the Rise and Progress of the Art in Greece. By the EARL OF ABERDEEN. 1s.

* *The two Preceding Works in One handsome Vol., half bound, entitled* "ANCIENT ARCHITECTURE." *Price 6s.*

132. *DWELLING-HOUSES,* a Rudimentary Treatise on the Erection of. By S. H. BROOKS, Architect. New Edition, with plates. 2s. 6d.

156. *QUANTITIES AND MEASUREMENTS,* How to Calculate and Take them in Bricklayers', Masons', Plasterers', Plumbers', Painters', Paperhangers', Gilders', Smiths', Carpenters', and Joiners' Work. By A. C. BEATON, Architect and Surveyor. New and Enlarged Edition. Illus. 1s. 6d.

175. *LOCKWOOD & CO.'S BUILDER'S AND CONTRACTOR'S* PRICE BOOK, with which is incorporated ATCHLEY'S and portions of the late G. R. Burnell's "BUILDER'S PRICE BOOKS," for 1875, published annually, containing the latest Prices of all kinds of Builders' Materials and Labour, and of all Trades connected with Building: with Memoranda and Tables required in making Estimates and taking out Quantities, &c. The whole Revised and Edited by FRANCIS T. W. MILLER, Architect and Surveyor. 3s. 6d.

182. *CARPENTRY AND JOINERY*—THE ELEMENTARY PRINCIPLES OF CARPENTRY. Chiefly composed from the Standard Work of THOMAS TREDGOLD, C.E. With Additions from the Works of the most Recent Authorities, and a TREATISE ON JOINERY by E. WYNDHAM TARN, M.A. Numerous Illustrations. 3s. 6d.

182*. *CARPENTRY AND JOINERY.* ATLAS of 35 Plates to accompany the foregoing book. With Descriptive Letterpress. 4to. 6s.

187. *HINTS TO YOUNG ARCHITECTS.* By GEORGE WIGHTWICK. New Edition, enlarged. By G. HUSKISSON GUILLAUME, Architect. With numerous Woodcuts. 3s. 6d.

189. *THE RUDIMENTS OF PRACTICAL BRICKLAYING.* In Six Sections. By ADAM HAMMOND. Illustrated with 68 Woodcuts. 1s. 6d.

CIVIL ENGINEERING, ETC.

13. *CIVIL ENGINEERING*, the Rudiments of; for the Use of Beginners, for Practical Engineers, and for the Army and Navy. By HENRY LAW, C.E. Including a Section on Hydraulic Engineering, by GEORGE R. BURNELL, C.E. 5th Edition, with Notes and Illustrations by ROBERT MALLET, A.M., F.R.S. Illustrated with Plates and Diagrams. 5s.

29. *THE DRAINAGE OF DISTRICTS AND LANDS.* By G. DRYSDALE DEMPSEY, C.E. New Edition, revised and enlarged. Illustrated. 1s. 6d.

30. *THE DRAINAGE OF TOWNS AND BUILDINGS.* By G. DRYSDALE DEMPSEY, C.E. New Edition. Illustrated. 2s. 6d.
. *With "Drainage of Districts and Lands," in One Vol., 3s. 6d.*

31. *WELL-DIGGING, BORING, AND PUMP-WORK.* By JOHN GEORGE SWINDELL, Assoc. R.I.B.A. New Edition, revised by G. R. BURNELL, C.E. Illustrated. 1s.

35. *THE BLASTING AND QUARRYING OF STONE*, Rudimentary Treatise on; for Building and other Purposes, with the Constituents and Analyses of Granite, Slate, Limestone, and Sandstone : to which is added some Remarks on the Blowing up of Bridges. By Gen. Sir JOHN BURGOYNE, Bart., K.C.B. Illustrated. 1s. 6d.

43. *TUBULAR AND OTHER IRON GIRDER BRIDGES.* Particularly describing the BRITANNIA and CONWAY TUBULAR BRIDGES. With a Sketch of Iron Bridges, and Illustrations of the Application of Malleable Iron to the Art of Bridge Building. By G. D. DEMPSEY, C.E., Author of "The Practical Railway Engineer," &c., &c. New Edition, with Illustrations. 1s. 6d.

46. *CONSTRUCTING AND REPAIRING COMMON ROADS*, [Papers on the Art of. Containing a Survey of the Metropolitan Roads, by S. HUGHES, C.E.; The Art of Constructing Common Roads, by HENRY LAW, C.E.; Remarks on the Maintenance of Macadamised Roads, by Field-Marshal Sir JOHN F. BURGOYNE, Bart., G.C.B., Royal Engineers, &c., &c. Illustrated. 1s. 6d.

62. *RAILWAY CONSTRUCTION*, Elementary and Practical Instruction on the Science of. By Sir MACDONALD STEPHENSON, C.E., Managing Director of the East India Railway Company. New Edition, revised and enlarged by EDWARD NUGENT, C.E. Plates and numerous Woodcuts. 3s.

62*. *RAILWAYS;* their Capital and Dividends. With Statistics of their Working in Great Britain, &c., &c. By E. D. CHATTAWAY. 1s.
. *62 and 62*, in One Vol., 3s. 6d.*

80*. *EMBANKING LANDS FROM THE SEA*, the Practice of. Treated as a Means of Profitable Employment for Capital. With Examples and Particulars of actual Embankments, and also Practical Remarks on the Repair of old Sea Walls. By JOHN WIGGINS, F.G.S. New Edition, with Notes by ROBERT MALLET, F.R.S. 2s.

81. *WATER WORKS*, for the Supply of Cities and Towns. With a Description of the Principal Geological Formations of England as influencing Supplies of Water; and Details of Engines and Pumping Machinery for raising Water. By SAMUEL HUGHES, F.G.S., C.E. New Edition, revised and enlarged, with numerous Illustrations. 4s.

82**. *GAS WORKS*, and the Practice of Manufacturing and Distributing Coal Gas. By SAMUEL HUGHES, C.E. New Edition, revised by W. RICHARDS, C.E. Illustrated. 3s.

117. *SUBTERRANEOUS SURVEYING;* an Elementary and Practical Treatise on. By THOMAS FENWICK. Also the Method of Conducting Subterraneous Surveys without the Use of the Magnetic Needle, and other modern Improvements. By THOMAS BAKER, C.E. Illustrated. 2s. 6d.

118. *CIVIL ENGINEERING IN NORTH AMERICA*, a Sketch of. By DAVID STEVENSON, F.R.S.E., &c. Plates and Diagrams. 3s.

Civil Engineering, etc., *continued.*

120. *HYDRAULIC ENGINEERING*, the Rudiments of. By G. R. BURNELL, C.E., F.G.S. Illustrated. 3s.

121. *RIVERS AND TORRENTS.* With the Method of Regulating their Courses and Channels. By Professor PAUL FRISI, F.R.S., of Milan. To which is added, AN ESSAY ON NAVIGABLE CANALS. Translated by Major-General JOHN GARSTIN, of the Bengal Engineers. Plates. 2s. 6d.

MECHANICAL ENGINEERING, ETC.

33. *CRANES*, the Construction of, and other Machinery for Raising Heavy Bodies for the Erection of Buildings, and for Hoisting Goods. By JOSEPH GLYNN, F.R.S., &c. Illustrated. 1s. 6d.

34. *THE STEAM ENGINE*, a Rudimentary Treatise on. By Dr. LARDNER. Illustrated. 1s.

59. *STEAM BOILERS:* Their Construction and Management. By R. ARMSTRONG, C.E. Illustrated. 1s. 6d.

63. *AGRICULTURAL ENGINEERING:* Farm Buildings, Motive Power, Field Machines, Machinery, and Implements. By G. H. ANDREWS, C.E. Illustrated. 3s.

67. *CLOCKS, WATCHES, AND BELLS*, a Rudimentary Treatise on. By Sir EDMUND BECKETT (late EDMUND BECKETT DENISON, LL.D., Q.C.) **** A *New, Revised, and considerably Enlarged Edition of the above Standard Treatise, with very numerous Illustrations, is now ready, price* 4s. 6d.   .

77*. *THE ECONOMY OF FUEL*, particularly with Reference to Reverbatory Furnaces for the Manufacture of Iron, and to Steam Boilers. By T. SYMES PRIDEAUX. 1s. 6d.

82. *THE POWER OF WATER*, as applied to drive Flour Mills, and to give motion to Turbines and other Hydrostatic Engines. By JOSEPH GLYNN, F.R.S., &c. New Edition, Illustrated. 2s.

98. *PRACTICAL MECHANISM*, the Elements of; and Machine Tools. By T. BAKER, C.E. With Remarks on Tools and Machinery, by J. NASMYTH, C.E. Plates. 2s. 6d.

114. *MACHINERY*, Elementary Principles of, in its Construction and Working. Illustrated by numerous Examples of Modern Machinery for different Branches of Manufacture. By C. D. ABEL, C.E. 1s. 6d.

115. *ATLAS OF PLATES.* Illustrating the above Treatise. By C. D. ABEL, C.E. 7s. 6d.

125. *THE COMBUSTION OF COAL AND THE PREVENTION* OF SMOKE, Chemically and Practically Considered. With an Appendix. By C. WYE WILLIAMS, A.I.C.E. Plates. 3s.

139. *THE STEAM ENGINE*, a Treatise on the Mathematical Theory of, with Rules at length, and Examples for the Use of Practical Men. By T. BAKER, C.E. Illustrated. 1s.

162. *THE BRASS FOUNDER'S MANUAL;* Instructions for Modelling, Pattern-Making, Moulding, Turning, Filing, Burnishing, Bronzing, &c. With copious Receipts, numerous Tables, and Notes on Prime Costs and Estimates. By WALTER GRAHAM. Illustrated. 2s. 6d.

164. *MODERN WORKSHOP PRACTICE*, as applied to Marine, Land, and Locomotive Engines, Floating Docks, Dredging Machines, Bridges, Cranes, Ship-building, &c., &c. By J. G. WINTON. Illustrated. 3s.

165. *IRON AND HEAT*, exhibiting the Principles concerned in the Construction of Iron Beams, Pillars, and Bridge Girders, and the Action of Heat in the Smelting Furnace. By J. ARMOUR, C.E. Numerous Woodcuts. 2s. 6d.

LONDON : LOCKWOOD AND CO.,

Mechanical Engineering, etc., *continued.*

166. *POWER IN MOTION:* Horse-Power, Motion, Toothed-Wheel Gearing, Long and Short Driving Bands, Angular Forces. By JAMES ARMOUR, C.E. With 73 Diagrams. 2s. 6d.

167. *THE APPLICATION OF IRON TO THE CONSTRUCTION* OF BRIDGES, GIRDERS, ROOFS, AND OTHER WORKS. Showing the Principles upon which such Structures are designed, and their Practical Application. By FRANCIS CAMPIN, C.E. Numerous Woodcuts. 2s.

171. *THE WORKMAN'S MANUAL OF ENGINEERING* DRAWING. By JOHN MAXTON, Engineer, Instructor in Engineering Drawing, Royal School of Naval Architecture and Marine Engineering, South Kensington. Illustrated with 7 Plates and nearly 350 Woodcuts. 3s.6d.

SHIPBUILDING, NAVIGATION, MARINE ENGINEERING, ETC.

51. *NAVAL ARCHITECTURE,* the Rudiments of; or, an Exposition of the Elementary Principles of the Science, and their Practical Application to Naval Construction. Compiled for the Use of Beginners. By JAMES PEAKE, School of Naval Architecture, H.M. Dockyard, Portsmouth. Fourth Edition, corrected, with Plates and Diagrams. 3s. 6d.

53*. *SHIPS FOR OCEAN AND RIVER SERVICE,* Elementary and Practical Principles of the Construction of. By HAKON A. SOMMERFELDT, Surveyor of the Royal Norwegian Navy. With an Appendix. 1s.

53**. *AN ATLAS OF ENGRAVINGS* to Illustrate the above. Twelve large folding plates. Royal 4to, cloth. 7s. 6d.

54. *MASTING, MAST-MAKING, AND RIGGING OF SHIPS,* Rudimentary Treatise on. Also Tables of Spars, Rigging, Blocks; Chain, Wire, and Hemp Ropes, &c., relative to every class of vessels. Together with an Appendix of Dimensions of Masts and Yards of the Royal Navy of Great Britain and Ireland. By ROBERT KIPPING, N.A. Thirteenth Edition. Illustrated. 1s. 6d.

54*. *IRON SHIP-BUILDING.* With Practical Examples and Details for the Use of Ship Owners and Ship Builders. By JOHN GRANTHAM, Consulting Engineer and Naval Architect. Fifth Edition, with important Additions. 4s.

54**. *AN ATLAS OF FORTY PLATES* to Illustrate the above. Fifth Edition. Including the latest Examples, such as H.M. Steam Frigates "Warrior," "Hercules," "Bellerophon;" H.M. Troop Ship "Serapis," Iron Floating Dock, &c., &c. 4to, boards. 38s.

55. *THE SAILOR'S SEA BOOK:* A Rudimentary Treatise on Navigation. I. How to Keep the Log and Work it off. II. On Finding the Latitude and Longitude. By JAMES GREENWOOD, B.A., of Jesus College, Cambridge. To which are added, Directions for Great Circle Sailing; an Essay on the Law of Storms and Variable Winds; and Explanations of Terms used in Ship-building. Ninth Edition, with several Engravings and Coloured Illustrations of the Flags of Maritime Nations. 2s.

80. *MARINE ENGINES, AND STEAM VESSELS,* a Treatise on. Together with Practical Remarks on the Screw and Propelling Power, as used in the Royal and Merchant Navy. By ROBERT MURRAY, C.E., Engineer-Surveyor to the Board of Trade. With a Glossary of Technical Terms, and their Equivalents in French, German, and Spanish. Fifth Edition, revised and enlarged. Illustrated. 3s.

83*bis*. *THE FORMS OF SHIPS AND BOATS:* Hints, Experimentally Derived, on some of the Principles regulating Ship-building. By W. BLAND. Sixth Edition, revised, with numerous Illustrations and Models. 1s. 6d.

99. *NAVIGATION AND NAUTICAL ASTRONOMY,* in Theory and Practice. With Attempts to facilitate the Finding of the Time and the Longitude at Sea. By J. R. YOUNG, formerly Professor of Mathematics in Belfast College. Illustrated. 2s. 6d.

Shipbuilding, Navigation, etc., *continued*.

100*. *TABLES* intended to facilitate the Operations of Navigation and Nautical Astronomy, as an Accompaniment to the above Book. By J. R. YOUNG. 1s. 6d.

106. *SHIPS' ANCHORS*, a Treatise on. By GEORGE COTSELL, N.A. Illustrated. 1s. 6d.

149. *SAILS AND SAIL-MAKING*, an Elementary Treatise on. With Draughting, and the Centre of Effort of the Sails. Also, Weights and Sizes of Ropes ; Masting, Rigging, and Sails of Steam Vessels, &c., &c. Ninth Edition, enlarged, with an Appendix. By ROBERT KIPPING, N.A., Sailmaker, Quayside, Newcastle. Illustrated. 2s. 6d.

155. *THE ENGINEER'S GUIDE TO THE ROYAL AND* MERCANTILE NAVIES. By a PRACTICAL ENGINEER. Revised by D. F. M'CARTHY, late of the Ordnance Survey Office, Southampton. 3s.

PHYSICAL SCIENCE, NATURAL PHILO-SOPHY, ETC.

1. *CHEMISTRY*, for the Use of Beginners. By Professor GEORGE FOWNES, F.R.S. With an Appendix, on the Application of Chemistry to Agriculture. 1s.

2. *NATURAL PHILOSOPHY*, Introduction to the Study of; for the Use of Beginners. By C. TOMLINSON, Lecturer on Natural Science in King's College School, London. Woodcuts. 1s. 6d.

4. *MINERALOGY*, Rudiments of; a concise View of the Properties of Minerals. By A. RAMSEY, Jun. Woodcuts and Steel Plates. 3s.

6. *MECHANICS*, Rudimentary Treatise on; Being a concise Exposition of the General Principles of Mechanical Science, and their Applications. By CHARLES TOMLINSON, Lecturer on Natural Science in King's College School, London. Illustrated. 1s. 6d.

7. *ELECTRICITY;* showing the General Principles of Electrical Science, and the purposes to which it has been applied. By Sir W. SNOW HARRIS, F.R.S., &c. With considerable Additions by R. SABINE, C.E., F.S.A. Woodcuts. 1s. 6d.

7*. *GALVANISM*, Rudimentary Treatise on, and the General Principles of Animal and Voltaic Electricity. By Sir W. SNOW HARRIS. New Edition, revised, with considerable Additions, by ROBERT SABINE, C.E., F.S.A. Woodcuts. 1s. 6d.

8. *MAGNETISM;* being a concise Exposition of the General Principles of Magnetical Science, and the Purposes to which it has been applied. By Sir W. SNOW HARRIS. New Edition, revised and enlarged by H. M. NOAD, Ph.D., Vice-President of the Chemical Society, Author of "A Manual of Electricity," &c., &c. With 165 Woodcuts. 3s. 6d.

11. *THE ELECTRIC TELEGRAPH;* its History and Progress; with Descriptions of some of the Apparatus. By R. SABINE, C.E., F.S.A., &c. Woodcuts. 3s

12. *PNEUMATICS*, for the Use of Beginners. By CHARLES TOMLINSON. Illustrated. 1s. 6d.

72. *MANUAL OF THE MOLLUSCA;* a Treatise on Recent and Fossil Shells. By Dr. S. P. WOODWARD, A.L.S. With Appendix by RALPH TATE, A.L.S., F.G.S. With numerous Plates and 300 Woodcuts, 6s. 6d. Cloth boards, 7s. 6d.

79**. *PHOTOGRAPHY*, Popular Treatise on; with a Description of the Stereoscope, &c. Translated from the French of D. VAN MONCKHOVEN, by W. H. THORNTHWAITE, Ph.D. Woodcuts. 1s. 6d.

96. *ASTRONOMY*. By the Rev. R. MAIN, M.A., F.R.S., &c. New and enlarged Edition, with an Appendix on "Spectrum Analysis." Woodcuts. 1s. 6d.

Physical Science, Natural Philosophy, etc., *continued.*

97. *STATICS AND DYNAMICS,* the Principles and Practice of; embracing also a clear development of Hydrostatics, Hydrodynamics, and Central Forces. By T. BAKER, C.E. 1s. 6d.

138. *TELEGRAPH,* Handbook of the; a Manual of Telegraphy, Telegraph Clerks' Remembrancer, and Guide to Candidates for Employ- ment in the Telegraph Service. By R. BOND. Fourth Edition, revised and enlarged; to which is appended, QUESTIONS on MAGNETISM, ELEC- TRICITY, and PRACTICAL TELEGRAPHY, for the Use of Students, by W. McGREGOR, First Assistant Superintendent, Indian Gov. Telegraphs. Woodcuts. 3s.

143. *EXPERIMENTAL ESSAYS.* By CHARLES TOMLINSON. I. On the Motions of Camphor on Water. II. On the Motion of Camphor towards the Light. III. History of the Modern Theory of Dew. Woodcuts. 1s.

173. *PHYSICAL GEOLOGY,* partly based on Major-General PORT- LOCK's " Rudiments of Geology." By RALPH TATE, A.L.S., &c. Numerous Woodcuts. 2s.

174. *HISTORICAL GEOLOGY,* partly based on Major-General PORTLOCK's "Rudiments." By RALPH TATE, A.L.S., &c. Woodcuts. 2s. 6d.

173 & 174. *RUDIMENTARY TREATISE ON GEOLOGY,* Physical and Historical. Partly based on Major-General PORTLOCK's "Rudiments of Geology." By RALPH TATE, A.L.S., F.G.S., &c., &c. Numerous Illustra- tions. In One Volume. 4s. 6d.

183 & 184. *ANIMAL PHYSICS,* Handbook of. By DIONYSIUS LARDNER, D.C.L., formerly Professor of Natural Philosophy and Astronomy in Uni- versity College, London. With 520 Illustrations. In One Volume, cloth boards. 7s. 6d.

** *Sold also in Two Parts, as follows :—*

183. ANIMAL PHYSICS. By Dr. LARDNER. Part I., Chapter I—VII. 4s.
184. ANIMAL PHYSICS. By Dr. LARDNER. Part II. Chapter VIII—XVIII. 3s.

MINING, METALLURGY, ETC.

117. *SUBTERRANEOUS SURVEYING,* Elementary and Practical Treatise on, with and without the Magnetic Needle. By THOMAS FENWICK, Surveyor of Mines, and THOMAS BAKER, C.E. Illustrated. 2s. 6d.

133. *METALLURGY OF COPPER ;* an Introduction to the Methods of Seeking, Mining, and Assaying Copper, and Manufacturing its Alloys. By ROBERT H. LAMBORN, Ph.D. Woodcuts. 2s.

134. *METALLURGY OF SILVER AND LEAD.* A Description of the Ores; their Assay and Treatment, and valuable Constituents. By Dr. R. H. LAMBORN. Woodcuts. 2s.

135. *ELECTRO-METALLURGY;* Practically Treated. By ALEX- ANDER WATT, F.R.S.S.A. New Edition. Woodcuts. 2s.

172. *MINING TOOLS,* Manual of. For the Use of Mine Managers, Agents, Students, &c. Comprising Observations on the Materials from, and Processes by which, they are manufactured ; their Special Uses, Applica- tions, Qualities, and Efficiency. By WILLIAM MORGANS, Lecturer on Mining at the Bristol School of Mines. 2s. 6d.

172*. *MINING TOOLS, ATLAS* of Engravings to Illustrate the above, containing 235 Illustrations of Mining Tools, drawn to Scale. 4to. 4s. 6d.

176. *METALLURGY OF IRON,* a Treatise on the. Containing Outlines of the History of Iron Manufacture, Methods of Assay, and Analyses of Iron Ores, Processes of Manufacture of Iron and Steel, &c. By H. BAUERMAN, F.G.S., Associate of the Royal School of Mines. Fourth Edition, revised and enlarged, with numerous Illustrations. 4s. 6d.

Mining, Metallurgy, etc., *continued.*

180. *COAL AND COAL MINING:* A Rudimentary Treatise on. By WARINGTON W. SMYTH, M.A., F.R.S., &c., Chief Inspector of the Mines of the Crown and of the Duchy of Cornwall. Second Edition, revised and corrected. With numerous Illustrations. 3s. 6d.

EMIGRATION.

154. *GENERAL HINTS TO EMIGRANTS.* Containing Notices of the various Fields for Emigration. With Hints on Preparation for Emigrating, Outfits, &c., &c. With Directions and Recipes useful to the Emigrant. With a Map of the World. 2s.

157. *THE EMIGRANT'S GUIDE TO NATAL.* By ROBERT JAMES MANN, F.R.A.S., F.M.S. Second Edition, carefully corrected to the present Date. Map. 2s.

159. *THE EMIGRANT'S GUIDE TO AUSTRALIA, New South Wales, Western Australia, South Australia, Victoria, and Queensland.* By the Rev. JAMES BAIRD, B.A. Map. 2s. 6d.

160. *THE EMIGRANT'S GUIDE TO TASMANIA and NEW ZEALAND.* By the Rev. JAMES BAIRD, B.A. With a Map. 2s.

159 & *THE EMIGRANT'S GUIDE .TO AUSTRALASIA.* By the
160. Rev. J. BAIRD, B.A. Comprising the above two volumes, 12mo, cloth boards. With Maps of Australia and New Zealand. 5s.

AGRICULTURE.

29. *THE DRAINAGE OF DISTRICTS AND LANDS.* By G. DRYSDALE DEMPSEY, C.E. Illustrated. 1s. 6d.
   *** *With "Drainage of Towns and Buildings," in One Vol.,* 3s.

63. *AGRICULTURAL ENGINEERING:* Farm Buildings, Motive Powers and Machinery of the Steading, Field Machines, and Implements. By G. H. ANDREWS, C.E. Illustrated. 3s.

66. *CLAY LANDS AND LOAMY SOILS.* By Professor DONALDSON. 1s.

131. *MILLER'S, MERCHANT'S, AND FARMER'S READY* RECKONER, for ascertaining at sight the value of any quantity of Corn, from One Bushel to One Hundred Quarters, at any given price, from £1 to £5 per quarter. Together with the approximate values of Millstones and Millwork, &c. 1s.

140. *SOILS, MANURES, AND CROPS* (Vol. 1. OUTLINES OF MODERN FARMING.) By R. SCOTT BURN. Woodcuts. 2s.

141. *FARMING AND FARMING ECONOMY,* Notes, Historical and Practical on. (Vol. 2. OUTLINES OF MODERN FARMING.) By R. SCOTT BURN. Woodcuts. 3s.

142. *STOCK; CATTLE, SHEEP, AND HORSES.* (Vol. 3. OUTLINES OF MODERN FARMING.) By R. SCOTT BURN. Woodcuts. 2s. 6d.

145. *DAIRY, PIGS, AND POULTRY,* Management of the. By R. SCOTT BURN. With Notes on the Diseases of Stock. (Vol. 4. OUTLINES OF MODERN FARMING.) Woodcuts. 2s.

146. *UTILIZATION OF SEWAGE, IRRIGATION, AND* RECLAMATION OF WASTE LAND. (Vol. 5. OUTLINES OF MODERN FARMING.) By R. SCOTT BURN. Woodcuts. 2s. 6d.
   *** Nos. 140-1-2-5-6, in One Vol., handsomely half-bound, entitled "OUTLINES OF MODERN FARMING." By ROBERT SCOTT BURN. Price 12s.

177. *FRUIT TREES;* The Scientific and Profitable Culture of. From the French of DU BREUIL, Revised by GEO. GLENNY. 187 Woodcuts. 3s. 6d.

FINE ARTS.

20. *PERSPECTIVE FOR BEGINNERS.* Adapted to Young Students and Amateurs in Architecture, Painting, &c. By GEORGE PYNE, Artist. Woodcuts. 2s.

27. *A GRAMMAR OF COLOURING*, applicable to House Painting, Decorative Architecture, and the Arts, for the Use of Practical Painters and Decorators. By GEORGE FIELD, Author of " Chromatics ; or, The Analogy, Harmony, and Philosophy of Colours," &c. Enlarged by ELLIS A. 'DAVIDSON. Coloured Illustrations. 2s. 6d.

40. *GLASS STAINING ;* or, Painting on Glass, The Art of. Comprising Directions for Preparing the Pigments and Fluxes, laying them upon the Glass, and Firing or Burning in the Colours. From the German of Dr. GESSERT. To which is added, an Appendix on THE ART OF ENAMELLING, &c. 1s.

41. *PAINTING ON GLASS*, The Art of. From the German of EMANUEL OTTO FROMBERG. 1s.

69. *MUSIC*, A Rudimentary and Practical Treatise on. With numerous Examples. By CHARLES CHILD SPENCER. 2s.

71. *PIANOFORTE*, The Art of Playing the. With numerous Exercises and Lessons. Written and Selected from the Best Masters, by CHARLES CHILD SPENCER. 1s. 6d.

181. *PAINTING POPULARLY EXPLAINED*, including Fresco, Oil, Mosaic, Water Colour, Water-Glass, Tempera, Encaustic, Miniature, Painting on Ivory, Vellum, Pottery, Enamel, Glass, &c. With Historical Sketches of the Progress of the Art by THOMAS JOHN GULLICK, assisted by JOHN TIMBS, F.S.A. Third Edition, revised and enlarged, with Frontispiece and Vignette. 5s.

ARITHMETIC, GEOMETRY, MATHEMATICS, ETC.

32. *MATHEMATICAL INSTRUMENTS*, a Treatise on ; in which their Construction, and the Methods of Testing, Adjusting, and Using them are concisely Explained. By J. F. HEATHER, M.A., of the Royal Military Academy, Woolwich. Original Edition, in 1 vol., Illustrated. 1s. 6d.
* *In ordering the above, be careful to say, "Original Edition," or give the number in the Series* (32) *to distinguish it from the Enlarged Edition in 3 vols.* (*Nos.* 168-9-70).

60. *LAND AND ENGINEERING SURVEYING*, a Treatise on ; with all the Modern Improvements. Arranged for the Use of Schools and Private Students ; also for Practical Land Surveyors and Engineers. By T. BAKER, C.E. New Edition, revised by EDWARD NUGENT, C.E. Illustrated with Plates and Diagrams. 2s.

61*. *READY RECKONER FOR THE ADMEASUREMENT* OF LAND. By ABRAHAM ARMAN, Schoolmaster, Thurleigh, Beds. To which is added a Table, showing the Price of Work, from 2s. 6d. to £1 per acre, and Tables for the Valuation of Land, from 1s. to £1,000 per acre, and from one pole to two thousand acres in extent, &c., &c. 1s. 6d.

76. *DESCRIPTIVE GEOMETRY*, an Elementary Treatise on ; with a Theory of Shadows and of Perspective, extracted from the French of G. MONGE. To which is added, a description of the Principles and Practice of Isometrical Projection ; the whole being intended as an introduction to the Application of Descriptive Geometry to various branches of the Arts. By J. F. HEATHER, M.A. Illustrated with 14 Plates. 2s.

178. *PRACTICAL PLANE GEOMETRY:* giving the Simplest Modes of Constructing Figures contained in one Plane and Geometrical Construction of the Ground. By J. F. HEATHER, M.A. With 215 Woodcuts. 2s.

179. *PROJECTION:* Orthographic, Topographic, and Perspective ; giving the various Modes of Delineating Solid Forms by Constructions on a Single Plane Surface. By J. F. HEATHER, M.A. [*In preparation.*
** *The above three volumes will form a* COMPLETE ELEMENTARY COURSE OF MATHEMATICAL DRAWING.

Arithmetic, Geometry, Mathematics, etc., *continued.*

83. *COMMERCIAL BOOK-KEEPING.* With Commercial Phrases and Forms in English, French, Italian, and German. By JAMES HADDON, M.A., Arithmetical Master of King's College School, London. 1s.

84. *ARITHMETIC,* a Rudimentary Treatise on : with full Explanations of its Theoretical Principles, and numerous Examples for Practice. For the Use of Schools and for Self-Instruction. By J. R. YOUNG, late Professor of Mathematics in Belfast College. New Edition, with Index. 1s. 6d.

84* A KEY to the above, containing Solutions in full to the Exercises, together with Comments, Explanations, and Improved Processes, for the Use of Teachers and Unassisted Learners. By J. R. YOUNG. 1s. 6d.

85. *EQUATIONAL ARITHMETIC,* applied to Questions of Interest,
85*. Annuities, Life Assurance, and General Commerce ; with various Tables by which all Calculations may be greatly facilitated. By W. HIPSLEY. In Two Parts, 1s. each ; or in One Vol. 2s.

86. *ALGEBRA,* the Elements of. By JAMES HADDON, M.A., Second Mathematical Master of King's College School. With Appendix, containing miscellaneous Investigations, and a Collection of Problems in various parts of Algebra. 2s.

86* A KEY AND COMPANION to the above Book, forming an extensive repository of Solved Examples and Problems in Illustration of the various Expedients necessary in Algebraical Operations. Especially adapted for Self-Instruction. By J. R. YOUNG. 1s. 6d.

88. *EUCLID,* THE ELEMENTS OF : with many additional Propositions
89. and Explanatory Notes : to which is prefixed, an Introductory Essay on Logic. By HENRY LAW, C.E. 2s. 6d.

** Sold also separately, viz. :—

88. EUCLID, The First Three Books. By HENRY LAW, C.E. 1s.
89. EUCLID, Books 4, 5, 6, 11, 12. By HENRY LAW, C.E. 1s. 6d.

90. *ANALYTICAL GEOMETRY AND CONICAL SECTIONS* a Rudimentary Treatise on. By JAMES HANN, late Mathematical Master of King's College School, London. A New Edition, re-written and enlarged by J. R. YOUNG, formerly Professor of Mathematics at Belfast College. 2s

91. *PLANE TRIGONOMETRY,* the Elements of. By JAMES HANN, formerly Mathematical Master of King's College, London. 1s.

92. *SPHERICAL TRIGONOMETRY,* the Elements of. By JAMES HANN. Revised by CHARLES H. DOWLING, C.E. 1s.
** Or with " The Elements of Plane Trigonometry," in One Volume, 2s.

93. *MENSURATION AND MEASURING,* for Students and Practical Use. With the Mensuration and Levelling of Land for the Purposes of Modern Engineering. By T. BAKER, C.E. New Edition, with Corrections and Additions by E. NUGENT, C.E. Illustrated. 1s. 6d.

94. *LOGARITHMS,* a Treatise on ; with Mathematical Tables for facilitating Astronomical, Nautical, Trigonometrical, and Logarithmic Calculations ; Tables of Natural Sines and Tangents and Natural Cosines. By HENRY LAW, C.E. Illustrated. 2s. 6d.

101*. *MEASURES, WEIGHTS, AND MONEYS OF ALL NATIONS,* and an Analysis of the Christian, Hebrew, and Mahometan Calendars. By W. S. B. WOOLHOUSE, F.R.A.S., &c. 1s. 6d.

102. *INTEGRAL CALCULUS,* Rudimentary Treatise on the. By HOMERSHAM COX, B.A. Illustrated. 1s.

103. *INTEGRAL CALCULUS,* Examples on the. By JAMES HANN, late of King's College, London. Illustrated. 1s.

101. *DIFFERENTIAL CALCULUS,* Examples of the. By W. S. B. WOOLHOUSE, F.R.A.S., &c. 1s. 6d.

104. *DIFFERENTIAL CALCULUS,* Examples and Solutions of the. By JAMES HADDON, M.A. 1s.

Arithmetic, Geometry, Mathematics, etc., *continued.*

105. *MNEMONICAL LESSONS.*—GEOMETRY, ALGEBRA, AND TRIGONOMETRY, in Easy Mnemonical Lessons. By the Rev. THOMAS PENYNGTON KIRKMAN, M.A. 1s. 6d.

136. *ARITHMETIC*, Rudimentary, for the Use of Schools and Self-Instruction. By JAMES HADDON, M.A. Revised by ABRAHAM ARMAN. 1s. 6d.

137. A KEY TO HADDON'S RUDIMENTARY ARITHMETIC. By A. ARMAN. 1s. 6d.

147. *ARITHMETIC*, STEPPING-STONE TO; Being a Complete Course of Exercises in the First Four Rules (Simple and Compound), on an entirely new principle. For the Use of Elementary Schools of every Grade. Intended as an Introduction to the more extended works on Arithmetic. By ABRAHAM ARMAN. 1s.

148. A KEY TO STEPPING-STONE TO ARITHMETIC. By A. ARMAN. 1s.

158. *THE SLIDE RULE, AND HOW TO USE IT;* Containing full, easy, and simple Instructions to perform all Business Calculations with unexampled rapidity and accuracy. By CHARLES HOARE, C.E. With a Slide Rule in tuck of cover. 3s.

168. *DRAWING AND MEASURING INSTRUMENTS.* Including—I. Instruments employed in Geometrical and Mechanical Drawing, and in the Construction, Copying, and Measurement of Maps and Plans. II. Instruments Used for the purposes of Accurate Measurement, and for Arithmetical Computations. By J. F. HEATHER, M.A., late of the Royal Military Academy, Woolwich, Author of "Descriptive Geometry," &c., &c. Illustrated. 1s. 6d.

169. *OPTICAL INSTRUMENTS.* Including (more especially) Telescopes, Microscopes, and Apparatus for producing copies of Maps and Plans by Photography. By J. F. HEATHER, M.A. Illustrated. 1s. 6d.

170. *SURVEYING AND ASTRONOMICAL INSTRUMENTS.* Including—I. Instruments Used for Determining the Geometrical Features of a portion of Ground. II. Instruments Employed in Astronomical Observations. By J. F. HEATHER, M.A. Illustrated. 1s. 6d.

. *The above three volumes form an enlargement of the Author's original work, "Mathematical Instruments: their Construction, Adjustment, Testing, and Use," the Eleventh Edition of which is on sale, price 1s. 6d. (See No. 32 in the Series.)*

168.}
169.} *MATHEMATICAL INSTRUMENTS.* By J. F. HEATHER,
170.} M.A. Enlarged Edition, for the most part entirely re-written. The 3 Parts as above, in One thick Volume. With numerous Illustrations. Cloth boards. 5s.

LEGAL TREATISES.

50. *THE LAW OF CONTRACTS FOR WORKS AND SER-VICES.* By DAVID GIBBONS. Third Edition, Enlarged. 3s.

107. *COUNTY COURT GUIDE*, Plain Guide for Suitors in the County Court. By a BARRISTER. 1s. 6d.

108. *THE METROPOLIS LOCAL MANAGEMENT ACT*, 18th and 19th Vict., c. 120; 19th and 20th Vict., c. 112; 21st and 22nd Vict., c. 104; 24th and 25th Vict., c. 61; also, the last Pauper Removal Act, and the Parochial Assessment Act. 1s. 6d.

108*. *THE METROPOLIS LOCAL MANAGEMENT AMEND-MENT ACT*, 1862, 25th and 26th Vict., c. 120. Notes and an Index. 1s.
. *With the Local Management Act, in One Volume. 2s. 6d.*

151. *A HANDY BOOK ON THE LAW OF FRIENDLY, IN-DUSTRIAL & PROVIDENT BUILDING & LOAN SOCIETIES.* With copious Notes. By NATHANIEL WHITE, of H.M. Civil Service. 1s.

163. *THE LAW OF PATENTS FOR INVENTIONS;* and on the Protection of Designs and Trade Marks. By F. W. CAMPIN, Barrister-at-Law. 2s.

MISCELLANEOUS VOLUMES.

36. *A DICTIONARY OF TERMS used in ARCHITECTURE, BUILDING, ENGINEERING, MINING, METALLURGY, ARCHÆOLOGY, the FINE ARTS, &c.* With Explanatory Observations on various Subjects connected with Applied Science and Art. By JOHN WEALE. Fourth Edition, with numerous Additions. Edited by ROBERT HUNT, F.R.S., Keeper of Mining Records, Editor of Ure's "Dictionary of Arts, Manufactures, and Mines." Numerous Illustrations. 5s.

112. *MANUAL OF DOMESTIC MEDICINE.* Describing the Symptoms, Causes, and Treatment of the most common Medical and Surgical Affections. By R. GOODING, B.A., M.B.. The whole intended as a Family Guide in all Cases of Accident and Emergency. 2s.

112*. *MANAGEMENT OF HEALTH.* A Manual of Home and Personal Hygiene. Being Practical Hints on Air, Light, and Ventilation; Exercise, Diet, and Clothing; Rest, Sleep, and Mental Discipline; Bathing and Therapeutics. By the Rev. JAMES BAIRD, B.A. 1s.

113. *FIELD ARTILLERY ON SERVICE*, on the Use of. With especial Reference to that of an Army Corps. For Officers of all Arms. By TAUBERT, Captain, Prussian Artillery. Translated from the German by Lieut.-Col. HENRY HAMILTON MAXWELL, Bengal Artillery. 1s. 6d.

113*. *SWORDS, AND OTHER ARMS* used for Cutting and Thrusting, Memoir on. By Colonel MAREY. Translated from the French by Colonel H. H. MAXWELL. With Notes and Plates. 1s.

150. *LOGIC*, Pure and Applied. By S. H. EMMENS. Third Edition. 1s. 6d.

152. *PRACTICAL HINTS FOR INVESTING MONEY.* With an Explanation of the Mode of Transacting Business on the Stock Exchange. By FRANCIS PLAYFORD, Sworn Broker. 1s.

153. *SELECTIONS FROM LOCKE'S ESSAYS ON THE HUMAN UNDERSTANDING.* With Notes by S. H. EMMENS. 2s.

EDUCATIONAL AND CLASSICAL SERIES.

HISTORY.

1. **England, Outlines of the History of;** more especially with reference to the Origin and Progress of the English Constitution. A Text Book for Schools and Colleges. By WILLIAM DOUGLAS HAMILTON, F.S.A., of Her Majesty's Public Record Office. Fourth Edition, revised and brought down to 1872. Maps and Woodcuts. 5s.; cloth boards, 6s. Also in Five Parts, 1s. each.

5. **Greece, Outlines of the History of;** in connection with the Rise of the Arts and Civilization in Europe. By W. DOUGLAS HAMILTON, of University College, London, and EDWARD LEVIEN, M.A., of Balliol College, Oxford. 2s. 6d.; cloth boards, 3s. 6d.

7. **Rome, Outlines of the History of:** From the Earliest Period to the Christian Era and the Commencement of the Decline of the Empire. By EDWARD LEVIEN, of Balliol College, Oxford. Map, 2s. 6d.; cl. bds. 3s. 6d.

9. **Chronology of History, Art, Literature, and Progress,** from the Creation of the World to the Conclusion of the Franco-German War. The Continuation by W. D. HAMILTON, F.S.A., of Her Majesty's Record Office. 3s.; cloth boards, 3s. 6d.

50. **Dates and Events in English History,** for the use of Candidates in Public and Private Examinations. By the Rev. EDGAR RAND, B.A. 1s.

ENGLISH LANGUAGE AND MISCEL-LANEOUS.

11. **Grammar of the English Tongue,** Spoken and Written. With an Introduction to the Study of Comparative Philology. By HYDE CLARKE, D.C.L. Third Edition. 1s.

11*. **Philology:** Handbook of the Comparative Philology of English, Anglo-Saxon, Frisian, Flemish or Dutch, Low or Platt Dutch, High Dutch or German, Danish, Swedish, Icelandic, Latin, Italian, French, Spanish, and Portuguese Tongues. By HYDE CLARKE, D.C.L. 1s.

12. **Dictionary of the English Language,** as Spoken and Written. Containing above 100,000 Words. By HYDE CLARKE, D.C.L. 3s. 6d.; cloth boards, 4s. 6d.; complete with the GRAMMAR, cloth bds., 5s. 6d.

48. **Composition and Punctuation,** familiarly Explained for those who have neglected the Study of Grammar. By AUSTIN BRENAN. 16th Edition. 1s.

49. **Derivative Spelling-Book:** Giving the Origin of Every Word from the Greek, Latin, Saxon, German, Teutonic, Dutch, French, Spanish, and other Languages; with their present Acceptation and Pronunciation. By J. ROWBOTHAM, F.R.A.S. Improved Edition. 1s. 6d.

51. **The Art of Extempore Speaking:** Hints for the Pulpit, the Senate, and the Bar. By M. BAUTAIN, Vicar-General and Professor at the Sorbonne. Translated from the French. Fifth Edition, carefully corrected. 2s. 6d.

52. **Mining and Quarrying,** with the Sciences connected therewith. First Book of, for Schools. By J. H. COLLINS, F.G.S., Lecturer to the Miners' Association of Cornwall and Devon. 1s. 6d.

53. **Places and Facts in Political and Physical Geography,** for Candidates in Public and Private Examinations. By the Rev. EDGAR RAND, B.A. 1s.

54. **Analytical Chemistry,** Qualitative and Quantitative, a Course of. To which is prefixed, a Brief Treatise upon Modern Chemical Nomenclature and Notation. By WM. W. PINK, Practical Chemist, &c., and GEORGE E. WEBSTER, Lecturer on Metallurgy and the Applied Sciences, Nottingham. 2s.

THE SCHOOL MANAGERS' SERIES OF READING BOOKS,

Adapted to the Requirements of the New Code. Edited by the Rev. A. R. GRANT, Rector of Hitcham, and Honorary Canon of Ely; formerly H.M. Inspector of Schools.

	s.	d.					s.	d.
INTRODUCTORY PRIMER	0	3	THIRD STANDARD	.	.	.	1	0
FIRST STANDARD	0	6	FOURTH ,,	.	.	.	1	2
SECOND ,,	0	10	FIFTH ,,	.	.	.	1	6

„ *A Sixth Standard in Preparation.*

LESSONS FROM THE BIBLE. Part I. Old Testament. 1s.
LESSONS FROM THE BIBLE. Part II. New Testament, to which is added THE GEOGRAPHY OF THE BIBLE, for very young Children. By Rev. C. THORNTON FORSTER. 1s. 2d. *„* Or the Two Parts in One Volume. 2s.

FRENCh.

24. **French Grammar.** With Complete and Concise Rules on the Genders of French Nouns. By G. L. STRAUSS, Ph.D. 1s.

25. **French-English Dictionary.** Comprising a large number of New Terms used in Engineering, Mining, on Railways, &c. By ALFRED ELWES. 1s. 6d.

French, *continued.*

26. **English-French Dictionary.** By ALFRED ELWES. 2s.
25,26. **French Dictionary** (as above). Complete, in One Vol., 3s.; cloth boards, 3s. 6d. *⁎* Or with the GRAMMAR, cloth boards, 4s. 6d.
47. **French and English Phrase Book :** Containing Introductory Lessons, with Translations, for the convenience of Students; several Vocabularies of Words, a Collection of suitable Phrases, and Easy Familiar Dialogues. 1s.

GERMAN.

39. **German Grammar.** Adapted for English Students, from Heyse's Theoretical and Practical Grammar, by Dr. G. L. STRAUSS. 1s.
40. **German Reader :** A Series of Extracts, carefully culled from the most approved Authors of Germany; with Notes, Philological and Explanatory. By G. L. STRAUSS, Ph.D. 1s.
41. **German Triglot Dictionary.** By NICHOLAS ESTERHAZY, S. A. HAMILTON. Part I. English-German-French. 1s.
42. **German Triglot Dictionary.** Part II. German-French-English. 1s.
43. **German Triglot Dictionary.** Part III. French-German-English. 1s.
41-43. **German Triglot Dictionary** (as above), in One Vol., 3s.; cloth boards, 4s. *⁎* Or with the GERMAN GRAMMAR, cloth boards, 5s.

ITALIAN.

27. **Italian Grammar,** arranged in Twenty Lessons, with a Course of Exercises. By ALFRED ELWES. 1s.
28. **Italian Triglot Dictionary,** wherein the Genders of all the Italian and French Nouns are carefully noted down. By ALFRED ELWES. Vol. 1. Italian-English-French. 2s.
30. **Italian Triglot Dictionary.** By A. ELWES. Vol. 2. English-French-Italian. 2s.
32. **Italian Triglot Dictionary.** By ALFRED ELWES. Vol. 3. French-Italian-English. 2s.
28,30, **Italian Triglot Dictionary** (as above). In One Vol., 6s.; 32. cloth boards, 7s. 6d. *⁎* Or with the ITALIAN GRAMMAR, cloth bds., 8s. 6d.

SPANISH.

34. **Spanish Grammar,** in a Simple and Practical Form. With a Course of Exercises. By ALFRED ELWES. 1s.
35. **Spanish-English and English-Spanish Dictionary.** Including a large number of Technical Terms used in Mining, Engineering, &c., with the proper Accents and the Gender of every Noun. By ALFRED ELWES. 4s.; cloth boards, 5s. *⁎* Or with the GRAMMAR, cloth boards, 6s.

HEBREW.

46*. **Hebrew Grammar.** By Dr. BRESSLAU. 1s.
44. **Hebrew and English Dictionary,** Biblical and Rabbinical; containing the Hebrew and Chaldee Roots of the Old Testament Post-Rabbinical Writings. By Dr. BRESSLAU. 6s. *⁎* Or with the GRAMMAR, 7s.
46. **English and Hebrew Dictionary.** By Dr. BRESSLAU. 3s.
44,46. **Hebrew Dictionary** (as above), in Two Vols., complete, with 46*. the GRAMMAR, cloth boards. 12s.

LATIN.

19. Latin Grammar. Containing the Inflections and Elementary Principles of Translation and Construction. By the Rev. THOMAS GOODWIN, M.A., Head Master of the Greenwich Proprietary School. 1s.

20. Latin-English Dictionary. Compiled from the best Authorities. By the Rev. THOMAS GOODWIN, M.A. 2s.

22. English-Latin Dictionary; together with an Appendix of French and Italian Words which have their origin from the Latin. By the Rev. THOMAS GOODWIN, M.A. 1s. 6d.

20,22. Latin Dictionary (as above). Complete in One Vol., 3s. 6d.; cloth boards, 4s. 6d. *⁎* Or with the GRAMMAR, cloth boards, 5s. 6d.

LATIN CLASSICS. With Explanatory Notes in English.

1. Latin Delectus. Containing Extracts from Classical Authors, with Genealogical Vocabularies and Explanatory Notes, by HENRY YOUNG, lately Second Master of the Royal Grammar School, Guildford. 1s.

2. Cæsaris Commentarii de Bello Gallico. Notes, and a Geographical Register for the Use of Schools, by H. YOUNG. 2s.

12. Ciceronis Oratio pro Sexto Roscio Amerino. Edited, with an Introduction, Analysis, and Notes Explanatory and Critical, by the Rev. JAMES DAVIES, M.A. 1s.

14. Ciceronis Cato Major, Lælius, Brutus, sive de Senectute, de Amicitia, de Claris Oratoribus Dialogi. With Notes by W. BROWNRIGG SMITH, M.A., F.R.G.S. 2s

3. Cornelius Nepos. With Notes. Intended for the Use of Schools. By H. YOUNG. 1s.

6. Horace; Odes, Epode, and Carmen Sæculare. Notes by H. YOUNG. 1s. 6d.

7. Horace; Satires, Epistles, and Ars Poëtica. Notes by W. BROWNRIGG SMITH, M.A., F.R.G.S. 1s. 6d.

21. Juvenalis Satiræ. With Prolegomena and Notes by T. H. S. ESCOTT, B.A., Lecturer on Logic at King's College, London. 1s. 6d.

16. Livy: History of Rome. Notes by H. YOUNG and W. B. SMITH, M.A. Part 1. Books i., ii., 1s. 6d.

16⁎. ———— Part 2. Books iii., iv., v., 1s. 6d.

17. ———— Part 3. Books xxi. xxii., 1s. 6d.

8. Sallustii Crispi Catalina et Bellum Jugurthinum. Notes Critical and Explanatory, by W. M. DONNE, B.A., Trinity College, Cambridge. 1s. 6d.

10. Terentii Adelphi Hecyra, Phormio. Edited, with Notes, Critical and Explanatory, by the Rev. JAMES DAVIES, M.A. 2s.

9. Terentii Andria et Heautontimorumenos. With Notes, Critical and Explanatory, by the Rev. JAMES DAVIES, M.A. 1s. 6d.

11. Terentii Eunuchus, Comœdia. Edited, with Notes, by the Rev. JAMES DAVIES, M.A. 1s. 6d. Or the Adelphi, Andria, and Eunuchus, 3 vols. in 1, cloth boards, 6s.

4. Virgilii Maronis Bucolica et Georgica. With Notes on the Bucolics by W. RUSHTON, M.A., and on the Georgics by H. YOUNG. 1s. 6d.

5. Virgilii Maronis Æneis. Notes, Critical and Explanatory, by H. YOUNG. 2s.

19. Latin Verse Selections, from Catullus, Tibullus, Propertius, and Ovid. Notes by W. B. DONNE, M.A., Trinity College, Cambridge. s.

20. Latin Prose Selections, from Varro, Columella, Vitruvius, Seneca, Quintilian, Florus, Velleius Paterculus, Valerius Maximus Suetonius, Apuleius, &c. Notes by W. B. DONNE, M.A. 2s.

GREEK.

14. **Greek Grammar**, in accordance with the Principles and Philological Researches of the most eminent Scholars of our own day. By HANS CLAUDE HAMILTON. 1s.

15,17. **Greek Lexicon.** Containing all the Words in General Use, with their Significations, Inflections, and Doubtful Quantities. By HENRY R. HAMILTON. Vol. 1. Greek-English, 2s. ; Vol. 2. English-Greek, 2s. Or the Two Vols. in One, 4s. : cloth boards, 5s.

14,15. **Greek Lexicon** (as above). Complete, with the GRAMMAR, in
17. One Vol., cloth boards, 6s.

GREEK CLASSICS. With Explanatory Notes in English.

1. **Greek Delectus.** Containing Extracts from Classical Authors, with Genealogical Vocabularies and Explanatory Notes, by H. YOUNG. New Edition, with an improved and enlarged Supplementary Vocabulary, by JOHN HUTCHISON, M.A., of the High School, Glasgow. 1s.

30. **Æschylus: Prometheus Vinctus: The Prometheus Bound.** From the Text of DINDORF. Edited, with English Notes, Critical and Explanatory, by the Rev. JAMES DAVIES, M.A. 1s.

32. **Æschylus: Septem Contra Thebes: The Seven against Thebes.** From the Text of DINDORF. Edited, with English Notes, Critical and Explanatory, by the Rev. JAMES DAVIES, M A. 1s.

40. **Aristophanes: Acharnians.** Chiefly from the Text of C. H. WEISE. With Notes, by C. S. T. TOWNSHEND, M.A. 1s. 6d.

26. **Euripides: Alcestis.** Chiefly from the Text of DINDORF. With Notes, Critical and Explanatory, by JOHN MILNER, B.A. 1s.

23. **Euripides: Hecuba and Medea.** Chiefly from the Text of DINDORF. With Notes, Critical and Explanatory, by W. BROWNRIGG SMITH, M.A., F.R.G.S. 1s. 6d.

14-17. **Herodotus, The History of,** chiefly after the Text of GAISFORD. With Preliminary Observations and Appendices, and Notes, Critical and Explanatory, by T. H. L. LEARY, M.A., D.C.L.
Part 1.   Books i., ii. (The Clio and Euterpe), 1s. 6d.
Part 2.   Books iii., iv. (The Thalia and Melpomene), 1s. 6d.
Part 3.   Books v.-vii. (The Terpsichore, Erato, and Polymnia) 1s. 6d.
Part 4.   Books viii., iv. (The Urania and Calliope) and Index, 1s. 6d.

5-12. **Homer, The Works of.** According to the Text of BAEUMLEIN. With Notes, Critical and Explanatory, drawn from the best and latest Authorities, with Preliminary Observations and Appendices, by T. H. L. LEARY, M.A., D.C.L.

THE ILIAD :   Part 1. Books i. to vi., 1s.6d. | Part 3. Books xiii. to xviii., 1s. 6d.
              Part 2. Books vii. to xii., 1s.6d. | Part 4. Books xix. to xxiv., 1s. 6d.
THE ODYSSEY: Part 1. Books i. to vi., 1s. 6d. | Part 3. Books xiii. to xviii., 1s. 6d.
              Part 2. Books vii. to xii., 1s. 6d. | Part 4. Books xix. to xxiv., and Hymns, 2s.

4. **Lucian's Select Dialogues.** The Text carefully revised, with Grammatical and Explanatory Notes, by H. YOUNG. 1s.

13. **Plato's Dialogues: The Apology of Socrates, the Crito, and the Phædo.** From the Text of C. F. HERMANN. Edited with Notes, Critical and Explanatory, by the Rev. JAMES DAVIES, M.A. 2s.

18. **Sophocles: Œdipus Tyrannus.** Notes by H. YOUNG. 1s.

20. **Sophocles: Antigone.** From the Text of DINDORF. Notes, Critical and Explanatory, by the Rev. JOHN MILNER, B.A. 2s.

41. **Thucydides: History of the Peloponnesian War.** Notes by H. YOUNG. Book 1. 1s.

2, 3. **Xenophon's Anabasis; or, The Retreat of the Ten Thousand.** Notes and a Geographical Register, by H. YOUNG. Part 1. Books i. to iii., 1s. Part 2. Books iv. to vii., 1s.

42. **Xenophon's Panegyric on Agesilaus.** Notes and Introduction by LL. F. W. JEWITT. 1s. 6d.

LONDON, *May*, 1875.

A Catalogue of Books

INCLUDING MANY

NEW & STANDARD WORKS

IN

ENGINEERING, ARCHITECTURE, AGRICULTURE, MATHEMATICS, MECHANICS, SCIENCE, &c. &c.

PUBLISHED BY

LOCKWOOD & CO.,

7, STATIONERS'-HALL COURT, LUDGATE HILL, E.C.

ENGINEERING, SURVEYING, &c.

—✦—

Humber's New Work on Water-Supply.

A COMPREHENSIVE TREATISE on the WATER-SUPPLY of CITIES and TOWNS. By WILLIAM HUMBER, Assoc. Inst. C.E., and M. Inst. M.E. Author of "Cast and Wrought Iron Bridge Construction," &c. &c. This work, it is expected, will contain about 50 Double Plates, and upwards of 300 pages of Text. Imp. 4to, half bound in morocco. [*In the press.*

** *In accumulating information for this volume, the Author has been very liberally assisted by several professional friends, who have made this department of engineering their special study. He has thus been in a position to prepare a work which, within the limits of a single volume, will supply the reader with the most complete and reliable information upon all subjects, theoretical and practical, connected with water supply. Through the kindness of Messrs. Anderson, Bateman, Hawksley, Homersham, Baldwin Latham, Lawson, Milne, Quick, Rawlinson, Simpson, and others, several works, constructed and in course of construction, from the designs of these gentlemen, will be fully illustrated and described.*

AMONGST OTHER IMPORTANT SUBJECTS THE FOLLOWING WILL BE TREATED IN THE TEXT :—

Historical Sketch of the means that have been proposed and adopted for the Supply of Water.—Water and the Foreign Matter usually associated with it.—Rainfall and Evaporation.—Springs and Subterranean Lakes.—Hydraulics.—The Selection of Sites for Water Works.—Wells.—Reservoirs.—Filtration and Filter Beds.—Reservoir and Filter Bed Appendages.—Pumps and Appendages.—Pumping Machinery.—Culverts and Conduits, Aqueducts, Syphons, &c.—Distribution of Water.—Water Meters and general House Fittings.—Cost of Works for the Supply of Water.—Constant and Intermittent Supply.—Suggestions for preparing Plans, &c. &c., together with a Description of the numerous Works illustrated, viz :—Aberdeen, Bideford, Cockermouth, Dublin, Glasgow, Loch Katrine, Liverpool, Manchester, Rotherham, Sunderland, and several others; with copies of the Contract, Drawings and Specification in each case.

Humber's Modern Engineering.   First Series.

A RECORD of the PROGRESS of MODERN ENGINEER-ING, 1863. Comprising Civil, Mechanical, Marine, Hydraulic, Railway, Bridge, and other Engineering Works, &c. By WILLIAM HUMBER, Assoc. Inst. C.E., &c. Imp. 4to, with 36 Double Plates, drawn to a large scale, and Photographic Portrait of John Hawkshaw, C.E., F.R.S., &c. Price 3*l.* 3*s.* half morocco.

List of the Plates.

NAME AND DESCRIPTION.	PLATES.	NAME OF ENGINEER.
Victoria Station and Roof—L. B. & S. C. Rail.	1 to 8	Mr. R. Jacomb Hood, C.E.
Southport Pier	9 and 10	Mr. James Brunlees, C.E.
Victoria Station and Roof—L. C. & D. & G.W. Railways	11 to 15A	Mr. John Fowler, C.E.
Roof of Cremorne Music Hall	16	Mr. William Humber, C.E.
Bridge over the G. N. Railway	17	Mr. Joseph Cubitt, C.E.
Roof of Station—Dutch Rhenish Railway	18 and 19	Mr. Euschedi, C.E.
Bridge over the Thames—West London Extension Railway	20 to 24	Mr. William Baker, C.E.
Armour Plates	25	Mr. James Chalmers, C.E.
Suspension Bridge, Thames	26 to 29	Mr. Peter W. Barlow, C.E.
The Allen Engine	30	Mr. G. T. Porter, M.E.
Suspension Bridge, Avon	31 to 33	Mr. John Hawkshaw, C.E. and W. H. Barlow, C.E.
Underground Railway	34 to 36	Mr. John Fowler, C.E.

With copious Descriptive Letterpress, Specifications, &c.

" Handsomely lithographed and printed. It will find favour with many who desire to preserve in a permanent form copies of the plans and specifications prepared for the guidance of the contractors for many important engineering works."—*Engineer.*

Humber's Modern Engineering.   Second Series.

A RECORD of the PROGRESS of MODERN ENGINEER-ING, 1864; with Photographic Portrait of Robert Stephenson, C.E., M.P., F.R.S., &c. Price 3*l.* 3*s.* half morocco.

List of the Plates.

NAME AND DESCRIPTION.	PLATES.	NAME OF ENGINEER.
Birkenhead Docks, Low Water Basin	1 to 15	Mr. G. F. Lyster, C.E.
Charing Cross Station Roof—C. C. Railway.	16 to 18	Mr. Hawkshaw, C.E.
Digswell Viaduct—Great Northern Railway.	19	Mr. J. Cubitt, C.E.
Robbery Wood Viaduct—Great N. Railway.	20	Mr. J. Cubitt, C.E.
Iron Permanent Way	20a	
Clydach Viaduct—Merthyr, Tredegar, and Abergavenny Railway	21	Mr. Gardner, C.E.
Ebbw Viaduct ditto ditto ditto	22	Mr. Gardner, C.E.
College Wood Viaduct—Cornwall Railway	23	Mr. Brunel.
Dublin Winter Palace Roof	24 to 26	Messrs. Ordish & Le Feuvre.
Bridge over the Thames—L. C. & D. Railw.	27 to 32	Mr. J. Cubitt, C.E.
Albert Harbour, Greenock	33 to 36	Messrs. Bell & Miller.

With copious Descriptive Letterpress, Specifications, &c.

" A *resumé* of all the more interesting and important works lately completed in Great Britain ; and containing, as it does, carefully executed drawings, with full working details, it will be found a valuable accessory to the profession at large."—*Engineer.*

. "Mr. Humber has done the profession good and true service, by the fine collection of examples he has here brought before the profession and the public."—*Practical Mechanics' Journal.*

Humber's Modern Engineering. Third Series.

A RECORD of the PROGRESS of MODERN ENGINEER-
ING, 1865. Imp. 4to, with 40 Double Plates, drawn to a large
scale, and Photographic Portrait of J. R. M'Clean, Esq., late President of the Institution of Civil Engineers.   Price 3*l.* 3*s.* half
morocco.

List of Plates and Diagrams.

MAIN DRAINAGE, METROPOLIS.

NORTH SIDE.

Map showing Interception of Sewers.
Middle Level Sewer. Sewer under Re-
gent's Canal.
Middle Level Sewer. Junction with Fleet
Ditch.
Outfall Sewer. Bridge over River Lea.
Elevation.
Outfall Sewer. Bridge over River Lea.
Details.
Outfall Sewer. Bridge over River Lea.
Details.
Outfall Sewer. Bridge over Marsh Lane,
North Woolwich Railway, and Bow and
Barking Railway Junction.
Outfall Sewer. Bridge over Bow and
Barking Railway. Elevation.
Outfall Sewer. Bridge over Bow and
Barking Railway. Details.
Outfall Sewer. Bridge over Bow and
Barking Railway. Details.
Outfall Sewer. Bridge over East London
Waterworks' Feeder. Elevation.
Outfall Sewer. Bridge over East London
Waterworks' Feeder. Details.
Outfall Sewer. Reservoir. Plan.
Outfall Sewer. Reservoir. Section.
Outfall Sewer. Tumbling Bay and Outlet.
Outfall Sewer. Penstocks.

SOUTH SIDE.

Outfall Sewer. Bermondsey Branch.
Outfall Sewer. Bermondsey Branch.
Outfall Sewer. Reservoir and Outlet.
Plan.

MAIN DRAINAGE, METROPOLIS,
continued—

Outfall Sewer. Reservoir and Outlet.
Details.
Outfall Sewer. Reservoir and Outlet.
Details.
Outfall Sewer. Reservoir and Outlet.
Details.
Outfall Sewer. Filth Hoist.
Sections of Sewers (North and South
Sides).

THAMES EMBANKMENT.

Section of River Wall.
Steam-boat Pier, Westminster. Elevation.
Steam-boat Pier, Westminster. Details.
Landing Stairs between Charing Cross
and Waterloo Bridges.
York Gate. Front Elevation.
York Gate. Side Elevation and Details.
Overflow and Outlet at Savoy Street Sewer.
Details.
Overflow and Outlet at Savoy Street Sewer.
Penstock.
Overflow and Outlet at Savoy Street Sewer.
Penstock.
Steam-boat Pier, Waterloo Bridge. Eleva-
tion.
Steam-boat Pier, Waterloo Bridge. De-
tails.
Steam-boat Pier, Waterloo Bridge. De-
tails.
Junction of Sewers. Plans and Sections.
Gullies. Plans and Sections.
Rolling Stock.
Granite and Iron Forts.

With copious Descriptive Letterpress, Specifications, &c.

Opinions of the Press.

" Mr. Humber's works—especially his annual ' Record,' with which so many of our
readers are now familiar—fill a void occupied by no other branch of literature. . . . .
The drawings have a constantly increasing value, and whoever desires to possess clear
representations of the two great works carried out by our Metropolitan Board will
obtain Mr. Humber's last volume."—*Engineering.*

" No engineer, architect, or contractor should fail to preserve these records of works
which, for magnitude, have not their parallel in the present day, no student in the
profession but should carefully study the details of these great works, which he may be
one day called upon to imitate."—*Mechanics' Magazine.*

" A work highly creditable to the industry of its author. . . . . The volume is quite
an encyclopædia for the study of the student who desires to master the subject of
municipal drainage on its scale of greatest development."—*Practical Mechanics
Journal.*   •

Humber's Modern Engineering. Fourth Series.

A RECORD of the PROGRESS of MODERN ENGINEER-
ING, 1866. Imp. 4to, with 36 Double Plates, drawn to a large
scale, and Photographic Portrait of John Fowler, Esq., President
of the Institution of Civil Engineers. Price 3*l*. 3*s*. half-morocco.

List of the Plates and Diagrams.

NAME AND DESCRIPTION.	PLATES.	NAME OF ENGINEER.
Abbey Mills Pumping Station, Main Drainage, Metropolis	1 to 4	Mr. Bazalgette, C.E.
Barrow Docks	5 to 9	Messrs. M'Clean & Stillman, [C. E.
Manquis Viaduct, Santiago and Valparaiso Railway	10, 11	Mr. W. Loyd, C.E.
Adams' Locomotive, St. Helen's Canal Railw.	12, 13	Mr. H. Cross, C.E.
Cannon Street Station Roof, Charing Cross Railway	14 to 16	Mr. J. Hawkshaw, C.E.
Road Bridge over the River Moka	17, 18	Mr. H. Wakefield, C.E.
Telegraphic Apparatus for Mesopotamia	19	Mr. Siemens, C.E.
Viaduct over the River Wye, Midland Railw.	20 to 22	Mr. W. H. Barlow, C.E.
St. Germans Viaduct, Cornwall Railway	23, 24	Mr. Brunel, C.E.
Wrought-Iron Cylinder for Diving Bell	25	Mr. J. Coode, C.E.
Millwall Docks	26 to 31	Messrs. J. Fowler, C.E., and William Wilson, C.E.
Milroy's Patent Excavator	32	Mr. Milroy, C.E.
Metropolitan District Railway	33 to 38	Mr. J. Fowler, Engineer-in-Chief, and Mr. T. M. Johnson, C.E.
Harbours, Ports, and Breakwaters	A to C	

The Letterpress comprises—

A concluding article on Harbours, Ports, and Breakwaters, with
Illustrations and detailed descriptions of the Breakwater at Cher-
bourg, and other important modern works; an article on the
Telegraph Lines of Mesopotamia; a full description of the Wrought-
iron Diving Cylinder for Ceylon, the circumstances under which it
was used, and the means of working it; full description of the
Millwall Docks; &c., &c., &c.

Opinions of the Press.

"Mr. Humber's 'Record of Modern Engineering' is a work of peculiar value, as
well to those who design as to those who study the art of engineering construction.
It embodies a vast amount of practical information in the form of full descriptions and
working drawings of all the most recent and noteworthy engineering works. The
plates are excellently lithographed, and the present volume of the 'Record' is not a
whit behind its predecessors."—*Mechanics' Magazine.*

"We gladly welcome another year's issue of this valuable publication from the able
pen of Mr. Humber. The accuracy and general excellence of this work are well
known, while its usefulness in giving the measurements and details of some of the
latest examples of engineering, as carried out by the most eminent men in the profession, cannot be too highly prized."—*Artizan.*

"The volume forms a valuable companion to those which have preceded it, and
cannot fail to prove a most important addition to every engineering library."—*Mining
Journal.*

"No one of Mr. Humber's volumes was bad: all were worth their cost, from the
mass of plates from well-executed drawings which they contained. In this respect,
perhaps, this last volume is the most valuable that the author has produced."—*Practical Mechanics' Journal.*

Humber's Great Work on Bridge Construction.

A COMPLETE and PRACTICAL TREATISE on CAST and WROUGHT-IRON BRIDGE CONSTRUCTION, including Iron Foundations. In Three Parts—Theoretical, Practical, and Descriptive. By WILLIAM HUMBER, Assoc. Inst. C.E., and M. Inst. M.E. Third Edition, revised and much improved, with 115 Double Plates (20 of which now first appear in this edition), and numerous additions to the Text. In 2 vols. imp. 4to., price 6*l.* 16*s.* 6*d.* half bound in morocco.

"A very valuable contribution to the standard literature of civil engineering. In addition to elevations, plans, and sections, large scale details are given, which very much enhance the instructive worth of these illustrations. No engineer would be willingly be without so valuable a fund of information."—*Civil Engineer and Architect's Journal.*

"The First or Theoretical Part contains mathematical investigations of the principles involved in the various forms now adopted in bridge construction. These investigations are exceedingly complete, having evidently been very carefully considered and worked out to the utmost extent that can be desired by the practical man. The tables are of a very useful character, containing the results of the most recent experiments, and amongst them are some valuable tables of the weight and cost of cast and wrought-iron structures actually erected. The volume of text is amply illustrated by numerous woodcuts, plates, and diagrams : and the plates in the second volume do great credit to both draughtsmen and engravers. In conclusion, we have great pleasure in cordially recommending this work to our readers."—*Artizan.*

"Mr. Humber's stately volumes lately issued—in which the most important bridges erected during the last five years, under the direction of the late Mr. Brunel, Sir W. Cubitt, Mr. Hawkshaw, Mr. Page, Mr. Fowler, Mr. Hemans, and others among our most eminent engineers, are drawn and specified in great detail."—*Engineer.*

Weale's Engineers' Pocket-Book.

THE ENGINEERS', ARCHITECTS', and CONTRACTORS' POCKET-BOOK (LOCKWOOD & CO.'S; formerly WEALE'S). Published Annually. In roan tuck, gilt edges, with 10 Copper-Plates and numerous Woodcuts. Price 6*s.*

"A vast amount of really valuable matter condensed into the small dimensions of a book which is, in reality, what it professes to be—a pocket-book. . . . . We cordially recommend the book to the notice of the managers of coal and other mines ; to them it will prove a handy book of reference on a variety of subjects more or less intimately connected with their profession."—*Colliery Guardian.*

"Every branch of engineering is treated of, and facts, figures, and data of every kind abound."—*Mechanics' Mag.*

"It contains a large amount of information peculiarly valuable to those for whose use it is compiled. We cordially commend it to the engineering and architectural professions generally."—*Mining Journal.*

Iron Bridges, Girders, Roofs, &c.

A TREATISE on the APPLICATION of IRON to the CONSTRUCTION of BRIDGES, GIRDERS, ROOFS, and OTHER WORKS ; showing the Principles upon which such Structures are Designed, and their Practical Application. Especially arranged for the use of Students and Practical Mechanics, all Mathematical Formulæ and Symbols being excluded. By FRANCIS CAMPIN, C.E. With numerous Diagrams. 12mo., cloth boards, 3*s.*

"For numbers of young engineers the book is just the cheap, handy, first guide they want."—*Middlesborough Weekly News.*

"Invaluable to those who have not been educated in mathematics."—*Colliery Guardian.*

"Remarkably accurate and well written."—*Artizan.*

Barlow on the Strength of Materials, enlarged.

A TREATISE ON THE STRENGTH OF MATERIALS, with Rules for application in Architecture, the Construction of Suspension Bridges, Railways, &c. ; and an Appendix on the Power of Locomotive Engines, and the effect of Inclined Planes and Gradients. By PETER BARLOW, F.R.S. A New Edition, revised by his Sons, P. W. BARLOW, F.R.S., and W. H. BARLOW, F.R.S., to which are added Experiments by HODGKINSON, FAIR-BAIRN, and KIRKALDY ; an Essay (with Illustrations) on the effect produced by passing Weights over Elastic Bars, by the Rev. ROBERT WILLIS, M.A., F.R.S. And Formulæ for Calculating Girders, &c. The whole arranged and edited by W. HUMBER, Assoc. Inst. C.E., Author of " A Complete and Practical Treatise on Cast and Wrought-Iron Bridge Construction," &c. &c. Demy 8vo, 400 pp., with 19 large Plates, and numerous woodcuts, price 18s. cloth.

" Although issued as the sixth edition, the volume under consideration is worthy of being regarded, for all practical purposes, as an entirely new work . . . the book is undoubtedly worthy of the highest commendation."—*Mining Journal.*

"An increased value has been given to this very valuable work by the addition of a large amount of information, which cannot prove otherwise than highly useful to those who require to consult it. . . . . The arrangement and editing of this mass of information has been undertaken by Mr. Humber, who has most ably fulfilled a task requiring special care and ability to render it a success."—*Mechanics' Magazine.*

"The best book on the subject which has yet appeared. . . . . We know of no work that so completely fulfils its mission."—*English Mechanic.*

"There is not a pupil in an engineering school, an apprentice in an engineer's or architect's office, or a competent clerk of works, who will not recognise in the scientific volume newly given to circulation, an old and valued friend."—*Building News.*

"The standard treatise upon this particular subject."—*Engineer.*

Strains, Formulæ & Diagrams for Calculation of.

A HANDY BOOK for the CALCULATION of STRAINS in GIRDERS and SIMILAR STRUCTURES, and their STRENGTH ; consisting of Formulæ and Corresponding Diagrams, with numerous Details for Practical Application, &c. By WILLIAM HUMBER, Assoc. Inst. C.E., &c. Fcap. 8vo, with nearly 100 Woodcuts and 3 Plates, price 7s. 6d. cloth.

"The arrangement of the matter in this little volume is as convenient as it well could be. . . . . The system of employing diagrams as a substitute for complex computations is one justly coming into great favour, and in that respect Mr. Humber's volume is fully up to the times."—*Engineering.*

"The formulæ are neatly expressed, and the diagrams good."—*Athenæum.*

"We heartily commend this really *handy* book to our engineer and architect readers."—*English Mechanic.*

Mechanical Engineering.

A PRACTICAL TREATISE ON MECHANICAL ENGI-NEERING : comprising Metallurgy, Moulding, Casting, Forging, Tools, Workshop Machinery, Mechanical Manipulation, Manufacture of the Steam Engine, &c. &c. With an Appendix on the Analysis of Iron and Iron Ore, and Glossary of Terms. By FRANCIS CAMPIN, C.E. Illustrated with 91 Woodcuts and 28 Plates of Slotting, Shaping, Drilling, Punching, Shearing, and Riveting Machines—Blast, Refining, and Reverberatory Furnaces—Steam Engines, Governors, Boilers, Locomotives, &c. 8vo, cloth, 12s.

Strains.

THE STRAINS ON STRUCTURES OF IRONWORK; with Practical Remarks on Iron Construction. By F. W. SHIELDS, M. Inst. C. E. Second Edition, with 5 plates. Royal 8vo, 5*s.* cloth.

CONTENTS.—Introductory Remarks; Beams Loaded at Centre; Beams Loaded at unequal distances between supports; Beams uniformly Loaded; Girders with triangular bracing Loaded at centre; Ditto, Loaded at unequal distances between supports; Ditto, uniformly Loaded; Calculation of the Strains on Girders with triangular Basings; Cantilevers; Continuous Girders; Lattice Girders; Girders with Vertical Struts and Diagonal Ties; Calculation of the Strains on Ditto; Bow and String Girders; Girders of a form not belonging to any regular figure; Plate Girders; Apportionments of Material to Strain; Comparison of different Girders; Proportion of Length to Depth of Girders; Character of the Work; Iron Roofs.

Construction of Iron Beams, Pillars, &c.

IRON AND HEAT, Exhibiting the Principles concerned in the Construction of Iron Beams, Pillars, and Bridge Girders, and the Action of Heat in the Smelting Furnace. By JAMES ARMOUR, C.E. Woodcuts, 12mo, cloth boards, 3*s.* 6*d.* ; cloth limp, 2*s.* 6*d.*

" A very useful and thoroughly practical little volume, in every way deserving of circulation amongst working men."—*Mining Journal.*
" No ironworker who wishes to acquaint himself with the principles of his own trade can afford to be without it."—*South Durham Mercury.*

Power in Motion.

POWER IN MOTION : Horse Power, Motion, Toothed Wheel Gearing, Long and Short Driving Bands, Angular Forces, &c. By JAMES ARMOUR, C.E. With 73 Diagrams. 12mo, cloth boards, 3*s.* 6*d.*   [*Recently published.*

" Numerous illustrations enable the author to convey his meaning as explicitly as it is perhaps possible to be conveyed. The value of the theoretic and practical knowledge imparted cannot well be over estimated."—*Newcastle Weekly Chronicle.*

Metallurgy of Iron.

A TREATISE ON THE METALLURGY OF IRON : containing Outlines of the History of Iron Manufacture, Methods of Assay, and Analyses of Iron Ores, Processes of Manufacture of Iron and Steel, &c. By H. BAUERMAN, F.G.S., Associate of the Royal School of Mines. With numerous Illustrations. Fourth Edition, revised and much enlarged. 12mo., cloth boards, 5*s.* 6*d.*
[*Just published.*

" Carefully written, it has the merit of brevity and conciseness, as to less important points, while all material matters are very fully and thoroughly entered into."—*Standard.*

Trigonometrical Surveying.

AN OUTLINE OF THE METHOD OF CONDUCTING A TRIGONOMETRICAL SURVEY, for the Formation of Geographical and Topographical Maps and Plans, Military Reconnaissance, Levelling, &c., with the most useful Problems in Geodesy and Practical Astronomy, and Formulæ and Tables for Facilitating their Calculation. By LIEUT-GENERAL FROME, R.E., late Inspector-General of Fortifications, &c. Fourth Edition, Enlarged, thoroughly Revised, and partly Re-written. By CAPTAIN CHARLES WARREN, R.E., F.G.S. With 19 Plates and 115 Woodcuts, royal 8vo, price 16*s.* cloth.

Hydraulics.

HYDRAULIC TABLES, CO-EFFICIENTS, and FORMULÆ for finding the Discharge of Water from Orifices, Notches, Weirs, Pipes, and Rivers. With New Formulæ, Tables, and General Information on Rain-fall, Catchment-Basins, Drainage, Sewerage, Water Supply for Towns and Mill Power. By JOHN NEVILLE, Civil Engineer, M.R.I.A. Third Edition, carefully revised, with considerable Additions. Numerous Illustrations. Crown 8vo, 14s. cloth. [*Now ready.*

Drawing for Engineers, &c.

THE WORKMAN'S MANUAL OF ENGINEERING DRAWING. By JOHN MAXTON, Instructor in Engineering Drawing, South Kensington. Second Edition. carefully revised. With upwards of 300 Plates and Diagrams. 12mo, cloth, strongly bound, 4s. 6d.

"Even accomplished draughtsmen will find in it much that will be of use to them. A copy of it should be kept for reference in every drawing office."—*Engineering.*
"An indispensable book for teachers of engineering drawing." — *Mechanics' Magazine.*

Levelling.

A TREATISE on the PRINCIPLES and PRACTICE of LEVELLING; showing its Application to Purposes of Railway and Civil Engineering, in the Construction of Roads; with Mr. TELFORD'S Rules for the same. By FREDERICK W. SIMMS, F.G.S., M. Inst. C.E. Fifth Edition, very carefully revised, with the addition of Mr. LAW's Practical Examples for Setting out Railway Curves, and Mr. TRAUTWINE's Field Practice of Laying out Circular Curves. With 7 Plates and numerous Woodcuts. 8vo, 8s. 6d. cloth.   *** TRAUTWINE on Curves, separate, price 5s.

"One of the most important text-books for the general surveyor, and there is scarcely a question connected with levelling for which a solution would be sought but that would be satisfactorily answered by consulting the volume."—*Mining Journal.*
"The text-book on levelling in most of our engineering schools and colleges."—*Engineer.*
"The publishers have rendered a substantial service to the profession, especially to the younger members, by bringing out the present edition of Mr. Simms's useful work."—*Engineering.*

Earthwork.

EARTHWORK TABLES, showing the Contents in Cubic Yards of Embankments, Cuttings, &c., of Heights or Depths up to an average of 80 feet. By JOSEPH BROADBENT, C.E., and FRANCIS CAMPIN, C.E. Cr. 8vo. oblong, 5s. cloth. [*Just Published.*

"Creditable to both the authors and the publishers. . . . The way in which accuracy is attained, by a simple division of each cross section into three elements, two of which are constant and one variable, is ingenious."—*Athenæum.*
"Likely to be of considerable service to engineers."—*Building News.*
"Practical illustrations of the tabulated quantities are given, which make the working of the tables easy to the most inexperienced. The work is excellently got up, and the type is remarkably clear; and contractors, builders, and engineers should not be without it."—*Builders' Weekly Reporter.*
"Two additions, one subtraction, and four multiplications, with the use of the tables, suffice to determine the quantity with considerable accuracy in any piece of earthwork; and, as the tables are of pocket-book size and very legibly printed, they cannot fail to come into general use."—*Mining Journal.*

Strength of Cast Iron, &c.

A PRACTICAL ESSAY on the STRENGTH of CAST IRON and OTHER METALS. By the late THOMAS TREDGOLD, Mem. Inst. C.E., Author of "Elementary Principles of Carpentry," &c. Fifth Edition, Edited by EATON HODGKINSON, F.R.S. ; to which are added EXPERIMENTAL RESEARCHES on the STRENGTH and OTHER PROPERTIES of CAST IRON. By the EDITOR. The whole Illustrated with 9 Engravings and numerous Woodcuts. 8vo, 12s. cloth.

₊ HODGKINSON'S EXPERIMENTAL RESEARCHES ON THE STRENGTH AND OTHER PROPERTIES OF CAST IRON may be had separately. With Engravings and Woodcuts. 8vo, price 6s. cloth.

The High-Pressure Steam Engine.

THE HIGH-PRESSURE STEAM ENGINE ; an Exposition of its Comparative Merits, and an Essay towards an Improved System of Construction, adapted especially to secure Safety and Economy. By Dr. ERNST ALBAN, Practical Machine Maker, Plau, Mecklenberg. Translated from the German, with Notes, by Dr. POLE, F.R.S., M. Inst. C.E., &c. &c. With 28 fine Plates. 8vo, 16s. 6d. cloth.

"A work like this, which goes thoroughly into the examination of the high-pressure engine, the boiler, and its appendages, &c., is exceedingly useful, and deserves a place in every scientific library."—*Steam Shipping Chronicle.*

Steam Boilers.

A TREATISE ON STEAM BOILERS : their Strength, Construction, and Economical Working. By ROBERT WILSON, late Inspector for the Manchester Steam Users' Association for the Prevention of Steam Boiler Explosions, and for the Attainment of Economy in the Application of Steam. 12mo, cloth boards, 328 pages, price 6s.

Tables of Curves.

TABLES OF TANGENTIAL ANGLES and MULTIPLES for setting out Curves from 5 to 200 Radius. By ALEXANDER BEAZELEY, M. Inst. C.E. Printed on 48 Cards, and sold in a cloth box, waistcoat-pocket size, price 3s. 6d.

"Each table is printed on a small card, which, being placed on the theodolite, leaves the hands free to manipulate the instrument—no small advantage as regards the rapidity of work. They are clearly printed, and compactly fitted into a small case for the pocket—an arrangement that will recommend them to all practical men."—*Engineer.*

"Very handy : a man may know that all his day's work must fall on two of these cards, which he puts into his own card-case, and leaves the rest behind."—*Athenæum.*

Laying Out Curves.

THE FIELD PRACTICE of LAYING OUT CIRCULAR CURVES for RAILROADS. By JOHN C. TRAUTWINE, C.E. (Extracted from SIMMS's Work on Levelling). 8vo, 5s. sewed.

Estimate and Price Book.

THE CIVIL ENGINEER'S AND CONTRACTOR'S ESTI-
MATE AND PRICE BOOK for Home or Foreign Service :
in reference to Roads, Railways, Tramways, Docks, Harbours,
Forts, Fortifications, Bridges, Aqueducts, Tunnels, Sewers, Water-
works, Gasworks, Stations, Barracks, Warehouses, &c. &c. &c.
With Specifications for Permanent Way, Telegraph Materials,
Plant, Maintenance, and Working of a Railway ; and a Priced List
of Machinery, Plant, Tools, &c. By W. D. HASKOLL, C.E.
Plates and Woodcuts. Published annually. 8vo, cloth, 6s.

"As furnishing a variety of data on every conceivable want to civil engineers and
contractors, this book has ever stood perhaps unrivalled."—*Architect.*

Surveying (Land and Marine).

LAND AND MARINE SURVEYING, in Reference to the
Preparation of Plans for Roads and Railways, Canals, Rivers,
Towns' Water Supplies, Docks and Harbours ; with Description
and Use of Surveying Instruments. By W. DAVIS HASKOLL, C.E.,
Author of "The Engineer's Field Book," "Examples of Bridge
and Viaduct Construction," &c. Demy 8vo, price 12s. 6d. cloth,
with 14 folding Plates, and numerous Woodcuts.

"A most useful and well arranged book for the aid of a student. . . . . We
can strongly recommend it as a carefully-written and valuable text-book."—*Builder.*

"Mr. Haskoll has knowledge and experience, and can so give expression to it as
to make any matter on which he writes, clear to the youngest pupil in a surveyor's
office."—*Colliery Guardian.*

"A volume which cannot fail to prove of the utmost practical utility. . . . . It
is one which may be safely recommended to all students who aspire to become clean
and expert surveyors."—*Mining Journal.*

Engineering Fieldwork.

THE PRACTICE OF ENGINEERING FIELDWORK,
applied to Land and Hydraulic, Hydrographic, and Submarine
Surveying and Levelling. Second Edition, revised, with considerable additions, and a Supplementary Volume on WATER-
WORKS, SEWERS, SEWAGE, and IRRIGATION. By W.
DAVIS HASKOLL, C.E. Numerous folding Plates. Demy 8vo, 2
vols. in one, cloth boards, 1l. 1s. (published at 2l. 4s.)

Mining, Surveying and Valuing.

THE MINERAL SURVEYOR AND VALUER'S COM-
PLETE GUIDE, comprising a Treatise on Improved Mining
Surveying, with new Traverse Tables ; and Descriptions of Im-
proved Instruments ; also an Exposition of the Correct Principles
of Laying out and Valuing Home and Foreign Iron and Coal
Mineral Properties : to which is appended M. THOMAN'S (of
the Crédit Mobilier, Paris) TREATISE on COMPOUND IN-
TEREST and ANNUITIES, with LOGARITHMIC TABLES.
By WILLIAM LINTERN, Mining and Civil Engineer. 12mo,
strongly bound in cloth boards, with four Plates of Diagrams,
Plans, &c., price 10s. 6d.

"Contains much valuable information given in a small compass, and which, as far
as we have tested it, is thoroughly trustworthy."—*Iron and Coal Trades Review.*

"The matter, arrangement, and illustration of this work are all excellent, and make
it one of the best of its kind."—*Standard.*

Fire Engineering.

FIRES, FIRE-ENGINES, AND FIRE BRIGADES. With a History of Fire-Engines, their Construction, Use, and Management; Remarks on Fire-Proof Buildings, and the Preservation of Life from Fire; Statistics of the Fire Appliances in English Towns; Foreign Fire Systems; Hints on Fire Brigades, &c., &c. By CHARLES F. T. YOUNG, C.E. With numerous Illustrations, handsomely printed, 544 pp., demy 8vo, price 1*l*. 4*s*. cloth.

" We can most heartily commend this book. . . . . It is really the only English work we now have upon the subject."—*Engineering*.

' We strongly recommend the book to the notice of all who are in any way interested in fires, fire-engines, or fire-brigades."—*Mechanics' Magazine*.

Manual of Mining Tools.

MINING TOOLS. For the use of Mine Managers, Agents, Mining Students, &c. By WILLIAM MORGANS, Lecturer on Practical Mining at the Bristol School of Mines. Volume of Text. 12mo. With an Atlas of Plates, containing 235 Illustrations. 4to. Together, price 9*s*. cloth boards.   [*Recently published*.

" Students in the Science of Mining, and not only they, but subordinate officials in mines, and even Overmen, Captains, Managers, and Viewers may gain practical knowledge and useful hints by the study of Mr. Morgans's Manual."—*Colliery Guardian*.

" A very valuable work, which will tend materially to improve our mining literature."—*Mining Journal*.

Gas and Gasworks.

A TREATISE on GASWORKS and the PRACTICE of MANUFACTURING and DISTRIBUTING COAL GAS. By SAMUEL HUGHES, C.E. Fourth Edition, revised by W. RICHARDS, C.E. With 68 Woodcuts, bound in cloth boards, 12mo, price 4*s*.

Waterworks for Cities and Towns.

WATERWORKS for the SUPPLY of CITIES and TOWNS, with a Description of the Principal Geological Formations of England as influencing Supplies of Water. By SAMUEL HUGHES, F.G.S., Civil Engineer. New and enlarged edition, 12mo, cloth boards, with numerous Illustrations, price 5*s*.

" One of the most convenient, and at the same time reliable works on a subject, the vital importance of which cannot be over-estimated."—*Bradford Observer*.

Coal and Coal Mining.

COAL AND COAL MINING: a Rudimentary Treatise on. By WARINGTON W. SMYTH, M.A., F.R.S., &c., Chief Inspector of the Mines of the Crown and of the Duchy of Cornwall. New edition, revised and corrected. 12mo., cloth boards, with numerous Illustrations, price 4*s*. 6*d*.

" Every portion of the volume appears to have been prepared with much care, and as an outline is given of every known coal-field in this and other countries, as well as of the two principal methods of working, the book will doubtless interest a very large number of readers."—*Mining Journal*.

" Certainly experimental skill and rule-of-thumb practice would be greatly enriched by the addition of the theoretical knowledge and scientific information which Mr. Warington Smyth communicates in combination with the results of his own experience and personal research."—*Colliery Guardian*.

Field-Book for Engineers.

THE ENGINEER'S, MINING SURVEYOR'S, and CON-TRACTOR'S FIELD-BOOK. By W. DAVIS HASKOLL, Civil Engineer. Third Edition, much enlarged, consisting of a Series of Tables, with Rules, Explanations of Systems, and Use of Theodolite for Traverse Surveying and Plotting the Work with minute accuracy by means of Straight Edge and Set Square only; Levelling with the Theodolite, Casting out and Reducing Levels to Datum, and Plotting Sections in the ordinary manner; Setting out Curves with the Theodolite by Tangential Angles and Multiples with Right and Left-hand Readings of the Instrument; Setting out Curves without Theodolite on the System of Tangential Angles by Sets of Tangents and Offsets; and Earthwork Tables to 80 feet deep, calculated for every 6 inches in depth. With numerous wood-cuts, 12mo, price 12s. cloth.

"A very useful work for the practical engineer and surveyor. Every person engaged in engineering field operations will estimate the importance of such a work and the amount of valuable time which will be saved by reference to a set of reliable tables prepared with the accuracy and fulness of those given in this volume."—*Railway News.*

"The book is very handy, and the author might have added that the separate tables of sines and tangents to every minute will make it useful for many other purposes, the genuine traverse tables existing all the same."—*Athenæum.*

"The work forms a handsome pocket volume, and cannot fail, from its portability and utility, to be extensively patronised by the engineering profession."—*Mining Journal.*

"We strongly recommend this second edition of Mr. Haskoll's 'Field Book' to all classes of surveyors."—*Colliery Guardian.*

Earthwork, Measurement and Calculation of.

A MANUAL on EARTHWORK. By ALEX. J. S. GRAHAM, C.E., Resident Engineer, Forest of Dean Central Railway. With numerous Diagrams. 18mo, 2s. 6d. cloth.

"As a really handy book for reference, we know of no work equal to it; and the railway engineers and others employed in the measurement and calculation of earth work will find a great amount of practical information very admirably arranged, and available for general or rough estimates, as well as for the more exact calculations required in the engineers' contractor's offices."—*Artizan.*

Harbours.

THE DESIGN and CONSTRUCTION of HARBOURS: A Treatise on Maritime Engineering. By THOMAS STEVENSON, F.R.S.E., F.G.S., M.I.C.E. Second Edition, containing many additional subjects, and otherwise generally extended and revised. With 20 Plates and numerous Cuts. Small 4to, 15s. cloth.

Mathematical and Drawing Instruments.

A TREATISE ON THE PRINCIPAL MATHEMATICAL AND DRAWING INSTRUMENTS employed by the Engineer, Architect, and Surveyor. By FREDERICK W. SIMMS, M. Inst. C.E., Author of "Practical Tunnelling," &c. Third Edition, with numerous Cuts. 12mo, price 3s. 6d. cloth.

Bridge Construction in Masonry, Timber, & Iron.

EXAMPLES OF BRIDGE AND VIADUCT CONSTRUC-
TION OF MASONRY, TIMBER, AND IRON ; consisting of
46 Plates from the Contract Drawings or Admeasurement of select
Works. By W. DAVIS HASKOLL, C.E.   Second Edition, with
the addition of 554 Estimates, and the Practice of Setting out Works,
illustrated with 6 pages of Diagrams.   Imp. 4to, price 2*l*. 12*s*. 6*d*.
half-morocco.

"One of the very few works extant descending to the level of ordinary routine, and
treating on the common every-day practice of the railway engineer. . . . A work of
the present nature by a man of Mr. Haskoll's experience, must prove invaluable to
hundreds. The tables of estimates appended to this edition will considerably enhance
its value."—*Engineering.*

Mathematical Instruments, their Construction, &c.

MATHEMATICAL INSTRUMENTS : THEIR CONSTRUC-
TION, ADJUSTMENT, TESTING, AND USE; comprising
Drawing, Measuring, Optical, Surveying, and Astronomical Instruments.   By J. F. HEATHER, M.A., Author of "Practical Plane
Geometry," "Descriptive Geometry," &c.   Enlarged Edition, for
the most part entirely rewritten.   With numerous Wood-cuts.
12mo, cloth boards, price 5*s*.

Oblique Arches.

A PRACTICAL TREATISE ON THE CONSTRUCTION of
OBLIQUE ARCHES. By JOHN HART.   Third Edition, with
Plates. Imperial 8vo, price 8*s*. cloth.

Oblique Bridges.

A PRACTICAL and THEORETICAL ESSAY on OBLIQUE
BRIDGES, with 13 large folding Plates.   By GEO. WATSON
BUCK, M. Inst. C.E.   Second Edition, corrected by W. H.
BARLOW, M. Inst. C.E.   Imperial 8vo, 12*s*. cloth.

"The standard text-book for all engineers regarding skew arches, is Mr. Buck's
treatise, and it would be impossible to consult a better."—*Engineer.*

Pocket-Book for Marine Engineers.

A POCKET BOOK FOR MARINE ENGINEERS. Con-
taining useful Rules and Formulæ in a compact form.   By FRANK
PROCTOR, A.I.N.A.   Second Edition, revised and enlarged.
Royal 32mo, leather, gilt edges, with strap, price 4*s*.

"We recommend it to our readers as going far to supply a long-felt want."—
Naval Science.
"A most useful companion to all marine engineers."—*United Service Gazette.*
"Scarcely anything required by a naval engineer appears to have been for-
gotten.—*Iron.*
"A very valuable publication . . . a means of saving much time and labour."—
New York Monthly Record.

Weale's Dictionary of Terms.

A DICTIONARY of TERMS used in ARCHITECTURE,
BUILDING, ENGINEERING, MINING, METALLURGY,
ARCHÆOLOGY, the FINE ARTS, &c.   By JOHN WEALE.
Fourth Edition, enlarged and revised by ROBERT HUNT, F.R.S.,
Keeper of Mining Records, Editor of "Ure's Dictionary of Arts,"
&c.   12mo, cloth boards, price 6*s*.

Grantham's Iron Ship-Building, enlarged.

ON IRON SHIP-BUILDING ; with Practical Examples and Details. Fifth Edition. Imp. 4to, boards, enlarged from 24 to 40 Plates (21 quite new), including the latest Examples. Together with separate Text, 12mo, cloth limp, also considerably enlarged. By JOHN GRANTHAM, M. Inst. C.E., &c.   Price 2*l*. 2*s*. complete.

Description of Plates.

1. Hollow and Bar Keels, Stem and Stern Posts.   [Pieces.
2. Side Frames, Floorings, and Bilge
3. Floorings *continued*—Keelsons, Deck Beams, Gunwales, and Stringers.
4. Gunwales *continued* — Lower Decks, and Orlop Beams.
4*a*. Gunwales and Deck Beam Iron.
5. Angle-Iron, T Iron, Z Iron, Bulb Iron, as Rolled for Building.
6. Rivets, shown in section, natural size : Flush and Lapped Joints, with Single and Double Riveting.
7. Plating, three plans ; Bulkheads and Modes of Securing them.
8. Iron Masts, with Longitudinal and Transverse Sections.
9. Sliding Keel, Water Ballast, Moulding the Frames in Iron Ship Building, Levelling Plates.
10. Longitudinal Section, and Half-breadth Deck Plan of Large Vessels on a reduced Scale.
11. Midship Sections of Three Vessels.
12. *Large Vessel*, showing Details—*Fore End* in Section, and End View, with Stern Post, Crutches, &c.
13. *Large Vessel*, showing Details—*After End* in Section, with End View, Stern Frame for Screw, and Rudder.
14. *Large Vessel*, showing Details—*Midship Section*, half breadth.
15. *Machines* for Punching and Shearing Plates and Angle-Iron, and for Bending Plates ; Rivet Hearth.
15*a*. Beam-Bending Machine, Independent Shearing, Punching and Angle-Iron Machine.
15*b*. Double Lever Punching and Shearing Machine, arranged for cutting Angle and T Iron, with Dividing Table and Engine.
16. *Machines.*—Garforth's Riveting Machine, Drilling and Counter-Sinking Machine.
16*a*. Plate Planing Machine.
17. *Air Furnace* for Heating Plates and Angle-Iron ; Various Tools used in Riveting and Plating.
18. *Gunwale* ; Keel and Flooring ; Plan for Sheathing with Copper.
18*a*. Grantham's Improved Plan of Sheathing Iron Ships with Copper.
19. Illustrations of the Magnetic Condition of various Iron Ships.
20. Gray's Floating Compass and Binnacle, with Adjusting Magnets, &c.
21. Corroded Iron Bolt in Frame of Wooden Ship ; Jointing Plates.
22-4. *Great Eastern*—Longitudinal Sections and Half-breadth Plans—Midship Section, with Details—Section in Engine Room, and Paddle Boxes.
25-6. Paddle Steam Vessel of Steel.
27. *Scarbrough*—Paddle Vessel of Steel.
28-9. Proposed Passenger Steamer.
30. *Persian*—Iron Screw Steamer.
31. Midship Section of H.M. Steam Frigate, *Warrior*.
32. Midship Section of H.M. Steam Frigate, *Hercules*.
33. Stem, Stern, and Rudder of H.M. Steam Frigate, *Bellerophon*.
34. Midship Section of H.M. Troop Ship, *Serapis*.
35. Iron Floating Dock.

" A thoroughly practical work, and every question of the many in relation to iron shipping which admit of diversity of opinion, or have various and conflicting personal interests attached to them, is treated with sober and impartial wisdom and good sense. . . . . As good a volume for the instruction of the pupil or student of iron naval architecture as can be found in any language."—*Practical Mechanics' Journal.*

" A very elaborate work. . . . . It forms a most valuable addition to the history of iron shipbuilding, while its having been prepared by one who has made the subject his study for many years, and whose qualifications have been repeatedly recognised, will recommend it as one of practical utility to all interested in shipbuilding."—*Army and Navy Gazette.*

Steam.

THE SAFE USE OF STEAM : containing Rules for Unprofessional Steam Users. By an ENGINEER.

N. B.—*This little work should be in the hands of every person having to deal with a Steam Engine of any kind.*

" If steam-users would but learn this little book by heart, and then hand it to their stokers to do the same, and see that the latter do it, boiler explosions would become sensations by their rarity."—*English Mechanic.*

ARCHITECTURE, &c.

Construction.

THE SCIENCE of BUILDING : An Elementary Treatise on the Principles of Construction. By E. WYNDHAM TARN, M.A., Architect. Illustrated with 47 Wood Engravings. Demy 8vo, price 8s. 6d. cloth. [Recently published.

" A very valuable book, which we strongly recommend to all students."—Builder.

" While Mr. Tarn's valuable little volume is quite sufficiently scientific to answer the purposes intended, it is written in a style that will deservedly make it popular. The diagrams are numerous and exceedingly well executed, and the treatise does credit alike to the author and the publisher."—Engineer.

" No architectural student should be without this hand-book of constructional knowledge."—Architect.

" The book is very far from being a mere compilation ; it is an able digest of information which is only to be found scattered through various works, and contains more really original writing than many putting forth far stronger claims to originality." —Engineering.

Beaton's Pocket Estimator.

THE POCKET ESTIMATOR FOR THE BUILDING TRADES, being an easy method of estimating the various parts of a Building collectively, more especially applied to Carpenters' and Joiners' work, priced according to the present value of material and labour. By A. C. BEATON, Author of 'Quantities and Measurements.' 33 Woodcuts. Leather. Waistcoat-pocket size. 2s.

Beaton's Builders' and Surveyors' Technical Guide.

THE POCKET TECHNICAL GUIDE AND MEASURER FOR BUILDERS AND SURVEYORS: containing a Complete Explanation of the Terms used in Building Construction, Memoranda for Reference, Technical Directions for Measuring Work in all the Building Trades, with a Treatise on the Measurement of Timbers, and Complete Specifications for Houses, Roads, and Drains. By A. C. BEATON, Author of 'Quantities and Measurements.' With 19 Woodcuts. Leather. Waistcoat-pocket size. 2s.

Villa Architecture.

A HANDY BOOK of VILLA ARCHITECTURE ; being a Series of Designs for Villa Residences in various Styles. With Detailed Specifications and Estimates. By C. WICKES, Architect, Author of "The Spires and Towers of the Mediæval Churches of England," &c. First Series, consisting of 30 Plates ; Second Series, 31 Plates. Complete in 1 vol. 4to, price 2l. 10s. half morocco. Either Series separate, price 1l. 7s. each, half morocco.

" The whole of the designs bear evidence of their being the work of an artistic architect, and they will prove very valuable and suggestive to architects, students, and amateurs."—Building News.

The Architect's Guide.

THE ARCHITECT'S GUIDE ; or, Office and Pocket Companion for Engineers, Architects, Land and Building Surveyors, Contractors, Builders, Clerks of Works, &c. By W. DAVIS HASKOLL, C.E., R. W. BILLINGS, Architect, F. ROGERS, and P. THOMPSON. With numerous Experiments by G. RENNIE, C.E., &c. Woodcuts, 12mo, cloth, price 3s. 6d.

Architecture, Ancient and Modern.

RUDIMENTARY ARCHITECTURE, Ancient and Modern. Consisting of VITRUVIUS, translated by JOSEPH GWILT, F.S.A., &c., with 23 fine copper plates; GRECIAN Architecture, by the EARL of ABERDEEN; the ORDERS of Architecture, by W. H. LEEDS, Esq.; The STYLES of Architecture of Various Countries, by T. TALBOT BURY; The PRINCIPLES of DESIGN in Architecture, by E. L. GARBETT. In one handsome volume, half-bound (pp. 1,100), copiously illustrated, price 12*s.*

** Sold separately, in two vols., as follows, price 6s. each, hf.-bd.
ANCIENT ARCHITECTURE. Containing Gwilt's Vitruvius and Aberdeen's Grecian Architecture.

N.B.—*This is the only edition of VITRUVIUS procurable at a moderate price.*
MODERN ARCHITECTURE. Containing the Orders, by Leeds; The Styles, by Bury; and Principles of Design, by Garbett.

The Young Architect's Book.

HINTS TO YOUNG ARCHITECTS. By GEORGE WIGHTWICK, Architect, Author of "The Palace of Architecture," &c. &c. New Edition, revised and enlarged. By G. HUSKISSON GUILLAUME, Architect. With numerous illustrations. 12mo. cloth boards, 4*s.* [*Just Published.*

Drawing for Builders and Students.

PRACTICAL RULES ON DRAWING for the OPERATIVE BUILDER and YOUNG STUDENT in ARCHITECTURE. By GEORGE PYNE, Author of a "Rudimentary Treatise on Perspective for Beginners." With 14 Plates, 4to, 7*s.* 6*d.*, boards.
CONTENTS.—I. Practical Rules on Drawing—Outlines. II. Ditto—the Grecian and Roman Orders. III. Practical Rules on Drawing—Perspective. IV. Practical Rules on Light and Shade. V. Practical Rules on Colour, &c. &c.

Cottages, Villas, and Country Houses.

DESIGNS and EXAMPLES of COTTAGES, VILLAS, and COUNTRY HOUSES; being the Studies of several eminent Architects and Builders; consisting of Plans, Elevations, and Perspective Views; with approximate Estimates of the Cost of each. In 4to, with 67 plates, price 1*l.* 1*s.*, cloth.

Builder's Price Book.

LOCKWOOD & CO.'S BUILDER'S AND CONTRACTOR'S PRICE BOOK—with which is incorporated ATCHLEY'S, and portions of the late G. R. BURNELL's Builders' Price Books—for 1875, containing the latest prices of all kinds of Builders' Materials and Labour, and of all Trades connected with Building; with many useful and important Memoranda and Tables; Lists of the Members of the Metropolitan Board of Works, of Districts, District Officers, and District Surveyors, and the Metropolitan Bye-laws. The whole revised and edited by FRANCIS T. W. MILLER, Architect and Surveyor. Fcap. 8vo, strongly half-bound, price 4*s.*

Handbook of Specifications.

THE HANDBOOK OF SPECIFICATIONS ; or, Practical Guide to the Architect, Engineer, Surveyor, and Builder, in drawing up Specifications and Contracts for Works and Constructions. Illustrated by Precedents of Buildings actually executed by eminent Architects and Engineers. Preceded by a Preliminary Essay, and Skeletons of Specifications and Contracts, &c., &c., and explained by numerous Lithograph Plates and Woodcuts. By Professor THOMAS L. DONALDSON, President of the Royal Institute of British Architects, Professor of Architecture and Construction, University College, London, M.I.B.A., Member of the various European Academies of the Fine Arts. With A REVIEW OF THE LAW OF CONTRACTS, and of the Responsibilities of Architects, Engineers, and Builders. By W. CUNNINGHAM GLEN, Barrister-at-Law, of the Middle Temple. 2 vols., 8vo, with upwards of 1100 pp. of text, and 33 Lithographic Plates, cloth, 2*l.* 2*s.* (Published at 4*l.*)

" In these two volumes of 1,100 pages (together), forty-four specifications of executed works are given, including the specifications for parts of the new Houses of Parliament, by Sir Charles Barry, and for the new Royal Exchange, by Mr. Tite, M.P.

"Amongst the other known buildings, the specifications of which are given, are the Wiltshire Lunatic Asylum (Wyatt and Brandon) ; Tothill Fields Prison (R. Abraham) ; the City Prison, Holloway (Bunning) ; the High School, Edinburgh (Hamilton) ; Clothworkers' Hall, London (Angel) ; Wellington College, Sandhurst (J. Shaw) ; Houses in Grosvenor Square, and elsewhere ; St. George's Church, Doncaster (Scott) ; several works of smaller size by the Author, including Messrs. Shaw's Warehouse in Fetter Lane, a very successful elevation ; the Newcastle-upon-Tyne Railway Station (J. Dobson) ; new Westminster Bridge (Page) ; the High Level Bridge, Newcastle (R. Stephenson) ; various works on the Great Northern Railway (Brydone) ; and one French specification for Houses in the Rue de Rivoli, Paris (MM. Armand, Hittorff, Pellechet, and Rohault de Fleury, architects). The majority of the specifications have illustrations in the shape of elevations and plans.

"About 140 pages of the second volume are appropriated to an exposition of the law in relation to the legal liabilities of engineers, architects, contractors, and builders, by Mr. W. Cunningham Glen, Barrister-at-law. Donaldson's Handbook of Specifications must be bought by all architects."—*Builder.*

Specifications for Practical Architecture.

SPECIFICATIONS FOR PRACTICAL ARCHITECTURE: A Guide to the Architect, Engineer, Surveyor, and Builder ; with an Essay on the Structure and Science of Modern Buildings. By FREDERICK ROGERS, Architect. With numerous Illustrations. Demy 8vo, price 15*s.*, cloth. (Published at 1*l.* 10*s.*)

*** A volume of specifications of a practical character being greatly required, and the old standard work of Alfred Bartholomew being out of print, the author, on the basis of that work, has produced the above. Some of the specifications he has so altered as to bring in the now universal use of concrete, the improvements in drainage, the use of iron, glass, asphalte, and other material. He has also inserted specifications of works that have been erected in his own practice.

The House-Owner's Estimator.

THE HOUSE-OWNER'S ESTIMATOR ; or, What will it Cost to Build, Alter, or Repair ? A Price-Book adapted to the Use of Unprofessional People as well as for the Architectural Surveyor and Builder. By the late JAMES D. SIMON, A.R.I.B.A. Edited and Revised by FRANCIS T. W. MILLER, Surveyor. With numerous Illustrations. Second Edition, with the prices carefully revised to 1875. Crown 8vo, cloth, price 3*s.* 6*d.*

CARPENTRY, TIMBER, &c.

Tredgold's Carpentry, new, enlarged, and cheaper Edition.

THE ELEMENTARY PRINCIPLES OF CARPENTRY : a Treatise on the Pressure and Equilibrium of Timber Framing, the Resistance of Timber, and the Construction of Floors, Arches, Bridges, Roofs, Uniting Iron and Stone with Timber, &c. To which is added an Essay on the Nature and Properties of Timber, &c., with Descriptions of the Kinds of Wood used in Building ; also numerous Tables of the Scantlings of Timber for different purposes, the Specific Gravities of Materials, &c. By THOMAS TREDGOLD, C.E. Edited by PETER BARLOW, F.R.S. Fifth Edition, corrected and enlarged. With 64 Plates (11 of which now first appear in this edition), Portrait of the Author, and several Woodcuts. In 1 vol., 4to, published at 2*l.* 2*s.*, reduced to 1*l.* 5*s.*, cloth.

" 'Tredgold's Carpentry' ought to be in every architect's and every builder's library, and those who do not already possess it ought to avail themselves of the new issue."—*Builder.*

"A work whose monumental excellence must commend it wherever skilful carpentry is concerned. The Author's principles are rather confirmed than impaired by time, and, as now presented, combine the surest base with the most interesting display of progressive science. The additional plates are of great intrinsic value."—*Building News.*

Grandy's Timber Tables.

THE TIMBER IMPORTER'S, TIMBER MERCHANT'S, and BUILDER'S STANDARD GUIDE. By RICHARD E. GRANDY. Comprising :—An Analysis of Deal Standards, Home and Foreign, with comparative Values and Tabular Arrangements for Fixing Nett Landed Cost on Baltic and North American Deals, including all intermediate Expenses, Freight, Insurance, Duty, &c., &c. ; together with Copious Information for the Retailer and Builder. 12mo, price 7*s.* 6*d.* cloth.

"Everything it pretends to be: built up gradually, it leads one from a forest to a treenail, and throws in, as a makeweight, a host of material concerning bricks, columns, cisterns, &c.—all that the class to whom it appeals requires."—*English Mechanic.*

"The only difficulty we have is as to what is NOT in its pages. What we have tested of the contents, taken at random, is invariably correct."—*Illustrated Builder's Journal.*

Tables for Packing-Case Makers.

PACKING-CASE TABLES ; showing the number of Superficial Feet in Boxes or Packing-Cases, from six inches square and upwards. Compiled by WILLIAM RICHARDSON, Accountant. Oblong 4to, cloth, price 3*s.* 6*d.*

"Will save much labour and calculation to packing-case makers and those who use packing-cases."—*Grocer.*   "Invaluable labour-saving tables."—*Ironmonger.*

Nicholson's Carpenter's Guide.

THE CARPENTER'S NEW GUIDE ; or, BOOK of LINES for CARPENTERS : comprising all the Elementary Principles essential for acquiring a knowledge of Carpentry. Founded on the late PETER NICHOLSON'S standard work. A new Edition, revised by ARTHUR ASHPITEL, F.S.A., together with Practical Rules on Drawing, by GEORGE PYNE. With 74 Plates, 4to, 1*l.* 1*s.* cloth.

Dowsing's Timber Merchant's Companion.

THE TIMBER MERCHANT'S AND BUILDER'S COM-
PANION ; containing New and Copious Tables of the Reduced
Weight and Measurement of Deals and Battens, of all sizes, from
One to a Thousand Pieces, and the relative Price that each size
bears per Lineal Foot to any given Price per Petersburgh Standard
Hundred ; the Price per Cube Foot of Square Timber to any given
Price per Load of 50 Feet ; the proportionate Value of Deals and
Battens by the Standard, to Square Timber by the Load of 50 Feet ;
the readiest mode of ascertaining the Price of Scantling per Lineal
Foot of any size, to any given Figure per Cube Foot.   Also a
variety of other valuable information.   By WILLIAM DOWSING,
Timber Merchant.   Second Edition.   Crown 8vo, 3*s*. cloth.

"Everything is as concise and clear as it can possibly be made.   There can be no
doubt that every timber merchant and builder ought to possess it."— *Hull Advertiser.*

Timber Freight Book.

THE TIMBER IMPORTERS' AND SHIPOWNERS'
FREIGHT BOOK : Being a Comprehensive Series of Tables for
the Use of Timber Importers, Captains of Ships, Shipbrokers,
Builders, and all Dealers in Wood whatsoever.   By WILLIAM
RICHARDSON, Timber Broker, author of " Packing Case Tables,"
&c.   Crown 8vo, cloth, price 6*s*.

MECHANICS, &c.

Horton's Measurer.

THE COMPLETE MEASURER ; setting forth the Measurement of Boards, Glass, &c., &c. ; Unequal-sided, Square-sided,
Octagonal-sided, Round Timber and Stone, and Standing Timber.
With just allowances for the bark in the respective species of
trees, and proper deductions for the waste in hewing the trees,
&c. ; also a Table showing the solidity of hewn or eight-sided
timber, or of any octagonal-sided column.   Compiled for the
accommodation of Timber-growers, Merchants, and Surveyors,
Stonemasons, Architects, and others.   By RICHARD HORTON.
Second edition, with considerable and valuable additions, 12mo,
strongly bound in leather, 5*s*.

"The office of the architect, engineer, building surveyor, or land agent that is
without this excellent and useful work cannot truly be considered perfect in its
furnishing."—*Irish Builder.*

"We have used the improved and other tables in this volume, and have not
observed any unfairness or inaccuracy."—*Builder.*

"The tables we have tested are accurate. . . . . To the builder and estate
agents this work will be most acceptable."—*British Architect.*

"Not only are the best methods of measurement shown, and in some instances
illustrated by means of woodcuts, but the erroneous systems pursued by dishonest
dealers are fully exposed. . . . . The work must be considered to be a valuable addition to every gardener's library.—*Garden.*

Superficial Measurement.

THE TRADESMAN'S GUIDE TO SUPERFICIAL MEA-
SUREMENT.   Tables calculated from 1 to 200 inches in length,
by 1 to 108 inches in breadth.   For the use of Architects, Surveyors,
Engineers, Timber Merchants, Builders, &c.   By JAMES HAW-
KINGS.   Fcp. 3*s*. 6*d*. cloth.

Mechanic's Workshop Companion.

THE OPERATIVE MECHANIC'S WORKSHOP COM-
PANION, and THE SCIENTIFIC GENTLEMAN'S PRAC-
TICAL ASSISTANT ; comprising a great variety of the most
useful Rules in Mechanical Science; with numerous Tables of Practical Data and Calculated Results. By W. TEMPLETON, Author
of "The Engineer's, Millwright's, and Machinist's Practical Assistant." Eleventh Edition, with Mechanical Tables for Operative
Smiths, Millwrights, Engineers, &c. ; together with several Useful
and Practical Rules in Hydraulics and Hydrodynamics, a variety
of Experimental Results, and an Extensive Table of Powers and
Roots. 11 Plates. 12mo, 5s. bound.

"As a text-book of reference, in which mechanical and commercial demands are
judiciously met, TEMPLETON'S COMPANION stands unrivalled."—*Mechanics' Magazine.*
"Admirably adapted to the wants of a very large class. It has met with great
success in the engineering workshop, as we can testify ; and there are a great many
men who, in a great measure, owe their rise in life to this little work."—*Building News.*

Engineer's Assistant.

THE ENGINEER'S, MILLWRIGHT'S, and MACHINIST'S
PRACTICAL ASSISTANT ; comprising a Collection of Useful
Tables, Rules, and Data. Compiled and Arranged, with Original
Matter, by W. TEMPLETON. 5th Edition. 18mo, 2s. 6d. cloth.

"So much varied information compressed into so small a space, and published at a
price which places it within the reach of the humblest mechanic, cannot fail to command the sale which it deserves. With the utmost confidence we commend this book
to the attention of our readers.—*Mechanics' Magazine.*
"Every mechanic should become the possessor of the volume, and a more suitable
present to an apprentice to any of the mechanical trades could not possibly be made."
—*Building News.*

Designing, Measuring, and Valuing.

THE STUDENT'S GUIDE to the PRACTICE of MEA-
SURING, and VALUING ARTIFICERS' WORKS; containing
Directions for taking Dimensions, Abstracting the same, and bringing
the Quantities into Bill, with Tables of Constants, and copious
Memoranda for the Valuation of Labour and Materials in the respective Trades of Bricklayer and Slater, Carpenter and Joiner,
Painter and Glazier, Paperhanger, &c. With 43 Plates and Woodcuts. Originally edited by EDWARD DOBSON, Architect. New
Edition, re-written, with Additions on Mensuration and Construction, and useful Tables for facilitating Calculations and Measurements. By E. WYNDHAM TARN, M.A., 8vo, 10s. 6d. cloth.

"This useful book should be in every architect's and builder's office. It contains
a vast amount of information absolutely necessary to be known."—*The Irish Builder.*
"We have failed to discover anything connected with the building trade, from ex-
cavating foundations to bell-hanging, that is not fully treated upon in this valuable
work."—*The Artizan.*
"Mr. Tarn has well performed the task imposed upon him, and has made many
further and valuable additions, embodying a large amount of information relating to
the technicalities and modes of construction employed in the several branches of the
building trade."—*Colliery Guardian.*
"Altogether the book is one which well fulfils the promise of its title-page, and we
can thoroughly recommend it to the class for whose use it has been compiled. Mr.
Tarn's additions and revisions have much increased the usefulness of the work, and
have especially augmented its value to students."—*Engineering.*

MATHEMATICS, &c.

Gregory's Practical Mathematics.

MATHEMATICS for PRACTICAL MEN ; being a Common-place Book of Pure and Mixed Mathematics. Designed chiefly for the Use of Civil Engineers, Architects, and Surveyors. Part I. PURE MATHEMATICS—comprising Arithmetic, Algebra, Geometry, Mensuration, Trigonometry, Conic Sections, Properties of Curves. Part II. MIXED MATHEMATICS—comprising Mechanics in general, Statics, Dynamics, Hydrostatics, Hydrodynamics, Pneumatics, Mechanical Agents, Strength of Materials. With an Appendix of copious Logarithmic and other Tables. By OLINTHUS GREGORY, LL.D., F.R.A.S. Enlarged by HENRY LAW, C.E. 4th Edition, carefully revised and corrected by J. R. YOUNG, formerly Professor of Mathematics, Belfast College ; Author of "A Course of Mathematics," &c. With 13 Plates. Medium 8vo, 1l. 1s. cloth.

" As a standard work on mathematics it has not been excelled."—*Artizan*.

" The engineer or architect will here find ready to his hand, rules for solving nearly every mathematical difficulty that may arise in his practice. As a moderate acquaintance with arithmetic, algebra, and elementary geometry is absolutely necessary to the proper understanding of the most useful portions of this book, the author very wisely has devoted the first three chapters to those subjects, so that the most ignorant may be enabled to master the whole of the book, without aid from any other. The rules are in all cases explained by means of examples, in which every step of the process is clearly worked out."—*Builder*.

" One of the most serviceable books to the practical mechanics of the country. . . . The edition of 1847 was fortunately entrusted to the able hands of Mr. Law, who revised it thoroughly, re-wrote many chapters, and added several sections to those which had been rendered imperfect by advanced knowledge. On examining the various and many improvements which he introduced into the work, they seem almost like a new structure on an old plan, or rather like the restoration of an old ruin, not only to its former substance, but to an extent which meets the larger requirements of modern times. . . . . In the edition just brought out, the work has again been revised by Professor Young. He has modernised the notation throughout, introduced a few paragraphs here and there, and corrected the numerous typographical errors which have escaped the eyes of the former Editor. The book is now as complete as it is possible to make it. . . . . We have carried our notice of this book to a greater length than the space allowed us justified, but the experiments it contains are so interesting, and the method of describing them so clear, that we may be excused for overstepping our limit. It is an instructive book for the student, and a Text-book for him who having once mastered the subjects it treats of, needs occasionally to refresh his memory upon them."—*Building News*.

The Metric System.

A SERIES OF METRIC TABLES, in which the British Standard Measures and Weights are compared with those of the Metric System at present in use on the Continent. By C. H. DOWLING, C. E. Second Edition, revised and enlarged. 8vo, 10s. 6d. strongly bound.

" Mr. Dowling's Tables, which are well put together, come just in time as a ready reckoner for the conversion of one system into the other."—*Athenæum*.

" Their accuracy has been certified by Professor Airy, the Astronomer-Royal."—*Builder*.

" Resolution 8.—That advantage will be derived from the recent publication of Metric Tables, by C. H. Dowling, C.E."—*Report of Section F, British Association, Bath.*

Inwood's Tables, greatly enlarged and improved.

TABLES FOR THE PURCHASING of ESTATES, Freehold,
Copyhold, or Leasehold; Annuities, Advowsons, &c., and for the
Renewing of Leases held under Cathedral Churches, Colleges, or
other corporate bodies; for Terms of Years certain, and for Lives;
also for Valuing Reversionary Estates, Deferred Annuities, Next
Presentations, &c., together with Smart's Five Tables of Compound
Interest, and an Extension of the same to Lower and Intermediate
Rates. By WILLIAM INWOOD, Architect. The 19th edition, with
considerable additions, and new and valuable Tables of Logarithms
for the more Difficult Computations of the Interest of Money, Discount, Annuities, &c., by M. FÉDOR THOMAN, of the Société
Crédit Mobilier of Paris.   12mo, 8s. cloth.

₊ *This edition (the 19th) differs in many important particulars
from former ones. The changes consist, first, in a more convenient
and systematic arrangement of the original Tables, and in the removal
of certain numerical errors which a very careful revision of the whole
has enabled the present editor to discover; and secondly, in the
extension of practical utility conferred on the work by the introduction
of Tables now inserted for the first time. This new and important
matter is all so much actually added to* INWOOD'S TABLES; *nothing
has been abstracted from the original collection: so that those who have
been long in the habit of consulting* INWOOD *for any special professional purpose will, as heretofore, find the information sought still in
its pages.*

" Those interested in the purchase and sale of estates, and in the adjustment of
-compensation cases, as well as in transactions in annuities, life insurances, &c., will
find the present edition of eminent service."—*Engineering.*

Geometry for the Architect, Engineer, &c.

PRACTICAL GEOMETRY, for the Architect, Engineer, and
Mechanic; giving Rules for the Delineation and Application of
various Geometrical Lines, Figures and Curves. By E. W. TARN,
M.A., Architect, Author of " The Science of Building," &c.
With 164 Illustrations. Demy 8vo.   12s. 6d.

" No book with the same objects in view has ever been published in which the
clearness of the rules laid down and the illustrative diagrams have been so satis-
factory."—*Scotsman.*

Compound Interest and Annuities.

THEORY of COMPOUND INTEREST and ANNUITIES;
with Tables of Logarithms for the more Difficult Computations of
Interest, Discount, Annuities, &c., in all their Applications and
Uses for Mercantile and State Purposes. With an elaborate Intro-
duction. By FÉDOR THOMAN, of the Société Crédit Mobilier,
Paris. 12mo, cloth, 5s.

" A very powerful work, and the Author has a very remarkable command of his
subject."—*Professor A. de Morgan.*

" We recommend it to the notice of actuaries and accountants."—*Athenæum.*

SCIENCE AND ART.

The Military Sciences.

AIDE-MÉMOIRE to the MILITARY SCIENCES. Framed from Contributions of Officers and others connected with the different Services. Originally edited by a Committee of the Corps of Royal Engineers. Second Edition, most carefully revised by an Officer of the Corps, with many additions; containing nearly 350 Engravings and many hundred Woodcuts. 3 vols. royal 8vo, extra. cloth boards, and lettered, price 4*l.* 10*s.*

"A compendious encyclopædia of military knowledge, to which we are greatly indebted."—*Edinburgh Review.*

"The most comprehensive work of reference to the military and collateral sciences. Among the list of contributors, some seventy-seven in number, will be found names of the highest distinction in the services."—*Volunteer Service Gazette.*

Field Fortification.

A TREATISE on FIELD FORTIFICATION, the ATTACK of FORTRESSES, MILITARY, MINING, and RECONNOITRING. By Colonel I. S. MACAULAY, late Professor of Fortification in the R. M. A., Woolwich. Sixth Edition, crown 8vo, cloth, with separate Atlas of 12 Plates, price 12*s.* complete.

Naval Science.

NAVAL SCIENCE: a Quarterly Magazine for Promoting the Improvement of Naval Architecture, Marine Engineering, Steam Navigation, Seamanship. Edited by E. J. REED, C.B., M.P., and late Chief Constructor of the Navy, and JOSEPH WOOLLEY, M.A., LL.D., F.R.A.S. Copiously illustrated. Price 2*s.* 6*d.* Now ready, Vols. II. & III., each containing 4 Nos. cloth boards, price 12*s.* 6*d.* each.

** The Contributors include the most Eminent Authorities in the several branches of the above subjects.

Dye-Wares and Colours.

THE MANUAL of COLOURS and DYE-WARES: their Properties, Applications, Valuation, Impurities, and Sophistications. For the Use of Dyers, Printers, Dry Salters, Brokers, &c. By J. W. SLATER. Post 8vo, cloth, price 7*s.* 6*d.*

"A complete encyclopædia of the *materia tinctoria.* The information given respecting each article is full and precise, and the methods of determining the value of articles such as these, so liable to sophistication, are given with clearness, and are practical as well as valuable."—*Chemist and Druggist.*

Electricity.

A MANUAL of ELECTRICITY; including Galvanism, Magnetism, Diamagnetism, Electro-Dynamics, Magno-Electricity, and the Electric Telegraph. By HENRY M. NOAD, Ph.D., F.C.S., Lecturer on Chemistry at St. George's Hospital. Fourth Edition, entirely rewritten. Illustrated by 500 Woodcuts. 8vo, 1*l.* 4*s.* cloth.

"The commendations already bestowed in the pages of the *Lancet* on the former editions of this work are more than ever merited by the present. The accounts given of electricity and galvanism are not only complete in a scientific sense, but, which is a rarer thing, are popular and interesting."—*Lancet.*

Text-Book of Electricity.

THE STUDENT'S TEXT-BOOK OF ELECTRICITY: including Magnetism, Voltaic Electricity, Electro-Magnetism, Diamagnetism, Magneto-Electricity, Thermo-Electricity, and Electric Telegraphy. Being a Condensed Résumé of the Theory and Application of Electrical Science, including its latest Practical Developments, particularly as relating to Aërial and Submarine Telegraphy. By HENRY M. NOAD, Ph.D., Lecturer on Chemistry at St. George's Hospital. Post 8vo, 400 Illustrations, 12s. 6d. cloth.

"We can recommend Dr. Noad's book for clear style, great range of subject, a good index, and a plethora of woodcuts."—*Athenæum.*

"A most elaborate compilation of the facts of electricity and magnetism, and of the theories which have been advanced concerning them."—*Popular Science Review.*

"Clear, compendious, compact, well illustrated, and well printed."—*Lancet.*

"We can strongly recommend the work, as an admirable text-book, to every student —beginner or advanced—of electricity."—*Engineering.*

"Nothing of value has been passed over, and nothing given but what will lead to a correct, and even an exact, knowledge of the present state of electrical science."—*Mechanics' Magazine.*

"We know of no book on electricity containing so much information on experimental facts as this does, for the size of it, and no book of any size that contains so complete a range of facts."—*English Mechanic.*

Rudimentary Magnetism.

RUDIMENTARY MAGNETISM: being a concise exposition of the general principles of Magnetical Science, and the purposes to which it has been applied. By Sir W. SNOW HARRIS, F.R.S. New and enlarged Edition, with considerable additions by Dr. NOAD, Ph.D. With 165 Woodcuts. 12mo, cloth, 4s. 6d.

"There is a good index, and this volume of 412 pages may be considered the best possible manual on the subject of magnetism."—*Mechanics' Magazine.*

"As concise and lucid an exposition of the phenomena of magnetism as we believe it is possible to write."—*English Mechanic.*

"Not only will the scientific student find this volume an invaluable book of reference, but the general reader will find in it as much to interest as to inform his mind. Though a strictly scientific work, its subject is handled in a simple and readable style."—*Illustrated Review.*

Chemical Analysis.

THE COMMERCIAL HANDBOOK of CHEMICAL ANALYSIS; or Practical Instructions for the determination of the Intrinsic or Commercial Value of Substances used in Manufactures, in Trades, and in the Arts. By A. NORMANDY, Author of "Practical Introduction to Rose's Chemistry," and Editor of Rose's "Treatise of Chemical Analysis." *New Edition.* Enlarged, and to a great extent re-written, by Henry M. Noad, Ph.D., F.R.S. With numerous Illustrations. Crown 8vo, 12s. 6d. cloth.

[*Just ready.*]

"We recommend this book to the careful perusal of every one; it may be truly affirmed to be of universal interest, and we strongly recommend it to our readers as a guide, alike indispensable to the housewife as to the pharmaceutical practitioner."—*Medical Times.*

"The very best work on the subject the English press has yet produced."—*Mechanics' Magazine.*

Clocks, Watches, and Bells.

RUDIMENTARY TREATISE on CLOCKS, WATCHES, and BELLS. By Sir Edmund Beckett, Bart. (late E. B. Denison), LL.D., Q.C., F.R.A.S., Author of "Astronomy without Mathematics," &c. Sixth edition, thoroughly revised and enlarged, with numerous Illustrations. Limp cloth (No. 67, Weale's Series), 4s. 6d.; cloth boards, 5s. 6d.

"As a popular, and, at the same time, practical treatise on clocks and bells, it is unapproached."—*English Mechanic.*

"The best work on the subject probably extant . . . So far as we know it has no competitor worthy of the name. The treatise on bells is undoubtedly the best in the language. It shows that the author has contributed very much to their modern improvement, if indeed he has not revived this art, which was decaying here . . . To call it a rudimentary treatise is a misnomer, at least as respects clocks and bells. It is something more. It is the most important work of its kind in English."—*Engineering.*

"The only modern treatise on clock-making."—*Horological Journal.*

"Without having any special interest in the subject, and even without possessing any general aptitude for mechanical studies, a reader must be very unintelligent who cannot find matter to engage his attention in this work. The little book now appears revised and enlarged, being one of the most praiseworthy volumes in Weale's admirable scientific and educational series."—*Daily Telegraph.*

"We do not know whether to wonder most at the extraordinary cheapness of this admirable treatise on clocks, by the most able authority on such a subject, or the thorough completeness of his work even to the minutest details. The chapter on bells is singular and amusing, and will be a real treat even to the uninitiated general reader. The illustrations, notes, and indices, make the work completely perfect of its kind."—*Standard.*

"There is probably no book in the English language on a technical subject so easy to read, and to read through, as the treatise on clocks, watches, and bells, written by the eminent Parliamentary Counsel, Mr. E. B. Denison—now Sir Edmund Beckett, Bart."—*Architect.*

Science and Scripture.

SCIENCE ELUCIDATIVE OF SCRIPTURE, AND NOT ANTAGONISTIC TO IT; being a Series of Essays on—1. Alleged Discrepancies; 2. The Theory of the Geologists and Figure of the Earth; 3. The Mosaic Cosmogony; 4. Miracles in general—Views of Hume and Powell; 5. The Miracle of Joshua—Views of Dr. Colenso: The Supernaturally Impossible; 6. The Age of the Fixed Stars—their Distances and Masses. By Professor J. R. Young, Author of "A Course of Elementary Mathematics," &c. &c. Fcap. 8vo, price 5s. cloth lettered.

"Professor Young's examination of the early verses of Genesis, in connection with modern scientific hypotheses, is excellent."—*English Churchman.*

"Distinguished by the true spirit of scientific inquiry, by great knowledge, by keen logical ability, and by a style peculiarly clear, easy, and energetic."—*Nonconformist.*

"No one can rise from its perusal without being impressed with a sense of the singular weakness of modern scepticism."—*Baptist Magazine.*

"A valuable contribution to controversial theological literature."—*City Press.*

Practical Philosophy.

A SYNOPSIS of PRACTICAL PHILOSOPHY. By the Rev. John Carr, M.A., late Fellow of Trin. Coll., Cambridge. Second Edition. 18mo, 5s. cloth.

Dr. Lardner's Museum of Science and Art.

THE MUSEUM OF SCIENCE AND ART. Edited by DIONYSIUS LARDNER, D.C.L., formerly Professor of Natural Philosophy and Astronomy in University College, London. CONTENTS: The Planets; are they inhabited Worlds?—Weather Prognostics—Popular Fallacies in Questions of Physical Science—Latitudes and Longitudes—Lunar Influences—Meteoric Stones and Shooting Stars — Railway Accidents — Light—Common Things:—Air—Locomotion in the United States—Cometary Influences—Common Things: Water—The Potter's Art—Common Things: Fire—Locomotion and Transport, their Influence and Progress—The Moon—Common Things: The Earth—The Electric Telegraph—Terrestrial Heat—The Sun—Earthquakes and Volcanoes—Barometer, Safety Lamp, and Whitworth's Micrometric Apparatus—Steam—The Steam Engine—The Eye—The Atmosphere—Time—Common Things: Pumps—Common Things: Spectacles, the Kaleidoscope—Clocks and Watches—Microscopic Drawing and Engraving—Locomotive—Thermometer—New Planets: Leverrier and Adams's Planet—Magnitude and Minuteness—Common Things: The Almanack—Optical Images—How to observe the Heavens—Common Things: the Looking-glass—Stellar Universe—The Tides — Colour — Common Things: Man — Magnifying Glasses—Instinct and Intelligence—The Solar Microscope—The Camera Lucida—The Magic Lantern—The Camera Obscura—The Microscope—The White Ants: their Manners and Habits—The Surface of the Earth, or First Notions of Geography—Science and Poetry—The Bee — Steam Navigation — Electro-Motive Power—Thunder, Lightning, and the Aurora Borealis—The Printing Press—The Crust of the Earth—Comets—The Stereoscope—The Pre-Adamite Earth—Eclipses—Sound. With upwards of 1200 Engravings on Wood. In 6 Double Volumes, handsomely bound in cloth, gilt, price £1 1s.

"The 'Museum of Science and Art' is the most valuable contribution that has ever been made to the Scientific Instruction of every class of society."—*Sir David Brewster in the North British Review.*

"Whether we consider the liberality and beauty of the illustrations, the charm of the writing, or the durable interest of the matter, we must express our belief that there is hardly to be found among the new books, one that would be welcomed by people of so many ages and classes as a valuable present."—*Examiner.*

⁎⁎ *Separate books formed from the above, suitable for Workmen's Libraries, Science Classes, &c.*

COMMON THINGS EXPLAINED. With 233 Illustrations, 5s. cloth.

THE ELECTRIC TELEGRAPH POPULARIZED. 100 Illustrations, 1s. 6d. cloth.

THE MICROSCOPE. With 147 Illustrations, 2s. cloth.

POPULAR GEOLOGY. With 201 Illustrations, 2s. 6d. cloth.

POPULAR PHYSICS. With 85 Illustrations. 2s. 6d. cloth.

POPULAR ASTRONOMY. With 182 Illustrations, 4s. 6d. cloth.

STEAM AND ITS USES. With 89 Illustrations, 2s. cloth.

THE BEE AND WHITE ANTS. With 135 Illustrations, cloth, 2s.

DR. LARDNER'S SCIENTIFIC HANDBOOKS.

Astronomy.

THE HANDBOOK OF ASTRONOMY. By DIONYSIUS LARDNER, D.C.L., formerly Professor of Natural Philosophy and Astronomy in University College, London. Third Edition. Revised and Edited by EDWIN DUNKEN, F.R.A.S., Superintendent of the Altazimuth Department, Royal Observatory, Greenwich. With 37 plates and upwards of 100 Woodcuts. In 1 vol., small 8vo, cloth, 550 pages, price 7s. 6d.

"We can cordially recommend it to all those who desire to possess a complete manual of the science and practice of astronomy."—*Astronomical Reporter.*

Optics.

THE HANDBOOK OF OPTICS. New Edition. Edited by T. OLVER HARDING, B.A. Lond., of University College, London. With 298 Illustrations. Small 8vo, cloth, 448 pages, price 5s.

Electricity.

THE HANDBOOK of ELECTRICITY, MAGNETISM, and ACOUSTICS. New Edition. Edited by GEO. CAREY FOSTER, B.A., F.C.S. With 400 Illustrations. Small 8vo, cloth, price 5s.

"The book could not have been entrusted to any one better calculated to preserve the terse and lucid style of Lardner, while correcting his errors and bringing up his work to the present state of scientific knowledge."—*Popular Science Review.*

Mechanics.

THE HANDBOOK OF MECHANICS. [*Reprinting.*

Hydrostatics.

THE HANDBOOK of HYDROSTATICS and PNEUMATICS. New Edition, Revised and Enlarged by BENJAMIN LOEWY, F.R.A.S. With numerous Illustrations. 5s. [*Just published.*

Heat.

THE HANDBOOK OF HEAT. New Edition, Re-written and Enlarged. By BENJAMIN LOEWY, F.R.A.S. [*Preparing.*

Animal Physics.

THE HANDBOOK OF ANIMAL PHYSICS. With 520 Illustrations. New edition, small 8vo, cloth, 7s. 6d. 732 pages. [*Just published.*

Electric Telegraph.

THE ELECTRIC TELEGRAPH. New Edition. Revised and Re-written by E. B. BRIGHT, F.R.A.S. 140 Illustrations. Small 8vo, 2s. 6d. cloth.

"One of the most readable books extant on the Electric Telegraph."—*Eng. Mechanic.*

NATURAL PHILOSOPHY FOR SCHOOLS. By DR. LARDNER. 328 Illustrations. Fifth Edition. 1 vol. 3s. 6d. cloth.

"A very convenient class-book for junior students in private schools. It is intended to convey, in clear and precise terms, general notions of all the principal divisions of Physical Science."—*British Quarterly Review.*

ANIMAL PHYSIOLOGY FOR SCHOOLS. By DR. LARDNER. With 190 Illustrations. Second Edition. 1 vol. 3s. 6d. cloth.

"Clearly written, well arranged, and excellently illustrated."—*Gardeners' Chronicle.*

Geology and Genesis Harmonised.

THE TWIN RECORDS of CREATION; or, Geology and Genesis, their Perfect Harmony and Wonderful Concord. By GEORGE W. VICTOR LE VAUX. With numerous Illustrations. Fcap. 8vo, price 5s. cloth.

"We can recommend Mr. Le Vaux as an able and interesting guide to a popular appreciation of geological science."—*Spectator.*

"The author combines an unbounded admiration of science with an unbounded admiration of the Written Record. The two impulses are balanced to a nicety; and the consequence is, that difficulties, which to minds less evenly poised, would be serious, find immediate solutions of the happiest kinds."—*London Review.*

"Vigorously written, reverent in spirit, stored with instructive geological facts, and designed to show that there is no discrepancy or inconsistency between the Word and the works of the Creator. The future of Nature, in connexion with the glorious destiny of man, is vividly conceived."—*Watchman.*

"No real difficulty is shirked, and no sophistry is left unexposed."—*The Rock.*

Geology, Physical.

PHYSICAL GEOLOGY. (Partly based on Major-General Portlock's Rudiments of Geology.) By RALPH TATE, A.L.S., F.G.S. Numerous Woodcuts. 12mo, 2s. [*Ready.*

Geology, Historical.

HISTORICAL GEOLOGY. (Partly based on Major-General Portlock's Rudiments of Geology.) By RALPH TATE, A.L.S., F.G.S. Numerous Woodcuts. 12mo, 2s. 6d. [*Ready.*

** Or PHYSICAL *and* HISTORICAL GEOLOGY, *bound in One Volume, price 5s.*

Wood-Carving.

INSTRUCTIONS in WOOD-CARVING, for Amateurs; with Hints on Design. By A LADY. In emblematic wrapper, handsomely printed, with Ten large Plates, price 2s. 6d.

"The handicraft of the wood-carver, so well as a book can impart it, may be learnt from 'A Lady's' publication."—*Athenæum.*

"A real *practical guide.* It is very complete."—*Literary Churchman.*

"The directions given are plain and easily understood, and it forms a very good introduction to the practical part of the carver's art."—*English Mechanic.*

Popular Work on Painting.

PAINTING POPULARLY EXPLAINED; with Historical Sketches of the Progress of the Art. By THOMAS JOHN GULLICK, Painter, and JOHN TIMBS, F.S.A. Second Edition, revised and enlarged. With Frontispiece and Vignette. In small 8vo, 6s. cloth.

** *This Work has been adopted as a Prize-book in the Schools of Art at South Kensington.*

"A work that may be advantageously consulted. Much may be learned, even by those who fancy they do not require to be taught, from the careful perusal of this unpretending but comprehensive treatise."—*Art Journal.*

"A valuable book, which supplies a want. It contains a large amount of original matter, agreeably conveyed, and will be found of value, as well by the young artist seeking information as by the general reader. We give a cordial welcome to the book, and augur for it an increasing reputation."—*Builder.*

"This volume is one that we can heartily recommend to all who are desirous of understanding what they admire in a good painting."—*Daily News.*

Delamotte's Works on Illumination & Alphabets.

A PRIMER OF THE ART OF ILLUMINATION ; for the use of Beginners : with a Rudimentary Treatise on the Art, Practical Directions for its Exercise, and numerous Examples taken from Illuminated MSS., printed in Gold and Colours. By F. DELAMOTTE. Small 4to, price 9s. Elegantly bound, cloth antique.

"A handy book, beautifully illustrated ; the text of which is well written, and calculated to be useful. . . . The examples of ancient MSS. recommended to the student, which, with much good sense, the author chooses from collections accessible to all, are selected with judgment and knowledge, as well as taste."—Athenæum.

ORNAMENTAL ALPHABETS, ANCIENT and MEDIÆVAL ; from the Eighth Century, with Numerals ; including Gothic, Church-Text, large and small, German, Italian, Arabesque, Initials for Illumination, Monograms, Crosses, &c. &c., for the use of Architectural and Engineering Draughtsmen, Missal Painters, Masons, Decorative Painters, Lithographers, Engravers, Carvers, &c. &c. &c. Collected and engraved by F. DELAMOTTE, and printed in Colours. Royal 8vo, oblong, price 4s. cloth.

"A well-known engraver and draughtsman has enrolled in this useful book the result of many years' study and research. For those who insert enamelled sentences round gilded chalices, who blazon shop legends over shop-doors, who letter church walls with pithy sentences from the Decalogue, this book will be useful."—Athenæum.

EXAMPLES OF MODERN ALPHABETS, PLAIN and ORNAMENTAL ; including German, Old English, Saxon, Italic, Perspective, Greek, Hebrew, Court Hand, Engrossing, Tuscan, Riband, Gothic, Rustic, and Arabesque ; with several Original Designs, and an Analysis of the Roman and Old English Alphabets, large and small, and Numerals, for the use of Draughtsmen, Surveyors, Masons, Decorative Painters, Lithographers, Engravers, Carvers, &c. Collected and engraved by F. DELAMOTTE, and printed in Colours. Royal 8vo, oblong, price 4s. cloth.

"To artists of all classes, but more especially to architects and engravers, this very handsome book will be invaluable. There is comprised in it every possible shape into which the letters of the alphabet and numerals can be formed, and the talent which has been expended in the conception of the various plain and ornamental letters is wonderful."—Standard.

MEDIÆVAL ALPHABETS AND INITIALS FOR ILLUMINATORS. By F. DELAMOTTE, Illuminator, Designer, and Engraver on Wood. Containing 21 Plates, and Illuminated Title, printed in Gold and Colours. With an Introduction by J. WILLIS BROOKS. Small 4to, 6s. cloth gilt.

"A volume in which the letters of the alphabet come forth glorified in gilding and all the colours of the prism interwoven and intertwined and intermingled, sometimes with a sort of rainbow arabesque. A poem emblazoned in these characters would be only comparable to one of those delicious love letters symbolized in a bunch of flowers well selected and cleverly arranged."—Sun.

THE EMBROIDERER'S BOOK OF DESIGN ; containing Initials, Emblems, Cyphers, Monograms, Ornamental Borders, Ecclesiastical Devices, Mediæval and Modern Alphabets, and National Emblems. Collected and engraved by F. DELAMOTTE, and printed in Colours. Oblong royal 8vo, 2s. 6d. in ornamental boards.

AGRICULTURE, &c.

Youatt and Burn's Complete Grazier.

THE COMPLETE GRAZIER, and FARMER'S and CATTLE-BREEDER'S ASSISTANT. A Compendium of Husbandry. By WILLIAM YOUATT, ESQ., V.S. 11th Edition, enlarged by ROBERT SCOTT BURN, Author of "The Lessons of My Farm," &c. One large 8vo volume, 784 pp. with 215 Illustrations. 1*l*. 1*s*. half-bd.

"The standard and text-book, with the farmer and grazier."—*Farmer's Magazine.*
"A valuable repertory of intelligence for all who make agriculture a pursuit, and especially for those who aim at keeping pace with the improvements of the age."—*Bell's Weekly Messenger.*
"A treatise which will remain a standard work on the subject as long as British agriculture endures."—*Mark Lane Express.*
"One of the best books of reference that can be contained in the agriculturist's library. The word 'complete' expresses its character; since every detail of the subject finds a place, treated upon, and explained, in a clear, comprehensive, and practical manner."—*Magnet.*

Spooner on Sheep.

SHEEP; THE HISTORY, STRUCTURE, ECONOMY, AND DISEASES OF. By W. C. SPOONER, M.R.V.C., &c. Third Edition, considerably enlarged; with numerous fine engravings, including some specimens of New and Improved Breeds. Fcp. 8vo. 366 pp., price 6*s*. cloth. *(Just published.)*

"The book is decidedly the best of the kind in our language."—*Scotsman.*
"A reliable text-book."—*Stamford Mercury.*
"Mr. Spooner has conferred upon the agricultural class a lasting benefit by embodying in this work the improvements made in sheep stock by such men as Humphreys, Rawlence, Howard, and others."—*Hampshire Advertiser.*
"The work should be in possession of every flock-master."—*Banbury Guardian.*
"We can confidently recommend the work as useful and reliable, and of much practical utility to the class for whom it is intended."—*Salisbury and Winchester Journal.*
"Mr. Spooner has conferred a boon on agriculturists generally, and the farmer's library will be incomplete which does not include so admirable a guide to a very important branch of the business."—*Dorset County Chronicle.*

Scott Burn's System of Modern Farming.

OUTLINE OF MODERN FARMING. By R. SCOTT BURN. Soils, Manures, and Crops—Farming and Farming Economy, Historical and Practical—Cattle, Sheep, and Horses—Management of the Dairy, Pigs, and Poultry, with Notes on the Diseases of Stock—Utilisation of Town-Sewage, Irrigation, and Reclamation of Waste Land. New Edition. In 1 vol. 1250 pp., half-bound, profusely Illustrated, price 12*s*.

"There is sufficient stated within the limits of this treatise to prevent a farmer from going far wrong in any of his operations. . . . The author has had great personal experience, and his opinions are entitled to every respect."—*Observer.*

Horton's Underwood and Woodland Tables.

TABLES FOR PLANTING AND VALUING UNDERWOOD AND WOODLAND; also Lineal, Superficial, Cubical, Wages, Marketing, and Decimal Tables. Together with Tables for Converting Land-measure from one denomination to another, and instructions for Measuring Round Timber. By RICHARD HORTON. 12mo. 2*s*. strongly bound in leather.

Ewart's Land Improvers' Pocket-Book.

THE LAND IMPROVERS' POCKET-BOOK OF FOR-
MULÆ, TABLES, and MEMORANDA, required in any Com-
putation relating to the Permanent Improvement of Landed Property. By JOHN EWART, Land Surveyor and Agricultural Engineer.
Royal 32mo, oblong, leather, gilt edges, with elastic band, 4s.

"A compendium long required by land surveyors, agricultural engineers, &c."—
Sussex Daily News.
"It is admirably calculated to serve the purpose for which it was intended."—
Scotsman.
"A compendious and handy little volume . . . admirably arranged, and can
hardly fail to prove exceedingly useful to the class of professional men for whom it
is intended."—*Spectator.*
"Contains in a condensed form the essence of many a treatise, and will be found
of much service to the land agent and measurer."—*Newcastle Daily Journal.*
"Is a marvel of industrious compilation, containing everything requisite for computations relating to the permanent improvement of landed property; it is a perfect
vade-mecum for a surveyor."—*John Bull.*

Hudson's Tables for Land Valuers.

THE LAND VALUER'S BEST ASSISTANT: being Tables,
on a very much improved Plan, for Calculating the Value of
Estates. To which are added, Tables for reducing Scotch, Irish,
and Provincial Customary Acres to Statute Measure; also, Tables
of Square Measure, and of the various Dimensions of an Acre in
Perches and Yards, by which the Contents of any Plot of Ground
may be ascertained without the expense of a regular Survey; &c.
By R. HUDSON, C.E. New Edition, royal 32mo. oblong, leather,
gilt edges, with elastic band, 4s.

"This new edition includes tables for ascertaining the value of leases for any term
of years; and for showing how to lay out plots of ground of certain acres in forms,
square, round, &c., with valuable rules for ascertaining the probable worth of standing
timber to any amount; and is of incalculable value to the country gentleman and professional man."—*Farmer's Journal.*

Complete Agricultural Surveyors' Pocket-Book.

THE LAND VALUER'S AND LAND IMPROVER'S COM-
PLETE POCKET-BOOK; consisting of the above two works
bound together, leather, gilt edges, with strap, 7s. 6d.

☞ *The above forms an unequalled and most compendious Pocket
Vade-mecum for the Land Agent and Agricultural Engineer.*

"We consider Hudson's book to be the best ready-reckoner on matters relating to
the valuation of land and crops we have ever seen, and its combination with Mr.
Ewart's work greatly enhances the value and usefulness of the latter-mentioned . .
It is most useful as a manual for reference to those for whom it is intended."—
North of England Farmer.

Scott Burn's Introduction to Farming.

THE LESSONS of MY FARM: a Book for Amateur Agriculturists, being an Introduction to Farm Practice, in the Culture of
Crops, the Feeding of Cattle, Management of the Dairy, Poultry,
and Pigs, and in the Keeping of Farm-work Records. By ROBERT
SCOTT BURN. With numerous Illustrations. Fcp. 6s. cloth.

"A most complete introduction to the whole round of farming practice."—*John
Bull.*

"*A Complete Epitome of the Laws of this Country.*"

EVERY MAN'S OWN LAWYER; a Handy-Book of the Principles of Law and Equity. By A, BARRISTER. 12th Edition, carefully revised, including a Summary of The Building Societies Act, The Infants' Relief Act, The Married Women's Property Act, The Real Property Limitation Act, The Betting Act, The Hosiery Manufacture Act, a Summary of the Supreme Court of Judicature Act, &c., &c. With Notes and References to the Authorities. 12mo, price 6s. 8d. (saved at every consultation), strongly bound.

COMPRISING THE LAWS OF

BANKRUPTCY—BILLS OF EXCHANGE—CONTRACTS AND AGREEMENTS—COPYRIGHT —DOWER AND DIVORCE—ELECTIONS AND REGISTRATION—INSURANCE—LIBEL AND SLANDER—MORTGAGES—SETTLEMENTS—STOCK EXCHANGE PRACTICE— TRADE MARKS AND PATENTS—TRESPASS, NUISANCES, ETC.—TRANSFER OF LAND, ETC.—WARRANTY—WILLS AND AGREEMENTS, ETC. Also Law for Landlord and Tenant—Master and Servant—Workmen and Apprentices—Heirs, Devisees, and Legatees—Husband and Wife—Executors and Trustees—Guardian and Ward—Married Women and Infants—Partners and Agents—Lender and Borrower—Debtor and Creditor—Purchaser and Vendor—Companies and Associations—Friendly Societies—Clergymen, Churchwardens—Medical Practitioners, &c.—Bankers—Farmers—Contractors—Stock and Share Brokers—Sportsmen and Gamekeepers—Farriers and Horse-Dealers—Auctioneers, House-Agents— Innkeepers, &c.—Pawnbrokers—Surveyors—Railways and Carriers, &c. &c.

"*No Englishman ought to be without this book.*"—*Engineer.*

"It is a complete code of English Law, written in plain language which all can understand . . . should be in the hands of every business man, and all who wish to abolish lawyers' bills."—*Weekly Times.*

"A useful and concise epitome of the law."—*Law Magazine.*

"What it professes to be—a complete epitome of the laws of this country, thoroughly intelligible to non-professional readers."—*Bell's Life.*

Auctioneer's Assistant.

THE APPRAISER, AUCTIONEER, BROKER, HOUSE AND ESTATE AGENT, AND VALUER'S POCKET ASSISTANT, for the Valuation for Purchase, Sale, or Renewal of Leases, Annuities, and Reversions, and of property generally; with Prices for Inventories, &c. By JOHN WHEELER, Valuer, &c. Third Edition, enlarged, by C. NORRIS. Royal 32mo, cloth, 5s.

"A neat and concise book of reference, containing an admirable and clearly-arranged list of prices for inventories, and a very practical guide to determine the value of furniture, &c."—*Standard.*

Pawnbrokers' Legal Guide.

THE PAWNBROKERS', FACTORS', and MERCHANTS' GUIDE to the LAW of LOANS and PLEDGES. With the Statutes and a Digest of Cases on Rights and Liabilities, Civil and Criminal, as to Loans and Pledges of Goods, Debentures, Mercantile, and other Securities. By H. C. FOLKARD, Esq., of Lincoln's Inn, Barrister-at-Law, Author of the "Law of Slander and Libel," &c. 12mo, cloth boards, price 7s.

The Laws of Mines and Mining Companies.

A PRACTICAL TREATISE on the LAW RELATING to MINES and MINING COMPANIES. By WHITTON ARUNDELL, Attorney-at-Law. Crown 8vo. 4s. cloth.

www.ingramcontent.com/pod-product-compliance
Lightning Source LLC
Chambersburg PA
CBHW060608030726
47498CB00005B/1598